Bedlam South

A NOVEL

MARK GRISHAM
DAVID DONALDSON

STATE STREET PRESS

Published by State Street Press
by special arrangement with
Ann Arbor Media Group LLC
2500 S. State Street
Ann Arbor, MI 48104

Printed and bound in the United States of America.
ISBN 13: 978-0-681-49756-6
ISBN 10: 0-681-49756-4

10 9 8 7 6 5 4 3 2 1

Library of Congress Cataloging-in-Publication Data is on file.

To my wonderful parents John and Wanda Grisham
for their never-ending faith and support.
M. G.

In memory of my father and in honor of my mother,
W. D. "Buddy" and Ramona Donaldson. Dad, I thank God
for the assurance that I will one day see you again
in heaven, until that day …
D. D.

"*What a cruel thing is war,
to separate and destroy families and friends,
and mar the purest joys and happiness God has granted us
in this world. To fill our hearts with hatred instead of
love for our neighbors, and to devastate the
fair face of this beautiful world.*"

GENERAL ROBERT E. LEE,
letter to his wife,
DECEMBER 25, 1862

One

Distracted by the clanking shackles, moans, and screams that periodically pierced the darkness, Dr. Joseph Bryarly paused in his packing. Asylum residents were receiving their nightly therapies, really nothing more than retaliation for the day's misbehavior. He couldn't believe he had been in this God-forsaken place more than fifteen years. Three thousand miles separated him from his home and his past in Alabama.

His sparsely equipped study was little more than an alcove leading into a sleeping chamber. On this night, a large shipping trunk temporarily served as a makeshift desk, since most of his belongings had already been packed in crates for transport back to America. A flickering flame from a brass candleholder dimly lit the room. Joseph strained his eyes and returned to the letter he'd received three weeks earlier. His hands shook. This message sealed his fate. God had stepped in to take charge of the doctor's life:

RICHMOND, VIRGINIA

January 5, 1863

Honorable Doctor Joseph L. Bryarly,

I trust this message finds you in good health and excellent spirits. Having received no response to my previous inquiries,

I feel compelled once again to request your assistance on behalf of God, your family, and the Confederate States of America. The late Reverend Theodore J. Bryarly, your father and my dearest friend, assured me just before his unfortunate death of your loyalty to the State of Alabama and to the Confederacy.

A commission within the Confederate Army awaits your timely response, with a rank of Lieutenant and all the rights and privileges thereof. Your assigned post will be as Chief Superintendent of Wingate Asylum in Richmond, Virginia, a newly renovated hospital for war criminals and the mentally insane. May God speed your return. I look forward to seeing you once again and sharing stories with an old family friend.

As ever, truly yours,

Jefferson Davis, President

Confederate States of America

Dropping the letter, the doctor removed his reading glasses and sighed. Years of distractions within the confines of Bethlem Royal Hospital had shackled his childhood memories to the darkest corners of his soul ... until now. He was overwhelmed by a rush of emotions, torn between his loyalties to the Confederacy and his hesitancy about returning home. News of his father's death had freed him to accept this commission, just as it released him from his bondage with the past. He would never have considered returning to the South if the Reverend were still alive. He silently prayed to the God of his childhood, a habit he'd never managed to break in times of distress. Each time he prayed, he felt childish—another legacy from his father. *Dear Lord, forgive my hypocrisy. Truly, one man's death has brought peace to another man's soul. As my father has already trusted his eternal spirit to your care, so now I commit my fate into your hands as well ...*

When he rose from his knees, the doctor paced his office for a moment, then left his quarters. He walked down two flights of rickety stairs to the first-floor wing of the asylum. A frigid north wind howled through barred windows that remained open to ventilate the stench. As always, the ward was teeming with too many people. Along both sides of the narrow hallway, debtors lay on beds of malodorous straw or sat shivering, huddled like cattle, awaiting their fate. Frosty vapors billowed from every mouth and nostril. Fat rats scurried along a foul-smelling trench used to channel away the filth and water. Padlocked doors along each wall hid occupants with more serious histories.

The doctor's presence in the ward was the signal for demented madmen to scream obscenities from behind iron bars. Pressing a handkerchief over his nose, Joseph strained against a thick wooden door and descended into the bowels of what seemed to be hell itself. Hastily scrawled messages scratched into the wall expressed the heart of all Bedlamites sentenced to die in this god-forsaken place:

Abandon all hope, ye who enter here.
In Bedlam, all hope is lost.

At the bottom of the staircase, in one of many cramped holding cells, three men stood half naked, shackled to the walls, feet and wrists bound securely, arms stretched high overhead. The poorly lit room failed to illuminate the face of the pitiful wretch in the far corner. The prisoner's head hung limply on his chest and he made no effort to acknowledge his visitor. The doctor paused before speaking. Absorbed in the pitiful sight, Joseph realized for the thousandth time, *The physical resemblance between us is remarkable! We're the same age and height. We have the same lanky build and pepper-and-salt hair. I know that without God's grace, I would be the poor creature condemned to stand in his place.*

"Forbred Lytton," he said, speaking softly as he moved closer, "tomorrow I leave for America."

A weak, raspy voice whispered, "For duty to God and country." Then Forbred Lytton shifted his weight and moaned softly;

the open wounds oozing beneath the shackles caused him excruciating pain.

"I thought, perhaps as a special gift to mark my departure, we could once again visit together—in my quarters."

The patient slowly raised his head, his face completely covered by his long matted hair and unkempt beard. "Your ... quarters?" His weak voice reflected hope. "Yes. Please!"

The doctor removed all the shackles except for the steel collar bolted around the man's neck. Using a long chain as a makeshift leash, the doctor led the man through the maze of huddled bodies and back to his quarters. While Forbred Lytton settled himself on a flimsy stool, Joseph quickly bolted the door and let the chain fall loudly to the floor. For many years, these penitent acts of kindness had been the highlight of Forbred's miserable existence. He knew all too well that after tonight, even this dismal escape from reality would be gone ... forever.

Each meeting was unique. Sometimes the doctor would read stories of the Wild West or tales of adventure in the American South. Many times, the prisoner would read to himself quietly for hours. He was fascinated with the doctor's medical books, especially journals chronicling the advancements in the fledgling field of psychiatry. These encounters always took place in secret, after the asylum administrator, apothecary, and handlers had retired for the evening. If discovered, the consequences of Joseph's actions would be severe and might include his discharge from the hospital. Bethlem, as he was all too well aware, was the most notorious hospital in the civilized world—and well deserved its reputation for brutality, inhumanity, and misery. But the doctor couldn't bring himself to deny one last act of kindness to this man with the brilliant troubled mind.

Joseph rummaged through a crate of half-packed books, removing and replacing various volumes. Finally, he exclaimed, "Excellent! How about this book, Forbred? A wonderful tale of redemption and hope entitled *A Christmas Carol*, written by Mr. Charles Dickens."

"Begging your pardon," the patient said painfully, lowering his head, "seeing it's our last night together and my last time to *ever* receive such kindness, would you read from your journal?"

Joseph gazed into the man's bloodshot eyes and replied, "Why, yes! A splendid idea." He replaced the novel in the crate, headed to his bedside table, and returned with a volume from his personal journals, an early account of his childhood adventures in southern Alabama beginning thirty-five years ago. Before he began reading, however, he turned and laid his hand on the man's shoulder.

"Forbred," Joseph's voice was soothing and filled with compassion, "my greatest source of hope in this wretched place has been watching God's sovereign majesty at work restoring your mind. You must know, my dear brother, that God has forgiven your sins. Whatever debt you felt that you owed to this miserable society was surely repaid long ago. You don't deserve to remain imprisoned—I know that. Over and over again, I've written to Lord Kennington, begging him to approve my request to have you released. However, I have to be honest: I don't believe he'll ever allow it." Joseph added sadly, "My single greatest regret is leaving you, my friend, behind."

Tears filled both men's eyes as Joseph opened the volume and began reading aloud from the journal.

"JUNE 12TH, in the year of our Lord 1834. The air seems filled with excitement. For my 17th birthday, the Reverend surprised me with a most generous gift of a new winter coat and enough gold coins to finance my return to the university in the fall. The heaviness of this past year is mercifully lifting; my return home for the summer has found the Reverend in the best of spirits. My father seems kinder now …"

For many hours the two men escaped the realities of asylum life, transported back many years in time. In his mind, Joseph Bryarly once again walked the backcountry roads around

Andalusia in Covington County. Friends, family, and childhood adventures filled his thoughts and some brought a warm spirit of peace to his soul. *I wonder what it's like back home now that Father is gone? Surely, war has changed things. Where are my old friends? What price will the war cost all of us?*

• • • • •

In early May 1863, the Army of Northern Virginia was in high spirits, particularly new recruits like Private Ezekiel "Zeke" Gibson, who grinned non-stop as he marched in column from Richmond toward Fredericksburg. Wagons, cannons, and cavalry stretched for miles on the dusty road ahead. Occasionally, the thick wilderness canopy would break, to reveal masses of troops converging in the distance. Zeke couldn't wait to see his big brother Billy—it would be the first time in more than two years. Four years older, Billy had been Zeke's childhood hero, and the younger Gibson knew from sporadic letters that his brother had been involved in every major battle in the eastern theatre since the war began. Ever since the day Billy had grabbed his rifle, ruffled his kid brother's hair, and kissed their mother goodbye as he headed across the mountains to war, Zeke had counted the days until he, too, could go fight. Anticipating that the war would have ended within two years, his folks had set the age of seventeen as the time when their last remaining child could join General Robert E. Lee's army—but they were wrong, and Zeke was off to war. His chest could barely contain the pride that swelled within him as he thought, *I'm part of the greatest group of fighting men God ever assembled, the Army of Northern Virginia!*

Zeke's column of new recruits was dressed in every shade and style of butternut gray. The battle-scarred veterans marching alongside them who were returning to the front after medical leaves; they were dressed in anything they could scrounge. Even the most casual observer could easily identify who was new to war and who was not. As they marched, Zeke noticed one ragged veteran glancing curiously at him from time to time. *When we get our first break, I'm goin' to find out who that fella is!*

"Are you little Zeke Gibson, Billy's kid brother?" the soldier demanded to know before the new recruit could approach him.

"Yeah! Who're you?"

"Whaddya mean, who am I? Nate! Nate Webster, you old coon dog!" The dusty veteran with a week's worth of beard pounded the boy on the back while spitting a long and impressive stream of tobacco juice onto a nearby bush. "How're things in Calhoun County? How is it that the state of Mississippi decided it could survive without you keepin' watch over our womenfolk?"

If possible, the boy grinned even wider than before. "Sure has been a spell, ain't it, Nate? You've changed plenty. I wouldn't have recognized you if you'd been sittin' next to me in church! I'm hopin' to catch up with Billy. Do you know how he's doin'?"

"Reckon he's the luckiest man alive. Been in every scrap since Manassas and ain't got so much as a scratch. I tell him all the time, he's ten foot tall 'n' bulletproof. Heck, I done been wounded four times. The last skirmish was the worst. A lead ball plumb near took off my hand." He held up a stump missing three fingers and a portion of his palm, but wiggled his thumb and index finger and pointed out, "but I can still shoot."

"Did you get that at Chancellorsville?"

"Naw, McLaw's division weren't at Chancellorsville. We stayed put in Fredericksburg—kept them Yanks from crossing the Rappahannock River. Figured them dogs would try sneaking up from behind." Rubbing the dirty bandage on his hand, Nate continued, "We sure fought like the devil—two days solid, while ol' General Jackson got 'round behind their right flank. We flushed them Yanks clean back to Washington City!"

"Wow! I can't wait to see that kind of action!" Zeke said, grinning. *Lord, what an army! Outnumbered more than two to one and still whipped them Yanks proper! The Yanks may have better artillery, but they ain't got nothing like our General Robert E. Lee. Yes, sir, everybody knows there ain't nothing and no one that can stop General Lee!*

"On your feet! March!" The orders were shouted down the

line. Nate and Zeke fell in next to each other, so they could talk while they marched.

"Boy, why are you grinning like a mule eating briars?" Nate asked, as the column headed north.

"I couldn't wait till I turned seventeen!" Zeke confided, nearly trotting along to keep up with the veterans. "I was sure, sure as shootin', that the war would be over 'fore I got my chance to fight. But I made it!"

Nate looked at the boy with a mixture of humor and sorrow written on his face. "I heard that your Pa got part of his leg blown off at Antietam. And you're about to get your eyes opened to a whole lot of hurts, things you ain't never seen before. I've seen a heap of our boys from back home blown to bits. Even their mommas wouldn't have known them. Once you've seen that, war ain't nothin' you'll smile about."

Zeke paused, letting Nate's words sink in, before he said. "I meant no disrespect, Nate. But I ain't seen Billy for two years and I miss him something fierce. I've always been afraid he'd get killed before I could see him again ... That's all!"

"You Gibson boys must be all alike. Full of fury when y'all is poked at."

"What do you mean?"

"Your brother's something else. As soon as a battle commences, he sets to screaming and hollering—the whole dang time, like he's havin' fun! The air is thick with bullets. Folks're gettin' shot left 'n' right. The noise is so loud you think your ears blowed up. And there he'd be, fightin' like the devil, yellin' as though the Yanks could hear him!"

Nate paused for long moments as Zeke watched him curiously, then the veteran put his good hand on the boy's shoulder and added, "This fighting's scary, Zeke, the first time bein' the worst. You gotta keep your head, listen to what folks tells you, and y'all might get out of this war alive."

Once again, Nate lapsed into silence, chewing on his wad of tobacco while Zeke surveyed the countryside with the eagerness of a puppy. Finally, the veteran glanced up at the boy and was forced to grin in spite of himself. "Well, if your luck is like your brother's and your Pa's, you'll be all right," he conceded. "Your Pa's one tough old man."

"Pa's doing fine now," Zeke boasted. "That busted-up leg kept him in bed four months—'bout drove Momma crazy. When he got well enough to move around, she sent him to join up with General Forrest's cavalry. That way, he can ride a horse and still fight, plus he ain't so far from home. Last I heard, he was having a high ol' time raiding and burning Union supplies all over western Tennessee."

"Forrest's sure enough one tough ol' wildcat," Nate observed. "Reckon he's the best on both sides when it comes to fighting on horseback—maybe even better than Jeb Stuart hisself."

For the rest of the morning and into the afternoon, Zeke barraged his friend with questions about the military leaders and battles he'd heard about, and the supply wagons, ambulances, and artillery caissons he was passing along the very long line. *All this commotion must mean we're getting close to the main army!*

For hours, the column marched through dense forests, across open fields, splashing through shallow creek beds and skirting swamps. Suddenly, late in the afternoon as they neared a clearing in the woods, the earth suddenly exploded with repetitive volleys of cannon fire.

Terrified, Zeke and the other new recruits hit the ground and covered their heads. The veterans howled with laughter. In the clearing, the Confederates' First Corps artillerists were practicing with recently captured cannons. Grinning from ear to ear, Nate helped Zeke to his feet.

"Man that was loud!" Zeke exclaimed, bending down to retrieve his rifle and knapsack.

"Y'all better check your britches, boys—I reckon I smell something!" another veteran said, howling with laughter at the recruits' expense.

"Fall in!" The command echoed down the line as the column

moved toward Cedar Fork, where two roads crossed in the middle of nowhere. Several miles later, the column came to rest beside train tracks. Zeke, Nate, and a thousand other soldiers waited in the hot late-afternoon sun for equipment and supplies to be loaded onto flatcars before the men scrambled aboard, filling every inch of every car.

"We're headed for Fredericksburg!" Veterans passed the word through the ranks. When the last soldier had climbed aboard, the railcars jerked violently and then squealed into motion, causing their passengers to stagger and filling the air with thick black smoke.

The pace of their journey quickened considerably. Before long, the train was rolling past much of the Army of Northern Virginia, dusting riders and sightseers alike with a thick coating of ash. Recruits passed the word that their unit would soon reach First Corps Headquarters, where they'd be dispersed into regiments. Zeke hoped that somewhere in the sea of men he might find his brother Billy.

Sometime around dusk, the train slammed to a halt, sending the men tumbling forward. Anxious to stretch, the soldiers quickly leaped down from the railcars and tried to assemble with their original column. Following the barked orders of a staff sergeant, the men and boys marched in the general direction of the 13th Mississippi.

"This is General Barksdale's Mississippi brigade, General McLaw's division, General Longstreet's First Corps," Nate explained, as Zeke's head swung from side to side, hoping to catch a glimpse of his brother. Finally, as the sun began sinking below the horizon, Nate pointed to the flag that announced General Barksdale's headquarters. "Dang it, Zeke! It's gettin' darker than a witch's outhouse at midnight. Let's hightail it."

• • • • •

In a city renowned for its beautiful women, Mary Beth Greene still managed to turn the heads of every man who passed her by. Slender, petite, with a shape that was most often found only in men's dreams, the freeborn twenty-four-year-old had flawless almond skin, sparkling green eyes set under arched brows, and a smile that could light up a city block if she wanted to. At the moment, she was gently swaying on a porch swing on the verandah of the finest brothel in downtown Jackson, Mississippi. The well-tended brick building sat just two blocks east of the State Capitol building. A cluster of women ranging in age from their teens to early thirties waved fans or chatted quietly as Miss Lou Ellen Pompadour, the madam and surrogate mother to all of these lost souls, busied herself in preparations for another hectic night. When taps echoed in the distance, it was the signal warning the women of the imminent stampede of young, adventure-seeking soldiers. Several women stood to stretch their backs and legs and hurry upstairs to fix their hair and attire.

"Is it time … *already*?" Mary Beth sighed, adjusting her off-the-shoulder emerald green gown, chosen to compliment her eye color.

"I surely wish I had your blessings," a young friend said, enviously eyeing Mary Beth's curves.

"Yeah, Mary Beth," another woman giggled, "save some of the boys for us tonight."

"That's quite enough, ladies!" Miss Lou Ellen had appeared at the door. "Need I remind you that you are all endowed with grace, charm, and intelligence? Any man would be proud to take any of my girls home with him to meet his mama!"

"As long as he didn't tell her where he found us," a teenager whispered to her neighbor, who hid her grin behind her fan. High class or not, a brothel was a depressing place to waste away a life, any life, even the life of a prostitute—or, as Miss Lou Ellen insisted upon saying, a *courtesan*.

"I wonder what man invented all the funny substitutes we use for the word whoring," Mary Beth Greene speculated aloud, more to herself than to be heard.

"Miss Mary Beth! You know how I detest that *horrible* word!"

"Harlot, tart, strumpet, prostitute, camp follower. What does it matter? The words all mean the same thing," the woman pointed out, glancing down the street.

"When I was in Washington," another woman chimed in, "all those Federal boys called us *Hooker Girls*, on account of General Joe Hooker and his fondness for … well … us."

Mary Beth suddenly grinned and asked, "Hookers?" Then she turned to Miss Lou Ellen. "Ma'am, I now stand with you on your word choice. I believe I do prefer the sound of *courtesan*."

"Mary Beth," one of the older women asked abruptly, "why are you still here? You could make your fortune anywhere."

"Why, the money, sugar."

"You know perfectly well what I'm asking," the woman persisted. "You're from a good upbringing. You're not like the rest of us. My momma was a pros—" with a look at Miss Lou Ellen, she corrected herself, "—a courtesan, so I'm one. But you ain't like us."

Mary Beth pretended not to hear the question. "Now just hush up," snapped an older woman. "Y'all knows she don't like tellin' tales about her family."

Mary Beth and her defender were the only women left on the porch as the others hurried in to finish their preparations and settle themselves on the parlor settees. Mary Beth turned to her friend and said thoughtfully, "She's right. I don't belong here."

"Mary Beth! You're the only friend I've got. What would happen to me if you leave?"

"I miss the music at the balls in Washington, the government men from all over the country who had interesting things to say, the fancy meals … and most of all, I miss being treated like a lady," Mary Beth admitted, thinking aloud. "The word courtesan doesn't mean what we do; it means a different class of woman, someone who's graceful and elegant and able to serve as a hostess at grand events, not a prostitute who services wild-eyed common soldiers."

"Was it a lot different from this?" Susan asked wistfully.

"Dinner and dancing all night. Only a short time for *romancing*."

"A short time?" Susan chuckled. "Lord have mercy, some of these young farm boys want to pay two dollars and stay all night. The young soldier boys will make us old by the time we're thirty."

"I'm not goin' to let that happen."

"Mary Beth! Where on earth would you go?"

"I'd follow the money." Mary Beth put her arm around Susan as they turned to go indoors. "The Confederate capital's gone to Richmond. The money's gone to Richmond," she said, nodding her head as if suddenly coming to a life-changing decision, "so, I'm going to Richmond."

"How you gonna get all the way up north to Virginia?

"I'll take the train."

"That train's for soldiers only—you know that. No civilians can set foot on that train."

"I haven't met a man yet that I couldn't convince to see things my way."

Two

For hours, General Barksdale's brigade marched along heavily rutted wagon trails into Virginia's interior. Occasionally, sergeants would order the men to cross creeks or skirt through forests as the supply wagons and ambulances accompanying them became bogged down in the spring mud. As they approached the general's newly established headquarters, Zeke's head was swiveling left and right, excitedly searching the faces of soldiers clustered around cooking fires, standing guard, or cleaning their guns. To his amazement, he spotted Billy talking to a group of officers. Bursting with excitement, he fought back the urge to tackle his big brother. Nate elbowed him and said, "I forgot to tell you: Billy's gotten himself a promotion—to corporal."

Watching his unsuspecting brother, Zeke marveled at the changes two years and a war could exact on a man. *He's a half a head bigger than he was when he left, and his muscles look more powerful than a blacksmith's! I see what Nate means about bullet-proof ... I hope the war turns me into a man like Billy!*

"Hey! Corporal Gibson! About face! Forward, march!" Zeke shouted, with a broad grin on his face, as soon as his brother's conference with the officers had ended and the others had started to move away.

Billy's head pivoted on his shoulders. When he saw who had shouted the orders, his heart leaped into his throat. This was his first contact with home for more than two years.

"Look what just snuck into the chicken coop!" he shouted, grabbing his brother and pounding his back like a drum.

"Momma sent me to babysit you. Thought it was about time you had a little supervision," Zeke announced with a grin and a salute when the brothers finally broke apart.

The older brother was six inches taller and significantly broader than Zeke, but they shared the same blue eyes with a direct and open gaze. Their mother's Cherokee heritage was evident in the boys' straight black hair, athletic builds, and chiseled noses and cheekbones. When Zeke turned to Nate for a moment, Billy surveyed his brother from toe to head, like a farmer would evaluate a thoroughbred horse. *My God in heaven! The boy is almost a grown man! Look at him standing there, bright-eyed, full of hope, ready for a good time. He has no idea of what war can do to a man!*

When Zeke turned back to his brother, the corporal put his arm around the new recruit's shoulder. "It's sure good to see you, little brother! How's Momma?"

"Momma's fine, just fine. She gave me a million messages for you, and some new socks and shirts." Zeke gave his big brother another up-and-down look. "We didn't know you was an officer now. Dang if you don't look real important with that sword and pistol!"

"Just got it last week after Colonel Carter wrote in his dispatch that I'd 'performed bravely under fire,'" Billy said, with a grin. "Heck, Zeke, I was just fighting like Pop taught us. We Gibsons fight to win."

"Pops will sure be proud, Billy! Say, ain't it past dinner time?" Zeke asked. "All I've had all day is a handful of crackers—man, I'm starving!"

Billy laughed. "I'll find you something to eat, but don't get used to it. Oftentimes meals are hard to come by. We may go all day without food, longer when we're on a march."

Corporal William "Billy" Gibson stepped back and in his best officer's voice barked, "All men of Company C, 13th Mississippi, follow me."

· · · · ·

The 13th Mississippi had been formed in March of 1861, made up of volunteers from the north-central part of the state. Company C, composed mostly of boys and men from Calhoun County, started one hundred strong, but by the time Zeke arrived, the unit numbered only fifty-two. Some had deserted, others had died of disease, but most were killed on the battlefield. Those remaining were battle-hardened soldiers and as soon as they reached their campsite, they quickly dispersed; within minutes they had erected their tents, started fires, pulled supplies and frying pans out of their packs, and busied themselves with dinner.

Zeke gathered kindling and split firewood as his brother set up his tent, then set to work frying salt pork and something that looked like a cornmeal biscuit. "Sure wish you'd brought some of Momma's pies," Billy said, looking up from the fire with a grin, adding, "but if she gave you any, I'm sure you ate them soon as you were out of her sight!" Zeke laughed and nodded. Not much later, the brothers stretched out in Billy's two-man tent. Zeke was asleep as soon as his head hit the pack that served as his pillow. Before nodding off himself, Billy studied his brother's profile. *I'm going to make a soldier out of him, no matter what, because surviving this madness depends on just how good a soldier he becomes—and just how lucky he is.*

A bugle sounded reveille at five o'clock the next morning. Startled, Zeke sprang to his feet hurriedly, banging into the small tent's roof and nearly disassembling the shelter. Roaring laughter rose from a nearby group of men. Billy started to join in the laughter, but stopped when he saw his brother's embarrassment. During roll call, Zeke noticed other familiar faces in Company C, including Joshua Steele. When the official duties were over, the new recruit headed over to talk to old friends.

"Hey, Zeke, I heard you've been keeping an eye on my little

sister for me," Joshua said. "She's right fond of you! I hear y'all are quite the pair."

"Huh—what? Josh, you aren't talking about Peggy, are you?"

"Don't be coy with me, boy. I got lots of letters from back home. I ain't got no problem with you courting my little sister."

Zeke was speechless. He just nodded his head and walked away. Billy added to his misery by teasing him, "You and Peggy, huh? Sounds like a match made in heaven—*hog heaven*!"

"That ain't funny, dang it. You know I can't stand *Piggy* Steele. I've not seen that big ol' sow in six months. I can't believe she's telling folks that I'm courting her!"

"Don't worry, little brother. Everybody knows most of the Steeles are a bit touched in the head. Besides, I'll bet your true love's still in Nashville—the *lovely* Miss Katherine Stewart."

Zeke fumed, "Yeah, she's still in Nashville and some crazy Yankee captain's doing his dangest to court her. That rascal ain't taking no for an answer. There's been many a time I was ready to sneak off up to Nashville, whip his butt, get Katherine, and bring her back to our farm."

"So, why don't you?"

"'Cause Momma and Pops both threatened to tan my hide if I did," Zeke admitted with a grin. "You know well as me, once they said their piece, there's no arguing with them."

• • • • •

The port of Liverpool was bustling with people arranging passage, loading freight, seeking work, or bidding their loved ones farewell. The horizon to the west was filled with a steady stream of railcars, freight, and Irish Catholic emigrants all converging on the river port with few resources and very little hope of ever returning home. Hundreds of poor tenant farmers and their families poured onto the ships believing that the hardships involved in sailing across the Atlantic would pale in comparison to the lingering effects of the potato famine back in Ireland. Some agreed to two years of indentured servitude in the South in exchange for their passage, while others paid the sum of ten pounds apiece, but all boarded the ship anticipating a new and better life in America.

With tears and cheers, the crowd converged on the gangplanks of the *Guy Mannering*, jostling and hurrying past Joseph, who took his time breathing in the sea air and scanning the crowd on deck and at the pier. He stared at the modest two-masted schooner, comparing her to the other vessels in the harbor.

An old salt loitering on the pier told the doctor, "Ain't she a pretty lady? Square-rigged, three-masted, triple-decked, and American-made. One of the finest vessels in the Black Star Line." While the deckhands made final preparations for the voyage to America, the old man put out his hand to greet Joseph.

The doctor regained his focus and replied, "Ah—yes, forgive me. Please allow me to introduce myself." He shook hands and said, "I am Doctor L—Bryarly."

"Pleased to meet you, Gov'ner. They call me Scully."

Scully turned toward the ship, but Joseph grabbed his arm saying, "I couldn't help but overhear one of the young deckhands refer to the *Guy Mannering* as a 'coffin ship'?"

"Bloody micks, got brains no bigger than a mouse's diddy," scowling, Scully viciously slapped his knee. "My apologies, Doctor. Oughta drown 'em all, filthy beggars. Like I always say— cut a pauper and you'll find a bloody Irish Catholic underneath."

Joseph frowned, offended by the comments. "What I really want to know is the meaning of the term *coffin ship*."

"Well, you see, some of them Irish wankers call the smaller vessels coffin ships 'cause most people what sails on 'em die afore making it to port."

"Thank you, Scully, but *why* do so many people die on the voyage?"

"Some die of typhus, some die of dysentery, others … plain bad luck. But this here ship, *Guy Mannering*, she ain't no bloody coffin ship. She's as fine as what sails from these ports—" The old sailor stopped talking in mid-sentence. Thinking and scratching his long tangled beard, he asked, "Begging your pardon, Doctor, but what did you expect for ten pounds?"

Despite reaching the height of educational achievement possible within the medical world in the mid-nineteenth century, the doctor was leaving England with little money. Over the past two years, Joseph Bryarly had invested much of his modest fortune in the war effort by purchasing Confederate treasury bonds. He never dreamed he would one day be asked to return to America to work for his beloved South.

More than two hundred thirty souls crowded into the small, split-level holding areas below deck. Joseph remained topside. Sitting on a large pile of rigging ropes, soaking in the bright sunlight and fresh sea air, he reread his childhood journal. The doctor couldn't quite believe he had seen the last of the nightmarish asylum—he kept glancing at the pier, even now anticipating that someone from the asylum's staff would be seen rushing to hail him and bring him back. Even still, he felt a tremendous burden lifted from his shoulders; years of persecution were finally ending. Sailing on a broad blue ocean between two continents and two very separate lives, he felt a joy that his heart could barely contain. At last, he thought, perhaps he could find peace—even in the midst of war, in the heart of the Confederate capital.

· · · · ·

"Fall in—now!" Orders thundered from the throat of First Sergeant Bradford Cawley. Somewhere west of Fredericksburg, the newly recruited Confederates of Company C formed something resembling a straight line. The sergeant completed roll call and began bellowing again, "One hour for breakfast! One hour for policing!"

Zeke wasn't sure what to do next, but he knew one thing for sure: he was hungry again and a little leery about the authoritative sergeant. Billy watched his brother with a grin before explaining, "That's Sergeant Cawley. His bark is worse than his bite, but don't make him mad or he'll have you digging latrine ditches all day."

"I'll remember that—I ain't any fonder of digging than I was back at the farm," he told Billy with a grin. "Did I hear him say something about breakfast?"

"Follow me." Billy led Zeke to a cluster of men gathering around a fire. "You're about to be introduced to a campfire specialty. It's called *cush*."

"Come again? Did you say *cush*?"

"Yeah, it's good stuff. We mix cornmeal with a little water and bacon grease and fry it over a fire. Just like Momma's cornbread."

Zeke grabbed a hot handful when it came his way, quickly gulped it down, and began looking for more. "I think it's been too long since you've had Momma's cornbread," he told his brother. "But it'll do in a pinch!"

"You'd better get used to feeling hungry because there ain't no seconds like there were back home," Billy said, putting his arm around his brother's shoulder and moving him in the direction of a circle of wagons. "Come on with me. We'll see the quartermaster about getting you a new rifle. We've captured so many guns from the Yanks that our whole army now has rifled muskets, good as theirs."

"But I brought my old musket from home, and I can still outshoot you *any* day!"

"You ain't gonna be shooting squirrels around here, Zeke. These Yankee rifles shoot three times farther than your old musket and probably three times faster. And keep in mind that the Yanks will all be shooting back at you with rifles. Now ... do you still want to keep that musket?"

Zeke hesitated for a moment, then shook his head. He was issued an almost new Enfield rifle, a leather cartridge bag, a bayonet with scabbard, and a cotton haversack. His rubber blanket, canteen, and provisions had been provided during his short stay in Richmond. "Look at me, Billy!" he said, holding his rifle smartly at his shoulder. "I'm a genuine full-fledged Johnny Reb!" His ever-present grin widened as his brother shook his head and grabbed his arm.

"I know you were itching to get here, but war isn't a turkey shoot!" Billy said in exasperation. "You're about to see a lot of bad stuff."

"Nate says you get a little crazy when the fighting gets going."

"I guess maybe I do." Billy loosened his grip on his brother's arm and continued, "If you're gonna survive, you find your own way to handle the fear."

"Fear? You've gotta be kidding me! You ain't never been scared of nothing in your whole life!"

"That's what I'm trying to tell you. You got no idea what it's like until you see the *White Elephant*."

"What are you talking about? White Elephant?"

"It's what the veterans call combat, when there's bullets flying, artillery blasting, officers commanding, bugles sounding, and men getting shot to pieces all around you and the smoke is so thick you can't see what you're shooting at. There's just no other way to describe it proper. Some men are so scared that they run off and hide."

"You think I'll have to wait long before I see that there White Elephant?"

"Nope. Rumor is that General Lee wants to invade the North again. General Longstreet wants to take the First Corps out west to help in Tennessee or Mississippi. That would be fine by me. Maybe then I could get a furlough and go see Momma and baby sister. Heck, maybe I could even find Pops."

"General Lee'll probably get his way, won't he?"

"Probably. He's the most powerful man in the entire Confederacy and nobody wants to cross him. Besides, he's always right, so it's hard to argue with his way of thinking."

"You ever see him, Billy?"

"I saw him ride past me a few times. I tell you, he looks like I'd imagine God to look. Wherever he goes, the men cheer. When I see him take off his hat and bow the way he does, well, I get goose bumps all over." Coming back to the present, Billy cautioned, "Just remember. War ain't fun. Pay attention to your officers, especially when we're drilling. One more thing: *never* volunteer to be flag bearer. I know it's supposed to be an honor 'n' all, but the flag bearers get killed in every fight."

"Why?"

"The enemy shoots 'em on purpose, to make the flag fall and confuse us. But don't take offense. We do the same to their flag bearers."

As they approached the camp, Zeke saw a circle of men raising a fuss and hollered, "Come on, Billy! It's a fight!"

Two farm boys from Company C had thrown off their jackets and were wrestling in the black Virginia mud, each trying to choke the other to death.

"Break it up—," Billy started to shout, elbowing his way into the crowd. Sergeant Cawley pushed his way in from the opposite direction. The corporal and the sergeant each grabbed a wrestler by the back of his shirt. "Break it up, now!" Cawley commanded, the veins bulging in his forehead and thick neck. "Save it for the Yankees!"

· · · · ·

"Finish policing your camp and get ready for drill," the sergeant ordered later that afternoon. As the men assembled, Zeke squeezed next to Nate, and they headed to the open fields. For the next two hours, the regiment practiced deployment, advances, retreats, charges, and dressing the lines in battle—everything a boy could ever imagine doing on a battlefield, and much more.

"Pay attention!" Sergeant Cawley suddenly hollered, leaning in close to Zeke's face. "What are you smiling at, boy?"

Zeke quickly erased the grin from his face. He hadn't realized that he'd been smiling the entire time. "Sorry, sir! Won't happen again."

"It better not, or you'll be knee deep in crap for a week."

As the sergeant stalked off, Nate elbowed Zeke and warned, "Don't get on his bad side! He's a mean old cuss. I call him Old Holler."

Lunch was a biscuit, a thick slice of some half-cooked pork, and a sour apple. "How can y'all survive with rations like this?" Zeke asked, disappointed, looking around as though expecting the main course to appear.

"You've got no choice," Billy replied. "When we marched into Maryland last year, we only ate every other day—and that was just a handful of raw corn and some apples."

"Ain't nobody died from starving. Hot lead and scurvy'll kill you quicker," Nate replied. He broke wind and chuckled.

· · · · ·

For two days, the crew and all able-bodied passengers aboard the *Guy Mannering* labored below deck bailing water that threatened to capsize the ship. The mid-deck air was thick, sticky, and humid. With the hatches closed and hundreds of passengers who had not bathed in several weeks confined below decks, the stench became offensive to everyone. Many of the passengers tied cloths soaked in various spices around their faces in an effort to filter the stagnant air. In sharp contrast, the *Guy Mannering* shipmates seemed largely unaffected by the odors that permeated the ship as they wrestled with ropes and sails.

Children wailed continuously, held and hushed by mothers with white, pinched faces. Three men were washed overboard and lost to the seas before anyone could even make a move to rescue them. Dr. Joseph Bryarly was kept busy going from berth to berth below decks, holding basins for sick passengers, comforting children, wiping cool water across fevered foreheads, and assuring frightened mothers and grandmothers that the ship was seaworthy and would ride out the storm.

As he made his rounds, he noticed a beautiful red-haired, green-eyed woman doing the same. During those endless days and nights, he caught glimpses of her walking the decks with wailing babies, bringing broth to passengers too weak to feed themselves, and singing lullabies to small children. Once he overheard a young widow tell her, "You're a blessing to us all, Ana. God will bless you in return one day."

Finally, four days after the gale-force winds began to blow, the winds and waves subsided. Grieving friends and family gathered on deck around nine bodies wrapped in white sheets—passengers who hadn't survived the first month of their voyage. The priest led the crew and passengers in singing an old Irish dirge in honor of the loved ones who would be consigned to the ocean's depths, forever entrusted to God's merciful care. The priest committed their souls to God, and the bodies were slipped overboard into the sea. Sharks, cruising alongside the ship, waited for their daily meals of discarded fish or rotten garbage. On this occasion, they feasted on human flesh. The mourners cried out in grief and horror when the feeding frenzy began before the service had even ended.

With the ship nearly becalmed, the afternoon after the storm passed quietly. The seamen were unusually hospitable to the passengers who remained on deck. Some breathed in the fresh air gratefully, basking in the welcome sunshine; others clustered around mourners. The scene belowdecks seemed equally peaceful; most passengers were either sleeping or trying not to disturb those who were.

Joseph made his rounds yet again, then stretched out on his mid-deck pallet and immediately fell asleep from exhaustion. But his was not the restful sleep of a weary physician. He tossed and turned as his mind was attacked by yet another nightmare from his past, blending images of fantasy with reality. In his subconscious mind, he was propelled back in time to the place that haunted his dreams: Bethlem Royal Hospital.

Thrashing against the flat, rusted bars only inches from his face, Joseph moaned and screamed in terror and disbelief, "NO!... Dear God, no!" The doctor was being held captive by a medieval torture device horizontally hung from the ceiling, fifteen feet above a deep vat of frigid water. The asylum's newest torture equipment was secured by chains on all four corners that were connected through a series of pulleys leading to a large iron brake switch in the corner of the auditorium. Coal-oil lamps and torches illuminated the chamber, exposing pale gray walls covered with mold. Several onlookers participating in the popular asylum tour appeared awestruck by the spectacle.

"Lord Kennington … Please … I beg you … release me!"

Out of the corner of his eye, Joseph could see the smug grin on the administrator's face, refusing to acknowledge his pleas for help.

"Maniacs and lunatics often beg for release," his lordship announced, in a successful effort to impress his guests. "They don't possess the cognitive capacity to understand the physiological value of Drowning Therapy.

"This fascinating device is known as the Chinese Temple," he continued. "Dr. Joseph Guislain designed this latest advancement in curative medical treatments. By simulating drowning, asphyxia overcomes the madman—thus relieving his troubled mind, subduing his mania, and eventually curing his madness."

Two ladies of fashion stood nearby, impressed by the human freak show and the dashing, well-dressed Lord Kennington.

Tourists paid five pence each to visit the hospital and witness these displays of shameless voyeurism. Touring the Bedlam madhouse had become one of the trendy social events of the era. Glaring at madmen and wretched paupers helped idle aristocrats fill their days while their visits filled the pockets of corrupt administrators. Asylum administrators boasted that their tour rivaled England's other attractions, including the Tower of London.

This bizarre scene was all too familiar to Joseph, but this time something was different. Something was terribly wrong! This time, the poor madman being tortured under the pretense of psychiatric treatment was Joseph himself.

"Please … please, Lord Kennington, have mercy on me! There's been some terrible mistake. It's me … Dr. —!"

"Lower him, lads … let's give the devil his due."

The doctor, flinging his hands through the bars in an act of desperation to stop the device, cut his forearms. Overhead, chains whirred loudly as the mechanical brake was released, plunging the rectangular cage into the dark, frigid waters. Garbled sounds and bubbles slowly rose to the surface while the cage sank out of sight.

Joseph's lungs burned as he fought to hold his breath and cling to life. *Dear merciful God! Please ... please don't let me die! Please God ... don't let me die ... not like this!* A sudden gasp filled his nose and lungs with water. His head pounding, his pulse racing, hundreds of images flashed through his mind. Light from the water's surface slowly began fading into darkness.

Pausing for dramatic effect, Lord Kennington waited until the water was deathly calm and only then announced, "Haul him up, lads. We want to cure the poor lunatic, not kill him."

Clanking chains and rattling gears startled the spectators in the gallery and filled the air with excitement. As the cage was hoisted up, water poured out of the device. In an arrogant display of contempt, Lord Kennington raised his right heel to avoid soaking his shoe. The brawny handlers unlocked the padlock, swung wide the hinged iron-bar top, and removed the occupant's limp body, dropping him on the floor facedown. They shoved against his back until water spewed from his lungs. He gasped desperately. Labored breathing and heavy panting followed. When everyone realized the lunatic had survived his treatment, the small crowd erupted in applause for Lord Kennington, who bowed gracefully with self-righteous appreciation. One of the handlers looked up at Kennington and asked, "Do you reckon he's cured, Gov'ner?"

"I'm certain he is cured," Lord Kennington announced gaily to the crowd. In a quiet aside to the handlers, he shrugged and said, "At any rate, after he wakes, he'll be no worse for wear. Carry him back to the cellar and chain him." Waving the handlers and their burden off dismissively, he added with a wicked grin, "Let him drip dry!"

• • • • •

"NO!" Joseph screamed. Lurching into an upright position, he grabbed the hand in front of his face and shoved a young woman violently to the deck. In her hand, she held a sweat-soaked rag—Joseph's sweat.

"Doctor! It's me ... Ana Laoise MacIntyre."

Although he didn't recognize the name, her quiet, soothing voice calmed his tirade. Exhausted from the nightmare, he went limp, physically and emotionally. After what seemed like hours, he looked up into large round green eyes and whispered, "Please forgive me." Joseph reached for her hand, and she cautiously took his. "I beg you, please forgive me, I meant you no harm."

She soothed him saying, "Aye, I know, Doctor." She wiped his brow as he slumped against a wooden support beam. "You need your rest now. Try for some *sweet* dreams this time." She waited a moment by his side and leaned close to hear him whisper, more to himself than to her.

"These nightmares! They torment my soul! At times, I find myself performing strange treatments on helpless victims. Unspeakable things I never would do—and never have done—to any of my patients. But this time I was the one at the mercy of cruel handlers."

"You've seen harsh things, Doctor, and you can't forget them. But remember this: the good Lord knows your heart. You be a good man … a decent man." Ana stroked his hair. "I've seen the way you care for the passengers. Saving some 'n' grieving with others."

Joseph's voice was weak and fragmented, "But what can these nightmares mean? They only began after I received the commission from Jefferson Davis, ordering my return home."

"'Tis the devil's work, of that you can be sure."

She waited patiently as the doctor drifted slowly into a deep sleep. As she turned to leave, she heard him whisper, "Thank you."

This time he didn't dream.

· · · · ·

Ana Laoise Dougall MacIntyre, a striking thirty-three-year-old widow, was immigrating to America with her parents and only remaining brother. Three other brothers as well as her husband had died several years earlier when a fever had swept through their small village. Unlike many of her neighbors who had lost family members during the plague and, several years later, the famine, Ana had a small stash of pound notes hidden in her sugar bowl. Soon after the funeral, she had returned to her parents' ancient home several miles away, in Ballinglass, Galway County. More than three hundred years earlier, the home's original Dougall had proudly and optimistically carved his family name over the front door.

The family had flourished for generations, but by 1845, the Potato Famine had forced this industrious family to the brink of starvation. In desperation, they left their home and diseased fields behind and began a succession of moves from place to place, crossing over into England, then slowly working their way southeast, searching for food, for work, and for dignity. They hoarded Ana's pound notes carefully, but by 1861, when they arrived at the port of Liverpool, they were near despair. During the previous three years, they had buried thirteen kinsmen. The reward for all their struggles and hard labors had been a pitiful thirty-four pounds in savings and a rough shelter—barely more than a roof and four walls—on the outskirts of the teeming industrial city.

During the middle years of the nineteenth century, the Dougalls were following in the footsteps of hundreds of thousands of Irish men and women—and many thousands more would follow their path. Irish shanty towns had cropped up all across England, uninvited and unwelcome by the natives. Culture wars and crimes quickly followed. "We Dougalls are a proud lot with a fine Irish heritage. We won't live like this—we're not livin', we're barely survivin'," Patrick Dougall, the family patriarch, announced one cold night as the four surviving family members huddled around their fire. "America could be no worse for us, and there's talk that it can be much better!"

Like hundreds of thousands of other Irish men and women, the Dougall clan couldn't raise the ten pounds sterling per person to pay for the journey as well as a sum large enough to feed the family until work was obtained, so Patrick, his wife, and son agreed under duress to become indentured servants for two years after landing in America, to pay for their voyage. Ana, however, announced that she would seek employment as a nurse in the medical hospitals as a free woman before she would agree to servitude. "I'm too proud and too stubborn to become someone's servant," she had explained as the family finalized plans for their voyage. "I have funds enough to make a start and to help you when you're ready to accept help," she informed her parents, with her hands on her hips and her eyes flashing.

It wasn't until the night after the storm ceased that the doctor made the family's acquaintance. Hours after Ana had tiptoed away from his pallet, the doctor smelled the aroma of a fragrant stew and opened his eyes to find a plump, kindly woman holding a bowl smiling at him.

"My daughter thought that the doctor might need some doctorin' of his own," Mary Margaret Dougall informed him, handing him the bowl.

From that point on, the Dougall family welcomed the doctor into their family circle as though he were a long-lost son. When they learned that one of the doctor's cargo trunks had been lost or stolen at the pier and his only remaining possessions were two cases of medical books and his journals, Mrs. Dougall set to work sewing him shirts, while her son loaned him an extra pair of trousers. For nine weeks as the ship sailed across the ocean, the doctor shared poetry books with Mary Margaret, discussed English and American politics with Patrick, offered books and advice about America to Michael Dougall, and reviewed medical procedures with Ana Laoise Dougall MacIntyre.

Every so often, Ana would interrupt the doctor to ask about his home in Alabama, his childhood, or his friends in America. "I don't want to bore you with old stories of people long gone or places far away," he would tell her. But he would go into great detail about his work at Bethlem Asylum and the torturous, inhumane treatment of its unfortunate inmates.

"You have such a fine heart for those people," Ana marveled. "When you speak of their pain, I could almost believe you had been incarcerated yourself."

Joseph shuddered and Ana reached for his hand in sympathy. "Enough about me," the doctor would insist. "Tell me about your home in Ireland. Tell me about your family members I'll never meet. Tell me about the woman named Ana." While the beautiful red-haired woman laughed and chatted, the quiet, graying doctor would watch her with a glimmer in his eyes and a smile playing around his mouth.

The doctor was quietly falling in love.

And so was the woman who hoped to become a nurse.

Three

Secreted among hundreds of Confederate troops collected at every railroad stop between Jackson and Richmond, Mary Beth Greene quietly slipped out of the last car of the Central Virginia Railroad. She was followed closely by an infatuated young major named Ricky Gordon, who had helped "arrange" her passage by hiding her and an impressive collection of luggage in the cargo railcar, where she and her trunk and satchels shared space with rifles, powder kegs, provisions, and crates of chickens, all stacked nearly to the car's ceiling. "Let me help you hail a carriage, ma'am," Ricky called out, pushing his way through the crowd while two privates struggled with her luggage.

"I declare, Mister Gordon, you have been a godsend," she said, gently fanning her face with a French-made ivory creation and smiling sincerely up at the handsome young officer. Any woman other than a true courtesan would have batted her eyes or suggested she might soon swoon, but Mary Beth was too skilled at attracting men to employ commonplace techniques. "I intend to find Richmond's finest hotel—one that is sympathetic to the needs of officers and ladies such as myself." The jostling crowds and the confusion rampant in rail stations during a time of war made it easy for Mary Beth's presence to go undetected.

"May I escort you?" the major stammered.

"Why ... won't you get into trouble, leaving your company 'n' all?" she asked demurely. "You've done so much for me already that I wouldn't want you to avoid your duties."

The captivated look on the man's face was his only reply. Ricky leapt into the street to hail the first carriage that came his way, then helped Mary Beth climb into its interior as the two grinning privates turned her luggage over to the driver.

Mary Beth leaned out of the carriage window, offering her hand to the privates in gratitude. "You boys have been ever so kind to a single lady traveling by herself. Thank you ever so much!"

The tall private blushed. The other, a boy fresh out of the Tennessee hills, took her hand in his as though he were holding an exquisite piece of glassware. "You're my new reason for fighting in this war, Miss Mary Beth," he declared ardently. She winked at him, smiled once again, then waved as the driver called to his horses.

As the carriage made its way through the streets of Richmond, any worries the courtesan might have had about finding her way into the social fabric of the new Confederate capital faded. She counted at least five grogshops in three city blocks, two brothels, and one suspicious-looking house, *either a gambling house or a brothel*, she mused. Richmond more closely resembled a seedy, carnal resort town than a nation's capital. Main Street appeared to be a paradise for gamblers, prostitutes, and smugglers.

As the carriage turned the corner, the newcomers saw two Confederate artillerists sitting handcuffed beside a rain barrel in front of a blacksmith forge, while provost guards searched amongst the crowd, barking orders and stopping every soldier who passed near. "Major Gordon, what's all the fussing about?" Mary Beth asked, curiously.

"Looks like they're searching for deserters and stragglers," he explained just before the carriage halted in front of the hotel.

After her belongings were unloaded, Mary Beth turned once again to thank her escort, and the major planted a long, passionate kiss on the woman's immaculate gloved fingertips. "Miss Mary Beth, I want you to have this," he said, wrapping her fingers around a small satchel of gold and silver coins. "It's not so much, but it should help you get a good start here."

Without hesitation, she took the offering, cupping his cheek tenderly with her hand and gazing into his eyes with tears glistening in her own. The major had no way of knowing that Mary Beth Greene was already a wealthy woman—and fully intended to become Richmond's wealthiest woman before the war was over. But she had no intention of sharing that information. She was well trained in keeping secrets.

She turned to enter the hotel, reminding herself, *You just keep working, Mary Beth Greene. Soon, you'll have all the money you'll ever need. You can buy that place on the bayou just outside of New Orleans, raise a family, and put this horrible life far behind you—forever!*

A middle-aged officer opened the hotel door for her. Smiling up at him, she inquired, "Would you be so kind as to help me with my luggage?" The officer motioned to a private who had been standing nearby; he quickly threw the trunk over his shoulder and grabbed one of the satchels while the major held out his arm and escorted Mary Beth into the hotel. "I declare," she mused, acting more like a debutante than a prostitute, "it's just not proper for a lady to check into a hotel unescorted in these dangerous times, now is it, Major?"

· · · · ·

Shortly after General Stonewall Jackson's death at Chancellorsville in early May 1863, General Lee divided his army into three corps, the first led by General James Longstreet, the Second Corps by General Richard Ewell, and the Third Corps was assigned to Stonewall Jackson's second-in-command, General A. P. Hill. Each corps numbered about twenty thousand men.

"Stonewall was one fighting general, I tell y'all what," Nate said. "I seen him at Antietam, tall on his horse, right in the thick of things. He weren't scared of dying a-tall—but I hate like heck to hear of him dyin' from a bullet shot by one of his own men!"

"This army will miss him and his abilities," a speaker unknown to Zeke predicted.

When Zeke leaned forward to see the man behind the spectacles, he noticed the care that the middle-aged soldier had taken to shave and keep his butternut-gray uniform immaculate. "Who is that fella? He looks like he just dressed up for a parade or something," Zeke whispered to his brother.

Billy slowly walked away and motioned for Zeke to follow. Turning, he said, "That's Daniel Thomas. He and his two sons enlisted with Pops and me. The boys were both killed at Antietam, with Daniel fighting right next to them. He went a little crazy after that. And the truth is, I think he still ain't back to normal yet."

"Man," Zeke said in awe, "that must've been awful for him."

"That was a bad day all around. Thousands of brave men on both sides went down. I got a taste of what Daniel might have been feeling when Pops got hit. It scared the daylights out of me! He was bleeding something fierce, and his leg looked like it was plumb blown away. You know how tough our old man is. He was yelling for me to shut up because I was screaming louder than he was. I swear, Zeke, I thought he was a goner."

Zeke shook his head with a grin. "Pop's too ornery to die. I knew he was hurting bad when he came home, but he never let on like he was in pain. Momma wouldn't have listened to much bellyaching anyway. It was funny to watch Pops trying to get out of bed and get around just so's he could go outside and get away from Momma's fussing at him for getting shot."

"Pops never was one to sit still for very long."

Zeke changed the subject. "So this Daniel fella, is he gonna be all right?"

"He seemed fine at Fredericksburg and Chancellorsville, but he was real calm in battle—too calm—like nothing much mattered anymore. He is one smart man. Went to school up in the Northeast somewhere. He's got all kinds of book smarts, and when he speaks, smart men listen. I hope you will, too, Zeke."

"He even looks like he's smart, with his eyeglasses 'n' all—and he'd have to be a heap smarter than I am to figure out how to stay that clean," Zeke suggested, watching Daniel Thomas out of the corner of his eye. "In fact, he looks like a high-up officer."

"I've *never* figured out how he stays so clean, but you're right, he does look like officer material. The sergeant told me he's been offered promotions and he just turns them all down. Says he wants to fight next to the boys, not from the back of a horse or at a headquarters somewhere," Billy added. It was obvious to his brother that he highly respected the man.

Suddenly a bugle blasted through the clearing—and for the first time, Zeke proudly realized that he recognized the call. "Time for more drilling," he said enthusiastically, as several veterans turned and gave him dirty looks.

· · · · ·

"Fall in! Column of two!" shouted Sergeant Cawley, looking at Zeke and scowling.

"You better tighten up, boy," Nate warned as the two quickly moved into column formation. "Old Holler's just waitin' for you to mess up so's he can scream a little extra."

I won't mess up! I won't mess up! I won't mess up! Zeke repeated over and over to himself as the column headed down the same road to the same field where they had practiced earlier in the morning. This patch of Virginia reminded Zeke of Mississippi: more woods and swamps than open fields, mountains rising off in the distance, and family farms rather than plantations claiming the cleared fields.

"You're doing better already," Billy whispered as he marched past his brother. After two hours of drills in the hot sunshine, the column headed back to camp for what Zeke hoped would be an afternoon of napping and talking. But Billy had other plans. "Grab your rifle and ammunition pack, Zeke."

"Sure thing. As soon's I finish my nap."

"Get your butt up now, *boy*, or I'll give you an order to," Billy insisted, poking his brother with his foot.

"Billy! I already know how to shoot a rifle."

"How many times do I have to tell you that you're not at a coon hunt? This is different, Zeke. It's dead serious—and you'll be dead if you're not as serious about learning soldiering. You need to know how to shoot fast while you're being shot at and listening for commands."

"You gonna shoot at me, *Corporal*?"

"If you don't come on, I might. March!"

Making their way to a nearby hay field, Billy turned to confront Zeke face-to-face. "I can't tell you often enough: you gotta take all of this serious. A war is a dangerous place to find yourself in, and I don't want to see nothing happen to you."

Zeke nodded and pulled his new rifle off his shoulder. He'd spent the past day admiring it. Now he loaded it, fired it, and reloaded as quickly as he could.

"Not bad, Zeke, but you've got to be quicker'n that." Billy pulled out his pistol, walked behind Zeke, and started firing rounds over his head.

"What are you doing?" Zeke screamed and flinched. "Dang it, Billy! You're trying to shoot me!"

"I'm just teaching you to keep your cool. Now start loading—and be quick about it."

Zeke loaded and reloaded his rifle until it was smoking hot. The brothers practiced together relentlessly for more than an hour before Billy finally spoke again. "That's enough. Let's get back and see what's for supper."

• • • • •

Reveille came at five o'clock in the morning, long before the sun started illuminating the fields and woodlands covered in tents. Grumbling, coughing, sputtering, and cursing, the soldiers yawned and stretched as they emerged from their tents following yet another restless night in camp. Zeke was among the first up and moving, although his stomach still rebelled against the meager rations he received three times a day. Despite the daily drilling, shooting practices with Billy, and Sergeant Cawley's raspy orders shouted in his ears, Zeke's enthusiasm hadn't waned.

"Still smiling, boy? Reckon I'll call you Smiley," Nate teased Zeke after muster, as the column marched back to camp and breakfast. "Y'all greenhorns are all alike. Couldn't pour pee outta a boot with the directions on the bottom."

Zeke grinned. "I know one thing. I'm ready to shoot me some blue-bellies."

"It's coming soon enough," Billy announced to the men under him. "General Lee's back from Richmond, and it looks like we're heading up north into Maryland or Pennsylvania to pay a social call on our fine northern friends."

"Really? Are you sure, Billy? When do we leave? Should I start to pack up now?"

"Calm down and keep your mouth shut, for heaven's sake! You think this is all some big adventure—but it ain't. This is *war*, Zeke! Sometimes I wonder what possessed Momma to let you leave the farm."

"Well, pardon me, *Mister* Corporal William Gibson!"

Billy stopped in mid-stride, clenched his fists, gritted his teeth, and headed straight for his brother. It wasn't hard to read his intentions on his face.

Nate jumped in between the two at the last second, stretching out his hands between the brothers and saying, "Now, c'mon, Billy … Zeke was only funning. Don't do nothin' to get yourself in trouble."

Glaring at his brother fiercely, Billy moved on down the line, informing the men about the need to be prepared to move at any moment.

Billy and the rest of the officers were all absent from camp after supper. "Something's up and they've been told to keep quiet," Nate said to Zeke, as they milled around camp restlessly. "Billy told more than he oughta. 'Sides, you poked him pretty good! That ol' boy was madder than a wet hen."

"Why do they keep everything so secret?" Zeke asked.

"Spies, turncoats, men who might drink and then talk too much. Word can travel very fast—even to enemy lines." Daniel Thomas had been standing nearby and he spoke up when Nate hesitated to reply. "I sincerely believe that General Lee thinks this army is invincible," Daniel continued. "If we're successful at defeating the Federal Army now, Europe may realize our legitimacy and send aid. The Confederacy would have grounds to sue for peace."

Nate quickly changed the subject when he jumped to his feet hollering, "Dang it! If these darn lice get any bigger, I'm gonna have to start naming 'em, just like they was kinfolk!"

· · · · ·

The Virginia sky had looked threatening when the soldiers turned into their tents that night. Several hours later, the storm arrived. Streaks of lightning followed by booming thunder rocked the camp. Long before reveille, Zeke woke up, soaked to the skin and lying in a bed of mud; when he glanced at his brother, he realized that the storm hadn't caused him any discomfort—yet.

Torrents of hail rattled through the pitch-black trees where the soldiers took shelter as high winds demolished some of the cruder tents. Men scrambled frantically to make emergency tent repairs and save their rucksacks from getting soaked all the way through. And then, the bugles sounded reveille. That day, Zeke had his first taste of soldiering in the rain and mud.

"On your feet! Now!" Sergeant Cawley paced back and forth, shouting above the storm, seemingly unconcerned about the streaking lightning and punishing hail. "Fall in, ladies!" he taunted his troops. *This bulldog of a man is fearless*, Zeke marveled, hunching his shoulders against the onslaught of hail.

"Surely we won't have to drill in this," the boy moaned to Nate. "It's still dark outside. How we gonna drill in the dark? I ain't crazy enough to be marching around carrying a rifle on my shoulder in a thunderstorm!"

The hail had stopped bouncing off Sergeant Cawley's hat by the time he finished roll call and a Captain William Tuttle had arrived to announce, "We have orders to be ready to move out. We'll await further instructions from headquarters. In the meantime, return to your tents and prepare yourselves for a hard march."

Zeke searched through the gray gloom for Billy and found him staring back with a strange look on his face. Zeke pointed to the tent, which he had moved to a spot under a spreading oak. The brothers sat quietly for a minute, until Zeke asked, "What's bothering you? And don't say you're just worried about me."

"I'm just trying to get you home alive and in one piece."

"That's bull. Tell me the truth!"

"You wouldn't … You can't understand."

"'Course I can! This is your brother talking."

"I've never told anybody this, not even Pops."

"I swear, I won't tell a cotton-picking soul."

Billy fidgeted for a moment before he looked his brother in the eyes and admitted, "All right. It's about the fighting. I love it! I dread it until it begins and then I get all tingly. It's hard to describe, but when a battle starts I get almost … crazy. I know how the Good Book tells us to act, but when the cannons start booming and the bugles start blaring, I can't wait to begin killing other men. That bothers me mightily … because I enjoy it all."

"So, what's wrong with that? Those boys in blue are trying to kill you."

"I know that, but I don't see men when I start firing my gun. I see the deer or wild hogs we used to shoot back home. But these are people, Zeke! People with families who love them … same as you and me."

"It's a war, Billy! Why're you so upset about killing men who are trying to kill you?" Zeke scratched his head, trying to follow his brother's logic.

"It's not just that. Now that I'm an officer, I have to keep my head. I'm responsible for directing you and the other men. Keeping my head is something I've never done in a battle."

Zeke grinned. "You always enjoyed fighting—this war just

took it all to a higher level. Don't fret about that—I know that you can do anything you set your mind on doing. Do you want me to tell you some of Momma's old sayings—like 'Don't put the cart before the horse'?"

"I've got them all memorized, thanks," Billy said with a sigh. He paused for a moment and put his hand on his brother's shoulder. "Thanks for listening, Zeke. Maybe you're right. Maybe I'm just worrying too much."

As the rain continued to fall, water ran like a river through the tent. Zeke complained, and Billy quickly scolded him. "Just be glad it's not cold outside. There's nothing more miserable than being freezing cold and wet for hours—or even days—on end."

"Do you think we're headed to Pennsylvania, Billy?"

"Looks like it—and soon. How'd you figure that out?"

"Just keeping my ears open." Zeke grinned and then admitted, "Actually, Daniel predicted it. He's sure one smart fella."

"He's a good man," Billy agreed. "You'll learn a lot listening to him. He sees the big picture of the war, not just the day-to-day battles."

"He thinks the Yanks will quit if we defeat 'em in Pennsylvania. Do you think they'll give up?"

"You never know. Even if we defeat this army, there are still a lot of Yankees out in the West to deal with. I hear tell that General Ulysses Grant's prowling around Vicksburg. The South has to deal with him—and that won't be easy. But maybe, if we can scare Lincoln and a passel of Northerners enough, they'll negotiate a peace. But first things first. We have to do our job."

"How many boys do you reckon they have?" Zeke asked, with the impatience of youth. "How many do we have?"

"Our spies say a hundred thousand Yanks are camped just across the river. With General Longstreet's reinforcements, we might have sixty-five thousand infantry and artillery."

"And we're *still* gonna attack?"

"General Lee don't care much about numbers. We've been

outnumbered in every battle so far, and we haven't lost a fight yet. Remember what Pops used to say—'It ain't the size of the man in the fight, it's the size of the fight in the man!'"

Four

Secretary of War Edward M. Stanton, the forty-nine-year-old former Attorney General for the United States of America, stood in a congested hallway inside the Philadelphia Courthouse of the Judge Advocate, Captain Alfred U. Higginbotham. Angrily scratching his long black-and-gray beard, he paced the floor. Suddenly, the courtroom doors were flung open and a detail of garrison guards escorted a shackled private down the corridor, followed by a formidable procession of Union military officers. Stanton aggressively pushed his way through the crowd to ambush the young defense attorney.

His prey was an inexperienced twenty-two-year-old graduate of the Dickinson School of Law by the name of Steven A. Billings. His poorly prepared defense had just resulted in a court martial verdict of guilty—death by firing squad—for eighteen-year-old Private Benjamin Wiley.

"Mr. Billings, I must speak with you—*immediately!*"

Steven's heart froze in his broad chest when he saw the rage on Secretary Stanton's red face. He rubbed the back of his neck and fumbled with the brown derby hat in his hand. He could feel his sandy-blond hair rise on his head. Steven unconsciously stood straighter and tugged at the waistband of his trousers, pulling them higher over his potbelly before he gulped and nodded.

"Yes … yes, sir, Mr. Secretary."

Secretary Stanton slammed open a door leading into the judge's chambers and shoved Steven inside. The Secretary of War towered over the little man, further intimidating the already frightened young lawyer.

"Mr. Billings," the Secretary fumed. "I cannot begin to convey the deep—*deep*—disappointment I feel." Stanton began pacing the floor, waving his fists in the air. Steven stumbled backward into a seat and prepared himself for the tirade he knew he deserved.

"Guilty? That jury of military officers found a simpleminded youth *guilty*? That boy was frightened out of his mind and incapable of speaking in his own defense. He trusted you to protect him, Mr. Billings. You let that boy down!"

"Mr. Secretary, when you stormed out of the courtroom, I—"

Stanton interrupted the young attorney. "Why didn't you pursue a strategy based on a plea of temporary insanity?"

"Judge Advocate Higginbotham had warned me that a mental illness plea on behalf of deserters wouldn't stand up in his courtroom."

"Temporary insanity is not the same as mental illness."

"Sir, I honestly believe that in the heat of the intense emotions, a battle can cause some men to lose sound reason and commit acts that under normal circumstances they would never attempt or even consider. I just didn't think the judge would listen to that plea." Steven pulled out his handkerchief and wiped his brow. "I had no idea that you were concerned about this particular case, Sir."

Edward M. Stanton erupted in anger, slamming his fist on the desk and shouting, "I'm concerned about every case! Our military leaders are overwhelming our courts with trials for men they charge with desertion. The men you are expected to *defend* with all the intellectual means at your disposal have families, families that have friends, Mr. Billings! Families who write letters to President Lincoln—letters that I have to answer for!"

"I understand, sir. Please believe me! My failure today will haunt me—always."

"You march back to your desk and write a masterful appeal—and you save that boy's life. Now!"

"But, sir, Higginbotham strictly warned me that such a defense would not be tolerated. He has never mitigated, pardoned, or suspended a court martial for any cause."

"Son, last week I met with President Lincoln. I saw a man stricken with grief who asked me, 'Tell me which is the greater of two sorrows: a life lost on the battlefield or a life lost at the hands of a merciless judge advocate?'"

Defense Attorney Steven Billings swallowed hard and stared unblinkingly at the Secretary of War as the man continued speaking.

"Mr. Billings, I understand that you cannot save all the men you represent—but pray God that you save at least some of them!"

· · · · ·

Three miles off the coast of North Carolina, the *Guy Mannering* was preparing for a midnight run through the Union blockade. A calm sea and bright half-moon aided in navigation, while revealing little to the Federal forces that were undoubtedly scanning the horizon. With all lights out, all hands on deck, and all passengers below, the *Guy Mannering* crept into the harbor. Without armaments and without any intention of engaging the warships, the captain was taking a carefully calculated risk in running the blockade. As the sun climbed in the sky and the coastline grew visible, two shallow-draft iron steamers came into sight two miles northwest of the *Guy Mannering*, whose crew watched anxiously, softly making bets on the outcome of possible encounters and hoping that the steamers would provide a much-welcomed diversion for the Union Navy. Their hopes were justified. Cannon fire suddenly boomed in the distance as the slower of the two steamers fell victim to the Union's eighteen-pound guns.

With the warships' attention distracted, the *Guy Mannering* glided silently into a shallow river port north of Wilmington. Confederate work teams had managed to carve a narrow river passage through the dense wilderness leading into a small oxbow lake, and the port was well concealed and well fortified. The passage was lined with cannons and makeshift bunkers on both sides. The immigrants stared at these harbingers of war. Within two hours, all passengers, cargo, and livestock had been hurried off the ship and quickly dispersed into the surrounding countryside.

Destined for indentured servitude, the Irish immigrants were met by several six-mule freighter wagons, which would carry them to Richmond over backcountry roads and cattle trails, the safest travel routes in war-torn Carolina. After bribing the teamster with his carefully hoarded English silver coins, Joseph climbed aboard the wagon carrying the Dougall family and a cluster of other Irish clans.

As the wagons pulled away from the hidden port, bright blue skies and warm breezes welcomed the weary travelers. "'Tis a breathtakingly lovely morning, Joseph," the red-haired beauty whispered, with her face turned toward the sunrise.

"Ana, every morning since I met you has been breathtaking— I thank God that we have yet another day together."

Ana reached over and held Joseph's hand when the wagons topped a ridge and a panoramic view spread before their eyes. Lush green fields were bordered by a flowing brook. Deer grazed nearby. A covey of bobwhite quail, flushed from their hiding place, startled the wagonload of passengers, who were behaving more like tourists than indentured servants.

Joseph sat in a pleasant haze, amazed at his good fortune in finding Ana and at his departure from England. But the fear that had haunted him for three months lurked at the back of his mind. *I'm facing a future that only God fully understands.*

"Mrs. Dougall, the past two months have given me the happiest days of my life," Joseph said, casting a look at Ana's profile as he spoke to the kindly older woman.

"Does this look like your home in Alabama, Joseph?" Ana's twenty-four-year-old brother Michael asked. "Does all of America look like this?"

"America is vast, Michael; it has bogs like those in your beloved Ireland, vast green fields like those in Wales, majestic mountains higher than anything in the British Isles, sandy beaches, and rivers broader than the Thames."

Suddenly, the wagon lurched across the road's deep ruts, knocking passengers off their makeshift seats and sending trunks flying. The fourteen-year-old farm boy-turned-teamster leaped from his seat and straddled the left rear mule. "This road's a mite poorly," he called back to his passengers. "Next ten miles or so will shake your innards something fierce. Pa says y'all city folks might have soft bottoms." Those passengers who could understand the boy's accent laughed and the others joined in, happy to be back on firm ground with fresh air and beautiful views.

As the mules plodded their way up north, the passengers heard Casey's life story. He wove tales of his childhood on a small Tennessee farm near Pickwick, where his family had struggled to scratch out a living on rented land. "Then the war came," the boy said with a sigh. "Both of my big brothers, Ben and Samuel, were killed at Shiloh—and on the same day, in the same battle, Pa lost his right leg. Soon after we got the letter tellin' us the news, Ma and my baby sister caught the yellow fever and they died." When Casey's father arrived home to find his son scared and living on his own, struggling to survive, the man and boy left the farm for good. Now they were making more money than either had ever dreamed of, driving wagons for smugglers and blockade-runners trying to supply the South.

· · · · ·

For the next three weeks, the journey through Carolina and Virginia continued to be uneventful. Each night the mules would pull the wagons into a circle and the immigrants would set up camp, post guards, find kindling wood, light campfires, and cook meals. An occasional farmhouse or small town would offer comfort, an occasional treat, and news of the war. Whenever a newspaper was available, the doctor closely studied every page.

Back in Bedlam Asylum, the Confederacy's cause had seemed noble and majestic, but now Joseph Bryarly began to wonder. *For over fifteen years, I witnessed the deplorable treatment of God's most precious creation. I longed for the day when I would be free from Bedlam and the cruel Lord Kennington. Now, seeing a family like Casey's so ravaged by war, I can't help but wonder if any outcome is worth such a terribly high price.*

"Such a dear, sad little lad." Ana's soft voice startled Joseph from his dark thoughts. He glanced over the fire to see her watching Casey as he cared for the mules. "A young lad surely needs a mother's love."

"You're right." Joseph smiled—he always seemed to be smiling around Ana. "I was just wondering how many other families have been forever changed by this war."

"Aye, Joseph … ye be always thinking. Do you ever think of anything to do with me?" Her mischievous smile was irresistible.

Joseph wasted no time. He stood and held out his hand. "This is a lovely night for a walk, *Miss*! Might I have the pleasure of your company?"

"Well, aren't you bold 'n' chipper this evening," Ana said with another smile. She called over her shoulder as the couple headed off by themselves, "I'll be back directly to help with supper, Mama."

"What's to help?" Mr. Dougall called after them. "'Tis rabbit stew—it's been rabbit stew for days!"

Mrs. Dougall playfully slapped him with a ladle. "Patrick Dougall! You should be thankful for God's blessing."

They watched as Joseph and Ana disappeared down the narrow path. "Aye, thankful I am, Mary Margaret. Joseph is right when he says families will be changed forever by this war, 'tis certain." He walked over and hugged his wife, softly saying, "As for the Dougall clan, me thinks it will change us for the better. I give thanks to God for our deliverance from the troubles in our homeland."

· · · · ·

The third of June 1863 dawned bright and hot and still. *We'll be in Pennsylvania in no time!* Zeke exalted as he looked ahead at the long, seemingly endless column snaking its way toward Culpepper and to points beyond. Barksdale's Brigade was marching fast, despite the heat. Morning passed with no mention of breakfast, a fact that had not failed to escape Zeke's attention. "What about food? Maybe some cush?" he asked his brother.

Billy reached into his haversack, pulled out a big chunk of hardtack, and offered it with a grin. "Weren't you issued three days' rations just yesterday?"

"Yeah, but that stuff just don't fill me up."

"We may get some decent rations once we get to Culpepper, since we'll be the first division there. Maybe some provisions will be waiting."

"Dang it, Billy—you know all this stuff and you never hardly tell me any of it. What else is going on, if it won't ruin our cause by telling me?"

"I'm not supposed to go around blabbing. You never know who's listening, even when it's just me and you talking."

The brigade covered almost twenty miles that day before making camp in woodlands offering shade and the promise of game for their kettles. When Billy returned from a successful squirrel hunt and Zeke built a fire, the boy looked around the clearing at clusters of exhausted soldiers intent on making dinner and then falling asleep. "Nobody's close enough to hear now, so tell me some good stuff," Zeke whispered.

"We're gonna sit tight in Culpepper until General Hood's division joins us. I heard tell that ten thousand of our cavalry are riding just east of Culpepper, around Brandy Station, watching to see how the Yankees react to our movements."

"Do they know we're moving?"

"It's hard to hide sixty-five thousand men, Zeke," the corporal pointed out. "They got spies everywhere. They even got big balloons they can send up to scout what's happening with us. But, remember, they're scared of General Lee flanking them again. I heard the colonel say that they won't follow us until they're positive we're all headed north. That's why we're staying put at Culpepper for a few days, just to see what they do when General Ewell's Second Corps starts moving."

"Will we be the first corps there?"

"Probably not. The Second Corps is supposed to go up through the Shenandoah Valley to Maryland, followed by General Hill's Third Corps. We're gonna stay just east of the Blue Ridge Mountains and guard the mountain passes, to keep the Yanks from getting into the valley."

Unexpectedly, Sergeant Cawley barreled into the clearing, ordering "Fall in! One column of four! Now!"

The brigade marched until dusk, camped for the night, and arrived in Culpepper around noon the following day and set up camp near several clear-water springs. *These aren't like the muddy ones back in Mississippi*, Zeke mused. Though the countryside was scarred by earlier troop movements and skirmishes, spring was doing its best to cover the scars with a rich covering of spring green. Zeke asked Billy, "Will we have to drill while we're here?"

"Well, well! Tired of drilling after only a few weeks? I'm shocked! I thought you loved everything about being a soldier."

"Everything but the meals! I ain't tired of drilling. I'm just curious."

"Well, I doubt we'll be doing much drilling. The Yanks could pop up anywhere, especially their cavalry. Keep your eyes and ears open."

Settling into their temporary campsite, the Gibson boys saw a long column of Confederate cavalry spanning the horizon, then riding directly toward them. Zeke was fascinated by the officers in their dress uniforms, especially one with a big feather curving over the side of his hat.

"You know who that is talking to General Barksdale?" Billy asked, without taking his eyes off the horseman. "That's Jeb Stuart himself."

Zeke stared at the officer and then at his troops as they galloped past. "Man, is that what ten thousand cavalry riders look like? Sure is a pretty sight …." The boy thought for a moment, then pointed out, "That's forty thousand horseshoes! Whoa! That's a lot of steel!"

Finishing his conversation with General Barksdale, General Stuart mounted his magnificent horse and sped right past Zeke and Billy, flashing a quick salute. Zeke smartly saluted with, if possible, an even bigger grin. He turned to Billy and said, "I swear I got goose bumps, Billy. Feel my arm right there. I got little bumps on it!"

"I believe you! You've just seen a great general. He's always right where we need him."

· · · · ·

A full moon lit up the night sky—not that Joseph noticed. The nightly strolls with Ana were the highlight of his day. He tried to decide what he loved best about her: her charm, gentle spirit, soothing Irish tones, or her fiery support of those she cared for. He wanted to tell her what was in his heart, but the words always escaped him. He found himself stuttering like a schoolboy when he tried to speak of emotions. Yet to even the most casual observer, it was obvious that Joseph and Ana were falling in love.

Less than a quarter mile from camp, they came to an abandoned farmhouse. Joseph led Ana to a bench swing overlooking a small pond. The moonlight shimmered across the water's surface and its reflection danced within her sparkling green eyes. A gentle breeze stroked her hair. A pair of ducks glided across the pond, while the sounds of locusts, crickets, and bullfrogs filled the night air like a wilderness concert conducted by God himself.

Holding Ana's hand sent shivers of anticipation piercing deep into his soul as Joseph realized that he was hopelessly in love for the first time in his life. Meekly, slowly, he drew Ana closer. She teasingly pulled away, then leaned into the kiss she also desired. Unknown to Joseph, Ana had already decided that tonight would be the night they would share far more than just a kiss. Time, war, and the hardships of life all faded away in the moonlight. Ana stared deeply into his eyes, and Joseph instinctively lowered his head once again.

With a gentle touch, she raised his head and whispered, "'Tis the eyes, Joseph." Ana stroked his short gray beard. "What poet first noticed that eyes are the windows to our soul? Your eyes tell me that you've known hardship—there'd be no doubting that. But I've been wondering … Have you ever known love?"

Tears streamed down Joseph's face, coursing over Ana's fingers. He struggled within himself. *How can I tell her? How can I make her understand what this … what she … really means to me?*

"Ana, I have lived alone all my adult life, pouring myself into my duties because that is how I was raised. Whether that was folly or madness, I can no longer determine. I have never known love—as a boy or a man—until I met you."

"You're a lovely man. 'Tis true, Joseph Bryarly."

"Ana, I haven't always … what I mean to say is … I may not be the man you think I am … or need me to be," he confessed with genuine concern.

"I'll be the judge of that. Only the Lord knows the hearts of men, Joseph. I'll be trusting in Him to tell me who I'll be loving."

• • • • •

The abandoned farmhouse and swing became a lover's paradise that moonlit night. The woman who was no stranger to the physical pleasures of love established a new beginning in Joseph's arms.

When the moon began to sink in the sky, the man and the woman reluctantly returned to the camp. Neither had any desire to abandon the embrace or the warm spring evening in which they first unleashed their passions. They knew that their futures were uncertain, and that it might be a very long time before they were alone together again.

The camp was quiet. Most of their fellow travelers were asleep, with young children bedded inside the wagons for safety. Having taken the first watch of the night, Casey's silhouette could be seen in the distance standing on a tall rock. Ana's parents sat snuggling by the glowing embers of a dying fire.

"'Tis a good thing you're back, *Ana Laoise Dougall MacIntyre*," her father teased. "We were about to rouse the camp to go looking for the both of you!"

Joseph grinned, trying not to laugh.

"Hush your teasing, Patrick Dougall," his wife pinched his arm and stretched, then walked over to Ana and whispered, "Straighten your dress, darling. Some tales are better left untold." She added so Joseph could hear, "You'll find plenty of stew on the fire."

• • • • •

The war seemed to stand still while Company C was encamped at Culpepper. A small pond nearby yielded fish for three meals a day and a cool place to swim. One night, sitting around the campfire, Billy told the men that General Hood's division was camped just down the road. "General Hood's a brave fighter, but some boys in his old brigade were real hard to get along with. I once had a little run-in with a boy from Texas. We ended up squaring off outside of camp. Pops was laughing his butt off and betting more money on me than he had."

Zeke laughed. "I can just see him now. He'll bet on anything, so why not his own son whipping somebody?"

"I had to win because I knew Pops couldn't cover all his bets. Besides, this fool was really asking for it—and he got it real good. He was bleeding something fierce."

"He most certainly was," Daniel chimed in. "I was there, and it was a thorough victory for your brother, Zeke. However, I believe Billy's most impressive encounter was with that large fellow from Alabama."

In his own defense Billy claimed, "He started that fight—he just couldn't end it!"

"I never said anything to the contrary, my friend. I was simply boasting about your fistfights to your younger brother." Daniel turned to Zeke and added, "Some in the Northeast call it boxing. Billy has a major talent for boxing."

"Believe me, I've seen him in a scrap—he's dang good."

"Y'all need to shut up and find something to do," Billy replied. "Reckon we need to take a little march."

The men of Company C lined the south bank of the Rapidan River. Zeke swore several times that he saw Yankees hiding amongst the underbrush. *Maybe Zeke was just wishing he saw them*, Billy thought. *Soon enough, little brother, you'll see plenty of Yanks.* The rumblings of artillery could be heard faintly in the distance.

"What do you think, Smiley? If'n them was Yankee cannons, your britches would be full up again, huh?" Snickering, Nate remembered Zeke's first experience with cannon fire. Fanning one hand across his butt and holding his nose with the other, Nate danced around in a circle.

Ignoring Nate's antics, Zeke asked, "Whose fire is that, Billy?"

"Hard to tell, but that's over where General Stuart and the cavalry have been for some time now. I'll go see what's up."

Daniel spoke up. "I believe it's the Yankee cavalry. They've been getting bigger and bolder as every month of this war passes. They may be gearing up to test General Stuart and his boys."

"Is their cavalry bigger than ours? 'Cause ours has almost ten thousand troops," Zeke announced proudly.

"If I had to venture a guess, I would say yes. Everything else they have is bigger than ours, but not better. That's the difference, Zeke."

· · · · ·

It was almost dark when Billy came back full of details and eager to share good news with his men. "We whipped them again, boys! They got the jump on us. They even brought in some infantry to help the cavalry, but we rallied and held the field. Outnumbered again, and we still won!"

Nate arrived back at camp from his work detail. Covered in mud and sweat, he plopped down by the fire next to Daniel, Billy, and the rest.

"Where've you been, Nate?" Zeke asked, then suddenly frowned. "And what the devil is that God-awful smell?"

"Aw, dang, if Old Holler didn't catch me tossing a garter snake in the outhouse," Nate whined, scratching himself furiously. "How's I suppose to know Lieutenant Tipton was sittin' in there?"

Fighting back a grin, Billy asked, "So, what'd Cawley have you do?"

"Wade knee-deep in latrine duty all night." His friends hooted with laughter. "I been busier than a one-legged man in a butt-kicking contest," Nate added with a grin.

"Man, you reek, Nate! Go down to the creek and wash up," Zeke protested.

"Reckon you're right, Smiley. That's a right powerful smell—the kinda smell what'd bring a tear to a glass eye!"

Five

As the wagon train carrying the Dougall clan neared Richmond, the passengers began seeing increasing signs of war. Endless streams of displaced families, carrying or carting all the possessions left to them, clogged the roadways. Soldiers were on the move, singly, in units, or dashing across country on horseback. Shanty towns similar to those the Dougalls had known outside Liverpool teemed with ragged women, children, and old people whose homes had been destroyed. In the distance, the crack of gun shots and the booming of an occasional artillery barrage interrupted the human sounds of the city. Trains clanged and rumbled as they chugged out of the capital in every direction, and shrill locomotive whistles announced the arrival of yet another Weldon railroad delivery of dead soldiers, wounded veterans, and new recruits to the Confederate capital. A continuous column of battle-weary farmers and miners dressed in all shades of butternut brown and gray, carrying every make and vintage of weapon, streamed toward the old Richmond fairgrounds, which had hastily been converted into an army post at the start of the war. The wagon train lurched awkwardly down the dusty, rutted city streets on the final leg of the immigrants' journey.

"I reckon you best get out here, Doctor," Casey suggested,

pointing to the outline of buildings barely visible through a sparse pine thicket. "That there's the hospital you asked about. It's shore gonna be a long walk from Seventh Street."

While Mr. Dougall and Michael helped unload Joseph's bag and boxes, the doctor and Ana jumped down from the wagon. As a dozen onlookers watched curiously, Joseph looked into the glistening eyes of the woman he had come to love. "Ana, I don't know what's in store for either of us, so it's next to impossible to make plans right now—but I hope you know how I feel about you and your family. Send word to me at Wingate Asylum as soon as you've found lodging—and let me know where your parents and Michael will be working. I'll come as soon as I can."

As the mules snorted and stamped their feet and Casey called to the Dougalls to climb back onto the wagon, the couple quickly embraced, then Joseph turned to kiss Mrs. Dougall's cheek and shake the hands of Michael and Patrick Dougall. "Casey, take care of yourself—and if you ever need help, come by to see me," Joseph said, extending his hand to the fourteen-year-old who had become part of his extended family. Ana's father held her elbow as she climbed back into the wagon and he scrambled up behind her. Casey snapped the reins and shouted to the mules.

The wagon slowly pulled away, groaning in protest. The cloud of dust that rose from the wagon and the flow of people riding, running, or walking in the city street nearly choked Joseph as he stood alone in the midst of strangers, straining for the last glimpse of the departing caravan.

• • • • •

Across the busy street, a young and stunning mulatto woman watched Joseph curiously as he turned to a young teenage boy in the crowd and asked for his help in carrying his cartons and bag up to the Chimborazo Hospital complex. The woman's thoughtful emerald green eyes then turned to the major general at her side. She smiled sweetly up at him, linked arms, and suggested, "Shall we continue our afternoon together in a less-frequented part of town?"

"Your wish is my command, Miss Mary Beth!"

• • • • •

Together Joseph and his companion set off down the busy lane leading to what appeared to be a gigantic complex spreading across forty acres on Chimborazo Heights. *One hundred fifty buildings here, the news accounts said*, he marveled. Never before had Dr. Joseph Bryarly seen such a massive hospital, but that wasn't the sight that riveted his eyes. Hundreds of men—perhaps a thousand—were strewn on the ground, many begging for help. Women and walking-wounded soldiers could be seen distributing water from buckets and dippers as these soldiers waited for stretcher-bearers to claim them for treatment. Officers mounted on horseback dashed past in both directions, seemingly oblivious to the sight of wounded and dying men. Joseph's first instincts prompted him to roll up his sleeves and offer the wounded emergency assistance, but he knew that the hospital administration had been waiting impatiently for months for his arrival. He couldn't postpone the inevitable any longer.

"They say there's more 'n six *thousand* wounded inside them walls," the teenager told the doctor, his head swiveling as he took in the sights. "These boys came from the battle of Chancellorsville four days ago."

Joseph couldn't bring himself to respond. Aghast at what he was seeing and hearing, he trained his eyes on the path ahead, pondering war's meaning as he walked—and then he pondered his fate. *Dear Lord in heaven, never could I have imagined such a sight! Do you hear these cries for help? How could any of these men retain their sanity in such ghastly, pitiful conditions?*

Standing on the steps of the first official-looking building he reached, Joseph thanked his escort, paid him with a few coins, then stared at the panoramic view that spread before his eyes from the elevated bluff. The towering masts of warships and blockade-runners lined up in military precision along the docks bordering the James River as the ships were unloaded or prepared for action. To the west, Richmond's church spires pointed to the blue skies.

To the east, outside the city, could be glimpsed a vast green farmland as yet unaffected by the ravages of war. In the foreground, the roads leading to and from Chimborazo were clogged with wounded soldiers, ambulance wagons, merchant carts, and cavalry from the army post. The air was filled with shouts, curses, pleas for help, the snorting of mules, and the clip-clopping of animals' hooves. Not far from the hospital was the small—but quickly expanding—Oakwood Cemetery.

With so much frantic activity going on and no directional signs within view, Joseph was hard-pressed to decide which way to turn. He walked over to several officers chatting beneath a shade tree. "Pardon me," the doctor interrupted, reaching out his hand to a young sergeant sitting at a long wooden table, "I am in need of assistance. My orders require me to report to Chimborazo Hospital for …"

He was sharply interrupted. "Which division?"

"Sir?"

"Chimborazo has five divisions," the disgusted sergeant bellowed irately, while swatting at the green horseflies that were plaguing him. Then he repeated impatiently, "Which hospital division do you want? Virginia, Georgia, North Carolina, Alabama, or South Carolina?"

"I am the new superintendent of Wingate Asylum, by order of President Jefferson Davis."

"Heck, why didn't you say so in the first place?" The sergeant's foul mood seemed to dissipate as he considered the doctor's upper-class English accent. "You a Limey?"

Joseph cleared his throat in embarrassment. "I am a native of Alabama, but I've lived and worked in England so long that I must have taken on a British accent without being aware of the change—until now."

The sergeant stared at the doctor curiously for a moment before he yelled, "Private Johnson!"

A startled young boy dashed over. "Yes, sir! You call for me, Sergeant?"

"Take uhh ..." He turned again to Joseph and asked, "Say, what's your name?"

"Doctor Joseph Bryarly."

"Take Doc over to Bedlam South."

The blood running in Joseph's veins froze. *Please God, let this be some horrible coincidence. What sick person would nickname a mental hospital Bedlam?* He asked hesitantly, "Sergeant, what did you mean by Bedlam South?"

"Got no idea. I reckon it's some kind of nickname for the asylum. Wasn't opened more 'n a month or so when folks started calling it Bedlam South."

Before Private Johnson grabbed Joseph's bags and tossed them onto a nearby supply wagon bound for Wingate Asylum, the sergeant added, "You shorely do sound English—I reckon you'll pick up the right accent in a hurry, though, once you get used to livin' here." Joseph nodded, then followed the direction pointed out by Private Johnson. He climbed onto the front bench of the heavily loaded wagon just as a garrison detail arrived with two barefoot prisoners dressed in rags and bound in chains. Joseph realized with shock that they were boys barely in their teens, too young to grow more than fuzz on their cheeks. From out of grimy faces, their round eyes stared in terror at the shackles, the wagon, and the guards.

"Heard y'all are going over to Bedlam South," one of the guards roared. "Reckon we can hitch a ride? Captain Percy says we'll keep these prisoners for a spell—least until they's hanged." Shackled to rings attached to the wagon's exterior, the prisoners would either walk behind the wagon or be dragged through the streets. The guards looked as though they didn't care which means would get the prisoners to the asylum.

The mules strained against their heavy load and turned east. One of the prisoners stumbled and fell, but quickly spinning around, he managed to regain his footing before the mules had built up speed.

"Getting pretty good at that, ain't yah, boy?" The garrison guard spat tobacco juice at the prisoner's shell jacket.

"Pardon me," Joseph said loudly, trying to suppress his anger. "Why are these men being treated so harshly?"

The guards looked curiously at one another. "Well, what's it to yah?"

"What possible precipitating offense could warrant such barbaric treatment?"

Confused by the question, the men looked at one another and shrugged their shoulders. Finally, the young private spoke, "Doc wants to know what these here fellers did to deserve hanging."

"Oh," one guard grinned at Joseph, showing a mouthful of black, decaying teeth. "This here scum deserted back at Chancellorsville. While their units were whippin' them Yanks proper, these yella dogs ran for the hills."

For the rest of the ride, those bound for Wingate Asylum sat—or stumbled—lost in dark thoughts. Each one knew the fate reserved for soldiers who deserted the battlefield; Southern military justice was swift, certain, and without mercy. Joseph closed his eyes and silently prayed for these poor farm boys destined for the gallows.

• • • • •

Attorney Steven Billings rubbed his fatigued eyes, took another large gulp of mud-colored coffee, and continued working on his weekly report to Secretary of War Edward M. Stanton. Over the past six weeks, the young attorney had achieved a dismal record in defending soldiers on pleas of mental incompetence. Two of his clients had been judged innocent; twenty-one had been sent back to prison to await the gallows—unless President Lincoln could find an excuse to pardon them. Steven shook his head gloomily, took another gulp, then returned to his paperwork.

"Excuse me, sir?"

A postal courier knocked on the open door, handed the attorney an envelope, and wordlessly left on his rounds.

When the attorney opened the dispatch, his eyes scanned the

page and his face whitened. Hoping he had misinterpreted the message, he reread the important points:

The Honorable Steven A. Billings,
Defense Counsel
Army of the Potomac

Dear Sir,

You are hereby ordered to report to Turner's Lane Hospital in Philadelphia by week's end. You will serve as defense counsel for Corporal Forsythe and Private Gardner ... general court martial arraignment ... Mental competency review requested ... Judge Advocate Higginbotham presiding.

... charged with malingering and desertion ... Specifically, 'wounds of nerves' have been claimed by the defendants ... Particulars of each case will be provided by Army Surgeon General William A. Hammond ...

By personal order of General Joseph Hooker
Army of the Potomac

"Oh, my heavens, just when I thought my work couldn't get any worse!" he groaned.

• • • • •

Mailbags finally caught up with the men of Company C at Culpepper. The rugged and ragged warriors had been waiting for news from home like children wait for candy. After the sergeant had handed out the last letter and package, a hush fell over the camp while men eagerly read and reread the tender words from loved ones they longed to see. Some cried openly, not caring what anyone else would think of them. Zeke was luckier than many: he had received a large bundle from home. When he tore it open, he discovered that his mother had sent several letters, knitted socks, and a batch of sugar cookies.

"You gonna eat them all at once?" Billy teased, reading one of the letters hungrily.

"I'm thinking about it! I might should save some, but I been hungry ever since leaving home last month."

"Here," Billy tossed Zeke his cookies after removing two, "eat all of yours. You can save these for later."

"You crazy? Don't you want your cookies?"

"Enjoy them. Did you read Momma's letter?"

"Naw, I didn't get past the cookies. Why?"

"Read. You'll be glad you did."

Stuffing his mouth full of cookies, Zeke reached for the letter and read anxiously.

"Katherine's with Momma in Calhoun County—safe from the Yanks!" he called out joyously, not raising his eyes from the pages.

"Keep reading. It gets better."

Zeke pored over his mother's account of the exploits of General Nathan Bedford Forrest. "It says here that Pops and some others crept into Nashville and managed to sneak off with Katherine and her little sister!" Zeke said, shaking his head in wonder. "I say, God bless Pops and God bless Gen'l Forrest!" He turned and grinned at Billy.

"Can you believe that? Katherine, safe at our farm? Thank you, God! Now we surely gotta end this war quick, so's I can get back home."

"That there's a great enough reason for me! Let's go tell General Lee we need to get this fighting business over with so Zeke can hightail it to his Katherine!"

When Zeke reached the last page, he found that the letter writer had changed from Momma to Katherine herself. He read and re-read the letter eagerly.

"Hey! Zeke, old buddy, I just got me a letter from my little sister Peggy." Joshua Steele sauntered up and joined the brothers uninvited. "She says to tell you hey, and she'll be praying for you to come home safe to her."

Zeke was speechless as he looked up from Katherine's note blankly, then fought the urge to retort, *There ain't nothing "little" about your sister!*

"Boy, she's plumb ate up with you, Zeke!" Joshua said, grinning.

Leaving Billy to handle Joshua, Zeke moved away to read Katherine's news yet again, this time in private. But better even than the letter was the tintype that had been wrapped within it. Zeke hadn't seen Katherine since her father had moved his wife and daughters to Nashville fourteen months earlier, hoping to get them out of the path of war—that was two months before the Yankees captured Nashville. *A lot changes in a year*, Zeke told himself as he pored over every feature of the lovely young woman in the picture. He thought about her soft hazel eyes and the warm smile she always reserved just for him—*as if I was General Lee himself!* He studied the picture intently, willing the flesh-and-blood young woman to step out of the tintype and into the camp. *She is so beautiful! Even more beautiful than I remembered!*

Billy had to call to Zeke three times before the younger brother was roused from his thoughts. "Zeke! We're heading out! Looks like you may get to see some of them blue-bellies you've been waiting for."

· · · · ·

On the nineteenth of June, a day when the skies were as blue-gray as the mountains, Company C crossed the peaks of the Blue Ridge. The troops caught their breath, gulped tepid water from canteens, and stared at the mountains stretching out in unbroken waves to the far horizon.

"Sure is pretty up here—huh, Smiley?" Nate observed. "Reckon a man could spit down this here mountain today, and it'd land on another feller's head tomorrow!"

"It looks like we're on top of the world," Zeke marveled.

"Look over yonder!" Nate pointed to clouds of smoke toward the east. "I bet the Yankee cavalry's trying to see what we're doing, and it looks like old Jeb's keeping 'em from findin' the answer."

"Why're we stopping here? If we don't get movin', we gonna be the last ones to get to Pennsylvania."

"We've been ordered to hold Ashby's Gap," Billy told his brother as he moved past him down the line. "We're protecting the army's rear. Can't let the Yanks catch us off guard."

"But that means we're gonna be the last ones there!" Zeke wailed.

"Don't fret! I'm sure there'll be some Yankees left for you to shoot at."

• • • • •

Philadelphia's Turner Lane Hospital was established in 1862 on a large farm situated between 22nd Street and Columbia Avenue on the outskirts of the City of Brotherly Love. The first of its kind in the nation, this Federal hospital was dedicated to treating nerve injuries and nervous disorders. More than four hundred patients filled its impressive and stately corridors. Steven Billings was astonished to see the modern facility; he stood and stared for long moments before making his way to a desk in the receiving area, where a young woman smiled at him.

"My name is Steven Billings. I'm here to see Corporal John Forsythe and Private Richard Gardner."

"Sir," she informed him politely, "at this hospital, patients don't normally receive visitors. Many of them are unable to recognize their own friends and family."

"I'm an attorney for the Army of the Potomac, here by General Hooker's orders."

"I see," the woman murmured. "Perhaps Doctor Da Costa will be able to help you."

Following in her wake, Steven was led down one corridor, up a flight of stairs, around two corners, and through an immaculate gathering room filled with patients who stared vacantly out of windows, sat with their heads in their hands, or cried softly to themselves. Silently, the receptionist opened the door to an examination room. The doctor standing just inside the door turned quickly, put his finger across his lips, and turned back to the demonstration taking place.

The patient appeared dazed. He stretched his arms high, shook his head, and rubbed his neck. Glancing at the nearby table, he reached for a glass of whiskey and drank it in one long gulp.

"Corporal Whitten! It appears that we have miraculously cured your blindness!"

The doctor moved within view of the still-groggy patient.

"Huh?" The corporal turned his head and saw a room full of witnesses at the moment he realized his mistake.

"Corporal, you will report back to your unit by morning. I have no intention of reporting you as a malingerer—yet. However, if you fail to appear before your commanding officer for any reason—or if I ever see you back here again—I will personally attend your hanging!"

Within minutes, a guard arrived to escort the shame-faced man back to his regiment. In a nearby room, Dr. Jacob Mendez Da Costa laughed uproariously before shaking his visitor's hand.

"Doctor, if you don't mind my asking, what did I just witness?"

"A man who feigned blindness in one eye in order to avoid his duties," the doctor explained. "I suspected his complaint was nothing more than a poor attempt to receive a medical discharge from the army, so I etherized him. While he was unconscious, I applied an adhesive plaster over his good eye. Still groggy from the anesthetic, the corporal instinctively reached for the glass using only the eye he had claimed was blind."

"Very clever, sir!"

"Thank you—but you're probably not here to watch my antics. I understand you intend to see Corporal Forsythe and Private Gardner?

When Steven nodded, the doctor sighed. "The private died from disease earlier this week. You're welcome to visit with the corporal—but since when has the Army of the Potomac assigned legal counsel for common soldiers in general court martial hearings?"

"To my knowledge, Doctor, since six weeks prior to this moment."

Dr. Da Costa looked at him curiously before explaining, "For the past two years, I have been researching advancements in wounds of the nerves, the psychological attributes of emotional traumas experienced by battlefield veterans, which I call *Irritable Heart Syndrome* and others call *A Soldier's Heart*. Up until you stepped in the door, these men have been treated as malingerers or malfeasants and routinely executed for desertion and cowardice. Now your presence here raises hopes that hundreds—even thousands—of lives could be spared and minds could be treated!"

Steven Billings nodded, but felt compelled to point out, "I wouldn't get your hopes up too high yet. Unfortunately, the results of my defense cases have been dismal—and have gained wide notoriety."

The doctor interrupted him. "Just think, sir! What if we could prove through medical research that many of these men truly suffer from mental illness and were incapable of performing their duties? Think of what it would mean to the individuals and their families, who now suffer such shame and humiliation! We could rid you of your current assignment!"

• • • • •

Majestic oak trees lined both sides of the circle drive leading up to the old Wingate Manor, which had been donated to the Confederacy by an ardent secessionist immediately after Virginia's secession. Jefferson Davis himself had toured the building and designated it as a hospital. Army officers estimated that one hundred ninety-eight men could be housed in each wing, with administration offices, examining rooms, and quarters for administrators and patient handlers in the main building. The former home had rapidly been transformed into an army barracks filled to capacity—and then to overflowing—with wounded soldiers. In recent months, due to the lack of prison space, one wing had been fortified and transformed into a barracks for prisoners of war, Joseph knew from one of President Davis's letters. As the wagon lumbered up the drive, Joseph stared at his new home and wondered what his future held.

Built entirely of brick, the former plantation house had been designed along the lines of a grand early nineteenth-century English manor house. The main building was three stories high, with symmetrical recessed two-story wings jutting out from either side of the central structure. Ornate white columns supported the verandah roof, which ran across the entire front of the building. Joseph glimpsed brick outbuildings symmetrically positioned on either side of the former plantation house. Nearly obscured behind ornate trees, each was surrounded by a six-foot-tall brick wall, presumably intended to protect gardens.

From a distance, the manor looked pristine, but as the wagon pulled nearer, the doctor could see signs of wear and neglect. Paint was peeling from the windows, the porch floor, and columns. Two windows on the third floor had been broken and never replaced. Shreds of curtains flapped outside open windows. *I wonder if they're waving a welcome or waving me away? Joseph mused.*

Like the manor, the grounds of the vast estate hinted at its former days of glory. Formal gardens outlined the circular drive, but they were now choked with weeds. Neglected tobacco fields had turned into hayfields. More weeds outlined the house foundation. Dead trees and broken branches were scattered throughout the grounds around the buildings.

As the wagon pulled up to the porch, Joseph noticed a sign that read:

WINGATE ASYLUM
May all who enter find the grace of God.

Sloppy red paint brushed across the face of the sign screamed
BEDLAM SOUTH!

Joseph's eyes widened as he gazed at the sign. "Private Johnson, why does the hospital staff tolerate this offensive name for the asylum?"

"Fella told me last time I was here 'at Sergeant Pirou ordered the sign changed on account of nobody knew what Wingate Asylum was." The private thought for a moment, then added, "Reckon you'll want to change it, huh, Doc?"

"Indeed!"

When the wagon pulled up to the front steps, Dr. Joseph Bryarly jumped down from the buckboard, crossed his arms, and stared at his new assignment as attendants began unloading the freight.

• • • • •

During its short lifetime, Wingate Asylum had already managed to earn the dubious reputation for extreme cruelty to its patients. Within walls of faded affluence, the inmates' living conditions were appalling. Dr. Bryarly was about to discover that a British surgeon retained by Jefferson Davis to give the fledgling hospital a start also gave the institution its nickname, linking the asylum to England's Bethlem Royal Hospital. By the end of its first year, Bedlam South had become infamous to Confederate and Union soldiers alike, associated with tales of torture, pain, and cruelty uncommon even in the middle of a violent civil war.

"Welcome, *sir*, can I help yah?" The elderly black man standing before Joseph was the only living reminder of the plantation's pre-war existence. When Joseph turned to him and offered his right hand in greeting, the former butler pulled back. "Sir! Ain't fittin'. Ain't fitting a-tall. I'm Benjamin, the butler."

After the doctor introduced himself as the new superintendent, the butler hoisted several of Joseph's boxes, shaking his head.

"Is something wrong, Benjamin?"

"I's just the butler. I ain't got nothin' I needs to know." Benjamin led Joseph into the main house and walked him past administrative offices and meeting halls.

"You'll need to wait a spell till I find Cap'n Percy." Benjamin walked away, mumbling, "Oh, there's shore gonna be some trouble."

Within minutes, he reappeared. "Sir, I's still looking for the cap'n." Benjamin opened a door below the staircase and disappeared into the cellar.

Minutes later, the staircase door flew open and a formally dressed Confederate officer marched into the room and saluted. "Captain Samuel T. Percy," he said tersely.

The captain's appearance was startling, almost grotesque. Burn scars covered his cheek and neck. A long laceration went from his left eye across his nose. His scraggly silver-and-black beard only partially hid the unsightly disfigurement. The left sleeve of his dress coat was empty, folded neatly, and tacked to his shoulder. His strong, angry gait seemed to reflect his disposition.

Startled, Bryarly rose and reached out his hand. "Sir, I am Doctor Joseph Bryarly and I—"

"I know who you are, Doctor," the captain interrupted harshly. "I know that you're a family friend of President Davis. I also know you were ordered to report for duty more than five months ago!"

Intimidated by the confrontation, Joseph stammered, "My apologies, Captain. It takes several months to travel from London to America."

"Our country is at war, sir! We cannot delay our duty while you *malinger*."

"Captain, I strongly object to your tone and your implication!"

"You should know, Doctor," the captain stepped forward, stopping just inches from Joseph's nose, "thanks to your delay, I am the *new* superintendent of Bedlam South!"

· · · · ·

General Barksdale's brigade set out again through the upper end of the Shenandoah Valley. The corps led by generals Ewell and Hill had already passed by days before, leaving evidence behind. Empty ammunition crates, fire pits, abandoned tents, trash, and animals' carcasses littered the roadside. Because June had turned beastly hot, winter coats and spare blankets had been cast off. Fences had been torn apart for use as firewood. Farmers' fields had been trampled and livestock confiscated; not a chicken, horse, cow, or dog could be seen. After four days of hard marching, the brigade reached the Potomac River at Williamsport, Maryland, and prepared to cross. It was another new adventure for Zeke.

He watched as thousands of soldiers stripped from the waist down. Holding their rifles and rucksacks overhead, they cautiously ventured into the river. A roar of laughter erupted whenever someone slipped and disappeared under the water, requiring rescue by sympathetic comrades. Zeke crossed uneventfully, but Nate was not as lucky. Stepping on a sharp rock, he lost his balance and disappeared under the water.

"Dang it, Zeke! That feller behind me promised he'd catch me," Nate complained as he reached the riverbank, flopped to the ground, and poured water out of his boots. "That's the kinda fella that'd pee on your back and tell yah it was raining."

"I didn't know you couldn't swim," Zeke laughed, examining his friend's wet rifle.

"I tell yah, boy, that water's colder than a well digger's butt!"

"Welcome to Maryland," Billy announced as they dried themselves and made camp. "Enjoy it quick—we won't be here long."

Leaving early the next morning, Company C trudged twenty miles through the Maryland countryside, making camp in Pennsylvania by nightfall. Along the way, local citizens gathered in clusters to watch the soldiers pass. Some houses proudly flew Union flags and their inhabitants shouted insults at the Confederates, while in other communities, small boys ran alongside the Confederate forces singing "Dixie" and cheering for Robert E. Lee.

"Well, what do you think of Pennsylvania, Private Gibson?" Billy teased.

"These folks got some well-stocked farms. I'm thinking we should help ourselves to livestock, like them Yanks did back in Virginia."

"I reckon it would serve them right—but General Lee says no

foraging or pillaging. He wants to show these people that we are *fine Christian gentlemen*, who act better than their Yankee boys do."

Zeke protested, "Just a few outlaw pigs would sure be nice!"

"Don't even think it! Our commissary officers can purchase anything they need and pay with Confederate dollars, which are worthless to these people. So, if food can be found, they'll find it for us."

That night, a procession of wagons rolled into camp, packed full of requisitioned hams, corned beef, cheeses, breads, chickens, hay, and crocks of apple butter. "Nice welcome we're getting!" Nate shouted gleefully. The soldiers swarmed around the wagons and feasted long into the night.

"I'm kinda liking Pennsylvania," Zeke mumbled as he groaned and rubbed his swollen belly.

Nate chimed in, "Kinda makes me homesick. My wife's a real good cook—and a dang good thing, cuz she shore ain't much to look at."

"Nate, she ain't so bad!"

His friend snickered. "God slapped that woman silly with an ugly stick the day she was born."

Stars shone brightly in the clear night sky as the camp of contented soldiers settled down for a good night's sleep. But before the sun rose, Company C was marching on the road toward Chambersburg, past General Hill's Third Corps, some twenty thousand strong.

"Where's them Yanks?" Zeke asked his brother when he saw him briefly.

"The captain told me we're not sure because we've lost contact with Jeb Stuart. I'd guess they're headed this way."

"We don't know their position, but do they know ours?" Daniel questioned. Before Billy could answer, Captain Tuttle rode up and told the men gathered around Billy, "Everyone stay alert. We're in enemy country today, boys, without much cavalry to scout for us." He ordered Billy to send out small details to secure the perimeter, then rode off. Zeke volunteered and was soon making his way through the woods, expecting to find blue-bellies behind every tree. He didn't find Yankees, but he did find a rich stash of blackberries, which offered a rare treat. His thoughts caught up with him as he settled down to pick: thoughts of home, Mama's cooking, and Katherine. The fact that his amazing adventure had thus far only led him to a field full of blackberries somewhere in Pennsylvania brought a smile to his face.

Six

Midnight in Richmond, four blocks east of Clay Street. An entirely different breed of men in Confederate uniforms lurked about the scattered tents and fires. This camp housed a battalion of Zouaves, the last remnant of New Orleans' Louisiana Tiger Battalion. Flamboyant red dress trousers, Turkish fez caps, and fancy blue jackets often fooled the casual observer into believing the Zouaves were proud sons of the South. In reality, this battalion was a cesspool of men without morals, religion, or loyalty to anything except their own personal gain—they were nothing more than pardoned convicts released under oath to fight for the South. With them, life was cheap. They were quick to punish anyone who dared to interfere or testify against them.

Through God's providence, nearly the entire Louisiana Tiger battalion had been wiped out in the Peninsula campaign; only these thirty-five cretins survived. Led and protected by Captain Samuel T. Percy, these murderers worked as handlers at Bedlam South.

Late one night at the end of June, Percy arrived at the camp accompanied by five Zouaves. The first to approach Percy was a barrel-chested, dark-skinned Cajun man, shirtless and shoeless, his arms and back covered in thick black hair. "Cap'n Percy," his

French Creole accent was unmistakable, "the men be ornery and the whores are restless."

The riders roared in laughter. Percy smirked. "Sergeant Pirou Boudreaux, I declare it grieves my southern soul to hear my men complaining more than my whores!" The captain grabbed a bottle of whiskey and idly watched four prostitutes, drunk and in various states of undress, stagger out of the barracks, their night's work complete.

• • • • •

Mary Beth Greene was being escorted from the major general's quarters a half-mile away when her carriage lost a wheel just outside the Zouaves' camp. As the driver struggled to untangle the horses' bridles, the woman stepped down from the carriage, walked to the shelter of an overhanging tree, and with a blank face watched the nearby show. A sultry-looking prostitute sauntered over to Percy, slowly unbuttoned his jacket and shirt, and rubbed her hands across his chest and stomach. Then she did the same to herself. She stood before him bare-breasted as he appraised her. "I only like beautiful women—beautiful women who are fighters," he said harshly. Kissing his neck and giggling like a schoolgirl, she teasingly straddled his lap and pressed her breasts against his chest.

Unseen by the Zouaves, Mary Beth watched the spectacle with loathing, then turned to a middle-aged passerby who appeared out of the darkness and asked sweetly, "Sugar, I have fallen into difficulties. Could you help a lady in distress?" He gallantly offered his arm and she gratefully took it. Then the couple turned and walked away.

Hours later, when the captain emerged from a borrowed tent leaving his companion behind, he turned to the men dozing by the fire and ordered Boudreaux, "Grab those saddlebags beside my horse! What's inside is yours." The sergeant quickly emptied the stolen contents onto the ground: thousands of dollars in Confederate and Federal currency, jewelry, sterling tableware, gold coins, and mounds of pay vouchers stolen from the bodies of dead Confederates. He laughed derisively as the men fought over the treasure like dogs over a pile of bones.

"What's next, Captain?" a shout rose above the crowd.

"Going back out soon, boys—at the next full moon. Gonna be something real special."

· · · · ·

Quietly, Joseph descended the manor staircase leading into the cellar, where, according to a chatty Irish handler, four treatment chambers were housed. Since the increasingly hostile Captain Percy had not given Joseph permission to go beyond the packed wards in the east wing, this was his first foray downstairs. Joseph's new area of responsibility had been designed to house one hundred ninety-eight mental patients, but the war had swelled the number of occupants to more than two hundred forty-five. The west-wing garrison, designed to stockade insane war criminals, was now, by necessity, also housing mental patients and prisoners of war.

Shortly after arriving at Wingate, Joseph presented himself and his credentials at the Confederate White House—after learning that its occupants were attending a fundraising ball in Charlottesville. He quickly left his calling card and departed. By that time, he knew, wild rumors of torture, abuse, and neglect at the hands of merciless Wingate handlers had flooded Richmond. Piled on the desk he had inherited at the asylum was a stack of letters from citizens demanding to know if what they had heard was true—but Joseph soon learned that overworked local military officials ignored the rumors. In truth, most officers despised the residents of Wingate. One had been quoted in the newspaper as saying all Wingate inmates were "merely cowards, more deserving of a noose than a nod."

Joseph had been aghast—but not surprised—at the overcrowding and unsanitary conditions. Memories of Bethlem Royal Hospital plagued him. He did his best to respond to the issues, but ran into difficulties every time he crossed Captain Percy's orders, although a few handlers were sympathetic and tried harder to attend to the patients' needs. Joseph hired a small army of washerwomen and cooks, but that was the only major change he accomplished in his first month. A long series of shouting matches with Captain Percy had left him mentally, physically, and emotionally exhausted. *Surely, Bethlem Hospital was not so much worse than my current state of affairs!* Discouraged, he thought endlessly of Ana, but continued to press for change.

On the first night Percy left Joseph in charge of the asylum, Joseph decided to explore the mysterious "therapy chambers" lying deep beneath the house. Screams suddenly stopped his hand from reaching out to the first iron handle in the cellar, but the doctor caught his breath and swung the massive door open. A foul odor rushed to his nostrils and the obscene drama within the room caused bile to rise in his throat. "Dear God in heaven!" Joseph exclaimed.

A naked man knelt at the feet of a burly handler, who held him by his nape while he scrubbed a caustic mustard powder on the patient's shaved head and face. What Joseph could see of the man by the flickering lamplight was covered in raw, oozing blisters.

"Who ordered this barbaric therapy?" Joseph asked, sternly preventing himself from retching.

"Captain Percy."

At that moment, the patient fainted from the intense pain and the handler washed his hands in a basin, then wiped the towel over his dripping forehead before he turned to the doctor. At the look on Joseph's face, the handler pointed out kindly, "Don't be worried none, Doc. This ain't one of our boys. This here is a Yankee."

"What is your name, sergeant?"

"O'Malley. Thomas O'Malley."

"Well, Mr. O'Malley, blistering is an extreme and highly dubious therapy. Do you have any idea why the captain ordered such a harsh treatment?"

"Well, Doc—" the sergeant removed his hat and scratched his head. (Lice were constant companions to everyone at Bedlam

South, resident and visitor alike.) "If you're asking is Percy punishing this here Yank, well … I reckon that'd be true."

"What was his offense?"

"Has himself fits pretty regular. Last night he busted up his cot and whooped the feller chained close by. Dang near killed him."

"I see." Joseph took a deep breath and reminded himself, *Careful! Ask too many questions and Captain Percy will forbid future access to the treatment rooms. I must be able to help, not destroy, men—but how?* The doctor addressed the handler once again. "Mr. O'Malley, would you consider having mercy on this pitiful soul? In my professional opinion, I believe you have fully completed the treatment task assigned to you."

Expressionless, O'Malley looked at the doctor for long moments before nodding. He shouted down the corridor and another handler soon appeared to drag the patient up the stairs, feet banging on every step. To the handler's surprise, the doctor helped him sweep, then wash the treatment room before obtaining fresh straw for the stained floor. As they worked, the doctor watched his companion curiously.

Thomas O'Malley was at least three inches above six feet tall, with dark red hair. A genuine mountain of a man, he spoke blending Southern slang with a strong Irish lilt. When at last the two men wearily climbed the stairs, O'Malley turned to Joseph and whispered, "You know, Doc, I could lose me head for saying this, but you seem like a kind man, a man what cares for the poor devils locked up here. I've heard folks talking about how you been standing up to Percy 'n' all."

"Mr. O'Malley—Thomas," Joseph corrected himself quickly, "I believe that God cares for all of us equally: Rebel, Yankee, lunatic, or sane. Everyone deserves kindness, *especially* unfortunates who have lost their capacity for reasoning."

"Aye—reckon I agree," the handler said, once again scratching his head. "I'm not a learned man, Doc, so I can't rightly say if these treatments helps the boys. They always seems more peaceful afterwards, but I swear, I hate doing it. Some handlers—Percy's boys—enjoys it, but not me. They be the worst bunch of cut-throats and ruffians the devil ever assembled."

Joseph glanced around the deserted hall and whispered, "Careful, Thomas. I've already learned that the walls have ears. Come into my office and we'll talk."

Once the doctor closed his office door behind the handler, O'Malley warned, "Cap'n Percy and his men don't like your meddling."

"Meddling?"

"Watch your back, Doc! Watch it close. These thugs wouldn't think twice about killing on Percy's orders. You keep doing what you're doing, caring about the men and poking your nose around, and you'll disappear … same as the others."

"The others? Others have disappeared? Tell me, Mr. O'Malley, just who is this Captain Percy?"

"Besides bein' the greatest blackguard ever spawned?" O'Malley retorted. "He's part Creole, part devil, from New Orleans. Lost his arm at Bull Run. I heard tell that he was pinned under a piece of artillery that burst into flames, and that's how he got his scars. Now he lives in fear of fire—watch and you'll see he stays far from any fireplace. Instead, he uses whores to keep him warm."

A scraping noise could be heard coming from the hallway. The doctor put his finger to his lips and the two men waited until the sounds retreated. Joseph slowly opened the door a crack and peered out in time to see two Zouaves dragging a Confederate soldier to the cellar door. As he listened, he heard one tell the other, "This one will be blisterin' in the sweat box. It'll be standing shackles for twenty-four hours." They laughed mirthlessly as they went thumping down the stairs. Joseph softly closed the door and turned to the handler. "Mr. O'Malley, do you know that patient's name?"

"I ain't never asked. Just been doin' what the captain orders."

"I see … thank you."

Shortly after the noise died away, O'Malley peered once again into the hallway and quickly left the doctor's office.

· · · · ·

"Any news from General Stuart and his men?" Corporal Billy Gibson asked Captain William Tuttle, after reviewing the day's orders.

"None that I've heard of," the captain answered angrily, shaking his head. "Where in tarnation is he? He's supposed to be our eyes and ears! Sixty-five thousand men right in the middle of enemy territory, depending on him as never before, and he's left us blind and deaf!"

The last days of June almost crackled with tension for the Army of Northern Virginia. General Lee had no idea about the Yankees' positions and no idea where his finest cavalry forces could be. The anxiety at headquarters filtered down through the ranks. No longer did men gather to make cards or complain about food, lice, and living conditions. Like Private Zeke Gibson, they spent more time sitting quietly, thinking, wondering, writing letters of farewell, and worrying. *We been told to be prepared to march quickly, but it don't seem like the order is ever gonna come! Some say them Yanks is close and General Lee's all worried he'll have to battle without having the cavalry to scout for us. We're in enemy country, yet we can't find the blasted enemy!*

Lately, Zeke's duties included patrolling the surrounding countryside, and his meals consisted of an abundance of requisitioned food. "I never thought I'd have a full belly in this army! I'm getting mighty fond of these here cherries," he grinned, after sharing a huge lunch with Nate.

"You best pace yourself, Smiley, or you're gonna get the screaming squirts," Nate warned. "If'n you do, you'll be in the woods all day and miss all the fighting."

"I ain't gonna miss this battle," Zeke promised. "Why, it could be the last one. I got a feelin' we're gonna finish the blue-bellies off once and for all."

"You ain't even seen a Yankee yet, and you done got this war over with, boy," pointed out an old veteran who had overheard Zeke's prediction.

"Them Yanks ain't got a prayer when this brigade turns loose on them!" Zeke retorted.

"It won't be easy," Daniel cautioned. "We're in the enemy's neck of the woods, which means they may fight harder to defend their homes. We're a long way from our supply base—they're not. I'm worried about obtaining ammunition, unless we can capture supplies from the Yankees."

Late that night, Billy returned from headquarters with news. "General Lee has ordered all forces to march in the morning toward a little town called Gettysburg about fifteen miles from here. I hear tell that we'll find shoe factories there," he reported. "General Longstreet's scouts tell us that the Yankee Army is moving our way."

"Where is General Ewell's corps?" Daniel asked.

"North of here near Harrisburg, about a couple days' march from us—but they're already headed this way. However, General Hill's corps is still around here somewhere. We should meet up with them."

"Billy, how close you reckon them Yanks are?" Nate asked. "I don't wanna trip on a blue-belly tonight."

Billy smiled and shook his head. "This morning, General Heth's division of Hill's corps reported spotting some Yankee cavalry in Gettysburg, but we're still not sure where their closest infantry is."

Zeke climbed into his tent, stretched out on his blanket, and tried to picture what a battle might be like. *Thousands of strong men, lined up two or three deep on both sides for miles on end, charging at the same time. We'll be screaming the Rebels' yell at the top of our lungs. Those Yanks ain't got a chance.*

• • • • •

General Barksdale's Brigade could hear artillery off to the east, but no one knew whose artillery it was. Billy later learned that soldiers in the lead of Ewell's corps flanked Union forces, which then fled through town. The Battle of Gettysburg had officially begun.

The first day of July witnessed a glorious victory for the Rebels. Despite terrific losses, Confederate confidence and spirits soared. Company C camped along the Chambersburg Pike, only a few miles from the battlefield. Just beyond South Mountain lay Gettysburg, the Yanks, and the glory that Zeke had dreamed about for two long years.

Billy updated the men in his command. "It was a tough scrap, but we ran them through the town and up on the hills just to the east. There's only one problem: they have the higher ground."

"Is the whole Yankee army there?" Zeke asked, his face flushed and eyes sparkling.

"We don't know—there's still no word from General Stuart and the cavalry," Billy said tensely, so wound up that he couldn't sit or eat. "They say General Lee's fit to be tied because he has no idea where the Yanks are—they could be coming up behind us for all we know. They could all be around Gettysburg. We just don't know."

"What's happening tomorrow?" Zeke's voice sounded high-pitched.

"General Lee will attack. Everyone knows he loves a good fight—and that's what he came to do."

"He's the best there is!" Daniel interjected.

"No doubt about that," Billy nodded, then punched one fist into a nearby tree. "I just wish we weren't fighting blind! Maybe General Lee will wait on Stuart—or maybe not."

"Are you nervous, Billy?" Zeke asked when he was alone with his brother, watching him pace the ground in front of their tent relentlessly.

"Naw, just hoping we both get through this alive," Billy said, trying to sound care-free. Then he turned and grabbed Zeke's arm. "When we deploy for battle tomorrow, don't stay too close to me. I don't want to sound like Pops, but I would hate for one blast to get both Gibsons. Remember all you learned during the drills, listen to the officers, and keep your head, Zeke. If you get scared, turn your fear into anger and give it back to the Yanks."

"I ain't scared!"

"Now! Just don't try to win the war all by yourself."

Zeke looked curiously at his brother and said hesitantly, "Billy? I remember what you told me. You're an officer now, so don't get too crazy."

Billy interrupted him, "Say your prayers and catch some sleep, if you can—you'll need it. Don't think about anything but Katherine. Maybe after tomorrow this madness will end soon."

· · · · ·

Despite his brother's advice, Zeke spent a restless night listening to his brother pace and worrying about Billy and his reckless passion for fighting.

"You awake?" Billy asked softly, just outside the tent.

"Yeah."

"Zeke, I want to tell you something. I don't mean to sound sappy, but I'm proud of you, how you've become a man."

"Same here, Billy. I ain't never said this before, but ... I love you, Billy."

There was silence outside the tent for a long moment. Then, when Zeke strained his ears, he heard, "I love you, too."

Dawn was breaking and Zeke had only managed to doze fitfully. He climbed out of the tent and saw his brother bending over to gather an armload of wood for the morning's fire. Impulsively, he leaped onto Billy's back, knocking him—and their tent—down. The brothers wrestled like two bear cubs, laughing and scattering their few possessions. Men gathered around, but instead of cheering them on, they were silent. Glancing over his shoulder, Billy noticed Company C snap to attention as a large man astride a large horse stopped to watch the little tussle. Billy quickly stood and saluted. Zeke followed suit.

General Barksdale stared at the two young men who looked so much alike, then gently advised, "You boys need to save your strength. Today may be the most important day of the war. The whole Yankee Army is just over that mountain waiting on us, and Mississippi will need all of her sons." The general nodded at the Gibsons, then slowly rode out of sight just as the bugle sounded reveille and a huge orange sun crested over the horizon, signaling a blistering hot day.

"On your feet!" Sergeant Cawley barked. "We march in one hour!"

There was plenty of food for breakfast, but for once, Zeke wasn't hungry. He rounded up his belongings, nibbled on a biscuit, and tried to prepare himself for war.

Seven

At last! A letter from Ana had arrived at the asylum, informing Joseph of the family's whereabouts and their news—unexpectedly joyful news. When Casey brought the Dougalls to the home of the wealthy businessman who had paid their passage, they learned he had fled from the city with his family, freeing the Dougalls from their servitude even before it began. Ana's father and brother had both found work immediately at a foundry an easy walk from their home, she wrote. She had been hired as a nurse in the Alabama division of Chimborazo Hospital, and her mother volunteered her services at a ladies' sewing society, which was composed of socialites, middle-class women with young children, elderly grandmothers, and anyone else who could ply a needle. This was indeed a prosperous start in America for the Irish family—and an incredible contrast to Joseph's life at the place he, too, had begun calling Bedlam South.

Two nights after Ana's letter arrived, the doctor dressed himself with painstaking care and walked the two miles that separated the asylum from the Dougalls' boardinghouse near Franklin and Seventh Street. On the way, he bought a bouquet of summer flowers from a ragged child on a street corner. In the distance, he could hear catcalls and revelry from the troops stationed around the city. Taps announced the end of the military day and the start of a night of revelry. To the west of the city, an endless sea of white tents covered the countryside, illuminated by the glow cast by hundreds of campfires.

After checking the address on Ana's letter, Joseph raised his hand to knock on the boardinghouse door. Before he could rap, however, Ana threw open the door and rushed into his arms. For a moment, Joseph felt as though he had at last found his rightful home.

"Will you please let that dear man in the door, Ana Laoise?" Mary Margaret Dougall teased.

Blushing, the man and woman broke apart and after Joseph hugged Mrs. Dougall, Ana led the doctor into a small but cozy suite of rooms. "We were fortunate to find this place," Patrick Dougall explained after Joseph congratulated him on the family's good fortune. "I see now why Richmond is nicknamed the 'City of Refugees.' Our landlady has a dozen people a day knocking on her door, hoping to find shelter."

The night passed much too swiftly, as Michael and Patrick described the foundry work, Mary Margaret described her volunteer work, Ana discussed nursing practices at the hospital, and Joseph described the asylum. "Goodness gracious! That place sounds like a nightmare, Joseph!" Mrs. Dougall exclaimed, horrified. "Is there nothin' you can do? Why don't you go to your friend Jefferson Davis and speak to him about conditions there?"

Joseph froze for a moment, then bent his head to put another log on the fire and said quietly, "The President has enough problems to think about. This is something I'll have to handle myself."

The room fell silent for a moment, then Patrick Dougall lit his pipe and said slowly, "I've kept my ears open at the foundry and I've heard tell that your Captain Percy and his Zouaves are to blame for the raiding along Westham Plank Road. People seem to think they're stealing from their own country folk, the miserable beggars!"

"Joseph, why won't the law deal with the likes of Captain Percy?" Ana asked anxiously.

"These are lawless times, Ana," Joseph replied. "During crises—famine and war—life is cheapened. The military has the Yankees on their hands. The government has the war on its hands. No one has time to follow Percy and his men in order to prove the charges. Someone in the government considers Percy a war hero because of the terrible wounds he suffered on the battlefield. Without credible witnesses or evidence, Percy cannot be stopped."

As Joseph and the family fell silent, they could hear the clamor of young troopers heading toward the brothels and gambling houses on Main Street. "The boys be going out for a little fun tonight," Mr. Dougall observed dryly. "I hope the girls are ready!"

"Papa!" Ana objected. "You shouldn't speak o' such things."

"Thankful to God for the women of the night, I am," Mrs. Dougall interjected, shocking everyone in the room.

"Excuse me, ma'am?" Joseph asked, certain he hadn't heard her correctly.

"War's a terrible thing and sometimes there's no one to love them boys or to comfort them, except the prostitutes," she said quietly, not looking up from her knitting.

Without a word, Mr. Dougall stepped away from the table. Grinning from ear to ear, he sat in his rocking chair smoking his pipe.

After dinner, Joseph and Ana sat together on the front porch. The day had been sweltering, but the night brought a pleasant breeze, making the stifling humidity a little more tolerable. Lost in their thoughts—and wondering what the other was thinking— the couple watched an endless parade of humanity pass by the house. Random gunshots could be heard in the distance. No longer were travelers safe outside in Richmond after dark.

Finally, Joseph broke the silence on the porch. "I long for a better life," he revealed, as much to himself as to Ana. "Wouldn't it be wonderful if we could escape all this misery?"

Ana reached over and took Joseph's hand in her strong, warm hands. "Aye, Joseph, but the Lord knows our plight. I expect it will be Him deciding the time to move on. Meanwhile, you have a tremendous responsibility to those poor souls locked up at Wingate, bless their hearts."

Joseph turned to her and admitted, "I honestly believe that they may be the reason why God led me there—but that doesn't mean I don't hope for a better life one day, for you and me together."

"Together?" Ana sat up straighter and grinned mischievously. "Making plans for the two of us, are you now, Joseph?"

"Ana, I hope you know my heart," the doctor said, putting his arm around her shoulder.

"Aye, Joseph," she responded, leaning against him and turning her head to kiss him. "I love you, too." Ana sighed. "But God still has work for us to be doing here before our time together arrives."

For the first time in too many years to count, a spirit of hope flickered in the doctor's heart.

· · · · ·

By dawn of July second, soldiers throughout Pennsylvania knew that the day would be beastly, with the sun blazing down on legions of men who were preparing anxiously for battle. Early in the morning, many soldiers in Company C muttered about the heat as they trudged up South Mountain. But not Zeke. *This ain't hot like back home. These fellas must of forgot how hot it gets back in Mississippi in the summertime.* Marching beside the boy, Nate wiped the sweat from his forehead and whined, "Whew—man it's hotter than two rats in a wool sock!"

As Company C headed down the backside of the mountain, a panoramic view of the battle spread out before their eyes. Tremendous clouds of smoke hung over the town of Gettysburg. The fighting had resumed on the hills off to the east, the hills where the Yanks had retreated the day before. The scorched earth swarmed with flies feasting on the blood-soaked ground. Wounded, dying, and dead soldiers lay scattered in fields, woodland groves, and across the doorways of deserted homes and barns. Wounded horses, mules, and oxen screamed in pain. Piles of corpses were stacked along the road, waiting for burial. The stench of gunpowder, dead bodies, dying animals, decaying food-stuffs, and fires made men retch and vomit.

"Still smilin', Smiley?" Nate asked, studying the landscape, his gun held at the ready. When he glanced with a grin at the silent white-faced boy, he realized this wasn't a time to tease. Awkwardly, he put his hand on Zeke's shoulder, then turned away.

By mid-morning, Company C had halted on the Gettysburg road, awaiting instructions from General Barksdale. Billy was passing the news that Company C would attempt to flank the Federal forces. He passed Zeke without stopping to speak.

Daniel put his arm around the boy, "Don't worry about your brother. He's got a lot on his plate. His main concern is helping you—and the rest of us—survive this war. There isn't a better man to have on our side."

Zeke could only bring himself to nod.

Soon, the long column of soldiers began moving south once again. In the past, when they marched the men would joke or sing to pass the time. Today, they processed silently. Once, Captain Tuttle ordered them to stop, turn about-face, and take another route. "We're trying to conceal our movements from the enemy," Daniel explained to surprised recruits.

By early afternoon, General Barksdale's brigade reached the staging area for their attack. Behind a grove of trees less than a quarter of a mile away, blue uniforms were barely visible within a peach orchard.

Can they see us? Do they know we're here? Zeke wondered. The entire brigade—one thousand seven hundred men strong—was deployed in a single line stretching over a quarter-mile. Orders were quickly passed down the line: "Lie down and stay put!" The men didn't hesitate to obey. The earth beneath their bodies shook with the ferocious sounds of battle and the vibrations from artillery passing directly over their heads—whether Federal, Confederate, or both, they didn't know. New recruits covered their ears and tried to bury their faces in the hard-packed dirt. Veterans swiped blades of grass to chew or silently rummaged for their canteens or a chunk of bread.

"Hood's division is trying to take those hills where the Yanks are digging in," Zeke heard Captain Tuttle tell Billy. Then the boy stretched his neck to watch another long line of Confederate troops line up behind his brigade. "Who's that?" Zeke whispered to Daniel.

"I recognize General Wofford, the man on the chestnut horse, so that must be his brigade of Georgians," Daniel speculated, staring in the distance. "Yup! I see their flag. They're a fine bunch of fellows. We've fought alongside each other before. Evidently, someone has decided that our line might need strengthening."

· · · · ·

Out of the peach orchard came thunderous booms as cannonballs bombed the woodland just behind the prone soldiers. *I guess that answers my question about whether or not the Yanks see us!* Zeke told himself. Shortly afterwards, the Confederate artillery set up behind Company C on a small bald hill responded in kind, pouring fire power on the Yankees. Anxious to know what was happening, Zeke had to remind himself to keep his head down. *Why don't we move to the right, where the fighting keeps getting louder? Why's General Barksdale looking all crazy-like, riding up and down the line, straining his poor stallion in this heat? I'm sick of hearing him say, "Get ready, boys." I am ready!*

Daniel nudged Zeke and pointed to a general and his staff as they dashed past the regiment and halted before General Barksdale and Company C. "General Longstreet," Daniel pointed, watching closely. The soldiers could hear General Barksdale pleading, "Pete! Let us go in! We can take that artillery battery in five minutes."

"Wait just a little longer and we'll all go in," was the reply, then Longstreet and his aides galloped away. General Barksdale continued riding back and forth along the lines, waving his hat in front of his flushed face and looking dissatisfied.

"He's a good man and a good general," Daniel observed, "but he's aggressive—some say too aggressive. We almost had to drag the old man out of Fredericksburg last winter before he'd quit the fight."

Zeke nodded, his thoughts racing faster than the general's horse. *We're finally about to fight! I was almost close enough to touch two great generals! Whew! At last I'm facing the Yanks— this is my time to be a man.*

"Where's Billy?" Zeke suddenly realized that he hadn't seen his brother since the brigade had hit the ground.

· · · · ·

Billy was nowhere near his brother, which is just how Billy wanted it to be right now. *Load rifles, fix bayonets, and silently wait on the command to advance.* Zeke repeated the last set of orders over and over again, waiting for the word to move. Unable to bear the inaction any longer, he briefly raised his head and torso up far enough to search the line. Finally, he spotted his brother at the far end of the regiment with a pistol in one hand, sword in the other, and a fierce look of determination on his face. Zeke stared, willing his brother to look his way. Billy saw the boy, hesitated, then bent low and slowly made his way through the men, whispering a quick joke to some and words of encouragement to others. Zeke was almost jealous as he watched the men respond, but when Billy got close enough, Zeke realized with a start that he had never—in any scrape they had ever been in as kids—seen a look on Billy's face like the one he wore now.

Zeke opened his mouth to say something—what it would be, he wasn't sure—when suddenly the entire brigade erupted in whoops and yells and screams that sounded like all the demons from hell had been unleashed.

For General Barksdale's brigade, the battle of Gettysburg had commenced.

Zeke stared wild-eyed as Billy joined the screaming.

"It's the rebels' yell, Zeke!" Daniel shouted in the boy's ear before he too joined the clamor. "We're going to let the enemy know we're coming!"

· · · · ·

Each wagon ride back to Wingate Asylum seemed longer than the trip before. Tonight was no exception. The wagon bench, covered with early dew, was hard. The road was deeply rutted and covered with refuse. The mules were more ornery than ever—and Joseph knew just how they felt as he jolted past flaming barrels of tar that provided a cheap, but smelly, substitute for the gas streetlamps that had burned in the finest sections of the city before the war. The doctor had to navigate the wagon through the crowded streets carefully, in order to avoid the drunken men who wandered into his path. Leaving the city's congestion, he inhaled the country air and it seemed to improve his disposition.

Two of Joseph's patients were receiving therapeutic bloodletting on this night, so he decided to visit the second floor of the east wing. As he walked the narrow aisle separating the long rows of beds on the ward, his spirits sank once again. Lunatics were strapped together with melancholies, maniacs were chained to nostalgia sufferers. The conditions were inhumane and heartbreaking. Despite the doctor's pleas to Captain Percy, the intermingling of all forms of patient ailments allowed the aggressive to prey on the helpless. Night or day, the ward was filled with moans, groans, the rattle of chains, angry outbursts, hysterical laughter, and uncontrollable tears.

Without warning, a maniac screamed, yanked against his shackles, lurched, and viciously bit the ear of the helpless man sitting beside him. The victim whimpered, but remained motionless and defenseless. The scene was horrifying.

Joseph yelled for help. "Mr. Weller—collar that man! Mr. McGinnis, bring the cage!"

Weller struck the attacker solidly on the back of his neck, but it barely stunned him. The maniac attacked again. Weller raised his arm high overhead, this time bringing the full force of his strength and weight against the attacker's shoulder.

CRACK! The attacker's collarbone snapped under the impact of the blow. He cried out, releasing his teeth from his victim's neck, and McGinnis muzzled him by slamming a metal restraint cage around his head. He attached a choke collar, tightening the chain until the maniac began gasping for air.

"Shackle this man to the restraining table, Mr. Weller. Twenty-four hours without relief," Joseph ordered, then turned to the second handler. "Mr. McGinnis, take that poor fellow to the west-wing surgeon's office. See if one of the doctors can treat his wounds and stitch some of his ear back onto his head."

McGinnis quickly removed the shackles and escorted the bleeding man down the stairs. A third handler helped Weller hold the maniac in a death grip, using two short metal rods that squeezed his neck like a vise. The resulting shortage of oxygen caused him to gasp and choke and caused his head and ears to turn a faint blue. Contrary to his usual demeanor, tonight Joseph seemed to lack compassion—and that bothered Alastair Weller.

"Something wrong, Mr. Weller?"

Fearful of speaking in front of the other handler, Weller chose his words carefully. "Sir, if I strap this here devil to the restraining table, I … I reckon Captain Percy will hear tell of it."

"Thank you, Alastair, but I'm certain that Captain Percy would agree to any harsh punishment."

"Aye, reckon you're right."

The doctor leaned forward and whispered, "Alastair, make certain the treatment isn't too harsh. We want to discipline, not damage."

"No need to worry about that," the handler said as he and another man wrestled the maniac down the corridor and into the cellar.

· · · · ·

Wiping blood from his hands after an emergency surgery, Joseph headed to the basin at the far end of the ward. Private Albert Wright was lying on the cot nearby—or he had attempted to lie on it. Joseph paused to wipe his hands and realized,

Surely this is one of the largest men God ever created! Albert was massive, with a seven-foot-one-inch frame. A freeborn black man from the backwoods of southern Arkansas, he was a fighter greatly respected and feared by residents and staff alike. Albert's arms had been shackled to an iron cot bolted to the floor, with another chain around his neck secured to an iron ring hinged on the wall. Four thick belt straps were wrapped around his chest and waist, while both feet were secured to thirty-pound balls resting on the floor nearby. According to his military report, Wright had lost his sanity on the second day of the battle at Fredericksburg, lashing out and bayoneting anyone around him, friend or foe. Mercifully, his commander had ordered him bound, not killed. Garrison guards had delivered him to Wingate Asylum last month, shackled from head to foot. As Joseph tested the restraints, he thought to himself, *Percy's refusal to place Albert in a secured holding cell on the first floor is endangering the lives of every man on this ward. My God, if I didn't know better, I would swear Percy is trying to cause a bloody revolt. I know he hates Negroes, but what would he possibly gain by such an uprising?*

· · · · ·

Several hours earlier, horse-leeches had been applied to key areas of Private Wright's abdomen, neck, arms, and face. The theory was relatively simple: weakened from blood loss, the patient was less likely to become violent—at least for a while. Based on the materials he had read during his days at Bethlem Royal Hospital and his own observations, Joseph believed therapeutic bloodletting to be the least painful method of sedating a maniac and diminishing violent behavior. Thomas O'Malley joined Bryarly, and together they began removing the leeches.

"This big bloke fought like hell when he saw them leeches," he reported conversationally.

"I was afraid he would respond harshly."

"Harshly? Huh!" O'Malley pointed to massive black-and-blue welts on his forehead. "He smacked me something fierce! Took five of us, it did, to strap his carcass back down to that bed!"

Joseph grinned despite himself, then shook his head. "Imagine one man besting six handlers—men chosen for their strength!"

"Bloody hell, Doc, that's the strongest man what I ever met. We had to add three new chains, we did! I'd hate to piss that one off—that be God's honest truth."

The doctor looked at the man in chains compassionately, briefly touching his shoulder. "I genuinely believe his loss of sanity is temporary, Thomas. The trauma of his battlefield experiences caused his mania, but I believe that with the proper treatment, Albert Wright could one day regain his senses." Joseph sighed. "The problem is, men like these require thoughtful one-on-one attention, and that's nearly impossible in a place like this."

"You really think this bloke can be cured?"

"I've seen it happen many times. Madness is a treatable, manageable ailment, not unlike other diseases. Albert Wright is a perfect example of someone who succumbs to temporary insanity: a twenty-year-old farm boy who had never previously been more than a few miles from his home is coerced into horrific battle after being told to kill or be killed."

"Hope you're right, Doc! If this rascal gets loose again, Percy's done told his Zouaves to shoot the poor fool on sight."

Percy's threat infuriated Joseph. He thought for a moment, then whispered, "Thomas, get our carpenter friend to prepare a special restraining room in the first-floor storage bin. Put shackle irons in all four corners. Have him build a reinforced wooden cot with three sets of heavy belt straps across the center."

Thomas O'Malley stared at the doctor. Joseph nodded once again. "Don't worry, I'll deal with Percy."

· · · · ·

Glad for an excuse to be absent when Albert finally awoke, Thomas O'Malley left in search of the carpenter. As Albert began to regain consciousness, he blinked his eyes repeatedly, trying to clear his vision. Joseph watched closely, sitting on a stool beside the manacled private. "Albert, I'm Doctor Bryarly. Do you remember me?"

Albert slowly nodded.

"I want you to know you're safe here. No more battles, no more war. The treatment you received today was to help you, not to hurt you." As men in nearby cots watched, Joseph took a wet rag and wiped the clotted blood from Albert's face. "I want to help you regain your senses, so you can return home."

"Home? You gonna … let me go home?" Albert asked in a husky whisper.

"Soon, Albert. Once you regain control of your senses. When that happens, I promise you, you *will* go home."

Albert closed his eyes. Every muscle in his body had been tensed and knotted, flexed against his restraints, but they began to relax. Soon, the enormous patient was snoring loudly.

Since it was so late and Joseph had a stack of paperwork to complete, he decided to return to his office, which was situated just below Captain Percy's quarters. He could hear Percy's revelry upstairs. *The creaking of the bed should stop soon*, the doctor reminded himself wearily. He leaned back in his chair, slowly stretched his neck from side to side, and picked up his Bible. From beneath the book, a small piece of paper glided onto his desk. Unfolding the note, Joseph read:

Search the latrine ditch to find your answers. *Psalms 21:11.*

Puzzled and intrigued by the unsigned note, Joseph turned to Psalms, chapter 21, verse 11, and read aloud,
> For they intend evil against thee:
> they imagine a mischievous device …

Eight

"Forward! Advance! On the double—quick! **CHARGE!"**

General Barksdale's entire brigade burst out of the forest in
precision formation, then leaped over two split-rail fences while
screaming at the tops of their lungs. Their screams blended with
the Rebel yells resonating up and down the Gettysburg battlefield
as they faced a blue sea of enemy infantry. Artillery fire exploded
everywhere, a deafening high-pitched whine announcing its
arrival. Leading the charge, General Barksdale rode furiously
amidst the smoke, exploding canisters, and hail of musket balls,
shouting repeatedly, "Forward men! Forward!"

Zeke could feel the blood pumping through his veins. Men
fell out of line on either side of him, struck down by bullets and
artillery blasts. Violent explosions rocked the ground. Shrieks of
agony pierced through the racket of the artillery. Zeke began
tripping over dead and injured men in Confederate gray and
Union blue as he advanced on the run. The boy tried to focus
on the enemy before him, but all he could think of was finding
his brother. He glanced to his left and saw the flag bearer fall.
Instinctively, he moved toward the Mississippi banner, but
remembered his brother's words, and once again scanned the
battlefield. To his relief, on the right he saw Billy wielding

his sword at a cluster of Yankees and yelling like a madman.

Company C held together in formation until they approached the Union cannons. This same battery had pounded them unmercifully earlier, so the Confederates were eager to repay the favor. Without command, the men stopped, took aim, and started dropping the artillery crewmen. Zeke followed suit, and was certain he had hit a Yankee. Together with a dozen others, he charged ahead and surrounded the Yankee artillery unit, capturing a half-dozen men. Quickly re-forming its lines, Company C moved on the Yanks in the peach orchard.

"Charge, boys!" Sergeant Cawley shouted. "Bust through that Yankee line!"

Overpowered, clusters of Union soldiers were trapped. Others backed up, shooting steadily at the oncoming Mississippians. Some took shelter within a nearby farmhouse, but these soldiers were quickly surrounded and disarmed. As in a dream, Zeke watched the drama unfold before him, all the while loading and firing at anything blue that was still fighting back. *This is bedlam!* While his body strained to fight, one part of his mind remained clear and thoughtful. *What do we do now?* An artillery shell landed just a few feet from him—and with a prayer of thanks, he realized the shell was dead. *Where did that come from?* He scanned the area, trying to locate an active enemy artillery position. This huge, chaotic mess of a battle was being fought as far as the boy's eyes could see, by individuals one-on-one, by clusters of soldiers, and by thousands of creatures in blue and gray rolling and racing and leaping and tumbling in every direction.

"Form your line, men! Advance—now!" Sergeant Cawley's command snapped Zeke back into reality. A bugle sounded the charge and they were off again as a unit. *Listen to your officers ... Listen to your officers ... Listen ...* The boy repeated his brother's words as he followed the sergeant.

Straight ahead, twenty or thirty Yankee cannons were pounding away at the brigade. General Barksdale galloped up and shouted, "Take those batteries, men! Forward! We're going to crush our enemy this time!" He bolted ahead, brandishing his sword.

The general's enthusiasm inspired his soldiers and propelled them forward, toward victory or death. Out of the corner of his eye, Zeke was aware of the general fearlessly riding in the range of fire, urging his troops, slashing at Union soldiers in his way, and supervising the direction of the battle. Union artillerists kept up a constant barrage; Mississippi lost many a brave man because of their deadly accuracy. Once again, the men managed to encircle the artillery unit and take aim at the gunners as they closed in on the cannons.

The noise, confusion, and mounds of dead and dying soldiers caused the unit to break up into individuals or pairs. Fighting became hand-to-hand, bayonet-to-bayonet. It was combat with deadly results. Without thinking, Zeke thrust his bayonet through the stomach of a young Yankee who had grabbed his rifle and wouldn't let go. Time seemed to stand still as Zeke watched, horrified, as the boy died. His last words were haunting: "See you in hell, Johnny!"

Nate's scream of warning broke the spell. "Smiley! Look to your left!"

Zeke didn't move fast enough. The butt of a Yankee rifle crashed in his face, and he dropped hard to the ground. The soldier stood over him, raising his rifle to finish the job with his bayonet. Nate, too far away to stop him, hurled his rifle, bayonet forward, like a spear. It hit the Yankee right in the chest, knocking him backward. Nate ran to Zeke's motionless body and stood over him, firing until the fighting subsided and nearby Yankee batteries were captured. Though the general had ordered his troops not to stop and assist the wounded, it was an order Nate could not obey.

As soon as the sounds of battle moved off, Nate knelt to see if Zeke was still breathing—but couldn't tell. Daniel ran up, leaned down, and checked the boy's pulse. "He has a heartbeat, but he took a severe blow to the head. He may be out for a while.

We—you would be wise to inform Billy."

Nate nodded, but couldn't tear himself away from the boy.

Daniel stood up and spotted Billy heading their way with a look of desperate concern on his face.

"Where's Zeke? I told you to watch over him, Nate," Billy yelled as he ran up. He shouted in rage and fear when he recognized his brother's crumpled body, lying on the ground, bleeding. Seeing Zeke's broken nose, swelling face, and blackening eyes, he knelt and anxiously demanded to know, "That looks bad! Is he hurt anywhere else? Is he … dead?"

Daniel put his hand on his shoulder, "No—it's a serious injury, but he's still alive."

"Damn all Yankees to the hottest corner of hell!"

Suddenly, the three men heard a new order barked by Sergeant Cawley: "Fall in! Form your line! NOW!"

"You're sure he ain't dead, Daniel?" Billy demanded to know. Daniel nodded, his hand and neckerchief pressed to Zeke's temple, trying to staunch the flow of blood while Nate wrapped a rag clumsily around his head, to hold the neckerchief in place.

"FORM YOUR LINES—NOW!" the sergeant roared again.

"Oh God, Daniel, we've gotta move. How can I leave him lying here?"

"We have no choice! His best hope is for us to force the Yankees back and return to get him."

"I'll be back, Zeke," Billy promised as he rose and grabbed his rifle. "I swear I'll be back to get you! Hang on!"

• • • • •

What was left of the brigade rushed north once again, some seeking glory, some seeking revenge, some following orders blindly. Although they had swept everything before them, they were so far out in front of the other Southern troops that they were in danger of being flanked. But General Barksdale was determined.

"Forward, men! Forward!" he commanded, leading the way. The men of the brigade who were still standing covered almost a half-mile, destroying everything in their path, with Corporal Billy Gibson far ahead of the charge. Cresting the top of a small hill, the men in the lead stopped suddenly, and those behind them plowed into their backs. They were staring into what seemed to be a hundred Yankee cannons, wheel to wheel, backed by countless artillerymen and infantry dug into the hill. More Federal reinforcements were racing to the scene.

"Damn!" Nate breathed.

"Forward!"

General Barksdale's final command was shouted into the mouth of the cannons. At that instant, Union troops unleashed an extraordinary burst of fire power. All its fury concentrated on Company C. Immediately, the general careened backward off his horse, killed instantly. As a gigantic swarm of bluecoats surged down the hill, the Confederates met them in hand-to-hand fighting, but all too soon the overwhelming numbers of Yankees engulfed the decimated battalion of Confederates. Chaos ensued.

Company C's line advanced as far as possible, considering the odds the soldiers were facing, but there was no stopping the superior numbers of enemy forces. The general's second-in-command, Colonel Humphreys of the 21st Mississippi, ordered a retreat. Reluctantly, slowly, stubbornly, Company C backed over the same ground they had won only hours before.

They were left with the same results that the rest of General Lee's army faced this day: repulsion.

Fortunately for the few remaining survivors of Company C, the Yankees chose not to pursue Barksdale's brigade as the Confederates retreated. Able-bodied men searched the bodies on the field for the wounded and dead and carried the casualties back to their morning's campsite. A perpetual stream of exhausted, discouraged veterans slowly straggled in at the end of the day. Some tried to perform emergency aid until men could be carried to a hospital tent. Some frantically hunted for familiar faces. Some clustered to review the day's events and speculate on what General Lee would do next. Others sat by themselves and covered their faces.

Billy was nowhere to be seen.

As soon as the call to retreat sounded, Nate had run to Zeke's side, picked him up in his brawny arms, and carried him to safety. Desperately worried, he turned to Daniel, who was examining the bloody make-shift bandage on the boy's head, and observed, "He ain't moved a lick."

Daniel flagged down a harried medic, then turned back to Nate. "Have you seen Billy anywhere?"

"Not since the last bunch of Yanks we met. I saw Billy leap into a whole swarm of 'em blue-bellies. I hightailed it out when the bugle sounded, but I didn't see Billy take one step backwards—he jest kept firin' his pistol and screamin' all crazy like." Nate looked on the verge of tears, "I ain't seen him since then, Dan'l."

"Nor have I." The two men sat by the unconscious boy, without needing to express what each was thinking.

"Two Gibsons on the same day? No!" Nate choked out before remembering Daniel's own loss. "I'm sorry, Dan'l. I forgot about your boys."

"There is nothing fair or right about any of this, but don't give up hope yet. Neither Gibson is lost for sure."

Nine

Mary Beth Greene was a delightful study in contrasts: she could look as lovely and as comfortable pursuing her chosen profession on a barrack's cot with a rowdy young soldier, or in a sumptuous suite on a canopied four-poster bed following a society gala. Once a man—any man—had associated with this woman, he never forgot her charm, her intelligent conversation, or her special skills. One visit was never enough, a first-time customer would realize before his visit ended.

Part of her charm was her fastidious cleanliness. In an era when a weekly bath was a luxury, Mary Beth Greene would stroll the short distance from her hotel to an excusive private bathhouse every day without fail, in order to scrub and soak, sometimes for well over an hour. A world-shaking battle was raging up North on one of the days the stunning woman walked into La Fleur's ladies' chamber, but she didn't know that—and neither did the other guests.

The spa matron immediately rose and welcomed her best customer warmly. Mary Beth smiled at her and when the woman turned away, sighed wearily and asked her maid to help her undress. Steam rose from the hot water, and soaked mineral rocks filled the air with the exotic fragrances of aromatic spices. Several socialites glared at her over the tops of the colorful ceramic-tile tubs, but the newcomer ignored them. She was as accustomed to the jealousy of other women as she was to the attentions of their husbands, sons, and beaus. One portly middle-aged woman grumbled when the only remaining attendant deserted her in order to assist Mary Beth.

"Why, thank you, sugar." Miss Greene never failed to treat servants as graciously as she treated her customers, even when she was weary and worried.

The assistant relieved her of her parasol and new French bonnet. As her maid unbuttoned her gown, Mary Beth removed her immaculate white lace gloves slowly, finger by finger, while abstractedly staring at a painting of Paris. What she was thinking was impossible to guess by her expression, but what the other guests at the spa were thinking was blatantly apparent.

Wealthy women who had been deprived of new clothing and accessories since the war had started more than two years ago watched enviously as Mary Beth removed an exquisite new gown in the latest French fashion, then French silk undergarments, before standing nude in front of her reserved artesian-style tub, waiting for the attendant to test the water.

"Cover yourself!" a rotund bather protested, wiping sweat from her brow. "Dressing rooms are in the back, for women of *modest* discretion."

"Well, darlin'," Mary Beth replied, turning to the speaker in surprise, "if I meet such a woman, I will surely send her in that direction."

"Have you no shame?" a young widow asked. "We know who you are—and y'all don't belong among civilized women of refinement."

Mary Beth eased into the hot, sudsy bath and the attendant began soaping her back and arms.

"Answer the lady's question, you harlot!" the first woman insisted.

More amused than annoyed, Mary Beth ignored the widow

and asked the middle-aged busybody gently, "Ma'am, do I know you?"

"I am Mrs. Gloria Strebeck—of the Cumberland Strebecks."

"Strebeck? Your husband wouldn't be Lieutenant Jonathan Strebeck?"

"Yes, he is. He serves on General Lee's staff and he—," she said proudly, before she realized the implication of the question.

"A tall long drink of water, with thick, wavy black hair?"

"Yes, but I ..."

Mary Beth interrupted her, "Does he have dark blue eyes and an adorable schoolboy smile?"

"Yes, but what business that is of ..."

"With the cutest little ol' mole on the left cheek of his butt?"

Even the woman's friends in the bathhouse choked with laughter. The spa matron had to clasp her hands over her mouth and bustle out of the room before her customers noticed her silent laughter.

"Why I never in my life ...!"

"I know, honey," Mary Beth said gently, adding, "because if you had, I wouldn't be able to afford these delightful spa baths!"

A mass of quivering and indignant flesh, the woman hoisted herself over the side of the tub, slipping and sliding on the wet floor as she padded into the changing room muttering things that women of culture don't normally say.

"Miss Mary Beth," the attendant whispered, "did y'all really sleep with her husband?"

"No. But when the lieutenant next comes home, I imagine there'll be a search for a cute little ol' mole!"

• • • • •

Over the past two days, Joseph had taken every opportunity to walk the length of the latrine ditch from the east wing all the way down to the James River. He managed not to arouse suspicion by his odd behavior, but he still had nothing to show for his efforts. *What did the note writer expect me to find? the doctor wondered. And who wrote the note? The handwriting was that of an educated man, which eliminates any handlers. Obviously the writer held strong religious convictions...*

At sunset, Joseph decided to visit Ana and discuss his dilemma. As he started to leave his office, he heard Captain Percy's voice outdoors. Peering out his office window, the doctor saw the captain astride a horse, talking to Sergeant Boudreaux Pirou, a mean and short-tempered behemoth. The doctor leaned closer to listen.

"Pirou, are the boys finished with their task?"

"Too many cavalry boys on the roads until now. They're gittin' to it."

"Get moving, Sergeant! I promised the boys a midnight ride—so hurry up."

"Me and the boys'll meet back at camp soon's we finish."

Percy galloped away, and Pirou's boots thumped down the wooden planks leading toward the latrine ditch. Knowing that his curiosity could get him killed, Joseph waited a few minutes, and then followed Pirou. He hid behind a dilapidated corncrib, watching as the Cajun and four others kicked and rolled a long, large object wrapped in burlap into the ditch. Two men quickly covered it up with a shallow layer of dirt.

"Dang! That smells something fierce," one of the diggers complained.

Pirou threw a spade full of dirt into his face. "Then stand upwind!"

Joseph knew this was his chance. He forced himself to stand in the open, awkwardly cleared his throat, and spoke. "Good evening, gentlemen."

The Zouaves whipped around, startled by the voice in the darkness. One man drew his pistol and cocked the hammer. Joseph felt seconds away from death, but managed to identify himself calmly. Apparently trying to decide whether or not to shoot, Pirou hesitated, then gestured, and the Zouave reluctantly holstered his pistol.

"A little late for a work detail, isn't it, Sergeant?" Joseph's voice exuded an unexpected confidence.

"Too hot till now."

"Who ordered this detail?" Already knowing the answer to his question, Joseph stalled for time as he moved toward the edge of the ditch.

One digger snapped, "None of your business!"

"Hold your tongue, Private," the doctor commanded. Turning to the sergeant, he insisted, "Remind your men that I am a doctor and a lieutenant, sir. They could be charged with insubordination."

Pirou spat on the ground and motioned for the men to return to work.

"Sergeant! I gave you an order. I expect it to be obeyed."

"Cap'n Percy gives the orders." Pirou stopped shoveling and moved just inches away from Joseph's face. "They know who you are," he snarled. "Now go away!"

Joseph ignored the man, stepped around him, knelt, and peered into the ditch. Amongst the dark shadows, he could discern a much larger object than the routine refuse, filth, and fresh dirt.

And the object appeared to be human.

Faintly visible was the back of a badly burned and scarred bald head. Joseph panicked, *My God, it's the blister therapy patient—he's dead! They murdered him!*

"Stop! Stop shoveling this instant! That's an order!" Joseph grabbed the nearest shovel. "That man was a Union prisoner of war!"

"What man?" Pirou snarled. "There's no man—only dung."

Defying Joseph's order to stop, the Zouaves quickly heaved mounds of dirt into the latrine, and whatever it was that Joseph thought he saw disappeared from view. Then they turned to the doctor. One man slowly drew his pistol. Pirou knocked the doctor to the ground. "I told you to GO AWAY! You don't know what you saw."

"I know what I saw." Joseph obstinately jumped to his feet. "The head of a man."

"If it's a head," another Zouave smirked, "it come outta some-body's butt."

Although Joseph knew Pirou hated him, he also knew that Pirou was the only reason he was still alive. *Men die every day. Life is cheap during a war. No one would think twice if I fell victim to what appeared to be an accident. Careful, Joseph, dying won't help the poor men in Wingate Asylum. Think! Think of a way out of this mess.*

"I apologize, Sergeant. Obviously, I was mistaken." Joseph must have been convincing, for at that instant the pistol beside his head was pulled away. His life had been spared once again. For now.

Pirou threatened, "Time you was gone. Get away now! Last chance!"

Joseph nodded, then walked briskly around the east-wing corner, wondering if he'd arrive back in his office alive.

"Finish this up, boys. Percy needs to know about him."

"Should of let me kill him," the lanky man grumbled.

Pirou smashed him across the face with his shovel. "Percy orders killings, not you—not me. The Doc is a personal friend of President Jeff Davis and if anything happens to him, the gov'ment will come runnin'. We don't want that, do we?"

Two hours later, the ditch was completely covered with fresh dirt, and the Zouaves had ridden away.

• • • • •

"I just wish I could be absolutely sure of what I saw." Joseph was sitting in the Dougall apartment, talking with Ana's father and brother. "It looked like the Union soldier I met several weeks ago, but in the darkness I couldn't be certain."

"Did you see his body, Joseph?" Mr. Dougall asked.

"No, sir, only what appeared to be the outline of a body and a head covered in fresh dirt."

"I wish the whole lot of them Zouaves would get hanged—let them taste their own medicine!" Michael said angrily.

"If I could prove they murdered the Union prisoner, they'd

be on their way to the gallows," Joseph mused. "The real question is: Who can I trust?"

"I'll help find that body—or bodies," Michael offered.

"No! You'd be killed—the both of you," Mrs. Dougall joined the conversation.

"Oh, Joseph," Ana pleaded, "this war's not ours to fight. I couldn't bear to lose you."

The doctor turned to her. "This war is my fight, Ana. It's the reason I left England. I owe it to the Confederacy to help the patients at Wingate, and the only way to help them is to confront Captain Percy."

"He'll kill you, Joseph," Mr. Dougall warned. "Soldiers need to look into Percy's actions, not you."

"I've heard some disturbing stories about the provost office, but that's probably my only choice," he mused, more to himself than his listeners. Then he insisted they turn to happier topics. Later, he accepted Mrs. Dougall's offer to stay in town that night.

Ten

The men of Company C sat talking among themselves about the last charge of the day, the loss of General Barksdale, and how Billy refused to retreat when the order was given. Sergeant Cawley told the troops, "I reckon I was the last man to see Billy. He took a bullet through his face and at least one other through the shoulder. I figured he was dead."

"I just can't believe it," Nate moaned.

With rarely heard tones of compassion, the sergeant told them, "He was one tough son of a buck. I tell you, I never saw a better fighter than Billy Gibson."

"Zeke's gonna be heartbroke," Nate said. "He sure thought the world of Billy."

"We all did, Nate. We'll all miss him," Daniel added, his face wooden.

"How's the boy?" the sergeant asked.

"Still no change. Hasn't moved a muscle."

"How many men you reckon we done lost, Sarge?" Nate asked, not really wanting to know the answer.

"More than one-third of our regiment is wounded, missing, or dead, and I'd guess it's about the same for the entire brigade. Not only did we lose the general, we also lost Colonel Taylor on that last charge." Sergeant Cawley stood and shook his head in disbelief, "Damn! It was a very bad day for the sons of Mississippi."

• • • • •

By the third day of the Battle of Gettysburg, General Lee had yet to crush the Northern Army—but he still was confident his forces could do the job. All morning, Confederate artillery bombarded and blasted away at the middle of the Federal line. At one o'clock, one hundred seventy-five Confederate cannons commenced firing. Meanwhile, the Yankees were countering with almost as many big guns. For what seemed like an eternity, the earth shook with the cannonading. The painfully intense noises, shaking ground, and thunderous volleys eventually startled Zeke back to consciousness. He opened his eyes, staring blankly at the sky before managing to stagger to his feet. When his legs buckled under him, he dropped and vomited violently.

"Easy boy! Easy!" Nate called, hurrying over to him. "You've had a busted head and a long sleep, but I'm mighty glad to see ya." Turning to Daniel, he added, "Glory to God! He's okay, huh, Dan'l?"

"He'll be in some pain for a while yet, but it looks like he'll make it."

Zeke tried to focus on his surroundings. "What happened, Daniel? Where we at? Where's Billy?" Zeke fired questions without waiting for responses. "What's going on now—?" He stopped talking and grabbed his head in agony. Moments later, he added, "Where's my brother? Did we win?"

"Calm down, Zeke—it's not good for your head."

"Who's making all that noise?"

"General Lee is still feeling a mite aggressive," Daniel informed. "The battle is in its third day. I hope that brigade has better luck than we did."

"I think my head's gonna explode," Zeke groaned, repeating, "Where's Billy?"

Silently, Nate and Daniel looked at each other. Their faces spoke volumes.

"He's gone? Billy's gone? No way—I won't believe it! He's too tough to die or be captured. He must be out there wounded," Zeke insisted, painfully trying to rise. "I've gotta go find him!"

"You can't, Zeke. All the ground we covered yesterday is in Federal hands," Daniel warned. "Sergeant Cawley said he saw Billy go down during our last charge, a long way from here."

"I won't leave him to the Yankees!" Zeke shouted, trying again to rise. When he couldn't get his legs to move, he burst into tears. Between sobs, he insisted, "Billy's out there somewhere. He's not dead!"

· · · · ·

Billy was indeed out there, lying in a mound of dead and wounded soldiers from the Union army, most of whom he had fought single-handedly. The noise from the cannonade jolted him back to consciousness, just as it had awakened Zeke. The stabbing pain in his shoulder was excruciating, and his jaw throbbed at the slightest movement. Trying not to move his shoulder or his head, he felt for his canteen, for he was desperately thirsty. Scavengers had already stripped away his boots, a present from his mother last Christmas, along with his jacket, personal belongings, and identification.

Reckon they must have took me for dead. Billy slowly eased upward, trying to understand the situation. *There are Yankees everywhere. I must be behind enemy lines.*

A Union soldier noticed Billy moving. "I'm here to help you, Reb, if you want help. You'll be a prisoner either way."

Billy lay back down. *A prisoner? This ain't supposed to happen to me.* When the medic leaned over him, he spoke again. "I'll help you … if you let me. You have some pretty serious injuries."

Billy tried to speak, but could only make gurgling noises that hurt fiercely and threatened to choke him. *Feels like I swallowed a lit firecracker*, Billy thought as he nodded his head. A stretcher arrived, and the Confederate was carted to an old farmhouse that had been converted into a Federal field hospital. He was amazed to learn that the Northern doctors were willing to help him. They cleaned and stitched the shoulder wound, snapped the dislocated shoulder back into place, then studied the broken jaw. "There's not much we can do for that, Johnny," the doctor advised. "You're not going to be able to speak for quite some time." He liberally dosed Billy with a mixture of laudanum and whiskey to help him manage the pain, then moved on to his next patient. Burly blue-clad medics quickly moved him outside.

Lying for hours in the shade of an oak tree, Billy could hear the screams and cries from thousands of wounded men. *This is what hell itself must sound like!* Drifting in and out of consciousness, he worried about Zeke, praying that he had survived, knowing that his folks would worry themselves sick about them. In a moment of near clarity, he thought, *I've got to get out of here. I've got to find my brother ...*

· · · · ·

The Battle of Gettysburg ended on the third day, with a resounding defeat for the Confederacy. Both sides suffered appalling losses. Because the Confederates were running low on food and ammunition, General Lee decided to order the long, sad retreat back to Virginia.

Heavy rains drenched the countryside and the soldiers for most of the afternoon and early evening of July 4, 1863. "It's as if God is washing the blood off the land," Daniel observed quietly, surveying the horrible carnage as Company C lead the retreat, following the long wagon train carrying Confederate wounded. The line of soldiers stretched for miles. Despite a disastrous headache, Zeke managed to walk with his company. A doctor who passed him by noticed his facial injuries and asked how he was feeling. "Mighty bad headache, sir."

"All I've got for the pain is some whiskey, compliments of our generous Pennsylvania friends. It's yours if you want it."

Zeke, who had never tasted whiskey in his life, accepted the bottle gratefully.

The first drink made him choke and cough; the second and third went down more smoothly.

"Not too much," Daniel cautioned. "We have a long march ahead, and we don't want you staggering."

Zeke handed the bottle back to the doctor. "You keep it. A lot of our boys are going to need it."

Slowly, painfully, the Army of Northern Virginia retreated south, limping and stumbling past the same houses and villages they had proudly marched past just days earlier.

"Y'all ain't as full of yourselves as you were last week," a young woman taunted from her front porch.

"Go back South and don't come this way again!" another yelled.

Ignoring the locals' smirks and insults, General Lee's forces kept marching. When they approached the Potomac River, they suffered a rude shock. The water level had risen from the recent rains; they were unable to ford the river immediately.

"What'll we do now, Daniel?" Zeke asked.

"I'm positive Mr. Lincoln is pushing General Meade to crush us. Pray they don't attack us here, now. Backed up to the river with no way to retreat, we'd be sitting ducks."

That night, after making camp, a work detail began digging a defensive trench in preparation for the Yankee attack that never came. Apparently, both sides were licking their wounds. The river finally receded, and the men crossed. In despair, Zeke realized that every step he marched took him farther from Billy.

· · · · ·

At eight thirty on the morning after the fourth of July, Joseph stood outside the Provost Office near the old fairgrounds reading the posted bulletins. *This seems foolish. With all the concern about spies, why would the Provost Marshall post the names and strengths of Confederate regiments defending the peninsula?*

The doctor stepped inside and immediately realized he was probably wasting his time. The stench of whiskey, body odor, and stale cigar smoke was overwhelming. On the deserted desk facing the door, passes to travel freely throughout the Confederacy and dispatches from the Army of Northern Virginia lay in plain view. Through an open door, he could glimpse Brigadier General John Henry Winder, Richmond Provost Marshall, asleep. Startled by the sound of the office door slamming, he lurched upright and stared blankly at the visitor. He staggered into the office.

"Whiskey," he croaked. Joseph spotted a bottle and handed it to the general. After a few gulps and disgusting belching, Winder finally spoke, "Well—what do you want?"

"I have a delicate matter that requires some assistance—" Joseph started to explain, but sensing that he had made a mistake in coming here, he hesitated.

"Speak your piece." Regaining his senses, Winder added, "How did you get past my provost guards?"

"I didn't see any guards, General."

Winder walked over, peered out the door, and shouted, "Stupid sulkers, good for nothin' ..." He sat down heavily at his desk. "Speak."

"I have reason to believe that Union prisoners are being tortured and killed."

"We're supposed to kill Yankees, mister."

"Look, I'm Doctor Joseph Bryarly, a lieutenant assigned to Wingate Asylum—"

"Are you talking about Bedlam South?"

"Yes, sir."

"Why should I care if Yankees are dying at the lunatic house? Good riddance!"

"What if I told you that Confederate troops were in danger as well?"

Winder scowled. "What do you want from my office, *Doctor*? Isn't Captain Percy in charge over there? What *specific* charges are you bringing against him?"

"No charges, General. I am just asking you to conduct an investigation. Yesterday, I witnessed several soldiers covering what appeared to be a body in the latrine ditch. I recognized the head of the man—a Union prisoner."

"*Appeared? Appeared?*" Winder made no attempt to hide his anger. "You're not sure?"

"Yes—yes, I'm certain. All I am asking is for you to send a guard detail and some workers to dig up the latrine ditch. It is the duty of this office to investigate all matters relating to prisoners of war, isn't it, General?"

Winder fumed before pointing out, "I know the duties of this office, Doctor. I'll send a detail out this afternoon."

· · · · ·

Wondering about what the day would hold, Joseph returned to the asylum. Mid-afternoon, he walked out onto the old manor's verandah, anxious for the arrival of the general and his men. He glanced onto the lawn and froze, speechless. Under a magnolia sat Winder and Percy, sharing drinks and laughs as though they were lifelong friends. The guard detail moved on to the ditch and quickly uncovered the long, shallow trench.

Winder yelled, "C'mon over, Doctor. You'll probably want to see this. It's awful, just awful. In fact, it stinks to high heaven." He laughed raucously and the work detail and the captain joined in the jeers.

"Bryarly," Percy said with false joviality, "if I knew you was so interested in latrines, I would've given you a shovel."

Outraged, Joseph shot back, "I know what I saw, Captain Percy."

"What?" Percy shouted, grabbing Joseph by his collar and forcing his head downward. "Do you see anything now, *Doctor*? Any dead bodies contained in all that filth?"

Joseph wrested himself out of Percy's grip and stood nose-to-nose with him. General Winder laughed again. "If y'all got that much spunk, then fill this ditch up yourselves."

Grasping a spade and shoving it into Joseph's chest, Percy snarled, "Good idea. Here, Doctor. Make yourself useful—for once."

Joseph didn't take his eyes off the captain—and he didn't take the spade. General Winder pretended not to notice as he explained, "Doctor, my men excavated more than one hundred yards of this ditch and found nothing larger than a kidney stone. I hope that makes you happy." Turning to Percy he added, "It's time I returned to camp."

With a nod, the general quickly departed and a work detail began the task of refilling the ditch. Percy and Joseph were left alone. Percy gritted his teeth and whispered, "One day … one day, *Doctor*, you'll go too far and I'll enjoy killing you … personally."

"And if you do, Captain, you'll have my friend and neighbor, Jeff Davis, to answer to," Joseph said with false bravado.

Both men were reluctant to be the first to turn his back and leave.

· · · · ·

By the time Federal soldiers gathered the wounded Confederates from Gettysburg's battlefields and temporary hospitals, the stench of dead horses, mules, and humans was nauseating. The sun beat relentlessly on the battlefield carnage. Every house and barn in the small Pennsylvania town had been requisitioned for hospitals or holding pens for prisoners. Every able-bodied man set to work carrying stretchers with wounded soldiers, burying dead soldiers, or assisting in hospital work. Every able-bodied woman set to work cooking, baking, comforting, or nursing.

"Mama, I'm sick to death of chopping firewood and standing over the stove night and day cooking when there are men out there who need help," Sally Stearns informed her mother, stretching her tired back and twisting her neck with fatigue, watching a detail of army privates leave her kitchen toting huge kettles of stew and a burlap sack full of breads. "I think it's time I see what I can do in a hospital."

Her mother collapsed into a nearby rocker and fanned her face with her dishtowel. She only had the energy to nod.

That night, armed with a kerosene lamp and a basket full of hastily-rolled bandages and salves, Sally walked to the next farm, where the barn had been requisitioned for a hospital.

• • • • •

Billy didn't know how long he had slept—whether an hour, a day, or longer—after he was loaded onto a wagon and bumped over fields whose crops had been destroyed by the three-day battle. Exhausted farmers and their sons joined soldiers in unloading endless wagons crammed with severely wounded men. Billy Gibson was carried into the Webbers' barn, on the outskirts of Gettysburg village. Cushioned with piles of hastily strewn straw, the floor served as the bed for seventy-some soldiers. Burlap sacks filled with discarded clothing, books, bags of animal feed, and anything else desperate people could think of were called into service as pillows. Fortunately, the weather was warm enough that blankets could be dispensed with.

The homes, schoolrooms, barns, churches, and gathering places that had been transformed into hospitals were staffed by emergency nurses: homeowners, barn owners, members of the clergy, sympathetic Pennsylvanians, and soldiers' family members who had heard about the battle and arrived in the hopes of finding their sons. Occasionally an exhausted army medical officer and his aides would make the rounds, performing primitive surgeries, splinting broken limbs, sewing gaping wounds, checking for fevers and rashes, and offering remedies for everything from dysentery to sunstroke. But there were too many wounded and too few doctors. Silas and Una Webber, along with their three young sons, had struggled for two days and nights to offer seventy-some wounded guests in their barn food, water, safety, and attention. The Webbers greeted Sally Stearns' arrival with exhausted, but open, arms.

So, when the Confederate corporal finally awoke, he opened his eyes to see a vision silhouetted in the doorway of the barn. A young and shapely woman unconsciously posed in front of the blood-red sunset as she lit a lantern to illuminate the barn's dark interior. The Confederate corporal stared uncomprehendingly as the woman moved toward him. She dropped gracefully by his side, picked up his hand, and checked his pulse, then felt his forehead for fever.

"You've joined us at last, sir," she said softly. "I wasn't sure if I'd ever know the color of your eyes."

Thanks to his shoulder wounds and injuries, he moved his arm awkwardly; he gestured to indicate that he couldn't talk. But his eyes spoke volumes as he stared into the nurse's twinkling gray-blue eyes.

"There's many a woman who wished her man spoke a little less—would your wife be among them?" she teased as she wrung out a cool, clean cloth and washed his face and hands. The Confederate tried to smile, flinched at the pain a smile required, but shook his head in answer to her question, still keeping his eyes on hers. She nodded, smiled, and moved on to the next patient. As much as he could, without moving his head or shoulders, he kept Sally Stearns in his sights.

Billy Gibson wasn't the only injured man in that barn who thought he was beholding an angel—a guardian angel with a sweet and soothing voice, soft and capable hands, and great compassion. But Billy Gibson was the only man whose handsome good looks, strong body, and piercing blue-gray eyes caught the nurse's attention.

At the age of twenty-one, Sally Stearns had become engaged to her neighbor and childhood sweetheart when he was home on a three-day leave. They spent the precious days walking through orchards covered in apple and peach blossoms, kissing, laughing, and spinning dreams for the future. Two weeks later, after the battle of Fredericksburg, Sally received a letter from the Grand Army of the Republic informing her that James had died on the battlefield. No one—not even her fiancé's mother—ever saw her cry. But from that point on, she regarded time and love in a very different light.

"Does it bother you that you're nursing the enemy along with our soldiers?" Una Webber asked Sally as the two briefly collapsed in the Webber's kitchen, waiting for water to boil.

"I thought it would," Sally said slowly. "But I've come to understand that there is no difference between Union and Confederate men except for their uniforms."

"Does nursing make you miss James even more?" the neighbor woman asked.

"It makes me regret that we had so little time together after we talked of marriage—and it hurts that I'll never know if he had someone by his side wiping his brow and holding his hand when he died," the young woman admitted with tears in her eyes, adding to herself, *I'll always regret that he went to war without holding me in the way a husband holds a wife ...*

The kettle boiled and the women returned to their labors, each a little wiser.

After finishing a long day's work, Sally found herself gravitating back to Billy's side. "I wish I knew your name," she said, brushing the long black hair off his forehead. "If I gave you a pencil and paper, could you write? Would you want to write?" When he nodded, she pulled the tools out of her pocket and asked his name. Hours later, just before she headed home, Billy wrote, *By the time I'm healed—or imprisoned—I'll have written a book, thanks to you!* She laughed and waved her hand carelessly as she headed out the barn door.

But she returned with more paper the next day. And the next. By the fourth day, Sally knew that she could love again.

Billy hadn't taken that long. From the moment he saw Sally silhouetted in the barn door—even before he saw her face clearly—he somehow knew that he would be linked with that woman for the rest of his life. *Could this beautiful woman ever fancy me?* he wondered through long, lonely nights, as men coughed, choked, cried, snored, and moaned all around him.

Knowing how exhausted the Webbers were, Sally offered to sleep through the days and remain in the barn through the night so they could sleep. "I promise I'll come running if there's an emergency," she told the kindly Una as she gently pushed her toward her home.

As the men surrounding Billy fell asleep, Sally drew closer to the Confederate and opened her heart. "My James was trying to build a pontoon bridge across the river near Fredericksburg and

Rebel sharpshooters began picking off the unarmed engineers …
His death broke my heart."

A cold chill ran through Billy. *My brigade was the last one out
of Fredericksburg! We were the ones shooting the Yankee engineers! How horrible is this war? This woman is helping me,
and I might have been the sharpshooter who killed her fiancé.*
Guiltily, he chose not to share this information.

After a week, the Yankees rounded up prisoners who were
fit to travel. They sent the officers on a train to the North and
then returned for the enlisted men. Doctors made the rounds
of Gettysburg hospitals alongside soldiers, to determine which
wounded could be moved. When the guards approached Billy,
Sally looked pleadingly at the doctor she had come to know
so well.

"He has a broken jaw and can't speak, a dislocated shoulder,
and serious bullet holes. He's in no condition to travel. If he tears
open his stitches, he'll bleed to death," he told the officers, with a
wink at Sally.

"How soon before he's ready?"

"It's hard to tell. Every man's wounds heal differently," the
old doctor explained. "You don't have to worry about him
escaping. He wouldn't make it into the barnyard before he'd drop
dead."

"Why are you in such a hurry to move these men?" Sally
asked.

"Because there'll be a prisoner exchange soon. The more
Rebels we have to trade, the more of our boys we'll get back
before they starve to death in some southern prison."

"Well, he's no good for an exchange if he's dead, is he?" Sally
shot back.

The Federals moved two wounded Confederates, but left
Billy. During the next few days many of the Union soldiers died.
Others were claimed by family members or conveyed to a train
that would carry them to hospitals in Washington. That left more
time for Sally to spend with her Confederate patient. One night

she confessed, "I can't bear the thought of you being dragged off to a prison. If only I could hide you until this horrid war ends!"

Grinning, Billy scribbled, *And then what would you do with me?*

Sally couldn't help but blush. "I would take care of you as long as you'd let me."

Billy wrote, *That might be a very long time. Ever been to Mississippi?*

Staring deep into his steel-blue eyes, she shook her head no. He wrote again, *Ever want to go to Mississippi?* Before she could do more than nod, he slowly pulled her closer. Then he reached for the nape of her neck and pulled her face down to his mouth.

The kiss was soft and gentle at first, but quickly heated. Sally softly moaned and settled into the straw by Billy's side without breaking the kiss. When at last they came up for air, Billy knew that his heart was racing—and he strongly suspected that Sally's was too. Without another word, she slipped under his blanket, molded her body to his, and for the first time fell asleep feeling cherished.

Billy didn't sleep that night. In his twenty-two years, he had never made time for girls, and now he knew why. He had been waiting for this girl.

When his nurse woke up to the crowing of the lonely rooster, she found her Confederate patient trying gingerly to walk. In her hand he'd slipped a message:

I love you with all my heart, Sally.

"I love you, too—" She choked back her tears, rose on her tiptoes, and kissed her soldier.

At dusk the next night, when Sally returned to the barn, Billy had a request: *Sally, since prisoners can't correspond with anyone, could you send a letter to my mother for me? But please be careful.* He added his parents' address at the bottom of the page.

"I'll be happy to."

Billy smiled and forced a soft, guttural "Thank you." Those were his first words and they set his throat on fire. *Too much too soon*, he grimaced. Sally hurried to ask Una Webber for stationery. After her return, she helped Billy pen a letter.

> *Dear Momma,*
>
> *If this letter gets to you, it's because of a beautiful friend named Sally I met in my stay at the hospital in Gettysburg. Don't worry about me. I was wounded on my shoulder and jaw, but I'm healing up and should be out soon. Zeke was on the battlefield with me, but I don't know how or where he is. I hope he will write, too. You'll love Sally as much as I do, Momma. She's the girl you told me to wait for. Hope to see you soon—more than you know.*
>
> *Love, Billy*

Eleven

To the east of Richmond, Captain Percy and eighteen of his
Zouave raiders prowled about the countryside under the full
moon, riding alongside the dense tree line to conceal their presence from the night patrols and to avoid detection by the sentry
picket posts on Long Bridge Road. When they reached the
Chickahominy River, they waded downstream from the bridge,
leading their horses.

Safely past the outpost, they mounted and rode hard once
again. Within the hour, the raiders had arrived at Whispering
Pines Plantation. They dismounted and gathered under a thick
grove of weeping willows while Percy and Pirou discussed their
plan of attack and surveyed the grounds.

Ghostly silhouettes of trees lined the quarter-mile lane leading
to the war-ravaged estate. Most of the second-story windows
were shattered; the shutters hung loosely beside the French doors;
the balcony railings were broken; the grounds were unkempt. The
tobacco barns and grain storage bins were burned-out skeletons.
A broken wagon lay across the circle drive, and tall weeds surrounded every structure. Pasture fences had been torn down.
Livestock and crops had disappeared. Whispering Pines was a
casualty of war, an easy conquest for raiders.

"Pirou," Percy ordered, "take five men and see what you can find."

"You and y'all," Pirou pointed, "leave the horses. Come with me."

"Pirou, no witnesses," Percy ordered.

The man nodded and left with his riders.

Percy rubbed the long, puckered scar on his face and turned to the remaining Zouaves. "Let's take this real slow. It's supposed to be abandoned, but keep your eyes open."

The raiders crept up to the house, guns drawn. Two raiders held large canisters containing coal oil. In the rear, one Zouave led horses heavy laden with massive packs. The first raiders slipped into the house.

Suddenly, a woman's screams pierced the darkness. Panicked shouts were followed by gunshots and the sounds of a struggle. A man's voice cried out, "Oh Lord!" Four more gunshots, and then silence.

Percy took control. "Check every room. Nobody but us walks outta here alive!"

Except for the corpses, the house was empty. The raiders began filling sacks with plunder: paintings, sterling, jewelry, and tableware.

"Don't waste your time with trinkets, boys," Percy interrupted. "I know where the real prize is. Follow me!" The men circled the outside of the mansion and climbed down into the storm cellar. Stored goods and shelves were strewn about, evidence of earlier looting.

One Zouave complained, "Why'd we ride so far? It's done been raided."

"Not the good stuff." Percy ordered two men to move a massive set of storage shelves along the cellar wall. A fog of dirt and dust filled the air as the shelves crashed to the floor. Torchlight illuminated a three-foot-square iron door secured with a massive padlock.

"Stand clear!" The captain fired three shots at close range.

Bullets ricocheted, but the final shot exploded the lock. Percy pushed the heavy wooden door. Covered with dust, Percy crawled inside the storage bin, then emerged holding two large bags.

"Here's your treasure, boys!" he shouted, dumping a sack and sending gold and silver coins clanging across the floor at the raiders' feet. The Zouaves scrambled through the dust and dirt for the money.

Percy gloated. "There'll be eight more bags where these came from. You boys haul 'em out, and we'll get a fair split." Pirou and his men were waiting when Percy emerged from the cellar.

"Find trouble?"

"Not much," Pirou replied. "Two deserters, two old men, one whore."

Everyone erupted in laughter when Pirou joked, "Whore—bad ugly—shot her first."

Pirou pointed to the pouches. "How much?"

"Ten bags, gold and silver, just like we were told. There should be Yankee greenbacks and gold, land deeds, and Confederate bonds."

Pirou's brows shot up.

The Zouaves gathered on the porch to divide up what their twisted minds considered to be the spoils of war.

"Captain Percy, how'd y'all know that stash was in the cellar?"

"Corporal Richard Montgomery, a fine young man with a poor troubled soul, insisted that we share his family's secret." Percy snickered. The Zouaves roared with laughter, correctly interpreting the word "insisted."

"He may have been born on Whispering Pines Plantation, but he'll die at Bedlam South—very soon."

Before returning to Richmond, Percy motioned to the loads on the pack horses. "Peltret! Leave the guilty witnesses."

The Zouave unwrapped two bodies of Union soldiers killed earlier that night in a previous raid, dumping one corpse on the porch steps, and propping the second against the nearby well. Peltret then scattered Union rifles, haversacks, and even coat buttons for effect. By the time LaSalle returned from the slaves' quarters dragging one civilian body with him, the fire in the outbuildings had begun to spread. He placed that body in the front doorway. As the men rode away, the plantation manor and outbuildings erupted into flames, lighting the night sky with crimson flames and billowing black smoke.

"Damn Yankees!" Percy screamed gleefully, far away from the noise and heat of the flames.

· · · · ·

Every day, Billy felt stronger, and every day the barn held fewer occupants. Late one afternoon, anticipating Sally's arrival, he climbed into the loft to hide just as thunder cracked in the distance. The pounding of the rain drowned out the creaking of the barn door. Sally hurried in with a small lantern and a dripping shawl over her head. After checking on the few remaining soldiers, she made her way to the back of the barn, expecting to find Billy in the nook they had fashioned for privacy. He was nowhere to be found.

"Billy? Where are you?" Her concern was apparent. He teasingly threw a handful of hay at her feet. She glared up at the hayloft, hands on hips.

"What are you doing up there, Billy Gibson?"

No answer.

Curiously, Sally climbed the ladder to the loft. She found her Confederate stretched on a pile of hay, pretending to be asleep.

"What are you up to?" she whispered, running a straw around his ear playfully. "If you're asleep, I'll just have to leave ..." He rolled over, grabbed her, and pulled her down to him.

A bolt of lightning momentarily lit the loft, revealing the young woman lying beside him. *She is breathtakingly beautiful!* Billy realized yet again. Her yellow dress was fanned across the hay, as was her yellow hair, which had tumbled out of its bun when she dropped down. Eyes dark with mystery smiled invitingly up at him. Her teardrop earrings called attention to the fine lines of her face and her delicate ears. Her perfumed fragrance overcame his senses …

At daylight the next morning, the Union soldiers returned to the barn. Sally heard the wagons pull into the farmyard as she frantically finished dressing. "Stay here," she pleaded with Billy. "Maybe they won't find you."

The Federal soldiers carried or accompanied the few remaining prisoners to the waiting wagon, where an informer squealed about Billy's hiding place in the loft, hoping for preferred treatment. Knowing he had no choice and he would fare better if he went willingly, Billy climbed down from the loft without coercion. A sergeant and corporal pointed their weapons and moved toward him menacingly.

Sally ran into his arms.

"Well, aren't you a shameless hussy—are you that way with all soldier boys?" the sergeant growled as he grabbed her with one hand and forcibly kissed her. In a flash, Billy nailed him with a solid right fist square on the chin, rolling the big man backward onto a stack of hay bales. Billy's shoulder burned agonizingly from the effort. By the time he turned around, he was staring down the barrels of three rifles. "One more move, Reb, and you'll die right here."

Billy took one step in their direction.

Sally jumped between them. "Billy—please, Billy! They'll surely kill you!"

The big sergeant, groggy from the blow, slowly rose to his feet. Shaking his head, he looked up at Billy in disbelief and admitted, "I ain't never been hit like that!" He stretched his head from side to side, adding, "I'd hate to see you when you were at full strength, Johnny Reb." He motioned to his soldiers, "Now get them out of here."

Chained to the other prisoners, Billy mouthed the words *I love you!* Sally ran to him and grabbed his hand. "Please, please, come back to me," she pleaded, not caring who heard her or what the consequences might be.

The corporal shoved her aside. Billy clenched his fists.

The shackled Confederates climbed onto the back of the wagon with difficulty. Billy turned and watched the beautiful woman in the yellow dress until the wagon drove out of sight.

In despair, Sally climbed back up into the hay loft. On the spot where Billy had slept, she found his last note. *I love you, Sally Stearns. I'll be back for you just as soon as this war is over. Wait for me!*

· · · · ·

Percy and his raiders rode for three days, and during those three days, Bedlam South was unusually peaceful. The hospital operated more smoothly and the patients appeared to be calmer and more cooperative. Joseph relished the changes, enjoying the solitude of his office, the silence in the room above his, and the visits with patients. He felt effective, useful to these men and to God. After completing his rounds, he encountered O'Malley coming out of the apothecary supply room.

"Morning, Doc." O'Malley grinned and said, "Reckon you'd like to see Private Wright's new home."

The two men passed thirty-five restrained men, then the ward that housed most of the more violent residents. They stopped outside the former storage locker that had been transformed into a personalized restraint room for Private Albert Wright. O'Malley fumbled for a moment with the massive padlock, then opened the door.

The scene was nothing like Joseph had imagined. His head pounded, his hands began to shake, and sweat poured off his forehead. Feeling sick, he leaned against O'Malley while he stared at Albert and the device that cruelly held him captive—as though he had been a primitive beast. "T-t-thomas!" he stuttered, "where … what … what is this?"

"Feller what built it called it a *crib*."

"I know what it is," Joseph mumbled. "I meant how? … Why?"

The crib was a long, narrow casket-shaped cage that stood

three feet off the floor. Bars stretched all four sides. A large padlock secured the metal-hinged opening on top. Albert lay nearly naked on top of soiled straw, staring blankly into space. He failed to acknowledge his visitors' presence in the room.

Joseph's first concern was that the device had driven Albert deeper into a deranged state of mania. Scientific research he'd read in the doctor's office at Bethlem Royal Hospital had stressed that the crib's confinement increased patients' psychoses, causing irreversible madness. *Dear God, I dare not release Albert, not after so long inside the crib! He is more susceptible than ever to madness, violent behavior, and unspeakable actions. But what should I do? I promised him—and you, Lord—to do my best to help him recover and get released.*

"The formal name for this torture device is the Utica crib, Thomas," Joseph said in a wooden voice. "It was invented in 1845 by a French physician and named for the first institution to use it in America: the Utica Lunatic Asylum."

Joseph stood frozen in grisly memories, "I have seen this beast … this instrument of Satan … many times."

"Sorry, Doc! I figured you'd be pleased."

Pacing anxiously, Joseph prayed silently, in anguish, for wisdom, for Albert Wright, and for his own soul. Finally, he asked, "Thomas, why didn't you have the carpenter build the restraining table as I requested?"

"He figured this'd be the same thing, I reckon. Says he got the idea from the isolation room down in the cellar. Says he built something like it for Percy last year."

"Show me the room—and have Albert removed from this instrument of Satan immediately."

"But, Doc—you're knowing that Percy don't allow *nobody* in that room."

"Give me the keys. I'll go alone."

• • • • •

Thomas O'Malley hated the asylum's cellar and its damp walls, huge metal cages hanging from the ceiling, and eerie treatment rooms. *These'd make the devil himself squeamish!* he told himself every time he was forced to go down there. The oil lamp he carried failed to adequately light the rooms, and the patients'—or prisoners'—screams added to the terrifying atmosphere. The original stone cellar housed four treatment rooms and two solitary confinement cages, but Percy had ordered the cellar expanded the previous year to include a long tunnel blocked by an impenetrable iron door. Joseph had never been behind the iron door. Neither had O'Malley. Only the Zouaves had permission to enter the isolation rooms. The crude sign on the door was unmistakable: Trespass and Die.

"Doc," O'Malley was sweating profusely in the chill of the underground tomb, "are you sure we needs this trouble?"

"Not we, Thomas," Joseph said, as O'Malley fumbled with the stolen keys, "me. You stand outside the tunnel and watch, or return upstairs."

O'Malley straightened his back. "Look all you want. I'll be waiting right here when you return. Mother O'Malley never raised no coward."

Joseph nodded in appreciation, lifted his lamp high, and proceeded down the pitch-black corridor, his footsteps echoing hollowly. As he walked, he heard something stirring in the darkness straight ahead, just beyond his line of sight. Chills came over him; icy sensations raced down his back and arms. Without a doubt, this was an evil place. *I would be willing to bet this tunnel travels directly under the latrine ditch.*

Joseph came to a large opening, an underground room with two other passages ahead to the left and the right. Along the south wall, a ladder led to a wooden hatch on the ceiling. *I must figure out where that hatch comes out. It must be hidden somewhere near the east wing ...*

As Joseph's eyes adjusted to the dim, flickering light, he spied five Utica cribs lined up against the west wall near the chamber. He counted three Confederate and two Union soldiers, fully clothed in their uniforms, trapped like animals and lying in their own filth. The chamber reeked.

Fear, repulsion, and heartsickness buckled the doctor's knees. His first response was an intense desire to flee. *If Percy finds out I've seen this, he'll make good on his threat to personally kill me. If these men see me, we're all as good as dead!*

Joseph dimmed his lamp by covering it with his hat, turned, and hurried out of the tunnel, hoping to proceed silently to the next corridor without arousing the prisoners, but when his jacket brushed against the wall, its metal buttons made a metallic scraping sound. His heart sank when he heard a weak, pitiful whimper in the darkness, "Please, please, God, is someone out there?"

Joseph stopped in his tracks, struggling in his spirit. Though he longed to free these men, releasing them from their captivity now would mean certain death for all. Agonizing, he moved toward the cribs. His great fear of being discovered slowed his response.

Several of the men whimpered, and the lone voice spoke once again, "Please, please ... God, are you there? I thought I saw a light ... I thought I heard something. For God's sake, have mercy on us!"

In silent agony, Joseph lay face down on the floor of that isolation room, praying for the protection of these poor men. Unexpectedly, his prayer mingled with the pleas of another lost soul. "Dear God," the frail voice of a young Union soldier echoed in the darkness, "let us die. Have mercy, Lord; send someone to help us ... to help us die."

Joseph could barely contain his grief and fear and cowardice. He slowly rose to his feet and silently turned to leave. As he did, he glimpsed something shimmering in the darkness down the adjacent corridor. A barred window on an iron door admitted the light into the corridor. Although he felt compelled to investigate all Captain Percy's secrets, curiosity would have to wait. He could sense that time was running out. Joseph retrieved the lamp. His footsteps echoed his retreat. The man in the Utica crib cried out, "If anyone is out there, my name is Corporal Richard

Montgomery. Please, please, remember me!" And then he wept.

When he opened the door to find Thomas O'Malley loyally standing guard, the grief-stricken look on Joseph's face answered all the questions the handler had ever asked himself. O'Malley locked the door and put his arm around Joseph's shoulder. As the men climbed the stairs, Joseph wiped the tears streaming down his face.

Twelve

For Barksdale's Brigade, most of August was spent resting and refitting the four regiments. Zeke's headaches were subsiding, but he still spent long hours lying in his tent, half-drunk, wallowing in despair, wondering about Billy, and waiting for the next orders. "I sure miss the information Billy used to get from headquarters," Daniel sighed one day. Zeke stared at the ground, kicking his feet in the dirt. "Daniel, I miss Billy so much I feel as if my chest had been blown away."

"Son, we all do." The older man gripped Zeke's shoulder sympathetically.

"Hey, Daniel, I know it ain't likely, but just say he did survive, say he was taken prisoner at Gettysburg … How does this prisoner exchange thing work?"

"It's up to delegates in Richmond and Washington to decide the time and location for an exchange. It is usually man-for-man, depending on rank. They trade man-for-man on privates, two-for-one on noncommissioned officers like Billy, four privates for one lieutenant, and so on up the ladder."

"How long 'fore he could be exchanged?"

Daniel considered his words carefully so he wouldn't raise false hopes. "It would depend on how badly he was wounded and how long it took him to recover ... But that won't get us the information we need now. Maybe Sergeant Cawley can shed some light on our darkness."

Zeke gave Daniel a startled look. "You gotta be kidding! That old bearcat hates me."

"That's not true, son. He was worried about you when you were lying wounded at Gettysburg."

"Ol' Holler done got hisself a heart, huh, Dan'l?" Nate joked. "Yep—reckon he's as cuddly as a tote sack full of puppies now."

"Sergeant Cawley has a tough job—and a tough job requires a tough man. In his way of thinking, if he's too friendly, we might grow soft. In battle, weakness leads to death."

"Never thought of it like that. Maybe I'll go see if he can help me," Zeke replied, looking around the camp, hoping to spot the sergeant. "There he is chewing somebody out as we speak. Man, I must be crazy," he mumbled as he headed toward Cawley. "Real cuddly like a puppy, huh, Nate?"

Nate waved Zeke on and then looked at Daniel, "Dan'l, I reckon you're the smartest fella I ever knew. So please tell me: what do yah 'spect this here war is all about? Why's we fighting?"

Surprised by Nate's compliment, Daniel thought for a moment before speaking. "Well, Nate, this could take a while, even if I give you my short version. Here goes: It seems the government in Washington thinks it knows what is best for every state. Congressmen make laws governing states regardless of how the people in a particular state might feel about those laws."

"What you think about the slaves, Dan'l?"

"They should be freed and allowed to earn their own wages. God never intended for a man to be enslaved to another man," Daniel said flatly. "But I'm not fighting this war over the slaves, Nate. I've never owned one, unlike some people up North who still own slaves. I don't think many Confederate soldiers have fought and died for the right to keep slaves. They've fought and died to defend their homes and their homelands."

"Sorry, Dan'l—didn't mean to get y'all riled up."

"Thinking of my boys killed before my eyes at Antietam stirs me up. And it disturbs me to hear Lincoln claim that this war began because of his desire to free the slaves. During his presidential campaign he stated that he did not intend to free the slaves. In fact, blacks are not even allowed to *live* in his home state of Illinois. Yet Lincoln claims the a war was intended to set the black race free …"

Returning to his friends, Zeke was ready with his own questions. "Daniel, did Abe Lincoln really say he wasn't gonna free the slaves?"

"Yes. But he used the slavery issue as propaganda to keep Europe out of the war and to justify attacking us."

"What's prop … uh proper, propergander?"

"*Propaganda* is lies, Nate."

Daniel rose and stretched, then grinned, "So much for the short version."

"Thanks, Dan'l. As for me, I got no fuss with the slaves, but them Yanks ain't got no right coming down here telling folks how to live their lives."

Daniel had his own question for Zeke. "How did it go with the sergeant?"

"Strange. He said he'd be glad to help and asked about Pops. He was real nice—almost scary nice."

· · · · ·

General court-martials for eighteen Union officers, from corporals to major generals, had been convening for the past two weeks in Philadelphia. Offenses ranged from rape to violence against officers, conduct prejudicial to good order and military discipline, and conduct unbecoming an officer and a gentleman. Steven Billings had the rare good fortune to have sufficient time to prepare for his defense of Corporal John W. Forsythe. His defense rested heavily on the corporal's commanding officers' statements about his exemplary service prior to the battle of Fredericksburg and on testimony by Dr. Da Costa related to his groundbreaking "Soldier's Heart Syndrome" research.

Early on a Wednesday morning, Corporal Forsythe was marched from the hospital to the courtroom. A nine-man military board stared with contempt at the defendant as he entered and was asked to sit facing Judge Advocate Captain Alfred U. Higginbotham.

After the initial formalities, the charges were read: *Desertion in the face of the enemy.*

"How do you plead, Corporal?" the judge asked.

Before the man could speak, Attorney Steven Billings answered for him: "He pleads not guilty ..." Steven swallowed hard and continued, "by reason of ... temporary insanity."

• • • • •

The order was given, and the journey to northern Georgia began. The brigade arrived in Ringgold the night after the onset of the battle of Chickamauga. After unloading from the train and marching all night, Barksdale's former brigade joined the fray, rushing to support General Hood's division. The Confederates managed to break the Union lines, causing a rout of most of the Yankee army, with one notable exception. Union General George H. Thomas and his soldiers fought stubbornly until long after dark before retreating to the safety of Chattanooga a few miles to the north. The battle was a much-needed victory for the Confederacy, just as General Longstreet had predicted months ago. The losses for the brigade were relatively slight.

To Zeke's surprise, Sergeant Cawley walked up to him one morning and told him he'd heard that Forrest's cavalry was rumored to be in the area. "I'll try to help locate them—and your Pa—for you." Zeke stared open-mouthed as the sergeant walked away.

"I bet your Pa knows you're here somewhere and I reckon he's looking for his boy," Nate said.

Later, the sergeant returned with bad news. "Word is Forrest's troops were transferred out. I'm sorry, boy. Maybe soon we'll catch up with 'em again."

Zeke was disappointed and angry. "How'd this General Bragg get to be head of this army anyway?"

"He is a West Pointer and close to President Davis," Daniel replied. "Unfortunately, General Bragg has had several chances to hit the Federal army hard, but he never rises to the occasion."

"Why don't they turn the army over to General Forrest? He'd have 'em whooped in a month."

"Like I said, Bragg is a friend of President Davis. And, besides, they would never give such a high command to Forrest. He has no formal military training."

· · · · ·

For two hours, Dr. Da Costa held the attention of every military officer in the courtroom as he presented his theories about A Soldier's Heart. Several of the nine-man military panel at least entertained the idea of a soldier becoming so fatigued and terrified by the horrors of war that he could temporarily lose control of his senses. Then Corporal Forsythe was called to the stand.

"Corporal Forsythe, how many family members have you lost since the war began?" the defense attorney asked.

Forsythe hung his head and began weeping. Board President General A. P. Howe objected. "Answer his question, son! We've all lost friends or family in this war. For God's sake, you're an officer! Let's get on with this."

The corporal wiped his hands over his face, sat up straight, and answered. "All of them are dead. I've got no family left. My mother and baby brother were killed by smallpox while Mama cared for troops in our home near Washington. Pa died at the Battle of Seven Pines; he was fighting right next to me when his head was blowed off. I was covered in his blood."

Once again he broke down, and this time his were not the only tears in the courtroom. The members of the panel sat silent in sympathy. Presently, the corporal continued, "My brother Bobby got dysentery and died in camp the first morning at Fredericksburg. We shared the same tent. I tried to wake my brother, but he was dead! He died right beside me in the night and I didn't know until morning … When I ran from the battle, I ran back to Bobby, to dig his grave for him. It took me two hours, and by that time hundreds of wounded men were coming back to camp."

Attorney Steven Billings stood before the defendant silently for long moments, then turned to the panel and softly said, "Your witness."

· · · · ·

A miserably cold afternoon for a walk, Joseph thought, strolling down an unfamiliar path toward a fog-shrouded lake. All around him was dense forest, too thick to see beyond the edge of the tree line. *In fact, I really don't even remember why I'm out here or where I'm going.* Anxiety increased with every step. *Maybe I should turn back.* Short, panic-stricken gulps of air nearly caused him to hyperventilate. He felt as if some powerful force was driving him toward the lake, to the water's edge. Sweat poured from his forehead and neck. Chill bumps covered his arms and traveled down the back of his legs.

Joseph knelt beside the water, trying to pray, but all he could think about was the eerie stillness. No sounds, no woodland creatures stirring about, nothing but silence.

Across the lake, only visible for an instant, was a shadow outlined in the fog. A man was standing on the shore. Joseph squinted his eyes, and the figure disappeared. He squinted again, and the same figure reappeared several yards to the left. Faintly, he could make out a man dressed in a long dull-white hospital overshirt. Long gray hair covered his face, so there were no other distinguishable features. In his spirit, Joseph knew he was in the presence of something evil.

"You—you there," his voice cracked from fear, "who are you? Please, tell me your name."

No answer. The figure turned and disappeared into the forest once again. The lake fog grew thicker, enveloping the doctor up to his waist. Every instinct told Joseph to run, but he was paralyzed with terror. To his right, shrouded by the fog, he could see dozens of figures drawing closer—limbs snapping, leaves rustling, and several figures encircling him.

Dear God, help me! How can these people move so quickly? What do they want from me? Joseph tried to cry for help, but he was mute with fright. To his left were the outlines of four men, standing barely visible inside the fog. *Confederate soldiers!* Joseph could barely make out their features. Somehow, he knew these were men mortally wounded in combat. *Torn clothes. Powder-burned faces. These men are not among the living!* In a panic, Joseph struggled to rise to his feet and flee, but his knees were stuck fast to the shoreline. Frantically he rocked back and forth, trying to free himself, but the harder he pulled, the stronger his knees held fast in the soft, thick mud. *Must run—must flee—Oh Dear God—help me!*

Once again, he sensed movement in the fog. Joseph began weeping bitterly—because this time he recognized one of the figures. A ten-year-old girl, dressed in a funeral gown, sat on a small bench. Her long blond hair drooped over her shoulders, while her sweet blue eyes gazed blankly into the water. Her hands, feet, and face were tinted a ghastly gray-blue, the unmistakable color of death.

"Elizabeth?" Joseph struggled to speak through his tears, "Is that you, dear child? Please speak to me ..."

Nothing.

His trembling hand reached out to touch her, "This cannot be happening. You died! You died years ago. But you know it wasn't my fault!"

No response.

He looked up and found the far lakeshore lined with hundreds of patients, all men and women he knew at Bethlem Royal Hospital, all dead. Held captive by the mud, the doctor wailed in desperation, "Is this my sentence, God? To be haunted by the deaths of these poor souls?"

Exhausted, alone, and hopeless, Joseph bowed and buried his face in his hands and grieved. For the people he had left behind. For the people he had been unable to help. At last, his strength spent, Joseph reached into the lake for water to wash his tears away. He screamed when he saw the reflection staring back at him in the water.

It was the face of Forbred Lytton.

Suddenly Joseph jerked violently, freeing himself from the mud. He turned to escape, but struck something that sent him careening to the ground. He looked up and recognized his obstruction.

"Going somewhere, Doctor?" the unmistakable voice of Captain Percy rasped gleefully.

"What—what do you want from me?" Bryarly asked, unable to stand on feeble legs.

"What y'all running from?" Percy smirked, nodding at the ghostly figures in the mist. "Reckon you got a few demons in your past, huh, Doc?"

"Leave me, Percy ... let me pass." His demand sounded more like a cry for mercy.

"Don't think so, Doc—got me a promise to keep." Captain Percy stared at Joseph while loading cartridges into the pistol tucked under his belt.

"Stop! Please, please don't do this!"

Frantically crawling backward, Joseph stopped at the water's edge and begged for his life.

"Sorry, Doc," Percy grinned. "Nothing personal."

KABOOM! Percy's shot found its mark: the dead center of Joseph's chest. The impact sent him splashing backward into the water.

He floated for a moment before slowly sinking into the darkness with eyes wide open.

• • • • •

"Oh, dear God!"

Joseph tried to stand, but staggered against the bookcase, sending him and the books crashing to the floor. Frantically, he sprang up, feeling his chest for the fatal bullet wound. When he found nothing there, he surveyed his office and tried to convince himself it was yet another nightmare. *Another nightmare!*

They've plagued me ever since I arrived! Dear God, when will this torture end? Exhausted from the ordeal, Joseph slumped back in his desk chair and cradled his head in his hands, determined to stay awake until daylight. Three hours later, still shaken from the night's psychotic episode, the doctor made a visit to the apothecary. Utilizing a small dosage of mercury mixed with sulphate morphia, opium, and raspberry leaves, he once again used himself as a test subject. When he drank the concoction, he felt ashamed, remembering a prophecy from the Gospel of Luke, a quote from Jesus:

Surely you will say to me—physician, heal thyself.

How can I possibly hope to heal myself? Joseph pondered. *Am I truly going mad? Is there no hope to stop this madness? The hallucinations and nightmares torment my soul!*

"Top of the mornin', Doc! You all right?"

O'Malley was uncomfortable. He had witnessed Joseph turning to drugs for relief, and he didn't like it—he had seen others fall victim to drugs. By now, the doctor's frequent trips to the apothecary were common knowledge to most people in the asylum—except for Percy and his Zouaves.

"Yes—yes, Thomas," Joseph stammered. "I'm fine … just fine."

"Reckon it'd be none of my business," O'Malley fumbled for the right words, "but I hope you know what you're doing. I mean, experimenting on yourself 'n' all."

"Thomas, I've been haunted by nightmares and hallucinations ever since I arrived in America, and I know that some of my patients suffer from the same problem. If I experiment on myself, I can determine the therapeutic qualities of these treatments."

"Aye," O'Malley said in obvious disbelief, "like I said— weren't none of my affair."

"The nightmares seem to be similar to the nightmares soldiers with battlefield trauma suffer."

Thomas rubbed his neck, confused. "But Doc, have you ever been in battle?"

"No."

"Then how's it the same kind of nightmares?"

"There are many types of battlefields," Joseph said solemnly. "The battlefield of the mind is none the less vicious."

Thirteen

Point Lookout, a new Federal prison built on the shores of the Chesapeake Bay in Maryland, was designed to discourage escape. Barren, treeless, and shadeless, without the nooks and crannies designed into older fortifications, guards watched all the prisoners all the time. Scattered throughout the compound, men huddled beneath makeshift tents made of rusted tin, canvas, and rotten boards—anything that could offer some protection from the elements.

Yet another load of Confederate prisoners was herded from the train car by gunpoint and marched, shackled together, up to the gates of their new residence. They halted, staring anxiously at the stark walls and guard posts, hoping to postpone the inevitable for even another few minutes. But rifles poked into their backs propelled them through the gates. They clustered into a pen where they would spend the next several months struggling to stay alive.

"Anybody here from Barksdale's brigade?" a stout son of Mississippi called out from the crowd, anxiously scanning the faces of the newcomers. Billy Gibson and several others he vaguely recognized raised their hands and searched the sea of ragged prisoners for the speaker. A large-boned man with brown hair that reached his shoulders and a scruffy beard stepped out from the crowd and held out his hand. "I'm Sam Dawson, Twenty-first Mississippi, Barksdale's brigade. Pleased to meet'cha—but sorry to do it in a place like this," he said in a loud, jovial voice. "Follow me!"

The prisoner led the men from his division past hundreds of men, some wandering aimlessly, others obviously listless, bored, curious, sickly, and worried. Too many looked half-dead. "Y'all need to stick close around here until y'all figure this place out," Sam said, when he reached an outer wall and turned to his followers. "There are thieves and cutthroats in here, and they'll kill yah dead just for the fun of it. Anyone been a prisoner before?" No one nodded, so Sam Dawson proceeded to explain the routines of the prisoners' lives and the personalities of their captors. When he finished, he shook hands once again and offered, "If y'all need anything at all, just let Big Sam know—but don't be expecting much. This shore ain't no fancy hotel."

As the other members of his brigade talked among themselves, Billy slumped against the prison wall. He couldn't believe he was in a stinking Federal prison camp. *I gotta get out of here! Somehow, some way, I gotta get out of here.*

"What's your name, son?" Big Sam asked kindly, putting his hand on Billy's shoulder.

Billy pointed to the scar on his jawbone, partially concealed by his new beard, and shook his head, indicating to Sam that he couldn't talk.

"Get that at Gettysburg?" Sam asked, sympathetically. Billy nodded.

"You stay over here," he told Billy as he led him to a tent that was already overcrowded. "Watch your back 'n' try not to be caught alone. I'll keep an eye out for yah."

Billy was grateful, but he knew enough about conmen from his days in the army to remain suspicious of Big Sam until he proved himself. *Why is he being so nice? And why me in particular? Is it just because we're both from Mississippi?* Whatever the reason, Billy was determined to keep to himself and hope for a prisoner exchange before winter set in. *I bet this is a miserably cold place in the wintertime.*

· · · · ·

"What happens now, Mr. Billings?" Forsythe asked, fatigued. "Are they going to hang me?"

"I don't know, John. For now, all we can do is wait."

Weeks after the trial, the attorney sat in his office, face tense with anticipation, staring at a dispatch from the headquarters of the Army of the Potomac. This letter would mean life or death for Corporal John W. Forsythe. With trembling hands, he tore open the envelope and quickly scanned the three-page document. His eyes fell immediately to one line:

Of the specification, guilty. Of the charge, guilty.

Steven's heart sank in his chest and he closed his eyes for a moment in despair and disbelief. *How could they, in all conscience, have done this?* Sick at heart, he returned to the document and continued reading:

… The Court does therefore sentence him to no attachment of criminality thereto because of Corporal John W. Forsythe's utter, obvious, and gross intellectual impairment, predicating deficiency in mental capacity at the time of said offense.

Steven stopped reading, rubbed his eyes in astonishment, and then continued:

… Corporal John W. Forsythe will continue his treatment under the care of Dr. Da Costa at Turner's Lane Hospital in Philadelphia, until such a time as his mental capacity returns to normal. When released from care and thereafter, he will cease from that date to be an officer in the military service of the United States …

It was done! The door marked Military Justice had opened— just a crack, but it had opened. Sometime—years, maybe decades or even generations—in the future, soldiers like Corporal Forsythe suffering from extreme trauma would be treated with sympathy, caring, understanding, and respect, no longer having to face a gallows or firing squad. Attorney Steven J. Billings leaped up from his desk, vigorously shook the hand of a startled postal clerk, then went dashing down the corridors of Turner's Lane Hospital.

• • • • •

Days turned into weeks and weeks turned into months at Point Lookout. Every day, it seemed, more Confederate prisoners were herded into the prison compound, and every day conditions worsened. Despite the guards' best efforts, diseases, particularly dysentery and scurvy, were epidemic. Ankle-deep mud and overflowing latrine ditches provided a breeding ground for flies, maggots, and disease. By late October, the wind coming off the river was chilling.

Gradually, Billy's voice strengthened and then returned to normal. In time, he and Big Sam began reminiscing about home and family. Billy made Sam promise that if he were released from prison first, he would go looking for Zeke—if he were still alive— and let him know that Billy had survived Gettysburg. Sam swore he would if Billy would report to Sam's folks back home that Sam was a good soldier and a good Christian man. With nothing to do, much of Billy's days were spent reliving the July 2 battle. Over and over again he saw his brother bloodied and unconscious, lying on the ground at Nate's feet. When the grief and his endless round of "What if …" speculations became too difficult to bear, he turned his mind to the few weeks he had spent with Sally— most especially their last night together. Then Billy would close his eyes and wish himself back in the barn in Gettysburg or walking hand-in-hand with Sally down to the creek that ran past his family's farm in Mississippi. So he wouldn't forget what she looked like, he would paint her picture in his head, over and over again.

The prisoners did their best to stay warm, but it was difficult. Every day the leading topic of conversation was the possibility of a prisoner exchange—that was the only thing keeping their hopes alive. Some northern guards cruelly taunted the men with the words "There'll be another prisoner exchange any day now" or "All exchanges have been suspended." For variety, they would occasionally announce that Robert E. Lee was dead or that the Army of Northern Virginia had been destroyed. After awhile, only the more ignorant believed the Yankees' lies. Billy hated this place with a passion that burned red-hot. The guards' inhumane treatment only intensified his hatred for the Union Army.

• • • • •

Longstreet's Corps spent most of the fall camped at the foot of Lookout Mountain just south of Chattanooga. Autumn had never seemed more beautiful: valleys and mountainsides bloomed with brilliant shades of orange, red, and yellow as the trees prepared to undress for the winter. One Sunday afternoon, Zeke, Nate, and Daniel hiked to the crest of the mountain and marveled at the surrounding countryside. Zeke strolled around the peak, then suddenly pointed down into the valley. "Hey, Daniel, what's all that?"

His friend walked up to Zeke's side and looked. "Union Army," he said briefly. When Zeke stared at him, he added, "I imagine they're dug in, waiting for a ground attack. But we haven't heard even rumors about advancing on them. Maybe General Longstreet is content shelling their fortifications from a distance."

Several days later, the men of Company C saw Colonel Porter Alexander, the head of artillery for the First Corps, deep in a conversation with other officers. Shortly afterwards, word was passed through the camp that Porter's men had managed to hoist some rifled cannons to the summit of Lookout Mountain and began bombing the Yankee encampment below in Chattanooga. The battalion put on a remarkable display of fireworks as its skilled gunners shelled entrenchments and warehouses with deadly accuracy. The frustrated Federal batteries could not return fire because their guns couldn't elevate high enough.

"You think the shelling is busting 'em up, Daniel?" Zeke asked one night around a campfire.

"I doubt it, Nate. They're too far off to inflict much damage." Daniel smiled and patted him on the back. "But it will sure get the Yanks' attention."

. . . . .

By the first week of November, the First Corps headed to Knoxville to engage the Federal forces. Because heavy rains had made the roads almost impassable to wagons and artillery caissons, the march dragged on for almost two weeks. Many times the men were forced to halt and pull wagons and teams of mules or horses from the muddy quagmires. Longstreet and the First Corps arrived with about fifteen thousand men around the end of November. Once deployed, Rebel skirmishers probed the Federal defensive positions searching for weakness. But none could be found.

"This don't look too good, fellas," Zeke said gloomily as he stared at their objective.

Nate agreed. "Those're powerful high walls around that fort."

"There must be a better way to assault their position. We'll be slaughtered if we charge those walls," Daniel added.

Longstreet grew frustrated and finally ordered a limited assault that would include Barksdale's brigade. The 13th Mississippi, commanded by Colonel McElroy, a gallant man who was known to the soldiers as a man who led from the front, launched a successful attack. The Mississippi boys reached and scaled the walls of the fort, only to be shot down before they landed within the fort. Among the casualties was Colonel McElroy. Frustrated, Longstreet halted all attacks and retired his forces. They would fight again another day.

. . . . .

On Thanksgiving Day 1863, Joseph and Ana spent the morning worshiping together with the Dougall family at St. Paul's Episcopal Church on East Grace Street, near Capitol Square. The church was packed. Among the worshippers were President Davis and his family, as well as dozens of officers stationed in Richmond. The elaborately decorated church was crowded with countless women and elderly couples dressed in black, mourning the loss of men they had loved. Ana struggled to make her way through the crowd to meet the president, but he had been quickly escorted by armed troops to an awaiting carriage.

"Oh, come now, Joseph," Ana playfully protested, "quit your lollygagging! Don't you want to see your friend the president?"

"Ana, look at the crowd! Everyone here wants to see the president. We'll have to wait for another day. Come! Your family is waiting for us."

"But, Joseph, don't you want to introduce yourself? It's been years since you spoke to one another …"

Joseph sternly interrupted, "Ana, please! Let's go now!"

Ana looked at him curiously, but she was a patient woman, willing to wait for the right moment to continue the discussion. Still, she couldn't help but wonder about his reluctance to approach his family's friend. *Why is he so hesitant to see the president? He's supposed to be an old and trusted family friend—he's the reason Joseph returned to America.*

After church, Joseph surprised the Dougalls and excused himself at the steps to their boardinghouse. Patrick Dougall seemed to be the only one privy to the doctor's secret, although the others knew that he had insisted the family take the afternoon together to relax. Mrs. Dougall struggled with Joseph's instructions to forego preparing a holiday dinner.

"It don't seem right," Mrs. Dougall mumbled. "And that's all I'll be saying on the subject."

"Mary Margaret," Mr. Dougall hugged her and pointed out, "me thinks the Dougall clan won't go hungry. O' that you can be sure."

Late that afternoon, Joseph arrived at the Dougall boardinghouse driving a rented carriage. He had planned and saved for this evening for two months. He straightened his coat, dusted his immaculate lapels, and knocked on the door.

Joseph's voice almost cracked with nervousness when he announced, "I've arranged for you and your family to celebrate Thanksgiving dinner with me. This carriage will carry us to our destination."

Ana stared, then smiled warmly, "Well, Joseph! How lovely!" Joseph handed Ana, then Mrs. Dougall, into the carriage and waited for the others to follow. "You knew this all along, Patrick, 'n' not so much as a mutter," Mary Margaret said, shaking her finger at her husband.

He grinned. "I said ye wouldn't starve. It was the Lord's truth."

It was a short, cold ride from Franklin Street to the corner of Eighth and Main. Winds chilled everyone to the bone. The carriage drove past poverty-stricken refugees huddled around small fires. The faces of homeless widows and orphaned children were etched with the sorrowful look of hopelessness. *Most of these people won't survive the harsh Virginia winter. The war will be claiming many more lives without a single shot being fired!* Joseph thought.

He stopped the carriage in front of the elegant Spotswood Hotel, one of the only three remaining hotels in Richmond still catering to guests. The parlor of the Spotswood was filled with Confederate officers, government officials, wives, girlfriends, and ladies of the evening. The Thanksgiving dinner would be a highlight of the family's year. Somehow the cooks had managed to procure foods that had become rare delicacies to common folk: turkeys, mince pies, eggnog, sweet potatoes, white potatoes, preserves, greens, and corn bread. Most Virginians hadn't tasted sugar or salt for months, unless they were friends of blockade-runners.

The Dougall family surveyed the Spotswood's lobby as though they were visiting a palace. Joseph knew by their expressions that the family appreciated his gift to them. They all savored the evening: the foods, the conversation, the servants who waited on them, and the music softly playing in the background. "I haven't eaten like this since long, long ago, in the days before the famine," Mary Margaret Dougall said with tears in her eyes. Ana reached over and squeezed Joseph's hand in gratitude.

"Ana …" Joseph fumbled for the right words. "I have something I would like to … need to say to you."

Ana interrupted teasingly, "Joseph, are you sick? Do you need a doctor?"

Mrs. Dougall shushed her daughter, "Ana Laoise, stop your teasing, acting all gab 'n' guts, 'n' let the man speak."

Joseph knelt on one knee beside Ana. "I've never in my life loved anyone—until now. Ana Laoise Dougall MacIntyre, may I have the honor of your hand … in marriage?"

Tears streamed down the lovely woman's face. Her family anxiously awaited her answer—but no more anxiously than Joseph himself. Ana blushed and paused for what seemed like forever, finally turning, not to Joseph, but to her father. "Papa?"

"Joseph already asked me blessing," Mr. Dougall grinned. "I told him I'd be proud to have him in the family—if he can manage my beautiful, stubborn, headstrong daughter!"

"Aye, Joseph," Ana whispered. "I'll be proud to be your wife."

Eavesdroppers and nearby diners suddenly burst into applause. Such a joyous decision temporarily brightened everyone's mood when so much news recently had been dreary or sad. The pianist changed his tempo and with a grin played the wedding march, followed by a rousing rendition of "Dixie." Joseph grinned broadly as he looked at his future bride.

Mary Margaret Dougall reached for her son and kissed him on both cheeks. "Mama, why are ye slobbering all over me?" Michael joked. "Kiss them! They be the ones getting married."

· · · · ·

During the final dreary week of November, word came that a prisoner exchange was in the works—and this time the guards weren't lying. Two days later, two thousand Confederate prisoners, all privates, were put on a train bound for Richmond, where they would be exchanged for an equal number of Union soldiers. Billy had hidden his rank from the prison guards, hoping that if he were a private, he would more quickly be chosen for an exchange. It didn't work. Although he knew he should be happy that anyone was leaving the dismal camp, his heart sank as he watched the procession of soon-to-be-free men marching toward the rail station. Within days, however, another list of names was called. This time, Billy's name was included.

Early the following morning, the prisoners who had been chosen for the exchange were packed into the railcars like livestock. "Shut up! Keep moving or we'll find someone else who wants to leave more than you do," shouted one guard.

"Where do you think I am going to move to?" the feisty young man in front of Billy asked. "There isn't room for a flea to squeeze onto this train."

Someone from behind shouted, "I intend to get on this railcar, so pretend you're a flea, dang it, and push in before the Yanks change their minds!" Despite the rank odors rising from hundreds of unwashed men, Billy didn't mind the crush. "This is our shot at freedom, boys, so we need to squeeze as many on as we can," one man yelled reasonably. After that, no one heard a complaint. The train was locked and slowly pulled away from one station that a Confederate would never want to see again. To the men on board, time seemed to move more slowly than the train, until the train finally squealed to a stop many hours later near Capitol Square in downtown Richmond.

With whoops and cheers, the freed prisoners jubilantly poured out into the square amidst a mass of well-wishers. A brass band struck up a round of "Dixie"; guns were fired in celebration; shouts of praise and declarations of victory filled the streets.

"Welcome home, boys!"

"Boxes of clothing over here. Come get ya some clothes!"

"Food is being served at the inn. All you boys are welcome!!!"

The citizens of Richmond made the heroes of the South feel welcome, as though they truly were back at home.

Billy had not seen Richmond in more than two years, and he couldn't believe he was looking at the same place. As far as he could see, refugees were huddled in masses. The once-elegant city now resembled a seedy gold-rush town with a shady past.

Officers of all ranks tried to keep order as thousands of newly freed men wandered through the streets with empty pockets, but in the mood to celebrate before returning to the war. Billy headed down a dark alley alone, feeling adventurous—or "ten foot tall 'n' bulletproof," as Nate would say.

Out of the dark night, an attractive red-haired prostitute approached him and offered her services, "First time's free, honey, after you wash up."

His thoughts flew to Sally. "Thank you, ma'am, for your generous offer, but no thanks."

Insulted, the prostitute retorted, "You think you're too good for me? You smell like crap! What's your problem, soldier boy?"

Shocked, Billy stammered, "It's not you ..."

"You don't like girls? Is that it?" she yelled, then turned and disappeared into Locust Alley next to the Oxbow, a gathering place for many of the returning prisoners.

Forget that, he thought. *I'll just have a drink of something, maybe play a little poker, and have some fun.* He entered the Oxbow with a few Confederate dollars in his filthy pockets and twenty Yankee dollars that Sally had given him. As he made his way through the crowd of men clustered by the front doors, he was thinking, *Momma would be ashamed of me if she knew this was my first stop after prison, but Pops would just laugh—and join me!*

"Whiskey," Billy called out as he elbowed his way to the bar. Turning to the soldier next to him he grinned and explained, "I've had a powerful thirst for five months."

"Whiskey's all we got," the bartender answered with a thick Cajun accent that Billy hadn't heard in months.

"You're from south Louisiana ain't you? Met some boys back early in the war that talked just like you."

The dark-eyed, dark-skinned bartender ignored him rudely.

"Real nice talking to you, too, *mister*," Billy called after him.

After a few shots, he felt at ease and began to relax and take stock of the past half-year. Gettysburg was almost five months ago. He'd spent six weeks in the hospital, five weeks with Sally, and three hellish months at Point Lookout. Now he was finally in Richmond. *First thing tomorrow I'll write to Sally. Then, I've got to find out where First Corps is. I can't wait to see Zeke and the boys—I hope to God that Zeke is still with the boys!* He assumed that Sally's letter had been delivered and his family knew he was alive. Later, he'd make plans to find his way back to Gettysburg, but that would have to wait until he learned what had happened to the Army of Northern Virginia since July. *But tonight, I'm gonna have some fun!*

Billy noticed a card game in the back corner of the bar. Before long, he was sitting at a table with six nasty-looking thugs. The whiskey was hitting him hard on an empty stomach. Even though his thinking was cloudy from the alcohol, his playing was still going pretty well. Things seemed to be just fine with the world until …

"Well, if it's not Mr. *Too Good For Me*," shouted the redheaded prostitute from Locust Alley, moving toward the table. Billy tried to ignore her, but she was intent on causing a scene.

"Hey, you! Soldier boy! You got something against women?" she hollered drunkenly.

Several seedy-looking soldiers joined in the laugh at his expense. Even the men at the table began snickering. Billy felt his face flush and his temper rise.

"Hey, queer boy, I'm talking to you!"

That's it … she's gone too far! "Shut up, you stupid hooker!" The tavern quieted and Billy continued, "Ain't none of your business what I like!"

"You saying you *do* like women?" She pulled up her skirt and exposed two shapely legs with black garters and silk stockings. She taunted him, "Prove it!"

"I ain't got to prove nothing to a low-down street hooker like you," he raged.

Ignoring the prostitute, Billy sat back down. The tavern remained hushed. The men at the table were staring at him with piercing, bloodshot eyes. Only now did he take note that every-one around him had similar looking features: dark eyes and dark skin. He suddenly realized that he was the odd man out. Coolly—at least on the surface—he asked, "We gonna play poker, boys, or worry about some stupid hooker?"

The men exchanged glances. No one moved. Billy continued to fight his temper. "Forget this crap," he declared, gathering up his earnings. "I'm outta here."

The largest of the men at the table stood, blocking Billy's exit. With his blood boiling, Billy turned and headed toward him, actu-ally looking forward to an encounter. As Billy approached him, the Cajun spoke, "So you is queer? That right, *boy*?"

"Ain't none of your business what I like. Can you understand that, or do I need to explain it more simple like? Now, you *best* move out of my way."

The big man drew back to strike, but Billy struck him first. The quick left fist to the face instantly caused the Cajun's eye to swell and his vision to blur. Another fist to the chin, and he fell to the floor like he'd been shot by a gun. The tavern was silent, every eye on Billy.

This would have been the perfect time to walk out the door. But he didn't. The trouble was, with his sense of timing impaired by the whiskey, he just couldn't keep his mouth shut. "Any more of you idiots want to know if I like women?"

In an instant, men jumped on him from every direction. He swung at everything in his path and took a beating in return. Slowly, Billy backed into a corner to protect his rear, but things weren't looking the way he'd like them to. Suddenly, he heard a familiar voice shout out above the angry crowd, "That you, Billy?"

"Who's askin'?" Billy shouted back, fighting a half-dozen thugs at once. "If you're a friend, I could sure use some help!"

Several men staggered away, having had their fill of Billy's Mississippi fury, but others took their place. The voice came closer and now had a name and face: Big Sam. He and another stout brawler named Luther had shown up at just the right time, in Billy's estimation.

"Looks like you need some help," Sam shouted above the roar of the crowd, keeping his eyes on the Cajuns as the three Mississippians slowly backed toward the door together. "We better get outta here real quick like."

"Say, Billy, you must have some lead in those fists," Luther yelled, admiringly.

Billy grinned, "Got lots of practice growing up. There's a time for talking and a time for fighting. Reckon I was through talking."

Just as they stepped onto the soft dirt street, a stern voice commanded, "Turn around slowly, boys. Drop any weapons and raise your arms in the air. You're under arrest for disturbing the peace."

"You gotta be kidding," Billy said in disbelief as he turned to see three provost deputies with pistols cocked and ready.

These battle-hardened veterans couldn't help but laugh. They were being held at gunpoint by three young, scrawny provost guards who, because of their family connections or cowardice, had managed to stay behind when the army departed—although who or what they were guarding was questionable.

Big Sam raised his arms and said slowly, "All right, boys. Don't shoot. You done got us."

Billy looked over at Big Sam in disbelief. Disgusted, he and Luther followed Sam's lead. The provost deputies lowered their pistols and grinned at each other, not noticing Sam wink and turn. Billy suddenly spun, dropping one guard with his bruised left fist, then another with his right. Sam took out the third marshal with a solid blow to the head.

"Lickety-split!" Sam said, looking at the three guards crumpled at his feet. "Thunder and lightning at the same time! That was some fine work, boys. Guess we didn't lose our touch in prison!"

"We need to be moving quick-like," Billy said, dodging into a nearby alley. Sam and Luther raced behind him. "We got to avoid any more provost. They won't take too kindly to us hurting some of their own," Billy shouted to Sam as they raced through Richmond. After several blocks without pursuers in sight, the men slowed to a walk. Half-drunk and exhausted, they sought a safe place to rest and hide for the night. A nearby livery stable looked like it would fit the bill. As they stretched out on the hay, the only plan that came to mind was to sleep.

The three ex-prisoners were soon snoring, not caring who was looking for them or what trouble tomorrow might bring

Fourteen

The west wing of Wingate Asylum was overflowing with battle-trauma patients, and more were arriving each day. Military prisoners, deserters mainly, were shackled to every available post. Since privacy was impossible within the building, Thomas O'Malley motioned for Dr. Joseph Bryarly to follow him outside. They walked along the front of the manor beyond the west-wing complex, eventually reaching a small clearing in the woods.

O'Malley spoke first, "I needed to get you alone, Doc." Nervously looking around, the Irishman began to pace. "Something happened last night—something you need to know."

"What's wrong?"

"Percy 'n' his Zouaves got in last night—brought some *folks* back with 'em."

"Brought someone? Who?" Joseph demanded to know.

"Gamblers 'n' hookers."

The doctor breathed a sigh of relief. "Thomas, Captain Percy brings prostitutes into the manor almost every night! That's nothing new."

"Doc, Percy brought hookers for the *patients*."

Joseph stared at the handler wide-eyed. "Please tell me it's not what I'm thinking!"

"If you're thinking Percy's giving the patients hookers in trade for their pay vouchers, then yep, 'tis what you're thinking."

"Where are they now? The prostitutes? Are they still on the premises?"

"Gone. Some of them Zouaves snuck 'em out before reveille this morning. Percy didn't want regular army folks to see so many women leaving at one time."

"Who did these women visit?"

"The boys in the west wing, mostly Yankee prisoners and Rebel convicts."

Joseph felt sick. "Did Percy offer these prostitutes to the madmen locked in the west-wing holding cells?"

O'Malley whispered, "Yep, reckon so."

"Was … was anyone hurt?"

O'Malley shuffled his feet staring at the ground, not wanting to answer the question.

Joseph repeated himself, "Thomas, was anyone hurt?"

"Doc, some things you just don't need—or want—to know."

"Thomas, tell me!" the doctor commanded. "You and I, as well as McGinnis and Weller, already know enough to bring about our deaths."

O'Malley considered the options, then made up his mind. "Millie, Percy's favorite whore, was drunk out of her mind. She insisted on being let into the cell with that big fella. You know the one, what bit the ear off that little wiry fella a couple of months back?"

Joseph nodded.

"Them Zouaves thought it'd be funny to turn Millie loose with that wild man …" Distraught, Thomas stopped talking.

Finally, Joseph finished the sentence for him. "She's dead, isn't she, Thomas?"

"Torn to pieces."

"And the madman?"

"Shot dead. Once Percy heard his favorite whore'd been

killed, he shot the madman himself. Both bodies were hauled out early this morning."

"Any witnesses?"

"None what would talk. Most figure it's just one less crazy and one less hooker."

"And what do you think?"

"They deserved better. You said it, Doc. God don't see them no different from us."

· · · · ·

Before daylight the next morning, a rooster crowed in the livery stable, waking the three men. It was comforting to hear a familiar sound, a sound never heard in an army camp or a Yankee prison. On his first morning as a free man, Billy stirred and tried to piece together what happened the night before. "I wonder if they'll be looking for us?"

"Maybe all them provosts is off duty, and we'll sneak outta here unnoticed," Luther suggested hopefully. He was an odd-looking man, with broad shoulders and a thick chest. He seemed the same size all the way down to his feet—thick head, body, and legs.

"Why don't we lay low for a while? We'll just make sure we're in the clear," Billy offered. They all fell peacefully back to sleep.

In the late morning, the three were awakened abruptly by men's voices and the cocking of pistols at close range. "That's them, Captain," declared one of the unfortunate guards, sporting a bandage over his nose and two swollen black eyes. The three free men found themselves surrounded by angry provost deputies, just hoping they would try something stupid so they could shoot the men who had humiliated them the night before.

"That one right there," one guard said, pointing to Billy, "hit me and Lester at the same time. Lester still ain't woke up."

"Chain them up, boys," the captain ordered, "and then we'll see how tough this trash is."

The trio was paraded in leg irons and shackles from the livery stable down Front Street to the jailhouse. When bystanders were near, the provost deputies would jab their prisoners with their gun barrels, trying to humiliate the prisoners and regain some self-respect at the same time.

"Unbelievable," Billy shook his head in frustration. "Locked up again? And this time in Richmond, of all places!"

"What'll they do with us?" Luther asked.

"Don't know. Never been arrested before," Sam answered.

Billy shrugged. "Guess we'll just have to wait and see."

After a few miserable hours in a filthy jail cell, the guards returned with a different captain and the other private that Billy had assaulted. The captain, a sleazy-looking man decked out in a fine uniform, swaggered over to the holding cell. Staring at Billy with a smirk on his face, the captain spoke to the private. "You're dismissed." Without taking his eyes off the big men, he ordered, "Guard, take these three men to my quarters and get them some food."

Billy, Luther, and Big Sam were suspicious, but food always sounded good to Confederate soldiers. The Mississippians were led into a small, empty log building occupied by a small desk with a chair, a cot, and three additional chairs.

"Sit down," the captain ordered from the doorway. Once they were seated, the guards chained each man securely to his chair.

"Now bring these men something to eat," the captain ordered as he ambled into the room. A pear-shaped man with greasy, stringy brown hair and eyes that stared greedily and unblinkingly, he sat behind the desk, pulled a pistol from a drawer, and laid it in plain view of the men.

"I'm Captain Hurdle," he announced, as though expecting them to be impressed. "Welcome to my little slice of heaven."

"What's going on here?" Billy demanded to know.

"That's up to you, friend," the captain replied, reaching for a box of cigars. "Have a smoke?"

Luther and Sam grabbed cigars. Billy crossed his arms. The captain studied his prisoners, his face expressionless. When the private returned carrying plates with roast pork, roast potatoes, and buttermilk biscuits, the men devoured their dinner ravenously. Then Billy impatiently broke the silence. "You say it's up to us what happens? How is it up to us?"

"Well, let's see now. You boys disturbed the peace, assaulted my deputies, and fled the scene of a crime. I could have y'all court-martialed, so y'all would spend the rest of the war in prison. Or I could have you shot for attempting to escape—no questions would be asked …" He paused and deliberately changed the subject. "Would y'all care for a little Kentucky bourbon?"

"We're waitin' to hear why it's up to us," Billy said again, his arms crossed.

Hurdle leaned back in his chair and grinned unpleasantly, "Well, you see, gentlemen, if you will cooperate with me, I can make your remaining days in this war a lot more enjoyable."

"How?" Big Sam asked as he swallowed his third shot of the captain's best.

"It's like this," the captain said, leaning forward and lowering his voice. "Twice a month several of my friends and I have a little get-together at different locations. We all bring our best fighters for a little fun and entertainment." Hurdle addressed Billy specifically. "I heard that you're one tough son of a buck. You took down a man named LeBlanc at the Oxbow last night with two punches—that's impressive. I've never had a fighter that could stand up to LeBlanc and live to tell the tale."

"How'd you know about that?"

"I know everything in this part of town," Hurdle bragged.

"What if I refuse?"

"I've already explained that you really have no choice."

"What if I don't win?"

"You better win, or one of your friends might have a bad accident." Hurdle leaned closer to Billy and stared him in the eye. "You understand me?"

Billy nodded. "You mean I fight twice a month, win, and we'll be kept alive?"

"Exactly. That's all you have to do. And your skills will be *well* rewarded. Your quarters will be in jail, but separate from the other prisoners. I'll give you all the food you can eat, whiskey you can drink, and women you can use for your pleasure—and anything else you want, just so long as you win." He paused, then added, "You'll have no contact with anyone outside of my world. And if you try to escape, you'll be shot."

Billy looked at Sam and Luther, who stared back at him. *Their lives are in my hands!* "I got no choice, do I, Captain?"

Hurdle's grin grew wider. "I hoped you'd see things my way!" He proceeded to explain that the first "exhibition" of Billy's fighting skills would take place very soon. "I want to see you in action. You'll fight my current brawler … And we'll see what all the fuss is about."

· · · · ·

Suffering from endless sleepless nights, Joseph tried any and every possible antidote for relief, but many of them only worsened his condition. *Purging, emetics, even mercuric chloride have failed to relieve these hallucinations. What can I do? What can I do? I'll die if I don't have relief!* The grief on his face revealed the story of a man in personal torment. *Percy and his Zouaves must not find out about my weakness—or this decline into madness. As much as I hate the idea, bloodletting is my only remaining option. Dear God, is there no mercy for a man trying his best to help the wretched souls in his care? Am I destined to become one of them?*

"You sent for me?" Alastair Weller stood outside the office door.

"Yes, Mr. Weller! Please come in." Joseph motioned for the handler to take a seat next to him. "I need your assistance this evening, for another experimental therapy …"

Refusing to make eye contact, Weller hung his head.

"Is there a problem, Mr. Weller?"

"Doc, I think you'll be wanting Thomas to help." Weller's eyes darted around the room; it was obvious the subject made him uneasy. "I'm a simple man—a handler—nothing more."

"Nonsense, you've assisted me with dozens of patients. Why not with me?"

"You planning to do this here experiment on the crazies?"

"No. On myself."

"That'd be the reason right there."

"Mr. Weller, how else can I know the true effects of these therapies unless I use myself to test their effectiveness?"

Weller pondered Joseph's question while the doctor looked on anxiously. Finally, reluctantly, the handler said, "If you need me, aye, I'll help. But can't you wait till Thomas gets back?"

"It must be tonight. I don't think I can stand another night —" Joseph corrected himself and continued, "Please meet me here in my office at nine o'clock."

Arriving back at the doctor's office later that night, Alastair Weller quietly opened the door, and then recoiled in shock. Pale and white, Dr. Joseph Bryarly lay on a cot, sweating profusely, with his shirt opened and trousers rolled up. Dozens of horse leeches were attached to his neck, face, forearms, and legs.

"Doc! What the bloody hell are you doing?"

Stiffly, Joseph lifted his head. "It's alright, Mr. Weller. You've assisted me many times in bloodletting therapy."

"Aye, but never on yourself!"

"Alastair, please listen closely. Within the hour, I will lose consciousness. After the second application of leeches, I'll lose two or perhaps three pints of blood. That's when I'll need you to remove the leeches and stay by my side until I regain consciousness."

The man shuddered and watched as the doctor poured a powdery substance out of a small green corked bottle into a glass of water and gulped it down.

"Uh ... Doc, knowin' it be none of my business 'n' all ..." The handler looked at Joseph and then back to the empty glass, concern written all over his face.

"Alastair, that powder is chloral hydrate, a sedative, a drug that will bring me sleep. Nothing more." His speech beginning to slur, the doctor whispered, "Alastair, my friend, I must find ... ways to relieve nightmares ... stop running ... from the past." At last, the exhausted man succumbed to the effects of the sedative, leeches, and nightmares.

Weller picked up the glass and placed it back on the table. "Aye, we all be running from something. I hope God is looking down on the both o' us."

Trying to make himself comfortable, the handler sat down behind the desk and leaned back. Within the hour, the first application of leeches was complete. Knowing it would be several hours before the second round of leeches could be removed, Weller began reading an article in the *Richmond Dispatch*. He, too, was soon fast asleep.

"Well, ain't this a sight for sore eyes," the familiar, sinister voice startled the handler. Still groggy, he jumped to his feet, trying to focus his vision on the figure silhouetted in the doorway.

"You! Explain—*this*."

"Aye, Cap'n Percy!"

"I'm waiting!"

"Aye … well … you see, Doc wanted to experiment, treat himself, to see how them leeches helps the crazy boys."

Weller was scared. Percy paced around the room and then stood menacingly over Joseph's inert body. The two men were at the mercy of the sadistic captain—a man as mad as some of the patients in the asylum. The room was deathly silent.

"You say Doctor Bryarly wished to experiment on *himself*?"

"Aye, Cap'n," Weller said, walking over to the doctor's body. "'Tis time to remove them leeches." Weller reached out for the creatures on Joseph's arm, but was stopped by the barrel of Percy's revolver.

"I'll be taking over from here, Weller." Percy motioned the handler away from the cot with the movement of his pistol. "I would consider it an honor to help with this experiment."

"But, Cap'n! Them leeches needs removing *now*. Else he'll bleed to death."

Percy raised his revolver. "If you don't leave this room, Mr. Weller, you'll bleed to death—long before he does."

• • • • •

The small farmhouse just outside of Gettysburg once resounded with joy during Christmas—and singing, laughter, special foods, and gatherings of friends. But Christmas Eve of 1863 was bitterly cold. Indoors, despite the crackling fire, the atmosphere was almost as cold. An old woman and her only daughter silently stared at the fire after a hasty and meager meal. Sally Stearns was five-months pregnant with Billy Gibson's child, and her mother was decidedly unhappy about that.

"Would you like a cup of tea, dear?"

"No, Momma … Thank you."

"Would you like me to fix you something else to eat, Sally? You haven't had much all day, and you'll need to keep up your strength for the baby."

"For the baby?" Sally slowly turned to look at her mother, who quickly lowered her attention to the needlework in her lap. "Are you concerned about the baby? Or are you concerned about what those women are saying down at the church?"

"Sally … I meant no harm," her mother pleaded. This sensitive subject just kept getting worse, "And yes, I am concerned about what people are saying. For heaven's sake, you were almost arrested when the postmaster confiscated those letters to Billy's family."

"I love him, Mother."

"You don't even know him, Sally! How can you be in love with a man whose voice you've never even heard?"

"We've been over this a thousand times." Sally sighed, rose, and placed her hands on her mother's shoulders, "I just wish you could see Billy through my eyes."

"Sally, you're carrying the child of a man who fights against your country. The only thing I see is the misery that lies ahead … for all of us."

Hoping to brighten the conversation, Sally reached behind the sofa and retrieved a knitted sweater she had made for her mother. "Merry Christmas, Momma."

Fifteen

Alastair Weller stood defiantly, afraid that leaving the room would mean certain death for the doctor. Percy pulled back the hammer on his pistol, intending to make good on his threat. "Delay any longer, Weller, and I'll shoot you where you stand!"

The handler couldn't win this standoff, he realized. *If I defy Percy, he shoots me and the doctor, and we're both done for. If I can get out of here alive, maybe I can get some help. God, how I'd love to ram that pistol down Percy's throat! But it won't be today. Doc needs you to keep your wits.*

Never turning his back to Percy, Weller reluctantly retreated from the office. Turning the corner into the west wing, he jerked his head hard to the right and stared at something in the shadows, "Oh, bloody hell …!"

After closing and locking the door, Percy walked to the cot and stood gloating over Joseph's helpless form. "Well, Doctor *Bryarly*, I figured I'd stand over your dead body one day, but I never reckoned you'd be helping me do it." Percy gloated, "This has to be the best Christmas present I've ever got."

Retrieving the chair from behind the desk, Percy situated it beside the cot, slammed his feet onto the bedside table, and began puffing a cigar he had found on the bookshelf, blowing the smoke over the unconscious body.

After thirty minutes or so, a woman's voice called out from the second-floor hallway, "Captain Percy, sugar! Where are you? I declare, I can't wait one minute longer for you to join me."

Percy checked the clock, rose, and scraped one of the leeches off Joseph's arm, which was beginning to change to an alarming shade of blue. "You be sure and take your little *friends* here with you, Doc—straight to hell!" Percy's spine-tingling laughter echoed down the hallway as he locked the office door behind him and climbed the stairs to pleasure himself with one of Richmond's finest whores.

Later, shrouded by the darkness, a shadow slipped into Joseph Bryarly's office and locked the door. With only the moon's glow for illumination, the shadow rapidly tore the leeches from the doctor's body. The visitor knelt by the cot, appearing to pray, then rose and slipped a note in Joseph's shirt pocket before fleeing into the night.

• • • • •

Company C settled into winter quarters outside Strawberry Plains, just east of Knoxville. When a scout reported sighting Yankee infantry nearby shortly after Christmas, the brigade that had once been commanded by General Barksdale advanced to Clinch Mountain Gap. The men were soon rewarded for their efforts: they found spoils of war in the hastily built shacks where the Union forces had been living.

"Man, I sure could use some new boots and some of that fine Yankee food," Zeke said hopefully, while he and Nate pilfered one of the small huts. "I ain't had nothing good to eat since we left Pennsylvania."

"We always be needing shoes in this here army, 'cause they sure are fond of marching," Nate agreed, searching the shelter thoroughly, then saying with disappointment, "but these boys don't seem no better off than us."

"Take all you want, men," Major Donald commanded, "then burn the rest."

The regiment confiscated a few dozen rifles, some ammunition, and several cases of hardtack, along with a couple of wagons to transport their contraband before setting the Yankee camp ablaze. Company C then marched to rejoin its brigade.

"Them Yanks will be sleeping out in the cold tonight," Zeke chortled.

Zeke's first winter in the army was miserable. For three months, the Confederates did nothing but drill, try to stay warm, and dream of food. The soldiers threw together small wooden huts. Zeke bunked with Daniel, Nate, and one poor-looking soul whom Nate quickly nicknamed Skeeter, explaining, "That boy is dumber than a sack full of rocks and no bigger than a chigger, but boy, can he tell a story and make some right fine hooch."

· · · · ·

Sergeant Cawley silently shook the shoulders of the men one morning before reveille. A heavy snowfall had blanketed the earth during the night.

"What's up, Sarge?" Zeke asked. "Why're we being so quiet?"

Cawley grinned and explained, "We're gonna have us a little fun this morning boys! We're gonna attack General Wofford's Georgia boys, who are camped just over that hill."

The men were stunned. "Attack our own men?" Daniel asked incredulously. "Sergeant Cawley, have you lost your mind?"

"We're gonna hit 'em with snowballs instead of bullets, soon as they muster for reveille."

The men of Company C scrambled over the slick hill and then hid behind trees and rocks when they could see the Georgians' camp. Cawley directed, "Boys, make them snowballs nice and tight." They quickly prepared large mounds of snowballs, and then the bugle was blown for reveille. "Now!" the sergeant barked. "Let 'em have it!"

The Mississippians opened fire on the half-awake and startled Georgians. Hearing the commotion, other expert hurlers came to the rescue of their Georgian comrades, returning fire skillfully, and slowly forcing Zeke's unit to retreat. The combined brigades of Semmes and Wofford formed mock battle lines and headed toward Zeke's brigade with vengeance in mind.

"Watch this!" Nate said as he packed a snowball. "I'm gonna bust that flag bearer."

"Ain't no way you can throw that far," Zeke shouted.

"Just watch." Nate reared his long arm back and slung the frozen projectile, smacking the flag bearer in the head, sending his hat flying backward and his flag tumbling to the ground. Loud cheers erupted from the Mississippians.

"Good shot, Nate! Bet you can't do it again!"

"Let's just see." Nate hurled another snowball, this time hitting an unfortunate boy in his crotch, doubling him over. Another huge cheer erupted from the brigade.

Since the Georgians had twice the men, Zeke's brigade was forced to retreat back up the hill, all the while making their pursuers pay for their victory.

After the snowball fight, the boys started a fire to warm their hands. They drank Skeeter's homemade hooch, the best in the camp, and reminisced about their memorable victory.

"Now that was a good ol' time," Nate said, laughing. "I tell you, boys, I sure was having me some fun hitting them flag bearers. Almost felt sorry for a couple of 'em."

"If only war were like a snowball fight," Daniel said with a sigh.

· · · · ·

All around him, people were shouting and horses were neighing. The man's muffled screams echoed within the small cramped space. Hurtling end over end, tumbling in pitch-black darkness, he slammed violently against the walls of his confinement until finally coming to a sudden stop. He struggled to move, but his legs were drawn up tightly into his chest. Covered in sweat, he fought to free himself from the confines of this miniature coffin. He strained to move his right arm, pushing and shoving with every fiber of strength, so intensely that his shoulder suddenly snapped, the bone popping out of joint. He opened his mouth with a silent shriek in response to the intense pain.

With each passing moment, the man's resolve to free himself intensified. Eventually, daylight dispelled the darkness, shining through a small hole in the side of the box, a tiny hole not much larger than a keyhole—but large enough to peer through.

In the distance, he could see the dome and six pillars adorning the entrance to Bethlem Royal Hospital. Down the narrow road, perhaps a half-mile away, bright yellow carriages passed gaily along the gray stone wall surrounding the hospital. The man's view was blocked by the figures of two—no, three, men. Only yards away, dust rose from a scuffle, partially obscuring the man's view once again. He heard more shouting, then a familiar voice crying "Help!" The deafening gunshot that followed pierced his ears. He could smell the fresh gunpowder through the hole and hear a loud thud—the sound of a lifeless body falling to the ground. And then there was silence.

A loud squeak … a blinding light … freed from the box. Two figures stood above him, silhouetted by the brilliant sunlight. Evil … must run … must escape … no … must fight … kill … avenge his death!

"LET GO OF ME!—I'll kill you all!"

Terrified by Joseph's threats, Ana jumped backward, narrowly avoiding his body as he lunged out of bed, crashing into a washbasin, slamming his fist into the face reflected in the mirror, slashing his hand and wrist in the process.

"Joseph!" Mr. Dougall shouted, "Joseph!"

The doctor gave no verbal response, continuing to struggle with his unseen enemy. These were the actions of a maniac. He turned toward the figure nearest the bed. Panicked, Mrs. Dougall stumbled backward.

"Joseph Bryarly! No!" Michael Dougall tackled the doctor, sending both of them crashing to the floor.

Ana screamed, "You're safe, Joseph! Oh merciful Lord, help us!"

Mr. Dougall helped Michael press the doctor to the floor.

Weakened from blood loss, Joseph was eventually restrained.

"Ana! Cold water! Hurry!"

Ana ran outdoors to the rain barrel. Quickly returning, she dashed water on all three men wrestling on the floor; another trip outside, another dousing.

"Joseph, dear, it's all right. You're among family," Mrs. Dougall took a rag and wiped the man's face, soothing him as she would a small child.

The frigid water, soothing words, and restraint were taking affect. Joseph began to relax; gradually, his senses returned and the nightmare subsided.

Ana went over to him, knelt on the floor, and gently caressed his face. "It's Ana, Joseph. You've had a terrible dream, that's all."

"Ana?" Joseph's eyes opened and darted around the room. His pulse rate gradually slowed and his conscious mind once again took control.

"Ana … Where am I?"

"You're safe, Joseph, in our home."

Joseph's voice cracked from exhaustion. "Ana, have I done any harm?"

"My arm hurts like the devil," Michael teased as he and Mr. Dougall climbed off Joseph's chest. "Are you all right, Papa?"

"Nothing like a little scuffle to make a man feel spry—like a young man o' thirty again," Mr. Dougall bragged, wiping his forehead.

Joseph sat up, surrounded by puddles of water. "How did I get here?"

"Four days ago, Thomas O'Malley brought you for us to tend."

"I've been unconscious for *four days*?"

"Pretty much," Mr. Dougall answered.

"Joseph, I'll be tending to your hand." Ana firmly gripped his wrist, gently pulling small pieces of glass from his swollen hand.

For several minutes, no one spoke. Lost in his thoughts, Mr. Dougall returned to his chair and smoked his pipe. Joseph knew an explanation was in order. Searching for the right words, he stammered, "I have no way to ever repay your kindness. I believe you know my heart … you are my family. I'm truly sorry for the misery I've brought into your home."

Mr. Dougall spoke first, "You almost died, Joseph. That's what Thomas O'Malley said. Found you unconscious they did, in your office early one morning."

"What happened to Mr. Weller? He was supposed to stay with me until I regained consciousness."

Michael shrugged. "No one's seen hide nor hair o' him since that night."

"The treatment shouldn't have affected me so harshly—not like this." Joseph sat, lost in thought.

Mr. Dougall spoke again. "Thomas said that Mr. Weller was last seen at eleven o'clock that night—the same time as that Cap'n Percy came back to the asylum. Percy went into your office, and Alastair left."

Joseph slowly rose to his feet, feeling weak, battered, and frail. "Something has gone terribly wrong."

"Aye, Joseph," Ana said sternly, finishing the bandaging. "'Tis something wrong, and tonight we mean to find out what."

Sixteen

After weeks of waiting, orders arrived to march on to Bristol, Tennessee. "Another hundred miles of hard walking, boys," Sergeant Cawley announced. After camping there for weeks, General Longstreet's corps climbed onto railcars and headed for Charlottesville, Virginia. The historic town of Charlottesville was home to the University of Virginia and its founder, Thomas Jefferson. As the men marched through town, they could catch glimpses of Jefferson's Monticello high on the hill overlooking the town.

"This is some town! I think I've found my new home, boys. Don't get me wrong, Mississippi is just fine, but this town breathes history and culture," Daniel announced, looking around at the stately homes and university buildings appreciatively

"Don't do much for me," Zeke said. "I wanna see Mississippi real soon like. I got a gal back there I miss something awful. I wanna go home."

"Don't we all, son," Daniel replied, sighing, "don't we all."

· · · · ·

The stay in Charlottesville was much too short for Daniel, but General Lee had other plans. After several long days' marches, General Longstreet's entire corps was assembled again around

Gordonsville. Pleased with the rapid return of one of his best general's corps, General Lee honored the man and his men with a grand review. Sprucing themselves up as much as possible, the men formed long, single lines down the main road of the valley and stood at attention. Sitting tall on his horse Traveler, General Lee slowly moved down the lines, taking time to look each man in the eyes as he rode by.

Never were men more moved than when the general reined up his horse, took off his hat, and bowed to the soldiers. Words were not necessary. Tears flowed down the men's weathered faces, their hats removed in silent tribute. "I'd march through hell for General Lee," Zeke whispered to Daniel.

"That might be exactly what we'll have to do," Daniel muttered to himself.

· · · · ·

Though Joseph had been absent from Wingate Asylum for over two weeks, Thomas O'Malley kept him informed about the affairs of the hospital during regular visits to the Dougalls' apartment. The more Joseph considered Captain Percy's role in his ordeal, the angrier he became. Alastair Weller, he learned, was still missing, presumed dead—which could also be chalked up to Percy, Joseph knew. He wrestled with another dilemma: what to do about the tortured soldiers held captive in the isolation rooms?

One dark, gray day when shards of ice rained from the skies, Joseph returned to Wingate Asylum. Entering the foyer, he quickly looked around, his eyes searching the shadows with a foreboding feeling of doom. Turning and fleeing seemed the best option, but his feet appeared to be glued to the floor.

"Well, if it isn't a ghost from my past!"

Joseph quickly turned, chills running up his spine at the sound of his enemy's voice. Captain Percy swaggered up to the doctor, with three henchmen close behind.

"I heard tell you was dead."

"I'm not."

"Well, I sure am relieved," Percy snickered. He whispered,

"Reckon you're a harder man to kill than I thought."

Bitter disgust welled up inside of Joseph. His hands twitched, desperate to strangle the devil where he stood, but a quick glance around the foyer reminded him that any act of aggression would be suicide. Joseph gritted his teeth, "Percy, I'm not afraid of you or your bloody henchmen!"

Confused by the sudden tone of defiance in the normally docile doctor, Percy cocked his head. "Just what are you trying to say, Doctor? Looks like you found yourself some gumption during your long resting spell."

Joseph growled, "Richmond is changing. And I've changed. The citizens and the laws are demanding justice."

Percy interrupted, "*Justice? Justice, Doctor?*" Leaning in closely, his hat touching Joseph's forehead, he continued, "Justice is the *right* of every man to get his head blowed off if he stands in my way."

Furious, Joseph shoved Percy. Equally incensed, Percy held up his hand, stopping the Zouaves from coming closer. "I ought to kill you right where you stand," Percy hissed.

Joseph grabbed the folded left sleeve of Percy's jacket mockingly. "Careful, *Captain*, you only have one arm left to lose."

Percy snatched his sleeve away from Joseph while slapping him across the face with the riding glove he held in his hand. Instead of backing down, as the captain expected, Joseph stared directly into Percy's eyes and enunciated for all to hear, "You backwoods ignorant fool! You have no idea what I'm capable of."

Both men tensed, hatred burning in their eyes. The doctor drew back his fists, and Percy reached for his pistol. Several Zouaves lunged forward, anticipating a bloody brawl.

"Good afternoon, Doctor!" A well-dressed elderly woman carrying a small lace parasol stood in the doorway of the foyer, with a half-dozen others clustered around her. "Have we come at a bad time?"

Percy stood toe-to-toe with the doctor, neither man speaking or addressing the visitors. Knowing the contempt the citizens of Richmond held for their battalion, the Zouaves slipped away.

"No ... no, Mrs. Albright, I'm *delighted* you're here—there's so much for you to see and hear." Joseph cautiously turned his back on Percy to greet the ladies. "It's always a joy to welcome guests to Wingate Asylum."

"I've brought the ladies from the Richmond Chapter of the Christian Commission for a visit with our troops and to report on the conditions of the hospital. Is that all right, Doctor?"

"Splendid! Don't you think so, Captain Percy?" He turned everyone's attention to Percy, whose face grew scarlet. He gave no response.

"Perhaps you ladies would like to begin with a review of our cellar and the treatment rooms ..." Joseph defiantly offered this tour, knowing it would infuriate Percy. "Would you like to escort them, or should I—*Captain Percy*?"

"Cellar's off limits," he fumed. Walking out of the foyer, he locked the cellar door behind him. Two Zouaves moved in front of the heavy paneled door to stand guard.

"Is something wrong, Doctor?" Mrs. Albright asked, sensing the tension in the air and knowing there was more going on here than met the eye. "Perhaps we should return later ... with a *military* escort?"

Joseph smiled grimly at the thought of honest military troops discovering the horrors of Bedlam South. He looked over to Sergeant Pirou, who stood menacingly, staring back. Unseen by the women, the sergeant held his pistol hidden in the folds of his coat, cocked and ready. Joseph knew a positive response to her question would mean that none of these women would ever make it back to Richmond alive.

"No, ma'am—I don't believe military assistance will be necessary." The doctor offered his arm to Mrs. Albright and smiled at her delegation. "I couldn't possibly give away the privilege of escorting you lovely ladies on a tour of our hospital." Satisfied with his response, the remaining Zouaves dispersed. Pirou remained behind, guarding the cellar entrance.

Unlike the visitation policy at Bethlem Royal Hospital, where the public came for titillating views of near-torture and death by cruel instruments, Joseph escorted visitors through the quietest wards, including the wards containing Union prisoners of war. He talked about the history of therapies for unstable mental conditions; he talked about the great need for suitable reading materials, food, bedding, and clothing for the patients; and he talked about progress being made in treatments that could return some of these men to their homes and to productive lives. Mrs. Albright and her friends left with promises to aid the doctor in his quest to improve the lives and futures of his patients.

Once again, Bedlam South was relatively peaceful. Captain Percy and his band of outlaws had left around midnight, heavily provisioned for what appeared to be another long journey. On his knees and prostrate upon the floor, Joseph prayed all night, trying to build up the courage to strike back at Percy with a powerful declaration of war. No longer would his reign of terror go unchallenged.

Joseph stood alone in the narrow hallway that led to the isolation rooms. Not even Thomas O'Malley had been invited to assist him this night. Wearing a low-brimmed hat and a Confederate uniform he had borrowed from a patient, Joseph felt confident his identity was safely hidden. With a quickening pulse, he silently descended the cellar stairs, proceeded down the corridor, and entered the small chamber, ready for the grisly scene he'd witnessed before.

"Oh, Dear God!"

Frantically turning the coal oil lamp in every direction, he repeated dazedly, "Gone? They're gone?" More nervous than before, he feared a fiendish trap by Captain Percy when he hurried over to survey each filthy—but empty—Utica crib. *The men are all gone—but how?*

Joseph saw moonlight shining through an open escape hatch leading out into the compound yard. As he gazed once more around the room, he spotted a scrap of paper in the nearest crib.

Hands trembling, Joseph retrieved the paper and read, then reread, the note:

God knows your deeds. You will be punished.
Jeremiah 15:15

Shaking so hard he felt his bones rattling, Joseph never remembered how he managed to make his way out of the cellar and safely back to his office. Having decided not to leave the note in the Utica crib for Captain Percy to find, he had stuck it in his pocket. Wishing he could give himself another medical treatment, he pulled out the scrap of paper and once again stared at the Biblical quote. *Who is the person who wrote this note and set those men free? A braver soul than I am! I will not let Percy suspect that others in this asylum are seeking his destruction. My actions today in front of Percy's thugs were foolish … foolish enough to cause my death—and I can't die until I've managed to help my patients.*

Joseph turned in his Bible to Jeremiah 15:15 and read aloud, "*O Lord, remember me, and visit me, and revenge me of my persecutors; take me not away in thy longsuffering: know that for thy sake I have suffered rebuke.*" He found great comfort in knowing that somewhere out there was a worthy adversary for Percy, someone who was willing to risk his own life to save others, someone else who was aware of Percy's crimes and knew his secrets. Someone who hated him as much as Joseph did.

· · · · ·

Mary Beth Greene slipped quietly through the lobby of the Powhatan Hotel just before three in the morning. As she began climbing the staircase, a familiar voice called out from the parlor, "Miss Mary Beth, you sure are a sight for sore eyes."

"Why, Captain—I mean Lieutenant Colonel!—Ricky Gordon." Mary Beth forced her fatigued body to stand erect, posing on the staircase for her unexpected suitor. It had already been a long night, and she was drained, but she was, after all, a very successful businesswoman. "I do declare, surely you haven't been in Richmond all this time hiding from me?"

"Hiding?" Gordon seemed startled. "Heavens no, Miss Mary Beth! I just arrived this evening. I've been waiting all night for you to return to the hotel." They cast a quick look around the empty lobby and embraced, kissing passionately. "Would you do me the honor of joining me in the parlor?"

With her most charming debutante voice, Mary Beth cooed, "Why, I would have been forever offended if you hadn't offered." She was lying, but Ricky Gordon was more than just a high-paying customer.

"Our regiment is camped not more than eight miles to the west," Gordon explained as they took a table in the darkest corner of the empty room. A weary-looking bartender brought a bottle of Kentucky bourbon and two glasses. He left without saying a word.

"And you requisitioned a furlough just to come visit with me?"

"Well, not exactly, I took what they call a *French leave* from my regiment."

"You mean you deserted? I declare, Mister Gordon, don't you know the hardship the Army of Northern Virginia brings on those who desert the cause these days? I've heard tell of many hangings lately! Why, they're even prosecuting civilians who harbor deserters," Mary Beth teasingly scolded him, although she was truthfully worried for his safety—and her own, as well.

"I'll return presently. I just couldn't stand the war one moment longer." The lieutenant colonel moved his chair closer and continued, "It's been so long, Miss Mary Beth. When our regiment moved so close to Richmond, I just had to take the chance to see you."

This wasn't the first time a customer had deserted his regiment to visit her in Richmond. Her heart warmed with compassion for this handsome young man. "You finish your drink, sugar," she reached over and caressed his thigh. "I guess Miss Mary Beth knows what you need." As he tipped his glass, she breathed seductively in his ear, allowing her tongue to trail around its curves. "Come on up to my room. I'll take care of you tonight. But before daylight, you'll be returning to your regiment—promise? Cross my heart?" she added as she pressed his hand to her heart. Breathlessly, the soldier nodded in agreement. They climbed the staircase to her room.

· · · · ·

The second Saturday in April was fight night for Billy. Captain Hurdle visited the cell soon after the men had devoured a huge breakfast. "Eat up, Billy Boy! You're gonna need all your strength tonight," he said with a laugh. "I'm gonna step up your competition, put you in with some of the best."

"I've been content with my competition. Ain't had no problems yet, Captain, *sir*," Billy said sarcastically.

"Well, tonight you might. You're fighting a monster called 'The Beast.' He'll charge you and try to wrestle you to the ground so he can smother you. Remember, there no few rules in these fights, and you better be prepared for anything."

"I appreciate your *expert* advice, Captain, sir, but I've never fought any man of any size that I didn't come out on top. Save your speech for somebody else."

"Listen here. You just better remember one thing, Billy Boy. You lose this fight and somebody's gonna get hurt."

Never one to take idle threats, Billy shot back, "Lots of folks could get hurt, *real bad*, before this war's over. That crap goes both ways, Captain. If you think it scares me, then you better think again."

Visibly shaken by Billy's response, Hurdle stepped back nervously. He swallowed hard but spoke with bravado, "Save it for The Beast. I promise you one thing, though, you won't be out of here until I say so, Billy Boy."

"We'll see about that. We'll just see."

"Don't get no ideas about running," Hurdle warned as he walked away.

"Hey, Captain," Billy shouted down the hall. Hurdle stopped and turned his head. "I just figured something out."

"What's that, Billy?"

"You ain't afraid of me running away, are you? You're afraid of me breaking out and running after you!"

Ten hours later, Captain Hurdle and company returned to escort the trio to the fight. Unexpectedly, Hurdle ordered only Billy and Sam to be shackled.

"What about Luther?" Billy asked.

"Luther's staying behind," Hurdle grinned. "He'll be just fine right here."

"But—!"

Billy was shoved out the door before he could manage a protest. Traveling down several dark alleys to avoid contact with regular military officials, Captain Hurdle led the two shackled men into an old brick building. Hurdle banged twice, waited, then knocked again on the heavily guarded back door. The group was led to a small dark room, where Sam and Billy were chained to a thick steel bar that ran the length of the wall. Although it was too dark for the Mississippians to see much, they knew that others were chained to the opposite wall

"Hey, Billy, you worried about Luther being left behind?" Sam tried to whisper, but his voice echoed in the brick room.

"I was at first," Billy confided, "but I figure Hurdle's just trying to make it harder for us to make a break."

"Hurdle knows we won't leave Luther behind. He's like a brother. Billy, don't do nothing stupid, nothing what would get Luther killed."

"Me—do something stupid?"

"Well—we is chained up because you turned down a free whore."

"Good point, Sam."

The door to the dark room burst open, blinding the men with light. The cheers and jeers from the main warehouse room indicated that an overflow crowd had gathered. Handlers unchained two of the men lurking in the shadows and led them into the ring. They tried desperately to dismember each other. The louder the din, the harder they fought, much to the delight of the crowd.

About twenty minutes later, the noise died down, and those same handlers returned to the dark room to retrieve two more prisoners. This process went on for two hours, until the only ones left were Billy, Sam, and another man who sat in the darkness mumbling to himself.

"Looks like we're the main event tonight, Sam. That must mean the smelly fella sitting in the corner is *the beast*," Billy said.

"Reckon you're right. Good luck—and try to stay away from that fella. I can't see him good, but he sure looks like a whopper."

"Yes, *Mother*."

"Dang it, boy! Get serious! Ain't you even a little bit scared?"

"No sense being scared. Scared men don't think straight, and that's what gets them hurt."

"Or killed," Sam added.

When the crowd had quieted again, the door was flung wide. Still blinking from the glare of a dozen lights, Billy stood in the entrance to the room, flexing his arms and legs and scanning the crowd. Every male in Richmond seemed to be packed into the smoky, hazy room: elegantly dressed merchants and government officials, soldiers of every rank, a scattering of sailors, rich and poor. Billy's handler pushed him from the back and he threw back his shoulders, then strode into the center of the ring. Nearby, Hurdle sat with a fat cigar in his mouth, his arms wrapped around two voluptuous prostitutes.

Before the fight could begin, the bets must be wagered, and soon Hurdle was surrounded by men wagering against Billy. *I ought to lose this fight just so Hurdle will lose all that money he's betting. No wonder he left Luther behind tonight. But if I do something stupid, Hurdle will kill him—and me—for sure.*

Straining to hear the crowd noises and still chained to the wall, Sam was stunned when the lights burst into the storeroom and The Beast rose. *That's the biggest son-of-a-gun I ever seen! For the first time, I'm scared for Billy. Lord, what'll happen to Luther if Billy loses this fight?* Sam was still chained to the wall when The Beast's handlers wrestled him out to the ring.

The Beast, filthy and covered with hair, stood a full head above his handlers and was as wide as any two of them. When he saw the man led though the doorway into the ring, Billy looked first at his eyes—and was startled by what he saw: the crazed look that he had seen many times during battle. It was a look that said "you can only beat me by killing me."

The crowd hushed with anticipation. While everyone marveled at the size of his opponent, Billy shot a quick glance at Hurdle who, although grinning broadly, was wiping his brow with a handkerchief. Sturdy and muscular, Billy's physique had impressed the crowd—until The Beast appeared. Billy removed his shirt slowly, while his mind stayed calm, considering his strategy. At least his opponent would have one less thing to grab without the shirt. The men were put in opposite corners of the ring.

The bell rang.

The fight was on.

Seventeen

A sound sleep was hard to come by at Wingate Asylum. Knowing this, Thomas O'Malley paused outside the doctor's office, trying to decide whether to wake him. Finally, the excitement overcame him, and he shoved open the door, announcing, "Doc! Doc, I got a little surprise for you."

"Huh—what? What is it, Thomas?" Joseph shielded his eyes from the bright lantern O'Malley carried. "What's wrong?"

"Nothing's wrong," Thomas said, smiling like a kid with a big secret. "Reckon for the first time in ages, things is looking up." O'Malley handed Joseph his jacket. Within moments, the still groggy Joseph and the very excited O'Malley were walking down the first-floor hallway toward the west wing.

Suddenly, Joseph grabbed O'Malley's arm, saying, "Thomas, last night I went down to the isolation rooms and …"

O'Malley interrupted him, "'Tis true, Doc, them Zouaves is a handsome lot."

O'Malley grinned, tipping his hat to a man standing in the shadows of a nearby doorway. Sergeant Pirou said nothing, but gave O'Malley him his best "go to hell" look as they continued walking away.

"Doc, I admire your courage 'n' all, there's no doubting that,"

O'Malley began speaking again when they were safely out of hearing range, "but you take too many risks. You're gonna get killed and take some o' us right along with you."

Joseph stopped and asked, "Do you blame me for Alastair's fate?"

"Nobody's to blame but the devil himself. Alastair did what he thought he should. You need to be more careful. That's all I'm saying."

"Thomas," Joseph's voice rang with excitement, "I wanted to tell you—in the isolation room the other night, the prisoners weren't there! They'd gone! Escaped, I presume."

"Doc, what in the bloody hell have you done?"

"That's just it, I didn't *do* anything. They were set free by someone else—the same person who wrote the note about searching the latrine ditch ... I wonder whether it's the same person who took the leeches off me and saved my life?" the doctor mused for a moment, then added, "At any rate, we have allies." Joseph suddenly stopped, turned to O'Malley, and asked, "Where are we going at four in the morning?"

O'Malley laughed, pleased to add to the doctor's good news. "A new fella with his leg shot off came into the hospital. Says you be neighbors when you was growing up."

The news startled Joseph. Distracted, he entered the west wing behind O'Malley.

"What's wrong, Doc? Figured you'd be excited to see 'im."

"It's just, well, it's been over twenty years since I visited with anyone from my childhood. Since I didn't leave my father's home under the best of circumstances, I'm not even sure where to begin."

"No better place to start talking than with 'hello.' There's the fella, over in that bunk close to the window." O'Malley pointed to a Confederate cavalry trooper sleeping soundly in the corner of the room. Leaving the two men alone, he walked back outside.

Joseph stood in silence just staring at the man resting on the bunk. Despite the pain and stress etched onto his face, the man had handsome features. Thick graying hair waved off his forehead. The insignia on the tailored jacket flung over him indicated he was a colonel. Finally, Joseph cleared his throat several times and reached out to shake the man gently. When he didn't immediately stir, Joseph decided that the patient was heavily medicated after his amputation. He turned to sneak away, but the patient opened his eyes and mumbled, "Joseph? … Ol' Joe, is that really you?"

"Yes, it's *really* me."

The two men stared at each other for long moments. "You don't remember me, do you?" At first the man seemed dejected, but then reasoned, "Well, reckon it's been over thirty years. Can't expect a man to remember everyone." He pushed himself up in bed and held out his strong, tanned hand. "Frederick Hutch, from The Glade, on the east side of the town." He awaited a response from Joseph, but when none came, he added, "My father was good friends with the Reverend."

"Yes, please forgive me! Of course I remember you! How are your parents?"

"Mother died in the yellow fever outbreak back in forty-one, same year the lowlands around Montezuma flooded. Reckon it's been twenty-two years or more. My father died last spring, too old to fight and too hardheaded to be told any differently."

"I'm sorry to hear that."

"Thank you kindly. Say, how's the Reverend?"

"Also dead. Two years ago."

"Reckon we're all getting closer to the grave, thanks to the march of time and this war," the colonel observed somberly. "We sure had us some times back home in Alabama, didn't we, Joe? Home … that's the only thing what God ever made that's worth fighting and dying for!"

"Yes, we sure had some good times." Joseph quickly changed the subject from their childhood days in Alabama to the colonel's medical condition, asking about the skirmish where he'd been wounded, the battlefield hospital, and the conditions of the ward. He spent long moments detailing the trip to America.

"All that fancy education's robbed you of your Southern sound. You even look different—I always figured you were the spitting image of the Reverend." Frederick studied the doctor closely, then conceded, "but I reckon I look a mite different after all these years. Heck, we were just wide-eyed whippersnappers last time we saw one another."

"That was many years and many miles ago," Joseph said, rising and checking the patient's pulse. "You need your rest now."

"Hey, Joe, remember when the Reverend preached at Macedonia Church over on Rose Hill and we got into such a lot of mischief? I reckon we could talk for hours ..." he trailed off sleepily.

"And we will, colonel—soon—but for now, you need your rest, and I need to visit my patients back in the asylum."

• • • • •

The Beast lumbered toward Billy, stalking him. When he was in range, Billy turned loose with his left-right combination, the same strategy that had dropped so many men in the past. But The Beast wasn't moved. Billy fired again, this time splitting his opponent's nose wide open. The monster staggered back, wiping the flow of blood and snot. Seeing his own blood dripping from his hand, he let loose a cry of rage.

The few women in the crowd panicked and screamed as the raging bull charged the fleet-footed soldier. Twice Billy sidestepped him, delivering several rapid-fire shots to his head each time The Beast flew off the ropes. While the giant was still off balance, Billy aimed a shot square at his chin with all the force he could muster. The big man plopped down on his backside with a thud. But he never took his eyes off Billy. He was frustrated more than hurt.

The Beast's handlers responded quickly, guiding him back to the stool in his corner. They iced his face, trying to slow the bleeding and doused him with cold water, hoping to revive his senses. Since Billy's previous fights had ended quickly, he wasn't sure what to do with himself, so he stepped back to his corner to wait.

Leaving his women behind, Hurdle met Billy in his corner, urging him to sit and catch his breath. "No rules," Hurdle advised. "It ain't over 'til one man can't be revived." Several minutes passed before The Beast regained what little sense he had left. "He's hurt, so finish him off real quick-like. You're good, boy—real good!" Hurdle praised Billy enthusiastically, all the while calculating his winnings in his mind.

The Beast was up and ready, but wobbled. Billy tried his best to stay out of reach and to deliver as many blows as possible to the big head. He loaded up his right fist, but swung too hard. The Beast ducked the punch and bear-hugged Billy, picking him up off the ground. He threw Billy onto the mat and landed on top of him full force with his massive body weight.

Pinned to the ground beneath the deadly weight, Billy gasped for air, unable to move. The Beast choked him with two hands. Gurgling sounds spewed from Billy's throat, seeming to delight the monster. He had no intention of letting up, not while Billy was still conscious.

No rules—no rules—no rules. In his last moment of consciousness, Billy mustered all his strength. Swinging upward as hard as he could, he hit The Beast in his throat, crushing his Adam's apple with one blow. Several more blows to the throat, and The Beast's grip went limp.

With a Herculean effort, Billy knocked him off to the side, rolled over on top, and began pounding on The Beast's massive head over and over and over again wildly, imagining his opponent to be the bulk of the Union army and Captain Hurdle, all rolled into one. He was so enraged, so focused, that he failed to notice The Beast had ceased moving several minutes ago and that his fists and knuckles were breaking from the brutal punishment he had inflicted. He was back in that out-of-body place for the first time since Gettysburg. The crazed look in his eyes matched the look in The Beast's eyes earlier.

The crowd roared and rose to their feet, erupting in applause and cheers. Even those who had bet against Hurdle's fighter were cheering for him. Billy was king of the ring this evening. But Billy heard none of it.

Smiling confidently, Captain Hurdle made his way back to the ring to congratulate his boy, but seeing the look in Billy's eyes, he stopped a few feet away. Billy recognized the mask of fear on Hurdle's face and with great satisfaction threatened, "I told you, Hurdle—no problem!"

Captain Hurdle laughed nervously while Billy was put in chains. "Great show, Billy Boy, but I'm afraid you may have killed him."

"So? No rules, remember?"

"You okay, Billy?" Sam asked, staring at Billy's hands when he arrived back in the holding cell. Billy gave no reply, nor had he spoken on the hike back to the jail.

When Sam and Billy arrived back in their quarters, Luther was waiting anxiously. "How'd it go?" he asked hesitantly, sensing Billy's solemn mood and seeing his bleeding hands.

Sam spoke up, "Did real good, but his hands're all busted up."

"He was a tough one, eh, Billy?"

"He was. I think I killed him, Luther," Billy finally spoke.

Captain Hurdle arrived with a doctor in tow to examine Billy's hands. The doctor took a quick survey of the fighter's injuries and announced, "He's broken a couple of knuckles on each hand. May have broke some of them small bones in his hand. It's hard to tell until I get him cleaned up good and the swelling goes down.

"One thing's for sure, Captain Hurdle," he added. "This man don't need to be fighting until his hands have healed up."

"Hellfire," Hurdle complained, "I have big plans for that boy. I need him in good working order."

"Making plenty of money off me, eh, Hurdle?" Billy asked with no emotion in his voice.

"Plenty. The Beast was one of the top fighters in the city. Hardly anybody bet against him. When the crowd saw you, they was betting big odds."

"I'm real happy for you."

Even Billy's sarcasm couldn't dim Hurdle's delight tonight. He owned the king of the ring and had just made a small fortune on the fight. Two prostitutes and a bottle of whiskey were waiting in his quarters to help him celebrate. Smiling, he set a bottle on the cell's battered table and left with the doctor.

"Hand me that bottle, Luther. I need some pain relief."

"You okay? Your hands look awful. How'd you do that?"

"I couldn't hurt him. The man was strong as an ox. So I just kept pounding harder and harder," Billy held up his mangled hands, "and this is what happened."

"Looks like you'll be out of action for a while," Sam said.

"Fine by me," Billy replied. Three stiff drinks later, he was snoring.

"That boy scares me sometimes, Luther."

"Me, too. He's got too many things buzzing around in his head."

"Do you reckon that he really don't fear things the way most folks do?"

"I reckon that's it, Luther. Billy dang sure ain't scared of nothing—and maybe, for all our sakes, he should be."

• • • • •

Sally Sterns had endured other sleepless nights, but tonight the shooting pains across her lower stomach were more intense. "Mother, please come," she called out from her bedroom. "There's something wrong!"

Her mother rushed into the room with mixed emotions. "What is it, dear? What's wrong?"

"Every few minutes, I get these cramps down low. Almost like a real bad stomach ache, but Mama, the pains are so intense. Do you think the baby's all right?" she moaned.

"Must be contractions. You must be in labor, honey," her mother replied, still fighting within herself to accept this new baby.

Sally burst into tears thinking of Billy, wondering for the

thousandth time where he was. Little did she know that while Billy fought for his life many miles away, she was about to fight for the life of his son.

A midwife, Sally's mother could deliver this baby without help. She hoped to keep the birth quiet for as long as possible—as if anyone in this small town didn't already know about Sally and the Rebel soldier. Fighting her emotions, she prepared the bed for the birthing.

The contractions grew stronger and longer. During a lull in the pain, Sally stood and shuffled over to the straw mattress prepared for this moment. Her water broke, and the baby's head lodged in her pelvis. Sweating and panicked, Sally gasped for breath during the next intense contraction.

"It's all right, dear. It's all right. Everything's going to be fine," her mother cooed, using the words she had spoken so often when her daughter was a little girl. "It won't be long now."

"It hurts so bad," she moaned.

"I know, Baby. It's the way God designed it. Our greatest pain, our greatest labor, brings forth our greatest joys," her mother soothed, handing her daughter a glass of brandy for the pain.

"Drink this," she insisted. "It'll help some."

Sally drained the glass, almost choking. "This baby's gonna split me in two!" she screamed. "How I wish Billy was here!"

Finally, Sally convinced her little Gibson that it was time to make an appearance. Sally's mother delivered the screaming little boy with a head full of thick black hair like his father's. Crying, she stared at the newborn, and her heart melted. The months of embarrassment and arguments were forgotten as she held her grandchild in her arms.

In the midst of war and so many deaths, life and peace had interceded and brought joy.

Eighteen

By late May of 1864, Richmond was a city besieged. Columns of Union prisoners captured during the Wilderness Campaign were herded through the streets daily on their way to Belle Isle or Libby Prison. Deserters, runaway slaves, destitute soldiers' wives, homeless orphans, and Southern loyalists forced out of Federal-occupied territories descended upon the city in masses, swelling its population to standing-room only. Hundreds of clerks from the Treasury Department had been evacuated to Montgomery by executive order, fueling speculation that President Davis intended to move the capital to Alabama and abandon Richmond, leaving the city and its people to merciless Federal generals like Grant.

No longer were nights quiet. Drunken soldiers and prostitutes stumbled through the streets. The homeless took shelter in factory doorways and under bridges, with children and women crying piteously. Messengers galloped frantically through the streets with messages for the president and his cabinet members. Supply wagons lurched through town, with teamsters cursing and whipping their exhausted mules. Trains whistled shrilly. Railcars rumbled continuously, bringing fresh troops and supplies to reinforce the Army on the Rapidan River.

"'Tis a good morning, Michael," Mr. Dougall patted his son on the back as they wiped their faces, laid down their work gloves on a stack of empty shipping crates, and joined their coworkers leaving the Byrd Street Foundry around lunchtime.

"Papa, what's all the fuss?" Michael pointed to a crowd milling around near the Basin waterway. Dozens of heavily armed provost guards led by General Winder were fanning through the crowd of hundreds, shouting.

Standing on the bed of a supply wagon, surrounded by armed troops, a young and visibly nervous colonel from the Bureau of Conscription began reading from a prepared statement: "By executive order of President Jefferson Davis, a summons has been issued this day by Secretary of War James Seddon for all white able-bodied men capable of bearing arms, between the ages of seventeen and fifty-four years of age ..."

Catcalls and cussing erupted from the men in the crowd. Women screamed their objections. Frightened youngsters wailed. Men tried to flee, but realized they were surrounded by Confederate cavalry, which corralled the crowd around the speaker. They were dragged back to the assembly.

The colonel coughed nervously and continued, "You are hereby ordered to report for military duty, to be conscripted this day. You will be escorted to Franklin Street for weapons and provision, then on to Capitol Square for organization and further orders." He then added, "Any man refusing to obey this order will be seized, thrown in irons, and tried by a military court as an enemy of the Confederacy!"

The crowd erupted in chaos, pushing, shouting, and shoving. Fights broke out among men attempting to escape past the cavalry. Barking dogs caused horses to panic. Women ran into the crowd to save their husbands and sons, only to be rudely thrust aside by angry troops. Shopkeepers locked their doors when the massive horde of citizens and refugees fled in every direction. Within minutes, downtown Richmond was transformed into a riot zone. Two men leaped through a dry goods store window, only to be forced back out into the street at gunpoint.

General Winder shouted, "Fire over their heads. Settle 'em down, boys!"

Dozens of muskets simultaneously cracked, sending men, women, and children to take cover on the ground. Only a few men, including Michael and Patrick Dougall, defiantly remained standing.

"I've got a pass!" a well-dressed and now muddy man, obese and in his mid-thirties, shouted from his kneeling position. "A pass signed by President Davis. I do not have to report."

"All passes have been revoked," the colonel yelled back. "Y'all have heard the thunder from the cannonades on Drewery's Bluff. At this very moment, over seven thousand Yankees are within sixteen miles of Richmond."

Another man shouted, "I purchased my substitute five months ago! Paid the government two thousand dollars!"

"And you got to stay home five months longer than most folks. There will be no substitutes this time. The summons is clear—all able-bodied men will report for duty!"

A brigade of infantry traveled down Fifth and Seventh Streets, effectively surrounding the entire block. They lined both sides of Byrd Street, ready to escort the reluctant conscripts to the Franklin Street Armory. As the disorganized march progressed, provost guards moved through the crowd, removing women, children, the aged, and those obviously physically unfit for service.

The Dougalls joined in the march, their minds a whirlwind of mixed emotions. In America for less than a year, they had been ordered to fight and perhaps die for a cause neither of them fully understood or supported.

"You! Old man!" a provost guard shouted above the din to Patrick Dougall. "Only men seventeen to fifty-four are to report for duty."

"I'll be going with me son," he insisted.

The guard pushed through the crowd, struggling to separate the old man from the conscripts. "You're too old, mister," the guard shouted again. "Don't be a dang fool! Even if you get to Capitol Square, them doctors will throw you back like yesterday's dead fish!"

"I'm not a day over fifty-three," Mr. Dougall lied. Ignoring the guard, he stared straight ahead and struggled to keep pace with the mob.

"Papa, it'd be best for you to stay here. You need to look after Mama 'n' Ana."

"Nonsense."

"Please, Papa. Please, listen to them," begged Michael. Their pace slowed as the crowd rounded the corner and lined up at the armory.

I'll not leave me son. I'll hear no more of this."

By the end of the day, over one thousand five hundred men would be conscripted.

Two hours later, the Dougall men reached the front of the line and stood before the supply officer's table. Michael was quickly registered. The process deadlocked when the stubborn old Irishman refused to be separated from his son.

"Mr. Dougall, sir," the supply sergeant said respectfully, "please, go home. You're at least sixty-five-years old. We appreciate the fact that you are the only man here who insists on joining the service, but you're too old."

"Ahh—that's where you be wrong, son! I'm not a day over sixty-three," Mr. Dougall replied. Realizing his mistake, he corrected himself swiftly. "Did I say sixty-three? Forgive me lying heart! Truth be told, officer, I'll be fifty-four next month."

"Let the old man go in my place," a foul-smelling drunk offered, "'cause I'd hate to split up a paw and his boy."

A tall, thin Irish private smacked the drunk with the butt of his rifle. "Speak of that man again, and I'll split your head down the middle. Now get back into the ranks, you bloody coward."

"Mr. Dougall," the sergeant's tone was firm, "please—go home."

Tears flowed as a sympathetic sergeant and a nearby private

removed Mr. Dougall from the line with unusual gentleness. "This should be humbling for the cowards still trying to escape their duty," a corporal whispered to his sergeant, who nodded.

"Be strong, son," Mr. Dougall yelled as he followed the procession containing Michael until it turned off Franklin Street and headed to the army encampment. "You'll be going with God now!"

· · · · ·

Every Saturday afternoon, Mary Beth Greene visited an almshouse for war orphans on Leigh Street, just eight blocks west of President Jefferson Davis's home. Formerly the home of an affluent Richmond attorney, it had been donated to the church when its owner was immortalized as one of the first of Virginia's war casualties. For the past three years, Catholic nuns from Saint Timothy's Cathedral had run the orphanage and ministered to the eighteen children who were packed into the home.

Whenever the elegant carriage and its two glossy chestnut horses pulled up in front of the home, children from two to eleven years old poured out of every nook and every room, shouting excitedly, "Miss Mary Beth—Miss Mary Beth's here!"

"Children! *Remember* your place!" The unpleasant shrill of an ancient nun stopped the children in their tracks. She waved a wooden soup ladle in the children's direction, scolding them again. "There will be none of that noise. Not in this house!"

"She's right, children," Mary Beth said, smiling at the nun, who returned to the kitchen. She knelt in the foyer to hug and embrace children who so seldom received attention.

Mary Beth slowly rocked from side to side. Smiling, the children mimicked her movements, trying their best not to giggle. With a mischievous grin, she motioned for the children to join hands. Swaying to the rhythm, Mary Beth sang a playful tune to them.

"We musn't be *laughing*, and *running*, and *dancing*, and *playing* … Nnoooo—*not in this house*."

"We musn't be *smiling*, and *grinning*, and *joking* and *dreaming* ... *Where* children?" she prompted.

"*Nnoooo—not in this house!*"

"We musn't be *hugging*, and *squeezing*, and *hoping*, and *teasing* ..."

"*Nnoooo—not in this house!*" the children chimed in.

Mary Beth jumped to her feet and announced, "I have a special treat today! Two of my friends are waiting outside for y'all. Miss Lucy and Miss Rebecca have brought us fresh cookies, cakes and pies and ... well, what else now? Hmm, I declare, I just can't remember!"

"What, Miss Mary Beth?" a darling little four-year-old with blonde braids asked anxiously, "what else did you bring us?"

"Well, I do believe it might be shoes! New shoes, I think ..."

"Shoes? *New shoes?*

"New shoes for *everyone?*"

Mary Beth looked thoughtful for a moment, then nodded her head. "Yes, I do believe there are new shoes for *everyone!*"

With squeals of joy, the children rushed outdoors. Two beautiful, but very nervous, prostitutes waited with gifts of love.

"You are such a dear, sweet woman," Sister Mary Catherine said quietly, standing beside Mary Beth and watching the children and their new friends. "We should invite your friends inside and thank them properly."

"Thank you kindly, but no." Mary Beth slipped something into Sister Mary Catherine's hand as they walked outside. "You see, most women in my, well, shall we say *profession*," Mary Beth continued as the nun blushed, "become a little too nervous being this close to God and all."

They shared a laugh and then Sister Mary Catherine replied, "I understand, but please, do thank them for all of us."

"Remember our agreement, Sister?"

"I know! I mustn't tell anyone about your gifts." She beamed and hugged the woman. "But God knows your heart, that I promise you. God knows your heart."

The procession of children walked past carrying boxes and bags and giggling excitedly. After the three women drove away, Sister Mary Catherine burst through the kitchen doors, startling her elderly cook. "God is good—and so is Miss Mary Beth!" she cried joyously. "Those ladies—and I do mean ladies—have just given us enough money to pay for the children's needs for months! And shoes! At last the children have shoes!"

• • • • •

Mr. Dougall walked the streets of Richmond for hours, torn between facing his wife and Ana and searching for Joseph. He wandered down Byrd Street, past the State Penitentiary, and to the front of the Hollywood Cemetery, where seventy-five coffins constructed from tobacco crates were lined up along the wrought-iron fence. Troops and gravediggers wearily went about their gruesome daily task.

Compelled by a mysterious force, Mr. Dougall watched horrified as the gravediggers worked. Each had wrapped cloths around his face to filter the stench from the decaying bodies. They stacked six coffins, one upon the other, into each grave. Unable to restrain himself, he stopped a gravedigger briefly. "Young fella," Mr. Dougall said softly, "these soldier boys deserve a decent resting place, a place of their own."

The young private removed the cloth from his face and wiped the sweat from his brow. "Mister, these here ain't regular soldiers. These are officers."

"Where are the soldiers buried?"

"Troops? Privates, like me?"

Mr. Dougall nodded.

"If they die in battle and they're lucky, they're thrown into a big ditch, hundreds at a time, with some dirt throwed on top." As the young man put the cloth back over his face, he added, "But most boys just rot where they fall."

• • • • •

The sun was shining, the redbud, azaleas, and dogwood trees were blooming, and a scattering of puffy white clouds danced across the horizon. For a few short hours, the earth—and the two people snuggling in the park at the crest of Gamble's Hill—seemed to forget that a war was blazing. Ana and Joseph listened to the military band playing waltzes and sonatas and refused to allow war's harsh realities to spoil their afternoon. Joseph admired the way the sun glinted on Ana's auburn hair and Ana marveled at Joseph's range of intellectual interests as they talked. In time, they opened a generously laden picnic basket and ate until they could eat no more.

Shortly after they had repacked the basket, Ana saw her father walking slowly, almost painfully, up the crest of the hill. The peaceful scene on Gamble's Hill was a remarkable contrast to the chaos around Capitol Square just a few blocks away, Patrick Dougall thought, before anguish once again washed over him.

"Papa?" Ana's voice quivered, then rose in pitch as she stood up and ran to her father. Joseph turned in surprise, and then followed her. "Papa? What's the matter? Where's Momma? What's happened?"

"Michael's gone ... Them army boys took him," Mr. Dougall sobbed. "He'll be forced to fight."

"Oh, dear Lord, no!" Ana began weeping softly. Joseph awkwardly tried to comfort them both.

"Tried to stop 'em, I did—or go with my son if I couldn't stop them from takin' him. They wouldn't take an old man, but they took his only son. When war comes, it should only be fought by old men ..."

As the father and daughter consoled each other, Joseph noticed that other messengers were arriving and informing other families of the news. Before long, the scene on Gamble's Hill resembled the chaos on the city streets. Picnickers frantically packed up their belongings as the story of the Clay Street conscription spread rapidly. Even the band members dispersed, each concerned about loved ones and friends.

"Joseph," Ana's eyes brightened with hope, "you could save Michael!"

"How? I have no influence with the Secretary of War."

Mr. Dougall's countenance brightened. "The President! Joseph, you could speak to 'im for Michael. He would listen to you!"

"You … you want me to talk to President Davis?"

"Please, Joseph!"

"Joseph," Mr. Dougall pleaded, "help save me son."

Nineteen

Darkness fell over the battlefield. It was a relief to have the cannons stilled and the whine of rockets silenced, if only for a few blessed hours. Company C had scoured the scene of carnage for hours, retrieving their dead and wounded, carrying or supporting soldiers to the hospital tents. They had shot badly injured horses, gathered discarded or lost weapons and ammunition belts, and managed to catch their breath and realize, almost dazedly, that they were in one piece—or pretty much so.

At last, Zeke stumbled back to his place in line as darkness fell. Exhausted, he lay panting between Daniel and Nate. Rifles primed, loaded, and ready by their sides, they faced the enemy instinctively, silently, realizing the struggle they would have to resume. "Why's everybody so dang quiet?" Zeke finally asked, trying to hide his concern.

"You know as well as we do, Zeke," Daniel said quietly. "You can hear the Yanks amassing their forces just beyond those trees. This may be the last battle we ever fight. We're all—Yanks and Rebs—thinking the same thing: remembering lost comrades who were killed beside us and thinking of our families and what they've sacrificed back home—if they're still at home."

Restless and worried, Zeke turned to Nate, who uncharacteristically hadn't said a word all night.

"Who peed in your whiskey, Nate?" Zeke poked him in the side.

Nate just shook his head.

"Come on, not you, too?"

"I cain't explain it, but I ain't never felt like I do right now. This here Grant ain't gonna quit until we is all dead. I ain't afeared exactly, but somethin' inside me's tellin' me that something bad's about to happen."

The men stayed in line all the next day, waiting on an attack that didn't come. Until morning.

Just before dawn, bugles sounded the Yankee advance. Confederate skirmishers fell back hastily. As the sun broke the horizon, Zeke could see line after line of Yankee infantry moving across the fields like waves on a sandy beach. "There must be a million of 'em coming!" he whispered, as much to himself as to his friends.

Nate shouted above the screams and booms of artillery, "This is gonna be one helluva fight boys—get ready!"

"This Grant means business," Daniel said, gritting his teeth and checking his rifle. "He's not leaving until this army is finished—but it's not finished yet!"

Over and over again, throughout the day, Grant's forces charged the Rebel lines. And, miraculously, every time the lines held. As evening finally descended, the Federals retreated, and the Rebels erupted in victorious shouting.

"They can't break our lines! Daniel, they can't break our lines!" Zeke exalted.

"They'll keep trying. This Grant is nothing more than a butcher."

Two days later, Grant ordered his troops into battle once again—and this time with much greater force. The Federals managed to break the center of the Confederate line with much cost in lives, but their success was only temporary. General Lee committed all reserves forward. A brutal, bloody hand-to-hand fight lasted almost twenty hours. When rain started falling in sheets, the soldiers' misery magnified. Exhausted, the Confederates retreated to a new line of entrenchments and waited for another attack. The Yankees' last charge was by far their worst. The violent clash wiped out whole companies of soldiers.

Furiously, valiantly, Nate fought next to Zeke. A barrage of bullets whistled past their heads. Leaning forward to reload, Nate instinctively looked over at Zeke. Their eyes met for an instant—just before a bullet ripped through Nate's chest. He was thrown backwards into a crumpled heap.

"No!" Zeke screamed as he rushed over to his friend. "No! Get up, Nate! Get up, Nate, c'mon—get up!" Though Zeke tried to arouse his friend, Nate's limp body lay in his arms. Zeke cradled Nate's head in his lap, "Can you hear me, Nate?"

Nate's eyes flickered open and with his last breath he whispered with great effort, "See yah on … the other side … Smiley."

Zeke didn't move. Paralyzed with grief, he sobbed over his friend's body as the hail of gunfire continued. Men steadily fell all around him. When Sergeant Cawley nearly tripped over the mourning soldier, he yanked him up by the collar and roared, "Fire your weapon, boy, or we'll all be dead! Now get up! Join that firing line!"

"He's gone, son," Daniel shouted to Zeke, "but we still have work to do."

Heartbroken, Zeke fired and reloaded mechanically, not aiming or thinking of anything but Nate until he saw a cluster of bluecoats charging in his direction. "Stinking blue-bellies! Lousy stinking blue-bellies!" he screamed, dropping on one knee and firing as fast as he could prime, load, and aim.

Hours later, his face blackened by gunpowder and the grime of battle, Zeke searched the field for his friend. He bent over the body and sobbed quietly as the rains returned. When Daniel found him, the two friends wrapped Nate's limp arms around their shoulders and dragged him back to the Confederate line. "It's a brutal war, Zeke," Daniel sighed. "We should collect his effects before the scavengers do. I'll write his wife and folks a letter and send his things home with it."

"If it's okay, Daniel, I'll write the letter. I know Lizzie and I know his Pa—and he's gonna take this hard … real hard. Nate was his only boy."

Looking completely drained, Daniel just nodded.

The heavy rains soaked the weary warriors—but they welcomed the break in the action that the deluge provided. Up and down the lines, soldiers passed the names of the dead and wounded. Among the casualties was General Jeb Stuart. The now-legendary cavalry leader had been killed during an engagement at Yellow Tavern.

• • • • •

Bedlam South seemed to decline faster than the rest of the city of Richmond. Scurvy and dysentery were spreading among the east-wing mental patients. Pyemia, a debilitating blood poison, had infested the Officer's Hospital located in the Baptist Female College building in Richmond, forcing Captain Percy to accommodate thirty-one infected officers in the west wing of the asylum. Joseph was grateful for the presence of these army regulars, because it meant routine visits from Richmond nurses and the watchful eyes of the Christian Commission.

For the past ten hours, Joseph had worked his way through the first-floor ward of the east wing. Assisted by the apothecary, Doctor Charles Little, he administered new experimental remedies for patients suffering from battle trauma, more commonly known as nostalgia. These pitiful souls relived the nightmares of battle daily. Adding disgrace to their suffering, many fellow soldiers and military officers were openly contemptuous of them. Relieved from duty due to mental illness, they would forever be labeled as cowards, malingerers, and slackers.

Joseph stood over the bed of Private Jimmy Hicks, a sandy-haired kid, barely eighteen years old, who hailed from a family of Tennessee River ferryboat operators. "How are you feeling, Jimmy?" Joseph knelt down beside the cot.

Jimmy stared into the distance without response. His face was thin and sallow, with black circles under both eyes and ghostly skin that hung like loose fabric off his frail body. His slow, labored breathing silently shouted, "The end is near!"

"He ain't spoke in four days, Doc," the man strapped to the cot next to Jimmy offered. "The handlers done quit feeding him. Reckon it's been over a week now."

"Why? Who ordered his food to be stopped?"

"Doc, how many of our boys do you reckon will die of starvation in Bedlam South?" asked a tattered-looking man who sat shackled to the wall beneath an open window.

"I know you men have endured great hardship, and food is getting alarmingly scarce throughout the Confederacy, but we don't intentionally try to starve our patients."

Slowly, those who were not bedridden or shackled gathered near Joseph, sitting on the floor or leaning against the wall to talk. Doctor Little patted Joseph on the back, leaving him to what he loved doing: working with patients.

The tired and tattered man lying beside Jimmy's bed spoke up again, "Do ya mean the hospital won't starve us, or Captain Percy won't starve us? Everybody knows if it weren't for you and O'Malley, Percy would've killed us long ago just to get our pay vouchers."

"You mustn't speak of such things, Nicholas," Joseph cautioned. "I know things look grim here, but it's no better anywhere else in the Confederacy."

Many of the men nodded in agreement. They all respected Joseph and knew he was sincerely trying to help—though whether he could outlast Percy was the question that concerned them whenever they spoke together.

"Doc, do you think ... what I mean is," a young drummer boy, shaking uncontrollably since surviving the fight at Chancellorsville, tried to speak without crying, "do y'all really believe any of us will ever get to go home?"

"Yes! I promise you! Many of you men are making remarkable progress. My job is to make sure as many of you as possible will return home." Joseph's words offered renewed hope. "Now let's not entertain any more talk of conspiracy or intent to harm. This is a night to think on more pleasant things." He shook the patients' hands or patted a shoulder before turning to leave. The doctor was almost out of the ward when he heard something unusual.

Have I not commanded you? Be strong and of good courage. Do not be afraid nor be dismayed, for the Lord your God is with you wherever you go. Therefore, let us come boldly before the throne of grace to obtain mercy and find grace to help in a time of need.

A tall, silver-haired man with a long white beard, wearing torn trousers and an equally tattered shirt, spoke once again as his bare feet navigated the congested aisle toward Joseph. *Look upon our affliction and our pain, Lord, and forgive all our sins.*

Joseph motioned to O'Malley and asked the man's name.

"They call him Preacher. Wanders in for a spell from time to time. Percy lets him be. Even the Zouaves lets him be, since they're a bunch of superstitious wankers."

"What do you mean?"

"You know, voodoo, witchcraft, such as that. Them Zouaves is bad superstitious."

"What does that have to do with this man?"

"This here fella was a Baptist preacher. I heard tell the poor bloke lost his wits, showed up around Richmond back last winter. No shoes, no shirt, and crazier than most. Even Pirou won't mess with a man of God."

Preacher walked an erratic path among the men, stopping, stepping sideways, and occasionally retracing his steps, as if being guided by some unseen force. He came to stand beside the restraining cot of Private Albert Wright.

"He only speaks God's words," O'Malley said, anticipating Joseph's next question. "Mostly, though, he don't mutter a blooming word."

"Fascinating …" Joseph murmured, continuing to stare at the eccentric man. *Here is an educated man of God, feared by Captain Percy and allowed to roam freely throughout the hospital. That's it—he's the one! He must be the man who saved my life by removing the leeches and he must have freed those prisoners from the Utica cribs!*

"Doctor!" an orderly called, standing beside Jimmy Hick's bed. "Jimmy's dead. He's got no pulse."

With a face full of great sorrow, Preacher looked around the long corridor packed with men, walked briskly over to Jimmy, and said, *Precious in the sight of the Lord is the death of His saints.* He knelt down beside the young boy's body while several others in the room bowed their heads in silent prayer. Within moments, the entire ward was quiet. Preacher then quietly stood, dusted the dirt from his knees, and walked passed Joseph.

"Thank you, Preacher," Joseph whispered. "I am most grateful."

Preacher stared blankly at Joseph for a moment, and then turned to leave.

· · · · ·

On the morning of June sixth, believing that General Lee's exhausted army had little fight left in them, Grant charged the Rebel lines. At the Battle of Cold Harbor, which lasted little more than two hours, the Union losses totaled over seven thousand five hundred men. Many Union soldiers refused to charge the Confederate lines a second time.

"My God," Daniel exclaimed, as the smoke and fog of battle lifted, revealing thousands of dead or wounded Union soldiers. "Is there no end to this slaughter? How many will have to die?" he uncharacteristically screamed at the Yanks.

"If they keep this up, there won't be nobody left out there but Grant himself," Zeke agreed.

"What he asks of his troops is inhumane."

"Y'all okay?" Skeeter piped in from nowhere.

"We're better off than those boys," Zeke answered, pointing to the fields in front of them. "I just hope we got more bullets than they do men."

The two armies battled each other for almost a month with unprecedented casualties for each side. Grant lost more than fifty thousand men—almost as many men as were in Lee's army when the fighting began. Lee lost more than thirty thousand. Grant had the resources and recruits to keep fighting; Lee's were in short supply.

Somehow, if Lee could hold off Grant until the fall elections were over, maybe, just maybe, the Confederacy could negotiate a peace with a different president, the Confederates speculated and hoped, from the president down to the lowliest private.

· · · · ·

The foyer of Wingate was quiet. Tired and depressed, Joseph slipped up the winding stairs to his study to retire for the evening.

"Joseph?" a familiar voice called up the stairs.

"Ana? Oh, thank God!" Quickly descending the staircase, he embraced her, holding her tightly. "I'm so glad to see you! Did you travel alone?"

"Aye, I come alone, Joseph. Everyone be worried sick for Michael. Haven't heard so much as a word from him … or from you."

Joseph loosened his grip. "I'm sorry, Ana. I wish I could have done something for you and for Michael."

"Are ye giving up, Joseph? Have ye spoken to President Davis yet?"

"No, but I pled Michael's case with the Provost Marshall General Winder and at least a dozen other officers." Joseph tried to wrap his arms around her again, but she pulled away. "I went to the Bureau of Conscripts. I offered to pay them one thousand dollars and to take his place in service, but they rejected my offer and ordered me to leave."

"Why won't you speak with President Davis?" Her tear-filled eyes told a story too painful to express with words.

"The Attorney General and Postmaster General were conscripted along with Michael the very same day. How can I influence President Davis when his own staff has been sacrificed? He won't even meet with any of his cabinet members on this subject."

"Please, Joseph."

"I ... I'm sorry," Joseph tried again to console her, but she rejected him.

"Please, I'm begging you. Please talk to President Davis."

"Ana ... you don't know what you're asking of me."

"Please, if you truly love me, talk to him."

"I ... I can't," Joseph softly muttered while keeping his eyes on the floor.

Ana sank into a nearby chair, hiding her face in her hands while he shifted his weight from one foot to another. "You could, Joseph. If you loved me, you would."

"I love you more than I can ever express, but I cannot meet with President Davis!"

"Joseph, is fear of your past worth Michael dying? How long will you run from the memory of your dead father? Is it worth the price of Michael's death?" she demanded.

"I tried to trade my life in exchange for Michael's! What else can I do?"

"Talk to your old friend! Face your past, Joseph. Do this for Michael, for me, for my family. Please, Joseph!"

"I'm sorry, Ana. I can't. Someday, I'll be able to explain this to you." Joseph surrendered the fight.

"You're a coward!"

"Ana, please ..."

She stood abruptly, shouting, "A coward!" Her face red with anger, she ran to the door and flung it open. She turned and shouted again, "You're a bloody coward, Dr. Joseph Bryarly!"

"Ana—wait!"

"I hate cowards—and I hate you! I won't be staying with a coward! May Michael's fate be on your head, Doctor. God have mercy on your cowardly heart!"

Twenty

Standing in front of the fifteen-foot-high wooden gates of Point Lookout Federal Prison, seventy-five or so angry, worried, disgruntled visitors waited hopefully for news of their loved ones. Assistant Provost Marshall Major General Benjamin Butler had ordered his men to answer the pleas.

"Look, folks," a young lieutenant shouted above loud grumblings and angry shouts from the crowd, "no visitors are allowed inside—period."

The noise from the crowd escalated.

"If you will all line up at that table over there and wait your turn, we can check the log for any particular prisoner you're searching for."

In spite of the blistering heat, the weary seekers obeyed, forming a long line. Sally Stearns was among them; she scanned the barren yet beautiful peninsula of St. Mary's County, Maryland, as she clutched her four-month-old son and a worn satchel. Although an army canopy shaded the table, none of the shade reached the visitors. One by one, the travelers relayed the name of their loved one to the old sergeant. They anxiously waited as he flipped the sheets of paper, checking his list.

"Watch him," an old man in line whispered. "If he points to the left, toward the Provost Marshall's office, someone is safe within the compound. If he points to the right, toward the parson standing on the steps of that makeshift chapel, someone's loved one is dead." The direction the elderly sergeant pointed was an ominous gesture of judgment.

Carrying her baby boy in this stifling heat was more than Sally could bear. Flushed, she fanned herself, hoping that she wouldn't faint. "You okay, miss?" A thin private stepped through the crowd and put his arms around her waist just as Sally's knees went limp. "Let me help you find a seat."

"Thank you," she managed to whisper, grateful for his act of kindness. He supported her until they reached the tent canopy and seated her beside the sergeant. Each time the officer raised his hand and pointed, her heart skipped a beat.

The old man who had spoken earlier smiled and eagerly walked over to the guards standing in front of the provost office. "I've got cash in hand, and I'm hopin' to buy supplies for my brother," Sally heard him explain.

A woman cried out, "Oh no, not my son! They told me he was here … they told me he was here …"

Left. Another smile.

Left. Another sigh of relief.

Right. The sergeant never even looked up.

Left again. Another relieved traveler.

Sally watched the drama with an almost morbid fascination. The expressions on the visitors' faces ranged from terrified to confident as they drew closer to knowing the fate of their loved ones.

The young private soon returned with a glass of lukewarm water. "Here, miss, this is the best I can do. It's so hot out today that it's really not safe for you and your baby to be here."

"Thank you," Sally replied anxiously. Now that the line had been dispersed, she alone remained.

The old sergeant finally turned to Sally; she was the only person keeping him from returning to the officers' quarters and escaping the midday heat. "What name are you looking for?" he asked.

"Billy—Billy Gibson."

"What unit?"

"Unit? I'm not sure what you mean by …"

He interrupted her, "Then where was he captured?"

"Gettysburg."

As the sergeant scanned the prisoner logs, the gates on the smaller compound creaked open. Two ambulance wagons and a gravediggers' detail began the slow walk to the prisoner cemetery on the sandy banks of the Chesapeake Bay. Sally closed her eyes tightly and prayed, *God, please don't let this gruesome scene be an omen.*

"Don't see no Billy Gibson, Miss," the sergeant responded, snapping his book closed and walking away without another word.

Shocked, Sally finally managed to sputter, "What does that mean?" She looked over at the kind young private. "Please, sir, what does that mean?"

"It doesn't mean anything, ma'am," he replied, giving the sergeant's back a harsh look. "Didn't you say he was captured at Gettysburg?"

"Yes," Sally replied as a faint glimmer of hope returned. "Yes, he was probably among the last prisoners to arrive from Gettysburg. He was wounded and couldn't be transported right away."

"Miss, stay here for a minute. I'll be right back." The private walked over to the provost office, deliberately passing the slow-moving sergeant. He returned, reading a slip of paper. "Billy Gibson, Mississippi's Barksdale brigade. Is that right, ma'am?"

"Yes, Billy Gibson. He is from Mississippi."

The private smiled, "He's safe, miss. Must be one lucky guy."

"What do you mean?"

"Well, not only does he got a fine wife and baby, but also he was one of the last prisoners exchanged last fall. General Grant doesn't allow prisoner exchanges anymore."

"Exchanged? Where did he go? Can you tell me how to find him?"

"No, ma'am, but he was exchanged in Richmond about ten months ago. I guess he could be anywhere by now, probably back with his unit."

"Do you know where that might be?"

"Yes, Ma'am," visibly uncomfortable, the private rubbed the back of his neck and struggled with a gentle way to tell her. Finally, he replied, "Miss, what's *left* of General Lee's army is camped not too far from Richmond. I'd start looking there."

• • • • •

Attorney Steven Billings rubbed his fatigued eyes, took another large gulp of coffee, and continued recording his weekly report to Secretary of War Edward M. Stanton—a mindless task. The squeaky door to his office, now located in Harper's Ferry, opened and the courthouse's postal courier stepped inside to deliver a dispatch. Steven smiled, nodded, then tore open the envelope. His pleasant expression faded. Because of new assaults on the city, government officials, clerks, and supply wagons were ordered to retreat into Maryland, where they would be protected by Major General Lew Wallace, the dispatch informed him.

Not again! This is the second time in six weeks we've been ordered to evacuate the city. How can they possibly expect me to finish this backlog of malfeasance cases amid such turmoil?

Standing and arching his back, Steven gazed out the shattered window at the high bluffs just beyond the B&O Rail Station. This was an astonishing sight for someone who had rarely ventured beyond Pennsylvania's soil. The Blue Ridge Mountains painted a dramatic backdrop for a landscape that had suffered grievous devastation from the war. As far as the eye could see, the land was littered with destroyed buildings, massive piles of burning debris, broken railroad trusses, abandoned and burned-out remains of armaments, and splintered wagons.

Before the hour was up, Steven and thirty-five other clerks and officials had loaded trunks containing their files onto wagon beds and climbed into carriages clutching satchels holding important papers. The caravan hadn't managed to get five miles down the rutted road before they were surrounded by fast-moving Confederate forces. They were easily apprehended.

"Surrender immediately or you'll be shot," the Confederate captain ordered.

Two Union officials reached for pistols and were killed instantly.

"Anyone else doubt my word?" the captain shouted.

No one did.

A small cavalry detail escorted the remaining prisoners back across the valley, while General Early continued his march through Maryland on his way to Washington.

· · · · ·

Two weeks later, Steven and hundreds of other prisoners were offloaded onto the platform of the Virginia Central Railroad near Capitol Square in Richmond.

"Okay, Yanks, fall out over yonder—where them troops is waiting!"

He must be a Confederate officer, Steven thought, *but he has no uniform or rank insignia, just that artillerist cap.* Surveying his new surroundings, Steven assembled with the others in the appropriate place, over yonder. The masses of people were unlike anything he'd ever imagined. Poverty, starvation, and a thick atmosphere of depression filled Richmond's Capitol Square. The harsh conditions of the city concerned him. *If people here live on the verge of ruin, how much more will the prisoners be forced to endure?*

Sergeant Pirou and his Zouaves rode hard into the square, followed by two transport wagons. A dust cloud covered refugees and soldiers alike. "These boys, where do they go?" Pirou asked.

One of the two young troopers nearby replied, "We was told to take Yank officers and government folks and such over to Libby Prison, but the prison refused the last bunch. Said they ain't got no more room until some more Yanks die."

Pirou considered the prize. Thirty-five Yankee officers might be forced to give up some real treasures.

"Belle Isle ain't taking no more Yanks neither. Last bunch was held up this morning over at the warehouses on Front Street, but Lord knows that place ain't fit for even the likes of these Yanks."

"We'll take 'em. Load 'em up," Pirou waved his arm for the wagons to pull forward and begin loading. Steven, at the head of the pack, obeyed the orders to climb aboard. The other prisoners quickly followed his lead.

The young guard looked confused. "Sergeant, I was told yesterday that Bedlam South is full. Said y'all weren't taking no more prisoners, only retards and wounded men."

"We could shoot these men—then they'd be wounded," one of the other horsemen with red trousers suggested without skipping a beat.

"Naw, Sergeant," the trooper grimaced at the thought, "that ain't what I meant."

Pirou smiled and turned his horse back toward the east. The others followed suit. The fully loaded wagons creaked and turned in the square, scattering nearby refugees. More dust clouds filled the air.

"Was full," Pirou shouted over his shoulder, "but I 'spect more Yanks'll die tonight 'n' make room for these boys!"

Twenty-One

Ever since Ana's last visit to Wingate, Enan McGinnis and Thomas O'Malley rarely let Joseph out of their sight. Lost in a sea of sorrow and self-pity, his drinking and drug usage increased; he was a shadow of his former self, no longer the meticulously dressed man they had grown to respect. Fearing a suicide attempt, the apothecary refused Joseph access to medications unless O'Malley was present with him.

Leaving O'Malley behind him, Joseph wandered toward the patients' wing. His only remaining comfort was the thought that he might do his patients some good. "Among madmen, I find my only comfort," he mumbled as he shuffled along.

By order of Captain Percy, construction work crews, comprised mostly of cripples and mildly afflicted nostalgia patients, were busy adding rooms onto the east wing of Wingate Asylum. When completed, Percy planned to seal off the west-wing from outside influences, including the east-wing staff, O'Malley overheard one Zouave tell another.

Even though the doctor knew of Percy's plan to torture patients, he had lost his will to fight. His days were spent mourning the loss of Ana and any hope of future happiness. His nights were spent restlessly dozing in his office chair, dreaming of the day he would slowly choke the life from Captain Percy. Torture, long painful torment, was the only suitable way to kill the man Joseph now blamed for every failure in his life.

"Top o' the mornin', Doc," Enan McGinnis stood in the doorway of Joseph's office, letting the door swing open wide to allow the bright sunlight to penetrate the darkness.

"Enan, why wake me?" Joseph complained. "Please close the door. Leave me alone."

"Sorry, Doc, that just won't do." Enan walked over to the cot, pulled back the ragged blanket, and pulled Joseph upright.

"Thomas says he needs your help." Enan encouraged the doctor to change his shirt, but the effort was in vain. Joseph dressed in the same clothes he had worn all week. "Percy and the raiders have been gone two days, and Thomas found something in the cellar he thinks you need to come see."

Joseph wiped his face and ran his fingers through his oily, matted hair. "Don't you understand? I don't care what Thomas found. Whatever Percy is doing—for God's sake, let him do it."

"Aye, Doc," Enan helped him to his feet, "you're all busted up inside, but there's nothing so bad that it couldn't be worse. 'Sides, you're all the men got."

"I no longer believe it is possible to help these men. I can't even help myself."

"Blarney! We all be knowing your heart, Doc." Enan gently pushed him out the door and into the hallway.

"I need my medicine."

"Nope."

"Then get me a drink, Enan. Whiskey, I must have something."

"Nary a drop but coffee." Enan led Joseph down the foyer stairs and around the corner to the cellar's entrance. "For today, you're *my* patient. I swear, Doc, I believe you'd step over ten naked women to get at a pint!"

They descended the stairs together. Terrified, Enan quickly looked away from two men shackled to the wall, arms stretched high overhead with only the tips of their toes touching the floor. Moans and wails echoed throughout the narrow chamber. The stench of human waste was nauseating. To the handler's dismay, Joseph seemed callous and unaffected.

Enan pointed to the iron door leading into the isolation room. "Hey, Doc, what's back there?"

Percy's playground. "Now where is Thomas, and why the devil have you dragged me down here?"

"In room three, Doc," Thomas suddenly called out of the darkness. "Cover your nose 'n' come in."

Enan followed Thomas's instructions, but Joseph strolled into the room, believing nothing at this point could possibly affect him. He was wrong.

"My God!" Joseph exclaimed.

The stench and torturous, agonizing sights in therapy room three sent Enan back out to the hallway, gasping for air. In the middle of the room, the decomposing almost-naked body of Frederick Hutch, Joseph's childhood friend, was propped straight up and strapped to a large wooden chair. His head was enclosed in a wooden box secured by two straps around the back of the chair. His arms, wrists, chest, and leg were all securely bound with belt straps as well. A large bucket of water was stagnating next to the corpse; another bucket was situated directly beneath the seat. Disgusted and angry, Joseph leaned against the wall. Choking from the stench and the bile that had risen in his throat, he screamed, "Is there no end to Percy's madness?"

Handkerchief over his face, O'Malley waited several minutes for the doctor to regain his composure. "I ain't seen nothing like this, Doc."

Joseph replied in disgust, "Once again, Percy has revived an instrument of torture long ago forgotten: a tranquilizing chair."

"Huh?"

Joseph continued his explanation while he and O'Malley began the grisly task of removing Freddie's body. "More than one hundred years ago, Dr. Benjamin Rush suggested that immobilization would help equalize the blood flow to the body helping to heal mental illness … Hold his shoulders for a minute so I can remove this strap," Joseph worked swiftly, talking to take his mind off the grisly task as much as possible. "Percy added this bucket. A doctor might fill the bucket with cold or hot water to assist the patient in regaining his sense through non-intrusive, hydro-shock therapy."

Joseph and O'Malley carried the decaying body to the hall-way. Enan began wrapping the corpse in a thick fabric, while O'Malley sprinkled it with lime to cover the stench.

O'Malley said grimly, "Apologies, Doc, about your friend 'n' all." He and Enan carried the corpse up the stairs and out to the cemetery on the west lawn. Joseph followed closely behind.

"Thank you, Thomas, and you as well, Enan. I'm sorry that I've lost sight of what I need to do … of God's reason for me being here. And I'm sorry for the incredible burden I've placed on both of you."

"Do you think Percy did this because Colonel Hutch was your friend?" Enan asked, wondering about his own personal safety.

· · · · ·

An early autumn brought much-needed relief from the swelter-ing heat in the trenches south of Petersburg. Grant's half-hearted assaults were easily beaten back by a desperate Robert E. Lee, his well-concealed Rebels, and their excellent defensive positions.

"They ain't got too much fight left in them, do they, Daniel?" Zeke asked, as they watched yet another Federal assault end in retreat.

"They're beat down in mind and body. The Yanks must have lost their spirit—and I shouldn't wonder. They've lost more men in the last few months than they have in the whole war."

"Our boys seem to be holding up pretty good, but these trenches sure are getting old fast," Zeke said. The men were living in huge dug-out trenches that snaked across the countryside for miles, just deep enough to walk in a crouched position and not be picked off by enemy sharpshooters.

"Daniel, why do they bomb the town knowing we ain't in there?" Zeke asked during the middle of an artillery barrage. "They even hit a little ol' church in Petersburg during a Sunday morning service! What kind of animal does that?"

"They do it because they can—and because they want us to know that they can. That General Grant is something else. Like a mean old bulldog, he refuses to quit."

"But you said the other day it looked like they were beat down."

"I did say that, but they seem to keep getting back up. They have so many men, unlimited supplies, and a general who will not stop, no matter the cost of human lives," Daniel replied. 'In one sense, I admire that man."

"What's that? I thought you hated him! Said he was a butcher. What changed your mind?" Zeke demanded to know.

"His tenacity."

"His what?"

"Tenacity means a ferocious drive, stopping at nothing until his goal has been achieved. I hate the way he sacrifices his men, but I do admire his tenacity."

"Sounds like a couple of hens cackling over here! What y'all carrying on about?" Skeeter asked as he crawled up.

"Just talking about Grant, that's all," Zeke answered.

Skeeter put in confidently, "Grant's done got a gutful of Bobby Lee. He whooped all them other generals out west, but it's different here. Lee's boys don't run."

"We might not run, but we have to eat, and we need ammunition. It looks like Grant is trying to cut off our supply lines and starve us out. This could be Vicksburg all over again," Daniel admitted.

· · · · ·

Desperate for manpower, the Confederate government began conscripting recruits for the Petersburg trenches, relying upon veteran soldiers for on-the-job training. One humid night just after dark, Zeke's regiment received thirteen reluctant warriors.

Sergeant Cawley welcomed these men in his usual loving way. "You new scumbags split up. No two of y'all together. Keep an eye on 'em, boys. They don't want to be here, so they'll probably run when they get a chance."

One of the new recruits was a young Irish man. Skeeter greeted him with a grin, "Welcome to the war, boy. Betcha can't wait to run off?"

"Got no plans to run. Didn't ask to be here, that's the Lord's truth, but here I am. You won't see the likes o' Michael Dougall running like a bloody coward!"

"Calm down, fellow, we're on the same side," Daniel said, in his fatherly tone.

"Then tell your fellas not to be calling me a bloody coward," Michael shot back.

"Didn't mean no harm. Reckon we got off on the wrong foot," Skeeter apologized. He leaned over, shook Michael's hand, and introduced himself. Zeke and Daniel did the same. The trenches were too dangerous already, without having enemies sitting right next to them.

"Forgive me, lads. I've been torn away from me family 'n' told to kill men that's done me or mine no harm. Been in this country only little more than a year now. Stranger in a strange land, that's me," Michael replied.

"You can be at ease with us, son," Daniel assured him. The tension subsided. Michael kept them entertained with his funny accent as he told stories of Ireland and the journey over. Michael and Zeke spent many nights drinking hooch and sharing stories.

• • • • •

Company C's brigade was sent as reinforcements to the battle of Cedar Creek. There they attacked Sheridan's army one foggy morning and helped drive the Union forces from the field. Michael Dougall fought bravely in his first combat, and his determination did not go unnoticed.

"You seemed to enjoy yourself today, there *Red*," Skeeter joked, using Michael's new nickname. "Was yah scared?"

"Not a-tall. I just pictured them Yanks to be Englishmen I was a blowin' to bits. Lord, how I hate the bloody English," Michael confessed with a grin.

"We didn't blow away enough of the Yanks," Zeke said, exhausted, as he stretched out on his blanket, looking up at a full moon on a clear night. "They kicked our butts today."

"They have over forty thousand men; we have twenty thousand men. Do the math and you tell me who will win," Daniel warned in a quiet voice.

"We've always been outnumbered," Zeke said like a true veteran.

"Not like this. Never like this. Grant gets stronger every battle. He's able to field increasing numbers of men, while our ranks grow smaller by the day."

Skeeter grinned. "I don't care how many men they got. We got Billy Lee."

"Hopefully, General Lee can keep this army alive and dangerous, at least until the presidential elections have been decided," Daniel said, echoing the hope of all the South.

· · · · ·

The artillery fire in the trenches around Richmond and Petersburg seemed endless, as did the sharpshooters' barrages. Michael's recklessness almost cost him his life more than once.

"Get down, Michael!" Zeke hollered.

"If it be me time to depart, then let that be the end of it. I'm not afraid to die. 'Tis a bloody miracle I've lived this long."

"Never flirt with death, Michael. You'll eventually lose—and you may take one of us with you," Daniel warned as he ducked behind a nearby tree.

"Me whole life's been a dance with death. Seen hundreds of women and children starved to death back in Ireland in the famine, kinfolks and others I knew all me life. They'd just lie down and die from hunger. Nothing you could do for 'em." He spun to take a shot at the Yankee who was shooting at him.

"What about your folks and your sister back in Richmond?"

Zeke hollered again, scurrying for cover under the brush.

"Aye, you be right, Zeke. They deserve me best effort." Michael dove across the open space to join Zeke.

"We all done seen folks die, kinfolks and friends alike," Skeeter added. "But that don't mean we is trying to get ourselves killed."

The four men made a run back to the trenches again.

"Pass that hooch, Skeeter, 'n' get off me back. You all made your point. I'll be more careful. 'Tis nice to know you boys care enough to fuss."

"Daniel," Zeke confessed one day, "I'm trying my best to be a good soldier, but I'm sick of the trenches, sick of death, and sick and tired of being hungry and homesick."

"Focus on something positive," Daniel insisted, putting his hand on the boy's shoulder.

The company's one benefit from being stationed outside Richmond was the steady flow of mail, so Zeke thought about the letters he had written and received from his mother and Katherine. "Hey! Listen to this!" he urged Michael one day. "Katherine wrote: 'I am so proud of you, Zeke. Please stay alive and come home to me. I love you so! Hugs and kisses, Katherine.'" As he reread her latest letter one crisp autumn afternoon, tears filled his eyes.

Daniel tried to comfort his young friend, "This will all be over soon, Zeke. Then you and Katherine will have a long, prosperous life together, regardless of who wins this war."

"I hope you're right. I gotta tell you, Daniel, when I first got here and got to be with Billy in this great army, I was as happy as I'd ever been in my life, but after Gettysburg and losing him, then Nate, and now day after day rotting in these stinking trenches, I ain't that crazy about the army like I was."

"That's understandable, son, but you're doing an admirable job as a soldier."

"Thanks, but I'm sick of it all! Stonewall Jackson is dead. Jeb Stuart is dead. Longstreet was almost killed. General Hood has lost an arm and a leg. Looks like we're all gonna be dead before it's over."

"That's enough!" Sergeant Cawley barked, emerging from behind a nearby tree. "You sound like you're ready to quit, Private Gibson. What would Billy or your pa think if they heard you talk like that?"

"I was just thinking out loud, Sergeant. 'Sides, I ain't going nowhere until this is all over. Reckon there's still a lotta Yankees that needs killing."

"That's more like it, boy. Now you sound like a Gibson," Cawley replied, slapping him on the back.

Daniel fumed, more to himself than others. "Two months ago, Lincoln didn't have a prayer for re-election. Now there's a good chance he will be."

"Pardon the interruption, Daniel. But could you tell me why you don't want that Lincoln fella being president?" Michael asked.

"If Lincoln wins, then the war will go on until we are defeated. We cannot last another four years. If Lincoln loses the election, the Confederacy has a chance of negotiating peace."

"General Lee's done miracles before," Zeke replied, "so maybe he can do it again."

Twenty-Two

"Bryarly!" Captain Percy shouted from the second-floor balcony, spotting Joseph about to leave through the asylum's front door. The doctor turned slowly, forcing himself to suppress the rage and contempt he felt for that man.

"Yes, *Captain*?" Having again taken up the fight, Joseph answered sharply. "What do you want?"

"Get them retards out of the west wing and take the malingerers with them."

"And where do you propose I house those men? There are at least fifty mentally ill patients in that west wing, and the east wing is already dangerously over capacity."

"I don't care what you do with them. If you ain't got room, let the retards loose in the woods and shoot the rest."

"I'll do no such thing, Percy!"

Percy sneered, "Like I said, Doc, I don't care what you do with them. But come sundown, any retards or malingerers left in the west wing, Yank or Rebel, will be given to Sergeant Pirou. He'll show you how to empty some beds in a hurry. Hell, he'll even help you make room for some more of your beloved retards!"

I'll kill that man one day, Joseph vowed for the thousandth time, as he dropped his bag at the front door, walked across the foyer, and strode down the hallway leading into the east wing.

Thomas O'Malley sat in the former music room of the mansion talking with the sixteen new handlers Joseph had recently recruited from among the nostalgia patients. Using a combination of medication and talk therapy, the doctor had witnessed instances of remarkable recovery, and he felt that the men could return to a form of employment, still performing a valuable service to the Confederacy. He had been open with his patients about his own battle with alcohol and drug abuse. "I think these men can understand the doctor's suffering, and he theirs," O'Malley speculated with Ewan. "I think all them are clinging to their sanity and to the hope of someday returning home." Ewan nodded.

"Good morning, gentlemen," Joseph walked into the room and wearily took the seat opposite Thomas O'Malley.

"Ain't you supposed to be leaving for Richmond?" O'Malley asked. "Percy stop ya?"

"It appears the west-wing addition is complete, and Percy wants all the mentally ill men to be removed … *today*."

"Today, Doc?" repeated a short, pot-bellied man wearing frayed trousers and a tattered shirt. "How we gonna move so many folks? Where are we expected to put 'em?"

"I know it will be difficult, Jeremiah, but if we don't accommodate these men, Percy will evacuate them in his own way—and we don't want that."

"Reckon we'd better get going, then," Jeremiah said. He and the other new handlers left the music room, heading for the west wing.

Allowing them to walk away out of hearing distance, O'Malley stopped Joseph. "Are you all right this morning, Doc?" The concern on O'Malley's face was genuine. "Looked in on you last night. Another nightmare?"

Joseph nodded.

"From the looks of things, your treatments ain't helping. Maybe it's time to think o' something else."

"I understand your objections to my medications, Thomas," Joseph said, putting his hand on O'Malley's shoulder, guiding him gently toward the west wing. "I offer no excuses for my occasional over-indulgence."

O'Malley gave Joseph a stern, disapproving look.

"All right then. My daily drunkenness for the past two months." Now O'Malley nodded in agreement and they both grinned. "Thomas, my heart aches for Ana every day."

"You be always telling the men not to give up hope," O'Malley reminded him.

"I do believe there is hope for these men," Joseph hung his head, saying, "but I no longer believe there is any hope for me."

Nine hours later, Joseph and the handlers finished moving the fifty-two mentally ill patients out of the west-wing prisoner wards. The doctor also interviewed nearly a hundred men claiming to suffer from mental illness in the hopes of being removed from the west wing. They knew their chances of survival would improve dramatically if they could escape the Zouaves' brutal treatment.

Joseph peered into Percy's new addition on the west wing. The large room, perhaps fifty yards long, had no provisions for the comfort and hygiene of the inmates. *No surprises here*, Joseph thought. In the back of the room, five massive wooden doors lined the wall, heavy padlocks on each. There were few windows.

"I don't think you want to go in there, Doctor," a raspy but refined voice spoke.

Startled, Joseph blurted out, "Who are you?"

He saw that the speaker's jaw was swollen, undoubtedly from his most recent encounter with Pirou. The man spoke with an effort. "My name is Steven Billings. I'm an attorney for the Army of the Potomac."

Joseph gazed at the man silently for a moment. Steven's torn and tattered uniform reeked. His bruised face and lacerated shoulder told an all too common story of abuse.

"I see you've suffered at the hands of the Zouaves."

"Nasty fellas, red trousers and a fondness for assault?" Steven managed a faint smile, but only for a moment. He nodded.

"Tell me, sir. How does an attorney end up in a hellhole like this?"

"I arrived two weeks ago, along with thirty-four other Union officers captured at Harper's Ferry," Steven replied as moans echoed down the hallway.

Joseph counted the men chained with Steven. *Only twenty-six officers remain. The rest will probably disappear soon as well.* His countenance fell just thinking about so many officers at the mercy of Captain Percy. He drew nearer to Steven and whispered, "How did you know my name?"

"I worked at a hospital for soldiers with mind illnesses once. The doctor there, Da Costa, spoke of your work, and I recognized your name when I got here." Steven tried to continue, but his throat was so dry he had to stop talking for a moment. "In this place, you're a legend. A cross between hero and angel of mercy."

"Actually, I am neither—far from them."

"In a place so horrible, any ray of hope, any man who truly cares for his fellow man, Confederate or Union, deserves that reputation."

The doctor shrugged.

Fearing this might be his only chance to improve his circumstances, Steven asked, "Why are you here in the prisoner ward? Perhaps Providence sent you? Is there a chance you can help me?"

"I was ordered to remove the mentally ill from among the prisoners."

"Trying to distinguish madness, malingerers, and malfeasance among this chaos seems an impossible task."

Joseph's curiosity was piqued. "You sound as though you speak from personal experience. How is it that an attorney knows the difference between pretense and true mental illness?"

"I'm no authority," he coughed, "but I've studied diseases of the heart caused by battlefield trauma. Most of the soldiers I've defended have suffered from one form of nostalgia or another," Steven glanced around timidly and mused, "but I must admit, my fascination with mental illness is growing."

The doctor glanced at the padlocked doors.

Steven stared over his shoulder and whispered, "Dozens of men, Union and Confederate, have been dragged behind those wooden doors by those Cajun guards. I've never seen one of them return." Continuing after he caught his breath, Steven spoke barely above a whisper. "The men have a nickname for those massive doors ... 'The Gates of Hell.'"

Joseph stared at the doors, opened his mouth, then remained silent. He nodded and turned to leave. Something about Steven convinced the doctor that this young lawyer could help him in his fight against Captain Percy. *If I leave this man here, he will be dead by the end of the week and, although I cannot save them all, perhaps I can save this one.* He stopped moving and looked around the room at the desperate faces of men who feared for their lives.

"Jeremiah!"

"Yes, sir?"

"Please unlock this man's shackles and take him to the east wing, first floor. Put him at the far end of the hallway, next to the storage locker that houses Private Wright."

"But, Doc," Jeremiah objected, "Captain Percy said we can't take no officers—retarded or not."

"I understand, Jeremiah," he gently commanded, "so get him some civilian clothes—quickly—and put him next to Albert Wright."

Joseph turned to Steven. "You'll be safe next to Albert. Everyone in the hospital, including every Cajun, is scared to death of that enormous black man."

Shackles removed, Steven quickly shed his uniform and donned a long, tattered nightshirt. Pleas and muttering broke out amongst the other Union officers. "I promise that I will do my very best for all of you," the doctor said, warning, "but we'll have to move one man at a time." He left quickly, before he could see the anguish in one more pair of eyes.

Relief washed through Steven. "Thank you! Thank you, Doctor Bryarly! I'll never forget this act of kindness, I promise you. I will one day repay this debt."

As Joseph hurried the attorney to his new quarters, he added, "For your own safety, try not to bother Private Wright. Albert does not *play well* with others!"

• • • • •

Captain Hurdle made an unexpected and unwelcome visit to the three Mississippi soldiers in the city jail. He was full of energy and eager to resume the fight business.

"Hello, Billy Boy. It's good to see you. How are the hands?"

"*Lovely*, just *lovely*. We'd begun to think that you'd forgotten us."

"Still full of piss and vinegar, eh, boy? That's what I like about you."

"Well, I haven't found anything I like about you, *Captain*."

Ignoring the insult, Hurdle said, "Now, are you ready for some action? You've gotta be bored to death in here. The war should calm down during the winter months, which means I won't be working around the clock. I'll have more time to put together a fight or two when the time's right."

"I'm ready for some action, but it's the kind of action where I kill Yankees, not sit around killing time. Let me remind you, our army needs every soldier it can get."

"We've been over this before, so I won't waste my breath again."

"Say, Cap'n, don't mean to interrupt, but ... uh ... well, we ain't had no whores in here for three weeks," Luther said hesitantly.

Hurdle burst out laughing, "The whores of Richmond have been busy, Luther, with them refugees swarming in like cockroaches. But I'll see what I can do."

Sam tried his luck as well. "Cap'n, sir, we're outta whiskey and there ain't been much food neither. Billy here can't fight good if he ain't fed good."

Hurdle confronted his guards angrily, then turned and said sincerely, "My apologies, men. We had a deal, and these men let down their end. It *won't* happen again. You'll have all the food, whiskey, and women you want, as long as Billy Boy keeps winning."

"Can you keep us better supplied with newspapers, too, Captain?" Billy asked, knowing he was pushing their luck.

"Now that wasn't part of our deal, but I'll think on it."

"The war news'll get me in a fighting frame of mind. Captain, that's why it's so hard to sit here and do nothing to help our cause. You remember we're on the same side?"

"Three soldiers will not make or break our beloved cause even if you're *half* as good at soldiering as you are at prizefighting."

"If I'm a prizefighter, then why ain't I getting any of the prize?"

"Your prize is all the food, whiskey, and women you want, plus not rotting away in a regular prison somewhere."

Hurdle turned to leave, slamming the guard Luther called Butt-face against the wall as he exited.

That evening, a large basket of food and a case of sour mash whiskey were delivered to their door by the grim-faced guard. "Thank you kindly … *Butt-face*. Mighty nice of yah," Luther said with a huge grin, as he opened the case of whiskey. The guard was a soft, chubby fellow with pale features and scattered acne across his big round face. "Say, *Butt-face*, ain't seen your momma and lil sis in here for a spell. Ain't nothing ailing them, I hope?" Luther and Sam roared in laughter. Billy grinned, shaking his head at Luther's antics.

The man was furious. He turned quickly to get in Luther's face, ready to put an end to the insults. Glancing to his left, he spotted Billy standing there, and he froze. Anger gave way to sound reason. He backed away slowly, knowing the slightest mistake could cost him his life—or at least a few teeth. He never took his eyes off Billy until he was out of the room.

Sam started laughing, patting Billy on the back. "I told you, them provost guards are plumb scared to death of you. I believe old Butt-face would have messed in his pants if you'd come at him."

"Their fear of me might come in handy, if we was ever to try to make a break for it, you know."

"Don't start with that," Sam warned.

Minutes later, the door swung open. Three streetwalkers, drunk and ready for business, had arrived. Luther and Sam squealed like schoolboys, whooping and hollering, groping the ladies without so much as an introduction.

"Come on, won't you have a good time for once?" Sam pleaded.

"No thanks," Billy said, turning to the third lady cuddling up beside him. "I'm spoken for."

"That's okay, Cap'n Hurdle done paid us anyway. We can just sit 'n' talk if you want to, sugar."

Billy started to tell her to get lost, but he suddenly noticed how she resembled Sally, with the same build, big blue-green eyes, and coloring. He stared for a moment, not sure how to respond to her offer. It had been a long time since he had carried on a civil conversation with a woman.

"It's been a while since I talked to a female," he replied, taking her hand, "but let's go into the other room. These boys ain't got no modesty, and things are about to heat up out here." They walked into the small side room, formerly a broom closet, and sat down.

"I'm Lucy."

"Billy. Billy Gibson."

"Well, Billy-Billy," she said laughing, "tell me your story."

He hesitated, then for some unknown reason he opened up his heart to Lucy. He told her all about his family and home back in Mississippi, and how he longed to see Sally once again. He told her that ten thousand times he had wished for a way to write her, but that Captain Hurdle refused the three men contact with the outside world. By the night's end, he had said more to Lucy than he had in the past six months to Sam and Luther. Whatever the reason, she just sat, smiling and listening quietly, as he described the woman who haunted his dreams. She never spoke until he finished. "Where's Sally now?"

"Still in Gettysburg, I guess."

"She's a lucky girl to have such a handsome, faithful man like you," Lucy said with a smile and touch of envy in her voice.

"I just hope she's safe. They carted me off with not so much as a good-bye. We had so little time together. I even wonder if she still loves me."

"I'll bet she's waiting on her Johnny Reb to come get her as soon as the war's over."

Several days later, the guards told the three men that there would be no newspapers, but they did report that what was left of Longstreet's Corps had dug themselves into trenches just to the east of Richmond, and that General Kershaw was in command, although Longstreet had recovered from his injury.

"O' course you knew that Abraham Lincoln had been re-elected," the guard continued. "We've got four more years of war, boys, unless them Yankees up and quit, which ain't likely with that slave-driver of a general."

"We ain't got a snowball's chance in hell of lasting four more years," Billy said in disgust. "Grant will be in Richmond before next summer."

•　•　•　•　•

New Year's Day 1865, frozen in the trenches east of Richmond, Zeke decided his situation couldn't possibly get any worse. He was perpetually shivering, nearly starving, and was bored senseless. Rarely, if ever, was he able to stand up straight, thanks to the watchful eyes of the Yankee sharpshooters. He, like every other soldier in Longstreet's corps, knew that their lines had been stretched to match the length of the overwhelming Union forces entrenched less than one hundred yards away. In between lay a no-man's land, with a huge crater blown into the land by aborted Yankee ingenuity as they tried to tunnel underground to the Confederate trenches, then blow them up. The pitted, stinking ground was littered with dead animals, skeletons of splintered trees, and battlefield refuse. The weak rays of the morning sun brought Zeke no comfort.

"Happy New Year, Skeeter," Zeke hollered down the line, sounding cynical.

"Thank you *kindly*. Hey, Michael, pass this jug down to Zeke and Dan'l." Skeeter held up his canteen as if to make a toast. "Join me in a drink, boys, to the Confederacy!" A mumbled, half-hearted response came from the shivering men within earshot.

Taking the jug from Skeeter, Michael Dougall stood tall and held the jug high above his head, shouting, "To wives 'n' lovers, may they never meet—and to the end o' this miserable war!" Cheers erupted from both sides of the battlefield, Federal and Confederate alike.

"Dougall!" Sergeant Cawley shouted. "You dang fool! Get your head down!"

Before Michael could duck, a bullet dropped him heavily into the trench. The minié ball had ripped into the base of Michael's neck and exited through his chest, leaving a gaping hole. Blood splashed against the walls of the trench.

"NO!" Zeke screamed hysterically, scrambling through the frozen mud toward Michael. "Oh, God, not again! Please God, not again!"

Zeke cradled Michael's body as Daniel tried valiantly to stop the gushing wound with rags. Within seconds, Skeeter scurried over to pour some whiskey into Michael's mouth and wipe his face with a muddy rag. Sergeant Cawley followed closely behind.

"Zeke," Michael coughed, gurgling as he tried to speak, "Oh bloody hell … Looks like … they done me in, lads."

"Dang thick-headed Irishman," Sergeant Cawley grumbled, rapidly blinking his eyes, fighting back the tears. "If I told you once, I told you a hundred times: keep your head down!"

"Zzzeke …" Michael, still clinging to Zeke's trembling hand, moaned barely above a whisper, "I'll be tellin' … the good Lord you been a good friend to me …" A weak smile spread across Michael's face as he gazed beyond this life. "Me brother's here now… Zeke, 'spect … I'll … be … goin' … home." His voice faded away.

Hours later, after the men of Company C had gathered around Michael's shallow grave, dug under cover of darkness, Sergeant Cawley asked curiously, "His brother?"

Zeke choked up yet again. "His older brother Patrick. Michael told me how he died during the potato famine back in Ireland. Reckon the brothers are back together now … I wonder if death is the only way I'll ever see my brother again?"

Zeke was still mourning the loss of his friend when a letter arrived from his mother. Daniel could tell by the look on Zeke's face that the news wasn't good.

"Pops has been wounded again … at the Battle of Nashville."

Almost afraid to ask, Daniel mumbled, "How is he?"

"Sounds like he blowed his shoulder up pretty good. Momma says he'll live, but the Doc don't think he'll ever be able to use his right arm again."

"Zeke, I am sorry …"

Zeke interrupted him, "We lost your boys, Billy, Nate, Michael, and almost lost Pops. Who's next? When will all this cussed killing stop? When will we get to go home?"

Daniel put his arm around Zeke. "That's up to God, not us. Our job is to do our duty and try to live with the results."

Twenty-Three

Deep in the recesses of her mind lay the memory of a day Mary Beth longed to forget. In the heart of a Louisiana bayou, in a back room of the small Mount Zion Baptist Church, four drunken and loathsome Union cavalrymen from Camp Parapet near New Orleans stood passing a bottle of bourbon, talking filthy, and anxiously waiting for their turns.

A young mulatto girl, with a torn dress and a bruised face, lay pinned to the floor. Physically and emotionally exhausted, her virginity and dignity stripped away, she was no longer able to scream and too weak to fight back. Blood trickled from between her legs and tears streamed silently down her face. Cold, lifeless eyes stared blankly at the ceiling.

"Hurry up, Mickey," one of the soldiers shouted. "I want a poke at her afore someone comes looking."

"Me, too. Hurry up, let's have at her."

"Is she white or black?" asked one of the drunken bystanders.

"Who cares?" came a quick answer. The drunks roared with laughter and bickered about whose turn it would be next.

At that instant, a dark-skinned heavyset man wearing overalls and wielding a frontier musket burst through the back door with his young teenage son in tow.

The man cried out in disbelief, "Mary Beth! Dear God! Mary Beth!" Roaring like a bull, he fired his musket, sending the man atop Mary Beth careening to the floor, dead.

"Papa, help me," Mary Beth whimpered, "p-p-please help me, Papa."

Shoving the boy and the huge man aside as he was reloading his musket, one of the panicked soldiers ran outside along Metairie Ridge through the church cemetery, stumbling over the tombstones. The young boy followed in hot pursuit. The obese cretin, his belly bulging below his uniform shirt and his pants hanging open, tripped and fell headlong into a gothic cement cross. Stunned and tangled in Spanish moss, he lay still for a moment, a mistake he would not live to regret.

He screamed just before his head snapped back and his throat was cut from ear to ear. Gurgling sounds poured from his mouth as Mary Beth's brother Rufus stood over the soldier, savoring the revenge—but only for a moment. A Union rifle shot rang out, striking the young boy squarely in the back of the head, hurtling him forward. His limp, dead body draped over the cross-shaped tombstone.

Mary Beth screamed when she heard the gunshot, struggling to free herself from beneath the body of the dead rapist. Her father, his face etched with horror and rage, snatched the cane blade from his belt and raced up to the shooter, slicing it across his chest in one swift blow. The two remaining soldiers savagely attacked the father, wrestling his massive frame to the ground. Overpowered and outnumbered, his thrashing body succumbed to the pounding blows and merciless stabbings. The men were stumbling through the graveyard when Mary Beth at last managed to free herself of her blue-coated burden.

"Rufus! O, God, no! Papa, Papa ... I need you, Papa ..." Mary Beth sobbed while trying to rouse his lifeless body. "Oh, Papa ..."

"Now what are we gonna do?" a panicked weasel of a man whined to another soldier as the cowards gathered in a group, leaving the sobbing Mary Beth next to the body of her dead father.

"Private, get that boy and put him on the front porch of the church," directed the tall cavalryman wearing a sergeant's coat. He shoved the reluctant private, forcing him to obey.

"You, boy, drag the bodies into the church—and you over there! Pour that coal oil on the church and the bodies!" The sergeant soaked Mary Beth as the men moved quickly to cover their sins. After throwing the oil onto the bodies, they lit an oil lamp and threw it onto the floor, where it crashed. As the fire spread rapidly, they left the church, running.

"No! Please God, no!" Mary Beth tried in vain to wipe the oil off her face before she could rush to the steps. "Rufus! Rufus! Please, Rufus, wake up!" She tugged and pulled, but was unable to drag her father and brother from the flames. The Union soldiers glanced back from the other end of the graveyard in time to see Mary Beth's dress catch fire. Black smoke filled her lungs and blurred her vision as she stumbled back, watching the fire consume the church.

· · · · ·

"No! God, help me!!" Mary Beth shouted at the top of her lungs, jerking straight up in bed and fumbling around in the darkness in a state of panic. The nightstand crashed to the floor before she finally managed to light the small lamp on the dresser near the bed.

"Oh, dear me! It's okay." Mary Beth tried to calm herself, scanning the room for familiar signs. "It's okay, Mary Beth, you're safe, you're safe."

"It ain't *okay*," protested Captain Percy groggily. "Now shut up." He sat up and looked at Mary Beth, mumbling, "Crazy whores, every one of 'em, just plain crazy."

The woman trembled all over, still terrified from her nightmare and disgusted with herself at the thought of lying in the same bed with the man she despised most in the world. She staggered over to a nearby chair, pulled on her dress, and laced her boots, all the time staring at her bag on the floor. Glistening in the glow of the lamp was a small palm-sized pistol. *Do it, Mary Beth,* she wrestled with her thoughts. *Take the gun and kill him.*

"You still here?" Percy rolled over and sat up, perched on the edge of the bed stark naked. He lit a cigar and began blowing smoke rings, "Well?"

"I'm leaving," she replied, tying her shoes. His bare stump of a left arm and the burn scars across his chest, neck, and torso revolted her more every time she saw them.

"I paid for the whole night. And I'm ready for more." Percy exposed his manhood.

"Here," Mary Beth took his money out of the bag, pausing to look at her reflection in the mirror. "Take your money, Percy. You disgust me." She threw his money at him and left.

Percy smiled and lit a cigar, "You'll be back. They always come back."

At the bottom of the staircase in the foyer of Wingate Manor, Mary Beth collided with Dr. Bryarly in the darkness, knocking them both backward. Joseph, drunk, was returning from another late-night raid of the drug room. Their eyes met for a moment. Mary Beth looked him up and down with obvious contempt; Joseph returned her contempt.

"You're up late tonight ... *Doctor.*" Mary Beth's cynicism did not go unnoticed.

"I suppose the *prostitute's* nights and days are interchangeable," Joseph muttered with slurred speech, "until the last customer is *satisfied*—and that one is never satisfied." He jerked his head in the direction of Percy's room. They glared at each other for a moment before Mary Beth's face softened.

"We aren't that different, you and I," she whispered.

"What could we possibly have in common, the *prostitute* and the *doctor*?" In a stupor, Joseph swayed back and forth, trying to maintain his balance.

Mary Beth grabbed his arm with both her hands to stop his fall, then guided him toward his room. "I see two hurting people trying to escape from a something we can't escape."

Joseph hung his head against the door jamb, whispering in a raspy voice, "Loneliness truly is a fate worse than death, isn't it, Mary Beth?"

· · · · ·

Awakening bright and early on Saturday morning, Joseph traveled through slush and half-frozen mud to the Shockoe Valley section of Richmond, more commonly known as Butcher Town. Here, refugees, European immigrants, and freed slaves made their living working at hospitals, prisons, and brothels. Joseph held a three-day-old copy of the *Richmond Examiner* in his hand open to an auction advertisement. He was looking for the familiar red flag of the auctioneer.

"Excuse me, sir," he addressed one of the countless transients roaming the streets, trying to stay warm. "Can you tell me where to find this address?" He pointed to an advertisement for an estate auction that promised hundreds of rare-edition books.

"Yeah, sure thing, fella." The stench from the filthy little man made Joseph's eyes water. The stranger pointed to a side street next to a seedy looking tavern, "Turn down Broad Street, then that little alley there on the right. It's the house right beside Jenna's Brothel. Just look for the red flag."

The auction was in full swing by the time Joseph arrived. Outside, huddled masses were starving for food and freezing for want of clothes. Inside, greedy patrons were gorging themselves on the spoils of war.

"Come now, folks," the caller barked, standing behind an elaborate dresser, draped with a handwoven European rug and gold-green bed tapestries. "Mr. Robert Dabney," motioning toward the auction proprietor, "has graciously agreed out of the kindness of his heart to donate ten percent of today's proceeds to help the Richmond Soup Association. So what do you say? What do I hear for this handsome bedroom collection?"

"Five hundred Confederate dollars for the entire lot," a shout came from the back.

"Six twenty-five," chimed another new bidder.

A moment of silence as the caller raised his hammer, "Six twenty-five once ... six twenty-five twice ..."

Suddenly, just before the hammer hit, "One thousand Confederate dollars!" shouted a white, weasel-like bidder. He and his companion, a small, middle-aged black man, were both dressed in expensive suits with floral waistcoats and lapels.

"I have a bid of one thousand, a worthy price for a *fine* gentleman, going once ... going twice ... sold!"

Scattered conversations rose from the crowd while the weasel and his friend shook hands vigorously. Lonely, Joseph walked around the once-impressive home, waiting for a chance to bid on the large collection of books. In a back parlor, he came upon a weary man cradling his sobbing wife, while two little children huddled close. Saddened by the spectacle, Joseph overheard the bright-eyed little girl anxiously ask, "What will we do now, Daddy?" Her father scooped her up in his arms, settling her on his knee. The boy, standing motionless, said nothing.

"Jessica, darlin'," her father said, brushing the hair from her tear-swollen eyes, trying bravely to convey hope to his family, "y'all don't need to worry none. Why, this afternoon, once this here auction's over, we're all gonna visit Uncle Jeremiah down south in Pine Bluff, Arkansas."

"How we gonna get so far? Doc said you weren't fit to travel." His son finally spoke, patting the bandage around the stump that used to hold his father's leg.

"We've paid a high price for this war," the man said, grief suddenly washing across his face. "Cold Harbor took my leg; the auctioneers are taking everything else." Remembering who his listeners were, he summoned his courage again. "Jacob, son, even with just one leg, I can still outrun y'all kids and your maw." He leaned over to kiss his wife.

Joseph was close enough to hear the wife whisper, "Jason, I'm so scared. What's going to happen to us? We've nothing left, and no way to leave this dreadful city."

Joseph spotted the books being moved to the table and joined the bidders in the main room. He won the bid, and paid a young attendant a few coins to carry the crated books to his wagon for the return trip to Bedlam South. The doctor lagged behind. Discreetly, he pulled the children's father aside, out of earshot of his family and the noise of the bidders.

"You got a great deal on those books," the man told him. "Some of them have been in my family for over a hundred years."

"Yes, sir," Joseph said. "I'll take good care of them, I assure you." Despite his efforts, his eyes filled with tears.

The man seemed genuinely concerned. "You okay, mister? Do you need some water? 'Cause water's about the only thing that I've got left."

Joseph shook his head. "All my life, I have dreamed and prayed for a family just like yours. Fate has chosen a different path for me, but I overheard your conversation, and I'd like to help."

He handed a large leather pouch to the family man. "This should be enough to finance your travels."

"Mister, I still have my pride—"

"And you also have a family that loves and needs you," Joseph told him, putting his hat on his head. "There should be well over two thousand dollars in Confederate currency. Take your family and escape from this horrible war."

"I've got no way to repay you."

Joseph's face gleamed with joy for the first time in a long time. "Knowing your children will survive this misery will be considered payment in full."

• • • • •

Several blocks away, Sally Stearns mingled on the platform of the Central Railroad Depot with thousands of soldiers and refugees. She was penniless. Looking around, she saw beggars, cripples, transients, and others filling every sidewalk and the entrances to nearby abandoned buildings. Beside her, hundreds of tobacco-crate coffins were stacked five high and ten deep along the dilapidated loading ramps, with hundreds more piled high under an open-air warehouse across the narrow side street. To the north, the silhouettes of gravedigger details were painted on the horizon.

Swept along by the uncaring masses, Sally was shoved against the stack of crates, unable to move. Clutching her nine-month-old son to her chest, Sally peered between the slats of a coffin, just inches from her face. The lifeless, clouded eyes of an unknown soldier stared back. She gasped in fear. A few travelers callously stepped around her, ignoring her distress. Terrified, she looked down Broad Street, and then down Seventeenth. Having no idea of where to begin her search for Billy, she threw herself into the teeming mass of people, compelled to escape from the lifeless eyes and the nauseating stench of death. *Finding Billy among all these people will take a miracle of God.* She had overheard one Confederate official on the train say that tens of thousands of soldiers passed over Richmond's streets every day.

"Get outta the way," a foul-mouthed drunk shouted, "or you're gonna get stomped to death."

Sally was frantic, trying to drag a heavy bag while clinging to her son. "I'm sorry. Please …" Shoved once again, stumbling, trying to regain her feet, she plaintively asked, "Someone please, help me!"

"Here ma'am, grab this."

A one-legged corporal leaned against the doorway and thrust his wooden crutch into the crowd. Sally grabbed the crutch and held on tightly as he pulled her out of traffic and under a burned-out storefront's awning. Her once-stunning features now reflected the full effects of a single woman with a young child roaming the war-torn South alone. Her weather-worn dress was nearly in rags, her shoes were tattered. Sally looked no different from the widows and orphans who had flooded the city, outnumbering the natives.

"What are y'all doing here?" he asked. Sally failed to hear him. "Ma'am?"

"Oh," startled, Sally turned. "I'm so sorry. Thank you for helping us."

"I said what are y'all doing here?"

"I am looking for … we are trying to find … my husband. Yes, I'm looking for my husband, Corporal Billy Gibson."

"Look around you, lady: dozens of corporals out there," he turned his head slowly toward the coffin warehouse, "and hundreds of corporals stacked up over yonder."

"Oh, my." Thirsty, hungry, and sick at heart, Sally fainted, collapsing onto a stack of rotten lumber beside her, her baby still in her arms. When she came to, her breathing was labored. She coughed and shook for almost twenty minutes. To his credit, the convalescent stayed by her side, holding her infant in one arm and using his crutch to block the doorway and protect Sally from being trampled. The only comfort he could offer was a canteen of water and a dirty cloth to cover her mouth and wipe sweat from her brow.

"Whatcha got?" he asked, this time with sympathy.

"Got?"

"What disease, ma'am? What ails you?"

Sally protested, "No, no, sir. I'm not sick. I'm simply weak from my journey. We've been traveling for months."

He nodded his head in agreement for her sake, but the disbelieving look on his face told another story. "Yes, ma'am, reckon I was wrong. Anyhow, if'n you hurry five blocks down Broad Street, there's a soup kitchen that might still be open. They'll help you on account of your child. Sometimes, one of the army's doctors even drops by."

"Thank you! My baby and I are hungry, but I assure you, I am not in need of a doctor." Sally somehow managed to stand to her feet. Her face and hands were still a chalky white.

"Yes, ma'am," he replied, removing his crutch from the doorway. "Like I said, it's five blocks down Broad Street," pointing with his crutch, "down thatta way."

· · · · ·

A young boy waving his arms caught Joseph's attention just as he was reaching for the reins to leave Butcher Town. The boy strained against the heavy bundle strapped over his shoulder. In his hand was today's edition of the *Richmond Examiner*.

"Paper, sir?"

"Yes, please," Joseph reached for his pouch and realized it was now on its way to Pine Bluff, Arkansas. He smiled at the thought, fumbled around in his pocket, and managed to retrieve two coins.

"Thank you, sir. Big list today of the fellas what died this week around Petersburg. Them Yanks keeps pouring it on our boys. What do you think, mister? Do you think we can hold 'em?"

When no reply came, the paperboy quickly walked away, flagging down another would-be customer.

Petersburg? Joseph was lost in thought. Suddenly his warm mood changed to apprehension, his heart sinking in his chest. Nervous fingers scanned the back page, which had been printed on old wallpaper, making it difficult to read. Joseph squinted, his eyes straining to read the alphabetical list of casualties:

Dexter, Richard—*no, Lord, please ...*

Dillard, Charles—*it can't be ...*

"Oh, no ..."

Joseph set the paper on the bench seat next to him, not willing to read the last name aloud: Dougall, Michael.

Oh, my Lord! Michael ... dead? It can't be. I must see Ana! But what can I say? What can I say now? I know she will blame me for Michael's death ...

Forcing his wagon through the crowds, Joseph slowly traveled down Broad Street, too grief-stricken to notice a struggling Sally Stearns near the C.R.R. Depot. Straining against the heavy load and the child on her hip, Sally looked up, hoping the man in the wagon would consider her plight and come to her aid.

"Sir, please, would you be so kind as to let us ride with you?"

No response from the distracted man. Joseph continued west and was soon out of sight. He never heard Sally's cry for help.

After crossing Shockoe Creek, Joseph's wagon was forced to stop. Dozens of police officers ran in all directions, chasing hundreds of young boys through the streets and back across the creek over Church Hill. None of these young warriors was more than thirteen years old. Several rough-looking boys, white, black, and Irish, wearing sackcloth and fresh bruises and trying to avoid arrest, ran past Joseph. Lagging well behind was a pot-bellied policeman, out of breath and no longer desiring the chase. He leaned against the wagon, chest heaving, gasping for air. Joseph watched the spectacle and waited for his unwelcome visitor to speak.

"Mister," still panting, the officer asked, "why didn't you jump out and help?"

"Wasn't any of my concern," he responded coldly.

"Riots is everybody's concern," the officer fumed, pointing in the distance to several young boys lying on the ground wounded and bleeding. Nearby, a mother cradled her young daughter, who had been injured by a flying rock. Her father knelt beside her, trying to stop the bleeding from the dangerous-looking head laceration. Innocent victims in the wrong place at the wrong time. "Tell them folks this ain't none of your business."

Humbled, Joseph spoke more kindly, "Officer, what happened here?"

"Another riot, a fight between the Butcher Cats and Hill Cats."

"Butcher Cats? Hill Cats? What you are talking about?"

"Two rival gangs with hundreds of young boys. Bloody fights all the time. Bricks, sticks, rocks, anything they can find to bash each others' brains in."

The seriousness of the situation was now apparent. Joseph jumped to the ground and walked to the family. "I'm a doctor. What can I do to help?"

An hour later, Joseph set out again. Circling Capitol Square, he drew the wagon to a stop as an entire battalion recruited from Winder and Jackson Hospital residents lined up for a drill along

Capitol Street. Although a battalion of patients was unusual, the sight that captured the attention of most onlookers was an entire company composed of Negroes willing to fight for the Confederacy.

Joseph pondered the sight. *I never considered that the Confederacy would be willing to create an entire company of Negroes to serve in the army. Is this an act of desperation or could it signify something more? The voluntary end to slavery?* The thought of ending slavery brought a grim smile to his face.

• • • • •

At the Dougall apartment, mourners gathered on the porch. A black wreath hung from the open front door. Grief and humiliation filled Joseph's heart as he made his way through the crowd and stood before the Dougall family, a family he once believed would be his forever.

"Ah, Joseph," Mrs. Dougall embraced him. Seeing her tears and hearing the weeping that filled the room overwhelmed the doctor. He, too, sobbed openly. The unconditional love of Mrs. Dougall caused him to feel even guiltier for Michael's death.

"I am so sorry—"

"'Twas the Lord that took Michael," she said, looking deeply into Joseph's eyes. "You need to know that. 'Twas the Lord's will. There be no one to blame."

"Mama! There be blame, no denying that," Ana objected as the room became deathly quiet. "I told you afore, *Doctor*, Michael's fate be on your head."

"Ana Laoise," Mr. Dougall scolded.

"I'll be saying what I feel. He betrayed us—he did!" Ana remained obstinate.

Joseph hung his head in humiliation. Without offering an explanation, he turned toward the front door, aware of the whispers all around him. Mr. Dougall followed him and embraced him.

"'Tis a sad day for the Dougall clan," Mr. Dougall consoled. "Breaks me heart. I want you to know, Joseph, that Michael loved you. 'T weren't nothing you could do to save 'im."

"Thank you …"

"Lost *two* sons today and I'll be grieving you both," Mr. Dougall said before walking back indoors to comfort his wife.

An expensively dressed businessman, cane in one hand and flowers in the other, stepped up to the porch and embraced Ana. After kissing her, he motioned toward Joseph. "Darling, who is that man? Why is he staring at us?"

Glancing, Ana saw Joseph standing in the street staring at her and her emerald eyes turned cold and empty. Her piercing glare penetrated deep into Joseph's soul. He understood now that she truly hated him. "He's a coward," she snarled, taking the man's arm and turning toward the door, "nothing but a bloody coward."

Twenty-Four

Bitterly cold weather was taking its toll on the Army of Northern Virginia. On the worst of nights, several hundred men deserted, desperate to make their way home to distressed families, and desperate to leave the carnage behind. Even the firing squads couldn't stop the exodus, although they did serve to wound the remaining soldiers' morale far more than starvation or frostbite ever could. Entire army battalions were drawn up at dawn, stomping their feet and muttering under their breath to witness the day's catch of deserters executed one by one. Daniel spat on the ground in disgust while watching an execution.

"Those poor men! I suspect many of them received letters from back home begging them to return and save their families. Now how are these brave soldiers rewarded? Butchered like dogs by the country they have been fighting for."

"Just don't seem right," Skeeter agreed. "It'd be tough knowing your wife 'n' kids was starving, your house burned down, and you was hundreds of miles away."

Zeke shuddered. "Guess we're lucky that our farms back home weren't in Sherman's way or they'd be burnt down, too. If Momma or Katherine was begging me to come home, I don't know if I would stay."

Surprisingly, Daniel agreed. "You're right, Zeke, we are lucky. Even though we've suffered our share of hardship, our homes and farms in Mississippi haven't been torched like those in Georgia."

"Them boys might'a been from Georgia, just trying to get home," Skeeter added sadly, cringing as the executed men were dumped into a shallow grave.

Desperate, the Confederate government had begun offering slaves their freedom in exchange for joining the fight. A few Southern loyalists predicted this would mark the end of the Confederacy, and many were outraged at the thought of arming the slaves. But, with the blessing of General Lee, the plan had been instituted.

Reading the paper, Daniel mused, "Did you hear the government has armed the slaves, Zeke? I guess President Davis worries that if they don't fight for us, then they'll probably fight against us. Either way, giving the slaves a chance at freedom is long overdue. Every man, white or black, should be able to fight for his freedom. That's the only reason I'm still fighting. After my boys were killed, I decided that freedom is the only thing worth dying for."

"Makes sense to me," Zeke replied. "From what I've heard, the Negroes fight almost as good as the veteran Yanks do. Guess we won't know what to expect until we get into a scrap. Can you imagine being a Yankee soldier fighting to free the slaves, and then, in the middle of a battle, look up and see ex-slaves in Confederate uniforms screaming the Rebels' yell and chargin' at you? Now that's funny! The men you're fighting to free would be trying to kill you."

"Y'all figuring too much. Making my head hurt something awful," Skeeter said as he reached for his canteen. "Wanna shot?" he asked.

For once, Daniel took the canteen and with a solemn look said, "Here's to our lost comrades. May God have mercy on their souls."

Opening his canteen, Zeke added, "And here's to General Lee and another miracle—because we're sure gonna need one."

• • • • •

Thomas O'Malley stopped walking, staring straight ahead in silence. His menacing look and piercing black eyes betrayed a dark Irish fury that few men had ever witnessed. A five-minute tirade that even the asylum patients were able to diagnose as psychotic had stirred the compromised residents. Melancholies were pulling out their hair while banging their heads, and maniacs were screaming obscenities while thrashing against iron cell doors. Terrified, any residents not confined quickly scattered as O'Malley approached them. No one took their eyes off him. Some even wondered if Doctor Bryarly himself wasn't one step away from madness.

Enan McGinnis went running for the doctor, who stopped his medical rounds immediately to race to his friend's side. He gently took Thomas's arm and guided him on a walk through the wards. Together, the two men completed a full loop without saying a word. In a soothing calm voice, Joseph spoke at last. "Thomas, could we please stop for a moment? I seem to have a cramp in my leg."

The doctor dropped onto the foot of the nearest cot, rubbing his hamstring and appearing unaffected by the drama around him. "Nice day for a walk, don't you think so, Thomas?"

No reply.

"If you don't mind," the doctor suggested, "let's walk through the west wing. We'll go scare the hell out of those patients for a while."

Everyone breathed a sigh of relief when the two men left the ward. The more the doctor walked and the quieter he talked, the more O'Malley's rage began to dissipate. As the men headed out onto the grounds, Joseph switched to jokes and finally saw rage give way to a smirk, and then the smirk grew into a smile that slowly spread across the Irishman's face. Joseph knew that the rage was masking an even deeper emotion: grief. When the men stopped beneath an oak tree, Joseph turned to the burly handler and spoke gently. "Thomas, we've been friends for over two years. I owe you my life. As your friend and a man who suffers an *occasional* bout with madness," O'Malley looked into Joseph's face for the first time, "tell me, my friend—who died?"

At first, O'Malley seemed shocked by the question, but tears betrayed his secret. Joseph had hit the mark. O'Malley retrieved a tear-soaked crumpled note from his pocket and handed it to the doctor, who recognized the handwriting as the same person who had written him in the past. The short note read:

Alastair Weller now resides with God. You can find his body in a shallow, unmarked grave, ten paces east of the cypress tree near the pond. **"Do not fear them, for there is nothing covered that will not be revealed, and nothing hidden that will not be made known."**

Matthew 10:26

Joseph had suspected that Alastair had been killed, but he, like so many others, had avoided the realization, hoping they would one day meet again. He pondered other losses: an ever-tightening noose around Richmond, the impending defeat of the Confederacy, Ana's love, and the death of Michael Dougall.

"Like a brother, he was … from the same little town in Ireland," O'Malley said, choking back the tears.

"Perhaps, Thomas, if I had not demanded his assistance …"

O'Malley shook his head. "He chose to help, none could deny that. 'Sides, ain't an Irishman alive what could be made to do something he didn't want to. This evil is Percy's doing. He'll be the one what pays blood for blood."

For long moments, Joseph relished the thought of Percy's judgment day. "Thomas, I know the pain of losing a dear friend," he said at last. He put his arm around O'Malley's broad shoulders and told him the story of Michael Dougall, accounting for his role in Michael's conscription and death.

"The Lord knows your heart, Doc. You save some and lose others."

"Thomas, do you really believe in God? Even in all of this misery?"

O'Malley nodded. "I believe in the sun when it's not shining. I believe in love even when I feel it not. And I believe in God ... even when he is silent."

After a few minutes of quiet reflection, O'Malley looked up and noticed the haggard look on the doctor's face and his weak, fragile appearance. "Still having trouble sleeping, Doc? 'Tis them nightmares, eh?"

"Yes, my friend, although not nearly as often as before. Actually, I'm encouraged. Exhausted," Joseph said, rubbing the back of his neck, "but encouraged nonetheless."

"Why?"

"Why? Well, I suppose I'm encouraged because, with less frequency, there is hope I could one day be free of these night terrors ... forever."

"Is it always the same dream?"

"Not before, but it is now. It's now a single dreadful vision that torments my soul." In vivid detail, Joseph recounted the recurring nightmare. "After a deep snow, the frigid wind howls through the wrought-iron gates of England's Bedlam Asylum. Icicles hang from windows and lampposts; a frozen pond lies nearby. Thrashing about in the courtyard are two friends, Joseph Bryarly and Forbred Lytton, locked in mortal combat, slashing, cutting, and relentlessly pounding one another in a life-and-death struggle. They battle despite exhaustion, each man realizing that to quit means certain death; only one man can survive."

When Joseph stopped speaking, O'Malley had many questions. "Did that really happen, Doc? Who is Forbred and why would you be fighting a friend to his death?"

"That answer could very well mean the difference between *sanity* and *madness* for me."

"Sounds like you better figure this one out."

"Yes, I agree. Until then," Joseph sighed, "the memory of a friend I left behind will continue to haunt my soul."

"Aye," O'Malley agreed and removed a half-pint flask from his pocket, offering a toast, "Here's to your coffin, Doc ... may it be built from a hundred-year-old oak tree, which I will plant first thing in the morning!"

• • • • •

In the city jail, a young guard removed his hat and wrung it in his hands. "You got a fight next Saturday," he told Billy, ignoring the two other men in the cell. He mumbled softly, "Captain told me to tell you that you're gonna lose this fight."

Billy chuckled and boasted with confidence, "Ain't gonna happen, so tell him not to worry."

"You don't understand. Hurdle wants you to throw the fight. Let the other fellow win, only make it look good, so nobody suspects nothing." The private broke into a sweat, fear painted across his face.

"Like I said," Billy's grin quickly changed to a scowl, "ain't—gonna—happen."

Sam and Luther leaned forward on the edge of their cots to catch the rest of the conversation. The guard tried to reason with Billy, but Billy was adamant. Looking to Sam and Luther for help, the guard continued, "Hurdle knew you'd refuse, but he ain't playing around this time. He told me to tell you 'Don't make him do anything drastic to persuade you to lose on purpose.'"

"Like what? What's he threatening me with *this* time?"

"That's just it! I don't know what he's got in mind! All I know is you'd better listen to him. Don't do anything stupid. This war will be over soon and we can all head home—*if* we're still alive! You might want to stay alive!" The private was in a panic.

"Where's your home, son?" Sam asked, trying to change the subject and calm things down.

"Little town in Georgia, name of Cumming, nestled at the foothills of the Blue Ridge Mountains. My family lives around Booger Mountain, about fifty miles north of Atlanta. We've been there for generations. Why, it's the prettiest place in the world, and I can't wait to get back home."

"Sounds like a right fine place," Luther added, asking how the war was going.

"There ain't much going on in the war. Seems like Grant's just waiting for spring so the roads will dry. Then he'll start back trying to break our lines again."

"Is Longstreet's Corps still around Richmond?" Sam asked.

"Yep, they're dug in just east of here." But the private wouldn't be distracted from his mission. "Please, Billy, just throw the fight. It don't really matter, anyway. Think about how soon you could all be heading home."

"Okay, boy, I'll think about it. But I ain't promising nothing. The whole thing just goes against the grain. I ain't even sure I could throw the fight if I wanted to."

The guard left, and Sam and Luther looked at each other, wondering what to say. "Gee, Billy, I'm afraid you might get hurt if you ain't really trying to win," Sam said with concern. "I've seen it too many times. I mean, you win because you go nuts and refuse to quit. Take that away, and you might get killed."

"Yeah, but what's gonna happen if yah don't mind the captain?" Luther asked nervously. "He said first time you get out of line, I'm gonna get busted up."

"Just let me think on it."

The prostitutes arrived at the jail again that evening. Billy confided the new orders to Lucy. "What would you do, Lucy?"

"Honey, I've had to sell my body and lose my dignity just to stay alive. Losing one stupid little fight don't seem like nothing much to me."

"Maybe you're right … but I'm not sure if I can. Trouble is, if I don't lose, the captain will probably shoot Luther or find something else crazy to do."

"Cap'n Hurdle's crazy, Billy. Everybody knows that," Lucy replied, as she gently put her hand on his thigh and eased up next to him.

"Hey! What are you doing?"

"We can still be friends, just closer friends. I know it's been a while since you've had some loving. Why don't you let me comfort you?"

Billy warmed. Sally's smiling face flashed through his mind, but Lucy was here and willing, right now. He remembered how good it felt to hold a woman's body close to his. There was no doubt he was aroused. He closed his eyes and remembered the first time he had kissed Sally, and how she looked that night in the barn during the thunderstorm, with her blonde hair glimmering as the lightning flashed.

Pulling back from Lucy's embrace, Billy apologized. "Sorry. I just can't. I could never betray Sally."

"She's a very lucky woman," Lucy said, disappointed and envious, as she stood to leave.

"Don't leave here mad—I don't want that, either."

"I'm not mad. I just wished somebody loved me like that. If you can't lose for Luther and Sam, maybe you can lose for Sally."

Billy lay tossing on his narrow cot that night considering what Lucy had said and dreaming of seeing Sally again. At last, he made up his mind. For the first time in his life, he would lose a fight.

As hard as it was, Billy managed to make his loss look convincing. Captain Hurdle, betting against his own fighter, won another small fortune. "Great job, Billy Boy! Well done," Hurdle said jovially, as he slapped him on the back once they were back at the jail. "I'm happy you listened to reason."

Billy said nothing. He grabbed a bottle of whiskey and stretched out on his cot with his back toward everyone.

"Well, y'all are no fun," Hurdle joked as he turned to leave. "Suit yourself. My business here is done." Grinning, Hurdle departed.

"Thanks, Billy. I know that was tough," Luther said after Hurdle's escorts disappeared.

"That's okay, Luther, but I didn't do it just for you. I did it for all of us."

"We know why you did it, and we're grateful," Sam said quietly. "Just hang in there, Billy. Maybe soon this cussed war will be over, and we'll all be back in Mississippi tending to our farms."

• • • • •

At Bedlam South, the growing friendship between Albert Wright and attorney Steven Billings was an amusing study in contrasts. They were opposites in every way. Albert towered over most men and intimidated all men with his powerful presence. The pale, white man with the potbelly was physically small, but intellectually a giant.

For months, Steven had worked tirelessly and with great compassion to help Albert to regain his sanity and dignity. Dredging his memory for everything he'd ever seen or heard at the Philadelphia hospital, Steven taught him to release pain and heartache using therapy techniques the attorney had observed while working with Doctor Da Costa. It turned out to be time well spent.

Joseph was fascinated and challenged when he would sneak the attorney into his office late at night, discussing treatments for what the Philadelphia doctor had called A Soldier's Heart, a disease of the heart caused by war and trauma. Once he understood what Dr. Da Costa had identified as moral management therapy techniques, he taught the methods to his handlers. As a result, dozens of men suffering from the ailment were showing remarkable improvement.

"Good evening, Albert." Joseph found the attorney and his friend on the first floor of the west wing, helping dole out the meager food rations.

"Hey, Doc," Albert hugged Joseph with the strength of a bear and the heart of a child. "How are you?"

Smiling, Joseph struggled to breathe. "I'm well, Albert. But you might want to release me before you crush me."

"Hello, Dr. Bryarly," Steven smiled, but continued with his work. Albert picked up a large washtub weighing well over one hundred pounds filled with Indian peas, rice, hardtack, and some stale-smelling meat—a pitiful bounty that would need to be stretched in order to feed another two hundred men.

"Albert and I *borrowed* some food from Chimborazo's commissary. Hope you don't mind."

"Finally, an honest day's work from a lawyer!" They shared a chuckle before Joseph continued, "Steven, your collected *donations* are the only thing keeping these men alive. Can you increase your food raids? I have other men who could assist you."

The attorney nodded. "Anything to get fresh air! We've been traveling at night lately ... Albert's idea."

"Have you seen Percy?" Joseph was unable to mask his concern.

"Only twice in the past week," Steven replied, still walking and distributing the food among the starving patients. Albert's presence kept some of the more despicable characters from taking more than their fair share from the small man.

"They moved out. Gone away," Albert said.

"Gone away?" Joseph repeated.

Steven added some detail. "Albert overheard Percy telling his Zouaves to clear out the cellar, storage bins, and something he called the 'isolation rooms' yesterday evening. Mean anything to you?"

Joseph looked puzzled and then thoughtful. "Yes! I'll share the story with you some other time. Meanwhile, both of you need to be extremely careful. If either you or Albert is caught outside of Wingate stealing food, you'll be shot on sight."

Albert grinned. "Nobody left to do no shooting, Doc. Like I said, gone away."

Joseph and Steven stared at the giant in amazement. Joseph turned to the attorney after a moment and said, "I believe in the new therapies, but only God deserves credit for Albert's improvement."

Later that night, Joseph searched for Steven again, requesting his help.

"Anything! I am completely aware of the fact that Albert and I both owe you our lives."

"I want to move you and Albert into my room, at least for the next few weeks."

"I don't mind an upgrade in quarters—but may I ask why?"

"Percy promised a long time ago to kill me. And with this war ending soon, one way or another, Percy may make good on his threat." He paused to look around the room at the destitute prisoners and wounded soldiers, both Yankee and Rebel, before continuing, "I've been a thorn in Percy's side for over two years, and men like Percy always exact their revenge." He paused, adding coldly, "I intend to kill him, Steven, pure and simple. I don't fear that man, but I cannot withstand all the Zouaves. Percy is a coward at heart, and cowards never attack alone."

Steven's eyes scanned the room. "Every man in here hopes you'll succeed in dealing with Percy. You know, the day will come when I won't be able to stop Albert and the others from attacking Percy and his raiders. All they're waiting on is one word from you," he added, watching closely for Joseph's response.

"I can't say that the thought hasn't crossed my mind, but for now we have hundreds of mentally ill patients to consider, men too weak to defend themselves—men Percy would slaughter just for sport."

Before returning to the asylum, Joseph added, "Oh, I meant to tell you earlier: I mailed those letters for you to Harper's Ferry. The town is in Union hands once again."

"Thank you!"

"She must be someone special." Joseph's smile wavered briefly when he saw Steven nod. "Hold onto her, no matter the cost."

"I intend to."

Twenty-Five

"Lady, I said No! For the last time, the answer is no!"

The angry desk clerk called for the burly bartender, "Johnny! Come and throw this lady out before our *paying* guests start complaining."

"Sir, please! My baby's hungry," Sally Stearns leaned against the counter and begged. "I just need a room for a few days. When I find my husband, I know he'll repay you."

Five weeks of living on the streets, in and out of shelters and soup lines, had taken a dreadful toll on Sally's health. The Powhatan Hotel was her last hope. Deathly pale, dirty, and alone, she wept as Johnny forced her toward the door, her son and bag in tow.

"Am I one of those *paying* customers y'all are so *concerned* about upsetting?"

"Why, yes," the desk clerk replied, bowing, "certainly, Miss Mary Beth."

Fuming, Mary Beth Greene stood at the bottom of the stairs. "Well, I am upset. So what do y'all plan on doing about it?"

He fumbled, "Yes, ma'am. Why, we're trying to remove her, Miss Mary Beth, this very moment."

"Release her this instant!" Mary Beth commanded as she

stormed across the lobby, slapping at the bartender's arm.

Humiliated and furious, Johnny dropped Sally and she fell to the floor, barely managing to hang onto her son, who cried lustily. Turning quickly, he grabbed Mary Beth's wrist, twisting her arm and forcing her to her knees. "Let go!" she cried in pain.

"Why you—" Johnny stopped in mid-sentence, startled by the chorus of scraping chairs all around him. Every man within sight stood to defend Mary Beth and the helpless Sally Stearns.

Perhaps the loudest noise of all was the cocking hammer from Lieutenant Colonel Ricky Gordon's Colt revolver, only a few feet away from Johnny's head. "*Sir,*" Ricky said calmly, "I advise you to choose your next words *carefully* … for they very well may be your last."

Johnny immediately released Mary Beth. His eyes nervously darted around the room, toward the front door, and then around the crowded lobby. He anxiously wiped both hands on the dirty white apron tied around his waist while Mary Beth stood and retreated behind Ricky.

"I'd estimate it's at least ten paces to the door," Ricky replied sternly, reading Johnny's thoughts, "but I seriously doubt you'd live beyond the front step."

"Mister, please don't kill me! I swear I didn't know who she was."

Ricky growled, "I believe you forced both ladies to their knees. So, if you really want to live, beg for your life from Miss Mary Beth."

Johnny quickly dropped to his knees, pleading for his life.

"Well, I forgive you." Mary Beth smiled, leaning over and gently raising him up. As he stood, in a swift move, her knee connected with his crotch. Johnny gasped and fell limply to his side, laying in a fetal position.

Looking swiftly around the officers, Mary Beth didn't spy Sally in the foyer, but caught up to her on the front steps as she was wrapping a blanket over her son's head, preparing to go out in the rain. With a single glance, each woman seemed to understand the other. Without saying a word, Mary Beth guided the woman back inside, holding her son in her arms.

"What's your name, sugar?" she asked when they caught up to Ricky.

"Sally Stearns." The young mother barely had enough breath to whisper her name.

"I'm Mary Beth. This here's my friend … my fiancé … Lieutenant Colonel Ricky Gordon."

A surprised grin spread clear across the officer's face. It was the first time Mary Beth had referred to him as her fiancé.

Sally tried to speak through the tears. "Thank you for helping me." A heaving, guttural cough interrupted the tears. Sally's face paled and her knees gave way. Ricky caught her, cradled her in his arms, and carried her to a nearby sofa. Still carrying the baby in her arms, Mary Beth hurried off to the kitchen, returning minutes later with fresh goat's milk in an improvised baby bottle and a glass of brandy for Sally.

Mary Beth and Ricky shared a look that indicated each understood the severity of Sally's condition. At this point in the war, everyone was all too familiar with the guttural cough and labored breathing of a victim slowly dying from consumption.

"Let me talk to Ricky just for a minute, Miss Sally." Mary Beth took her fiancé by the arm and guided him onto the porch. "I should put Miss Sally in my room. She's far too sick to be left out on her own. Don't you think?"

Ricky nodded. "We can't turn her away—and you're a real sweetheart!" He returned to the sofa and picked up the ailing woman. Followed by Mary Beth, who was holding the baby and dragging the woman's heavy bag, he carried Sally gently up the stairs and into Mary Beth's suite.

By the time Sally opened her eyes, Mary Beth had washed her face and was sitting nearby in a rocking chair, feeding the baby bits of food and cooing softly while Ricky looked on thoughtfully. Sally glanced around the luxurious room in wonder, then worry, until she spotted her baby.

"Sally," Mary Beth whispered, sitting on the bed beside her, "you're awfully sick, so you and the baby will stay in my room until you're better. I've sent for the doctor and we'll find a crib for the baby."

Ricky leaned over and asked, "Miss Sally, tell me your husband's name. I can't promise anything, but maybe I can get some of my boys looking for him."

Barely above a whisper, Sally replied, "Bill … Billy Gibson. He's from Mississippi … General Longstreet's Corps."

• • • • •

Late Friday night on the last day of March, Joseph, Thomas O'Malley, Enan McGinnis, and two other handlers sat in the Wingate commissary kitchen feasting on mule meat and rice. Albert and Steven had left hours ago, off on another scavenger hunt along with five men handpicked by O'Malley, but rumbling stomachs couldn't wait any longer. Joseph had donated the two mules from his wagon team to feed the prisoners and his friends. Each man shared the news they had been collecting, news of the evacuation of Richmond, reports of rioting in the streets, and speculation about the location of the president and his cabinet members. "No doubt about it. Our beloved Confederacy is dyin'," O'Malley said, sighing. He held up his glass of whiskey and offered a toast: "To me dear friend, Alastair Weller: May you be across heaven's threshold before the devil knows you're dead."

"Having a little *party*, are we?" Captain Percy's hateful voice rang out as he unexpectedly appeared in the pantry doorway. Five Zouaves loomed behind him.

"I will speak to *you*, Doctor, outside," Percy growled.

Still in shock at the sight of the captain, Joseph stood to obey, but felt O'Malley's hand on his shoulder restraining him.

"You can speak your piece in here," the handler declared defiantly.

"This doesn't concern you!"

"It concerns all of us!" Enan shouted at Percy, fists clenched, now standing with Joseph and O'Malley.

Percy's grin broadened menacingly as he leaned against a set of shelves, considering his next move. *Five armed men against five unarmed. Not bad odds.*

"So, Doctor," Percy replied calmly, trying to pick a fight. "Is today *the* day? The day you test your mettle?"

"Why not?" Joseph could feel rage welling inside of him. Every fiber of his body tensed as he gripped the large butcher knife he had used to carve the dinner's meal.

Sounds of hammers being cocked emboldened Percy, the boldness a coward only feels when he has stacked the deck in his favor.

Percy smirked as he pulled his pistol. "Tell me, Doctor, where can we bury all your precious *retards* once I've finished killing you?"

CRASH! Percy and his raiders collapsed beneath a massive set of pantry shelves and their load of jars, bottles, and crockery. On top of the shelves lay Albert Wright. Cursing, wood smashing, and a single gunshot rang out behind Albert in the darkness beyond the doorway. Dr. Bryarly, Thomas O'Malley, and Enan McGinnis stood frozen in shock.

"I guess we arrived in a timely fashion, Joseph," Steven observed, standing in the shadows behind Albert. "One of Percy's boys is dead outside, the other cretins just wish they were."

"Now what?" Enan asked.

Joseph walked over to Albert and the men he had pinned beneath the shelves, staring at Percy with a raw, seething hatred.

"Let's finish this, Percy. Just you and me."

"Go to hell!"

The doctor viciously kicked Percy in the face, blood splattering on his boots.

"Do that again … and I kill you!" Sergeant Pirou appeared at that moment with several armed Zouaves. The doctor and his friends had been ambushed a second time.

"No! He's mine to kill!" Percy screamed. "Pirou! Get me up!"

"You! Get up!" Pirou motioned to Albert with his rifle, "Now!" Hands raised, Albert silently obeyed after a glance at Steven, who nodded.

The Zouaves threw aside the shelving, helped Percy to his feet, and quickly retrieved their rifles before shoving everyone into the kitchen area. Expecting the worst, Joseph offered a compromise. "Take me, Percy—your fight is with me. Let them go."

Percy wiped the blood from his mouth, pulling out one loose tooth and throwing it to the ground. Laughing menacingly, Percy surveyed the room again. Blocking the captain's path, Albert and O'Malley moved in front of Joseph while others closed in behind them. Percy smiled, "Two massive men willing to lay down their lives for their friend. How sweet!"

Never taking his eyes off the captain, Albert shouted, "You come by me, I eat your heart when I done killing you."

"Percy," O'Malley yelled, "some will die—but I swear to God you'll be first!"

"Well, *Doctor*. You have your own little army of *retards* and *wankers*." Percy paced the floor, slowly backing up to Pirou and his Zouaves. "I'm a patient man," Percy picked up his hat and straightened his jacket. "Plenty of time to finish this later. For now, I have some cargo to ship and some paperwork to destroy."

"What?" Pirou growled at Percy, astonished at his words. He, along with everyone else, was expecting a bloodbath.

"I said, *Sergeant Pirou*," the captain gritted his teeth against his swollen lips, "we have cargo to ship, and the boat leaves within the hour."

"What about him?" Pirou pointed his rifle once again at Joseph.

"Oh, all right," Percy drew his pistol, turning quickly toward Joseph and company, "we really don't have time for this."

Everyone in the front row instinctively hit the floor. The men in the back never saw it coming. The handler standing behind Steven careened backward, struck in the forehead by Percy's bullet. Shouts and screams and accusations followed as four men grabbed Albert, who lunged for Percy, not caring that he was staring down the barrels of five rifles.

"Satisfied, Pirou? They killed one of ours—we killed one of theirs."

"Not the same."

Percy put his arm around Pirou, walked him out of the kitchen, and delivered his plan while the other Zouaves guarded the men in the kitchen. "We'll finish clearing the storehouse, burn the papers, ship our cargo, and then come back next week to kill 'em all. I've got some unfinished business with the doctor, and I want him to worry before he feels my revenge. I want him to beg me for mercy before I kill him—understand?"

Pirou reluctantly agreed. The men in the kitchen listened silently.

"What will we do when they come back?" Steven asked, breaking the silence in the kitchen after listening to the horses ride away.

Joseph replied coldly, "Next time, we'll be ready."

· · · · ·

Addressing his men, Sergeant Cawley delivered a plan for retreat should the Yankees break through their lines. "We're supposed to cross the river on the Mayo Bridge, then go on through Richmond, and rendezvous with the rest of the army at Amelia Courthouse, some thirty-five miles west of here," he said without expression.

"This can only mean General Lee now plans to evacuate Petersburg and Richmond," Daniel speculated.

"It don't mean nothing like that, Dan'l," the sergeant growled. "The general's just making plans in case we have to pull back. It don't mean we're evacuating nothing." His face turned red as he stormed off, leaving the men to argue among themselves.

"Whatever it means, it don't sound too good to me," Skeeter whined.

Daniel tried to make sense of the orders. "We may have no choice. If the Federal forces break through at Petersburg, we'll have to retreat to the west, or be cut off from the rest of the army. Boys, this very well could be the beginning of the end for our Confederacy."

"Maybe we'll have a better chance of beating Grant if we ain't pinned down in these dang trenches all the time," Skeeter complained again.

"Skeeter, my friend, we have no chance of beating General Grant, period."

Zeke sat motionless. "What's bothering you, son?" Daniel asked gently.

"We can't lose, Daniel. It can't be over … not like this. So many men dead? And for what?"

Daniel sighed heavily, rubbed his hands over his face, and dropped down beside Zeke. "Sometimes we don't understand God's will, but we must somehow find comfort in knowing that we did our duty as best we could. And then we live with the consequences."

"I just don't get it! We're fighting for our rights, for our homes—and we're gonna lose?"

Skeeter joined in. "Makes yah wonder how things will be back home, if'n we make it back home. Bet them Yanks will never leave now. They might even show up in Calhoun County someday!"

"To the victor go the spoils," Daniel said blankly.

"What's that mean?"

"It means that the winner of this war gets to make all the rules, as well as enjoying the bounty of their victory. If the Federals win, we are no longer in charge of our own destiny."

"So, if we lose, they get to tell us what to do?" Skeeter asked, confused.

"Yes. The Southern states and their citizens, especially Confederate soldiers, will be punished for rebelling against the Federal government."

"I just hope folks knows how bad outnumbered we was and how we never had steady food for long," Skeeter observed.

Absorbed in their thoughts, the men of Company C sat silently. Zeke thought of home and Katherine and his family. He thought of the creek on their farm where he and Billy had spent so many happy days when they were boys, fishing and killing snakes. But when he thought of home, his memories gave way to grief. His stomach felt as if it were being torn out of his belly when he realized that he'd probably never see his big brother again. In anguish, he asked for his friend to look into the future. "You really think it's almost over, Daniel?"

"Yes, I do. They'll attack again, but we just can't hold them much longer. We'll retreat to the west and regroup, but Grant will not stop in Richmond. He'll hound us until we surrender."

Daniel paused, sighed, and added, "Yes, Zeke, it's almost over."

Twenty-Six

The once faint rumblings from the battlefields were now deafening, shaking the rafters and windows of Wingate Asylum. Joseph stood atop the hill, staring for miles into the valley below, watching the battle unfold. Waves of Yankee attacks pushed hard against the lines, only to be repelled by another miraculous Rebel defense. Robert E. Lee's grossly outnumbered forces were holding their position against unimaginably superior forces.

Joseph mused, *If our forces fail to withhold the Yankees, by tomorrow morning the only thing between the Federals and Richmond will be Wingate Asylum.* He turned to Thomas O'Malley, who was standing beside him and instructed, "Please gather all the remaining handlers and resident interns and have them meet me in the foyer."

"Aye." O'Malley went running.

Joseph wandered around the grounds, knowing it would take a while to assemble the workers. Soon, Steven Billings joined him, with Albert Wright close behind.

"Joseph, I honestly don't know what to say ..." Steven's sincerity was obvious.

"I understand. Neither of us had a part in starting this war. Thankfully, we'll soon be free from its ravages. I was told this morning that President Davis has ordered the evacuation of the government from Richmond. By Sunday evening, the capital of the Confederacy will be fleeing the Federals."

"How can I help you?"

"You can help release all of the prisoners in the west wing. We'll begin with the Federal prisoners and the less-violent Confederates."

"Joseph, that's suicide!" Steven exclaimed. "Either Captain Percy or the Confederate military officers will shoot you on sight for treason. I'll be shot for helping you!"

"What choice do we have?" Joseph shouted, startling Albert, who moved closer and looked around in confusion. "If we don't free these men today, right now, they will be murdered. Percy will return very soon—maybe tonight, maybe tomorrow night."

"Why can't we wait for the Federal troops? Let me ride out now and find someone to help us."

Joseph considered his words, vacillating as he weighed the options. Finally, he spoke. "There isn't time, Steven. Captain Percy cannot allow even *one* of these prisoners or patients to remain alive. All of them can testify to the crimes of Percy and his Zouaves. At least out in the open countryside, some of them will have a fighting chance, though Percy may hunt them down one by one until no one is left."

"But, Joseph …"

"He will kill them all, Steven. That means three hundred fifty-three men will be slaughtered. Do you want to spend the rest of your life knowing you could have helped save these men, but you stood by and did nothing?"

"You know I don't want anything to happen to them—"

"Then, for heaven's sake, help me release the prisoners now. Take Albert with you."

Steven reluctantly nodded. "All right. We'll get started right away, and then tomorrow we can help you with the more violent prisoners and madmen."

"No, Steven."

"What?"

"I want you to leave today, before sunset, with the released prisoners. Albert will go with you. Stay clear of Richmond. With his help, you'll be safe traveling through the wilderness."

"No!" Albert shouted, bear-hugging Joseph. "I stay here!"

"Albert, do you remember that I told you one day you could go home?" Joseph looked up and saw the tears filling Big Albert's eyes as he nodded. "I need you to protect Steven, and then, when he's safe, you can go home. Home, Albert!"

Steven put his hand on Albert's arm, guiding him toward the west wing. Before they were out of sight, the Yankee attorney shouted over his shoulder, "I'll see you again, Doctor Bryarly."

"Go with God, Steven, Albert," Joseph whispered as he walked toward the manor. The words of Jesus brought temporary comfort and he repeated them as he walked: *No greater love has any man, than to lay down his life for his friend.*

The scene in the Wingate foyer was solemn. Thoughts of defeat, starvation, and despair warred with thoughts of family members, home, and peace. Thirteen handlers assembled, waiting for orders. A few had already fled, leaving everything behind. Others were frantically packing their belongings. Trying to remain calm, Joseph stood before his staff for the last time.

"We'll release all of the patients in the east wing immediately—Federal prisoners and all non-violent Confederates," he explained, after confirming that the rumors about the war were true. "Everyone let go today should be patients capable of fending for themselves."

"But, Doc, don't you think—" O'Malley began, but was interrupted.

"We don't have time to debate. This decision is mine alone, and I alone will suffer the consequences."

"What about them crazy fellers in the holding cells? Some is still in the west wing and in the cellar," someone called out.

"I'll stay at the hospital with the madmen and patients too weak to travel. When the Federals arrive, I'll surrender Wingate

Asylum." Choked with emotion, Joseph paused for a moment, then added, "I want you to know that I love you all, and I'm grateful to God for your loyalty. Now," he said, with renewed energy, "it's time to return to your families and rebuild your lives. Make the horrors of these past four years mean something."

After the other handlers had dispersed to the ward, Thomas O'Malley stalked up to the doctor and declared, "I be knowing what you're doing. Ye be protecting us from Percy. You want us gone 'fore he returns."

"Go save our patients' lives, my friend! Set them—and your-self—free."

"Doc, these men're still sick in the head! What'll come of them?"

"Thomas, after seeing the war from outside the asylum, and seeing the war that has raged inside the asylum, I'm truly not certain who is sane and who is sick in the head!" Barely above a whisper, Joseph added, "Better to be insane and free."

· · · · ·

Zeke was startled from his nap by earthshaking blasts. Adrenaline rushed through his entire body. He could think of only one time in his life that he felt like this: Gettysburg. He grabbed his rifle, checked to make sure it was loaded and to see how much ammunition he had, all the while keeping an eye on the fields between the opposing armies' trenches. It was already dark outside. The Yankee artillery had never bombed them at night like this.

"Stay down, you fools!" Sergeant Cawley screamed over the noise, although most men failed to hear him. "They're just trying to soften us up for the infantry. Stay down!"

"It's like being back at Gettysburg," Zeke shouted.

"Worse! Much worse!" Daniel yelled, pulling Zeke down to a kneeling position. "Look back toward Petersburg." The night sky was alive with projectiles leaving shimmering trails of light, like a thousand shooting stars. Beneath them, the ground rumbled as the projectiles exploded.

"They'll be coming at us fast 'n' furious right about daylight," Skeeter predicted.

Although some sections of the battle lines were mercilessly pounded throughout the day, Zeke's brigade saw limited action. "It's just a diversion, boys. Grant's keeping us pinned down here so we can't be moved to help those boys defending Petersburg," Daniel suggested.

The Confederates' outer trenches were overrun the next day, but the Yankees paid dearly for every inch of ground they won. General A. P. Hill, one of Lee's most trusted lieutenants, rode toward the retreating men in a futile attempt to rally the soldiers and stem the tide of the invasion. He was shot dead by a Yankee sharpshooter. The South had lost yet another great general.

Twenty-Seven

Dr. Joseph Bryarly stood at the end of the long circular drive leading to Bedlam South, watching the continuous wave of nameless and panicked faces. Few seemed to care about the plight of the persons running alongside, behind, or in front of them. From livestock to children, from wheelbarrows to ambulances, everything that was not fixed to the ground fled the advancing firestorm of the Northern invaders. Suddenly, a speeding covered wagon failed to navigate the sharp curve. Snagging an overhanging oak limb sent the wagon crashing to its side on the ground. An entire family—a harried-looking man, his pregnant wife, and three young children, as well as all their remaining worldly possessions—was scattered across the dusty road. No one stopped to help. Several hurried travelers took full advantage, stealing anything they could pick up without breaking stride.

Joseph never moved.

Unknown to these refugees rushing away from town, the Yankees didn't pose the only threat to their safety. Mingling in the crowds were hundreds of the lunatics released from the asylum the day before; many were aimlessly wandering about in the masses being swept away from the asylum. *They're not very difficult to spot*, Joseph thought, watching several patients interact with the crowds, *if you know what you're looking for*. He looked up the hill. Still sitting beside an old well was Benjamin Jones, a young teenager who had recently arrived from the Petersburg trenches, diagnosed with "soldier's heart." Abandoned, homesick, and mentally exhausted, Benjamin had been sitting motionless ever since his release. As Joseph stared at him, he realized, *even in a sea of people, the loneliness is maddening.*

"Why, Doctor Bryarly! How lovely to see you," Mary Beth Greene crooned as her wagon turned hard into Wingate's drive, with Lieutenant Colonel Ricky Gordon at the reins. As soon as the horses halted, he quickly jumped from the bench to assist the family whose wagon had overturned.

"Why, Doctor, aren't you going to help?"

Without turning his head to look at her, Joseph responded coldly, "It's not my wagon."

"Do you only help people for personal gain, *Doctor*?"

Now facing her, Joseph snapped, "Do you only sleep with men who pay you, *Miss* Greene?"

Mary Beth looked at him unblinkingly, and Joseph's stone-cold mood began to warm. He rubbed his hands over his face, stooped to catch a toddler and return her to her distraught mother, then apologized. She then offered, "Why, Doctor, I shall surely miss our little banters. You are a worthy opponent in debate."

"Going somewhere?" She could sense the caring in Joseph's question.

"Yes, Doctor, I'm returning home to Louisiana. The only thing in this God-forsaken city worth saving—," she looked over at Ricky and others righting the wagon, "—is my fiancé, the former lieutenant colonel, so I'm taking him with me."

"Fiancé?" Joseph looked surprised, then smiled and stepped forward to shake her hand, as Ricky climbed back into the wagon. "Good luck, *Mrs. Mary Beth Gordon*. May God protect you in your travels."

"Thank you, Doctor, but I couldn't leave before asking for a little favor."

"A favor?"

"Yes, sir, I have a Yankee woman, Sally Stearns, living in my suite at the Powhatan Hotel. She's dying from consumption and she has an infant child. I've paid for her care and boarding. I've also arranged for the child to live at an almshouse with some friends of mine. They'll come by and take the baby on Monday afternoon."

"What can I do to help her?"

"Please just check on her, Doctor, whenever you travel through Richmond. I'm afraid she won't be long for this world."

Joseph nodded as Ricky slowly pulled the wagon forward into the wave of refugees.

Mary Beth turned and grinned, "You better stay clear of horse leeches from this day onwards, Doctor. You won't have ol' Mary Beth to swipe them off your body for you—you might be surprised what I didn't do for money!"

Joseph was speechless. By the time he regained his senses, the wagon was already driving away. He ran wildly across a small field, through a saw-brier thicket, and intercepted the wagon at the next bend in the road. Exhausted, he grabbed the horse's bridle, heaving for breath, and bent over double. Ricky was about to protest, but Mary Beth patted his hand and gave him a reassuring smile.

"Why, Joseph, surely you knew I was your *guardian angel*?"

Soaked in sweat from his sprint, Joseph could simply gasp and shake his head.

"And I thought we were friends, sharing letters 'n' all," she teased.

"I—I—"

"And you being an educated man! Well, I guess it's time for my little confessional," she laughed, as Ricky looked puzzled. "I am your mystery writer: the latrine ditch, the cellar, your coat pocket." She suddenly shivered. "They were little hints to help you and those Irishmen protect those poor boys from Percy and his Zouaves."

"You?" Joseph questioned, still very confused. "You wrote all of the notes?"

Mary Beth nodded. "I surely did. I also released those boys from those hideous cages down in the cellar. I had to spend the night with Percy more than once in order to figure out how to do it." She shivered again.

"But the notes. You're not a preacher, a man of God … ?"

"I was not born a *courtesan*, Doctor!" Mary Beth responded, insulted. "None of us is what we seem, are we, *Doctor*? I was born the daughter of a spirit-filled, God-fearing Baptist preacher."

Joseph bowed low. "I am deeply ashamed—and deeply impressed. You've taught me more than one valuable lesson, ma'am—and I'll never be able to pay you for them."

"This war forced me to become a hooker, Doctor, but I have the power to change, to become whatever I desire. And so do you. Starting today, it's a whole new world." She leaned over, offering her hand, and Joseph didn't hesitate to kiss her fingertips. "I reckon life is a lot like one of your precious books. Only this time," she laughed delightedly and looked over at Ricky, "I can write the ending any way I like!"

• • • • •

Billy, Sam, and Luther were growing restless and anxious as the once-familiar sounds of war grew louder at sunrise. "Reckon this is Grant's big assault that everybody's been a waiting on. Sounds like that old boy means business," Sam suggested, pacing the floor.

"Hey, Luther, see if you can convince your buddy to go get the young guard for us," Billy said, "and maybe we can find out what's happening."

Luther screamed at the guard posted outside the door, "Hey, Butt-face! Come here, ol' buddy, I need a favor. Go get Andrew for us."

"Shut up!" was the reply, as usual.

"Ah c'mon, Butt-face, I don't mean no harm. Tell you what, you go get Andrew and I'll stop talking about your momma—at least for the rest of the day."

No reply came back. Luther hurled another round of insults, including some rather lewd comments about the man's mother and breeding horses, but still no reply. "Reckon he done run off. I don't see old Butt-face out there nowheres," Luther said after a while, as he looked out the tiny window in the door.

"That's strange! There's always a guard outside the door," Billy said, as he yanked at the door handle, hoping for freedom. To his frustration, he found it locked.

The three Mississippians were beginning to worry about their immediate future when Andrew finally showed up. "What's going on?" Billy demanded to know.

Fidgeting and looking over his shoulder as if being followed, Andrew spoke softly, "Grant's hitting us real hard down Petersburg way … it don't look good."

"Then let us out! It's over, Andrew. Please let us out!"

"I can't, Billy. I was with Captain Hurdle when the guard said you wanted to see me, and he told me there was no way that y'all were getting out until he'd left town."

"Where's he going?" Luther asked.

"Everybody's evacuating Richmond. There's no way anyone in the military can stay here if we lose Petersburg. Some even talk about Grant torching the city."

"We need to get out of here," Sam said firmly.

"Look, the captain thinks y'all will come after him if you're set free, so he's not letting you out until he's long gone."

"I swear we won't go after Hurdle! Let us out!" Billy promised.

"You just don't get it!" Andrew shouted. "Hurdle wants to kill the three of you and be done with it! The only reason you're still alive is I swore to him you wouldn't budge until he was long gone. He made the other guards swear, too!"

"What about old Butt-face?" Luther asked, this time without a humorous grin.

"He'll kill you, Luther, if he gets the chance."

Billy begged—something he had never done before. "Please,

Andrew, let us out. At least give us a fighting chance!"

"I can't just yet, but I will before I leave town, I promise. I'll do my best to protect you boys, but you'd better keep your mouths shut." Andrew cut a hard look at Luther. "Now I've got to get back to Captain Hurdle before he sends someone after me."

The men were more nervous than ever as the noise from the cannonade continued. Outside their quarters, they could hear that all Richmond was in a panic. Riots were breaking out in every section of the city. An unexpected visit by the prostitutes that afternoon helped to relieve some of the tension that Sam and Luther were feeling. Billy spent his time more productively. He questioned Lucy in detail about the evacuation of Richmond, the exact location of the jail, what she knew about Longstreet's corps, and the position of the Federal troops.

"There ain't been many military men coming to call in the last few days, so I ain't heard much," she told him. "That's why we came over here today. Nobody seems to be in the mood for loving when they feel their lives are in danger."

"I've gotta get out of here, Lucy. Seems like the whole world is collapsing, and we're stuck in here, helpless. We need to find our brigade. They'll probably be coming through Richmond when they leave the trenches."

"Say, Billy, this Sally you told me about, what's her last name?" Lucy asked suddenly, changing the subject.

"Stearns, Sally Stearns. Why do you ask?"

"I just met a little Yankee girl who wandered into the Powhatan Hotel a while back begging for food and carrying a baby. One of my girlfriends, Mary Beth Greene, put her up in her room cause she's real sick and wore out. Her name is Sally and she's looking for her husband, a Rebel boy."

The world suddenly felt as though it was spinning. Dropping to his knees in front of Lucy, he completely forgot the war. "What does she look like?" he asked, staring fiercely into her eyes.

"She looked plumb pitiful when I saw her … about broke my heart," Lucy said.

"No, I mean describe her! Hair, body, face! What does she look like?"

"Oh, well, she's got blonde hair and she's real skinny, I guess 'cuz she's so sick and all. I didn't get a real good look at her, but I think she's about as tall as me, with eyes 'bout the color of mine, I'd say. The little boy is a doll baby—about a year old, black hair, bright blue eyes ..." her voice trailed away as she looked at Billy's black hair and blue eyes.

"Oh my God, could it be my Sally?" Distraught, Billy rose and began pacing the cell. "You said the baby is about a year old? I met Sally in July 1863. If I got her pregnant, then the baby would be about a year old ... But why would she risk her life to leave home and come here?"

"What you figuring on over there, Billy?" Luther asked, distracted from the company of his prostitute.

"It may be that Sally is here in Richmond with my baby in tow. I have got to get the hell out of here!"

"I ain't sure if it's her. I mean, what's the chance? There are probably hundreds of women named Sally around these parts," Lucy reminded him.

"You gotta go find out. Please, Lucy! Go to her and ask what her name is and if she's from Gettysburg," Billy pleaded with all his heart.

Lucy nodded and started to leave. He grabbed her hand as she walked past and whispered, "Can you help us get out of here? Richmond's gonna be overrun with Yankees, and this may be our last chance to escape. Otherwise, Hurdle may kill us."

"I don't know what I can do to help you escape, but I'll try to think of something," she promised. She looked with shining eyes at the one man who saw her as capable of more than her profession.

"Thank you, Lucy! You've been an angel. I'll never forget you," he said, grabbing her hand and kissing it.

Lucy blushed. "Well, I ain't never been called an angel before, that's for sure. I'll be remembering you as the most decent man

I've ever met—and the only one I ever tried to bed what turned me down." She banged on the door and a guard let her slip out, then locked the door again.

Billy frantically paced the cell like an animal in a cage, his mind a whirlwind of thoughts.

Twenty-Eight

Since midnight, the western skyline had glowed crimson red, as the burning and pillaging of Richmond began. Thunderous explosions rocked the night as Confederate forces set fire to their own supply warehouses and destroyed their ironclads and warships in the river. Around two in the morning, a singular blast erupted of such magnitude that it shattered every window in the west wing of Bedlam South. But the asylum was hauntingly quiet, even ghostlike. Rats scurried along the corridors searching for food. The crimson horizon gave their fur an ominous red glow, while their cold, black eyes reflected fiery red shimmers of light. Death and destruction for one species created a bountiful feast for another. The remaining residents, eleven in all, were shackled and chained in the west-wing security cells as a last act of service from Thomas O'Malley and Ewan McGinnis.

Joseph roamed the abandoned hallways alone, whiskey bottle in one hand, a well-worn Bible in the other, and a Colt revolver looped through his belt. He was patiently waiting for something to happen. What it was, he couldn't predict. As they followed his orders and left, the handlers whispered that he was like a captain going down with his ship, surrendering Bedlam South to the Federal forces. O'Malley knew that Joseph also waited for something far less noble: revenge.

Weary from his all-night vigil and feeling the effects of the alcohol, Joseph took a seat on the servants' entrance steps, stealing a few moments of rest before sunrise. Suddenly, creaking floor slats aroused the doctor. He whirled around, but his reflexes were still too slow.

Sober, he might have stood a fighting chance.

A rifle butt to the face sent Joseph plummeting backward off the steps and smashing to the ground. Blurred vision and a swollen face made it impossible to see his attacker, but it didn't matter. He knew who it was.

"A funny thing happened on the way to the boat, *Bryarly*," Percy gloated as he swaggered down the steps with several Zouaves following close behind and viciously kicked Joseph in the ribs, circling him like a savage animal. "There I was, ready to leave you, your precious *retards*, and this miserable war behind me." Another vicious kick.

Joseph moaned and writhed in pain, rolling on the ground.

"Ol' Pirou here," Percy strutted over and slapped his sergeant on the back, "was throwing papers into the fire—most of which were just lies you wrote about me." Percy leaped forward, crouching over Joseph and slapping him across the face.

"Everything I wrote about you was true," Joseph cried out. "You filthy pile of dung, every word of those letters was true!"

Percy stood up, obviously pleased with himself. "Well, okay, I reckon you're right. All them things about raping, murdering, pillaging 'n' such sure does *sound* like me!" His raiders joined him in his laughter.

"Yep, it's been a good life, boys," Percy bragged, grinning.

He is a disgusting, revolting, one-armed egomaniac! Joseph thought bitterly.

The captain continued his story. "Then I saw a little package that caught my eye … an old, dusty box from over yonder in England. The letter inside was dated October 12, 1863, from a place called Bethlem Royal Hospital …" Percy moved slowly back toward Joseph, studying his every move while stalking him.

Joseph stopped twisting on the ground and grew attentive.

"From a man called Lord Kennington ..."

Joseph's eyes darted nervously.

"That fella was your boss. Ain't that right, *Doctor Bryarly*?"

Joseph tightly shut his swollen eyes, appearing to be on the verge of another panic attack.

"Want me to read the letter, *Doctor Bryarly*?"

He covered his ears mumbling, "No, no, no ..."

Percy removed a crumpled letter from his folded left sleeve, snapping it twice to unfold it. Pompously, he paced around the yard, reveling in his theatrics. Percy shouted for all to hear: "*Dear President Jefferson Davis, It is with a sad heart that I report the untimely death of Doctor Joseph Bryarly. His corpse was discovered just last week, a full six months after his presumed departure for America, stuffed in a shipping trunk at the bottom of a recently drained canal less than a mile from Bethlem Royal Hospital.*"

Several Zouaves followed the captain's lead and even removed their hats in mock mourning for the doctor's death. He skipped down, and then began reading once again: "*I fear, President Davis, that you may have a far more serious, more deadly problem on your hands ...*"

Percy turned to his men grinning. "Serious and deadly—I like the sound of that, boys." Cheers erupted from the raiders.

Percy continued, "*On the same day as Doctor Bryarly's departure, a madman escaped from Bedlam. He had been institutionalized for more than twelve years after his conviction for drowning an eleven-year-old girl ...*"

"No, no ..." Joseph moaned.

"*... his niece, Elizabeth Milan ...*"

"No! No! Just more lies!" Joseph was losing his grip on reality.

"*This man is a cold-blooded murderer ...*"

"NO—NO—LIES—LIES!" Joseph grasped his head and yanked on his hair.

"I said a COLD-BLOODED KILLER ..." Percy added the emphasis for full effect, "*named ... Forbred Lytton!*"

Forbred lay motionless.

"It says here, boys, ol' Forbred Lytton is a murderer—just like us! Says here, ol' Forbred killed his good buddy, Doctor Bryarly, and stuffed him in a trunk, then stole the Doc's clothes and headed for America. Says ol' Forbred is fascinated by psychie—psychuh—well, *retards*."

Percy knelt on the ground beside Forbred while the Zouaves drew in closer. "Well, hell, Forbred, welcome to America!"

"Oh dear God ..." Forbred lay defeated, whispering, "Please, Percy ... kill me."

"Okay, ol' buddy, if that's what you want. But first, I wanna hear you say who you are."

Forbred whispered, "I'm ... Forbred ... Lytton."

"Louder!" Percy slapped him across the face.

"I'm Forbred Lytton."

"Louder!" Percy was enraged, viciously slapping him twice again.

"I'm Forbred Lytton!"

"All right, boys. Now we can hang him."

· · · · ·

Big guns rumbled off to the south of Zeke's position. Word spread throughout the trenches that the brigade was pulling out. The stubborn resistance by his hard-pressed army had given General Lee time to begin his retreat to the west. Lee had abandoned Petersburg, and he ordered Longstreet's division to retreat from Richmond. Men packed their few belongings and waited anxiously for the command to fall in. The retreat was bittersweet. Though grateful for the opportunity to remove his army from the trenches, Lee was grieved and humiliated at the loss of Richmond.

"Man it feels good to be able to walk around straight-up without worrying about getting your head blowed off," Zeke said, trying to raise his spirits.

"That's for dang sure," Skeeter piped in.

As the column came to a halt on a hill looking down over the city, Sergeant Cawley called them to attention. "You men need to listen up. Richmond is in full panic, and we have to march right through the middle of town. Folks may beg you to stay, or curse you for leaving, but pay them no mind. Stay in formation. The provost guards and city police are supposed to direct us and try to keep the roads clear in front of us, but there will be delays, with everyone and their brothers trying to leave the city. When we stop, stay in formation. Is that clear?"

Not one man answered; they just stared at the rioting city stretched out below them.

"That, my friends, is total bedlam," Daniel whispered. "Our country is dying right before our eyes."

· · · · ·

The fires set by the Confederates to destroy anything of military value had accidentally spread. The entire riverfront was in flames. Explosions from the ammunition depots shook the earth beneath the soldiers as they fell back in column and began the march through town. Thick black smoke covered the city; the veterans choked as they marched.

"Looks like we're marching straight through hell itself," Zeke exclaimed, choking on the smoke.

"I just hope we makes it out the other side," Skeeter worried.

The men marched silently through the eastern section of the city, shocked at the madness, clogged streets, women and children running frantically, sporadic fighting, and looting. They saw citizens attack one another and others fighting to defend their few remaining possessions. Zeke's brigade hadn't marched more than fifty yards when they were halted so the roads could be cleared. This became the morning's routine: march fifty yards, wait thirty minutes, march one hundred yards, wait twenty minutes.

"We ain't never gonna get through Richmond at this pace," Zeke said in disgust.

Daniel kept repeating to himself, "Bedlam, total bedlam."

Twenty-Nine

A wagon heavily loaded with chicken crates, barrels, tools, housewares, and supplies slowed to a crawl in front of Bedlam South, caught in the mass of humanity frantically trying to escape the city. Four thin army-surplus mules strained against the double-tree harness. Fires and destruction surrounded them. Lunatics and melancholies wandered about aimlessly, fading in and out of the ever-thickening smoke. The high tide of refugees had passed through late the night before, pillaging every morsel of food and anything else they could carry. The Federal forces steadily advanced on Richmond; they were within sight of the asylum.

"A bloody waste of time, if 'n' you ask me," Ana Dougall protested.

"Don't remember asking you, daughter," came her father's sharp reply. "We'll be making our peace with Joseph afore leaving." Defiant and fuming, Ana stared out the rear of the wagon, arms crossed.

"This is an evil place, Patrick," Mrs. Dougall whispered, looking around at the crowd. She grasped his arm. "These men be touched in the head and their poor minds is lost. Perhaps we should keep movin'?"

"I'll be here to protect the both—" Mr. Dougall, hearing

shouts of revelry from behind the asylum, slapped the reins, urging the mules forward. They strained against the heavy load as they labored up the hill to Bedlam South.

Riders wearing the Zouaves' colorful uniforms gathered around the spreading oak tree overlooking the latrine ditch. Mr. Dougall slowed his wagon and inched cautiously forward until the full effect of the despicable drama was evident.

Ana's scream pierced the air. Mrs. Dougall cried, "Oh merciful God in heaven! They're hanging Joseph!" The startled Zouaves turned, pulling pistols and pointing rifles.

Balanced on a rickety stool with a noose tightening around his neck, Forbred dared not move. He twisted ever so slightly until he could see the wagon out of the corner of his eye. Dirty, bloody, bruised, and defeated, his ultimate humiliation would take place in front of Ana.

"Oh, no ma'am! We're not hanging Doctor Bryarly," Percy sneered and trotted his horse over to the wagon so he could hand Lord Kennington's letter to Mr. Dougall. "Meet our friend *Forbred Lytton*, murderer, child killer, swindler, fraud, and drunk." Percy now addressed his raiders, "Hell, come to think of it, Forbred here sounds like my kind of man!" Mocking cheers and erupting shouts followed by pistols firing recklessly in the air accompanied Percy's speech. "Pirou, why are we hanging our buddy Forbred?" Percy teased, easing his horse over next to Forbred, bringing them eye-to-eye.

"Cuz we hate 'im?" Pirou played along.

"Oh, yeah, I almost forgot." Percy leaned over and whispered in Forbred's ear, "I told you one day I would kill you … *personally*."

"Get on with it, Percy," Forbred hissed.

"Joseph," Ana defended him, "tell them it isn't true, tell 'em!"

"Go ahead, Forbred! Tell us who you are," Percy challenged.

Forbred said nothing. His silence was confession enough. He watched Ana slump and the Dougalls stare in disbelief, too shocked to speak or look away.

"Okay, boys," Percy raised his pistol in the air behind Forbred, "let's finish this and skin out." When Percy pulled back the hammer on his revolver, Forbred began reciting the Lord's prayer, "Our Father, who art in heaven, hallowed be thy name, thy kingdom come, thy will be done ..."

Percy shook his head at Forbred's words. *A religious man—and a cold-blooded killer? What a hypocrite!*

• • • • •

Billy had paced the cell all night, waiting for word from Lucy and hoping to hear that his prayers had been answered. "Where is she?" he yelled in frustration over and over again as he paced.

"Billy, don't take this the wrong way," Sam offered, rubbing the sleep from his eyes, "but I reckon the chances of this girl being your Sally is one in a million."

"I know, I know. But what if it is, Sam? What if it's Sally and my baby? Dang it! Where are the guards?"

Luther joked, "They ain't been for some time. Guess Hurdle's got 'em busy packing all his stuff."

At last, Lucy returned and was let into their quarters by a guard they had never seen before.

"Where have you been, woman? I thought you would've been back hours ago!"

"Well, it's just plumb crazy out there, Billy. I tell you, soon as I got back to the hotel, I went to see Sally, but I had several customers to take care of first. Guess they needed a little loving before they left town."

"Did you get to talk to her?"

"Yeah, though that girl is bad sick. She was coughing something fierce the whole time I was in her room." Billy stared at her. Lucy smiled and touched his hand, "She's your Sally. And that little baby boy is the spitting image of you, Billy Gibson."

The soldier stood frozen in shock for a moment, then turned to Sam and Luther and shouted, "Hallelujah! I got me a boy! And my Sally's just down the road!" He wrapped them in bear hugs and they pounded him on the back.

Billy grabbed Lucy and squeezed her, tears flowing down his face. She held him close, happy for him, but envious of his kind of love. She pulled back and he asked anxiously, "Did you tell her about me and where I was?"

"Billy, she was coughing so bad, she was barely conscious. So I ain't sure what all she understood." Lucy mumbled softly, "She's bad sick, Billy."

He couldn't comprehend the sickness. Just knowing she was in Richmond had him ready to burst at the seams. He hugged the woman tightly. "Thank you, Lucy! I owe you more than I could ever tell you."

"I ain't done yet," she said with a big grin as she lifted up her dress, exposing two shapely legs and white stockings. She laughed when Billy looked away, then reached into her bloomers and pulled out two sticks of dynamite. Tapping Billy on his shoulder to get his attention, she handed the dynamite to him.

"I figure this oughta get y'all outta here. But wait till I'm gone before you light 'em!"

"Where in the devil did you get those?" Sam asked.

Lucy teased, "You talking about that dynamite or my legs? Never you mind, Big Sam. Just see that y'all put them to good use. You need to skedaddle, quick as possible. I hear the Yanks will be here soon."

"What about you, Lucy?" Billy asked as he grabbed his few possessions and stuffed them into a rucksack.

"Me? I'm staying. Them Yankee boys might need a little company when they get here."

"Where's the hotel?" Sam asked.

"It ain't a quarter-mile from here. Just stay on Broad Street and you can't miss it. The Powhatan Hotel, room two."

"Thank you, Lucy!" Billy said, pounding on the door. "I'm forever grateful."

"Good luck, Billy. I hope we meet again. Who knows? Maybe I'll come to Mississippi one day," she said, tears in her eyes, as the guard let her out. "Good-bye, boys."

As soon as the guard disappeared, Billy ordered, "Boys, we got work to do."

"Already on it, boss," Sam said, firing up a cigar. He peered out the front window and saw to his chagrin that Butt-face was leaning against the wall in front of their quarters. "Dangit! There's a guard out here, now that we need 'em gone."

"Okay, Luther, do your thing with Butt-face—and try not to get shot!"

With a big grin, Luther started badgering his buddy to get to Andrew. It worked once again. As soon as the guard disappeared, Sam lit both fuses with his cigar, then stuffed the dynamite into the far corner of the cell, hoping to blow a hole big enough.

In a moment, he realized he'd succeeded. The force of the explosion ripped out a massive section of the jail, debris flying for more than two city blocks. Dust, smoke, brick particles, blood, and lacerations covered the trio as they dashed through the cloud of rubble and ran wildly down Broad Street. To their surprise, no one seemed to notice or care that they had just blown their way out of City Jail, destroying most of the building in the process.

Concealed among thousands of refugees trying to escape, the trio headed for the Powhatan Hotel. Within the half hour, they stood nervously on the front steps.

Thirty

"Captain Percy!" A loud, authoritative voice from behind the Dougall wagon made all heads swivel. Steven Billings stepped out wielding a rifle, followed by Albert Wright, rifle and bayonet flashing in the sunlight. Steven mockingly used his best Creole Cajun accent, shouting, "Like your boy once said: Do that again and I kill you!"

"Two men against twenty?" Percy yelled back. "Mister, you're a bigger fool than I thought."

"Funny, I don't remember saying anything about two men. Do you, Albert?" Steven asked. Albert shook his head.

Both men simultaneously turned toward the windows along the first floor of the west wing. Peering out of twenty-four windows were Federal rifles fixed on Percy and company. Shouts alerted the Zouaves that another Federal company was racing to the second floor, filling those windows with more soldiers. "I count one hundred soldiers carrying one hundred rifles, all pointing at you," Steven told Percy with satisfaction. "I am hereby authorized, under direct orders from General Ulysses S. Grant, to arrest you for crimes committed against Federal prisoners of war commended into your care and charge."

"You got no proof," Percy shouted, his men and horses now

nervously wheeling, desperately searching for an escape. Forbred, still balanced on the rickety three-legged stool, could only focus on staying alive.

"Oh, well, you see, that's where you be wrong, Percy. *Dead* wrong!" Thomas O'Malley said accusingly as he walked out from behind the long row of outhouses, followed closely by Ewan McGinnis and eight other handlers. Each man was covered from the waist down in filth, having excavated a long section of the latrine ditch.

"We found eighteen bodies just this morning. 'Spect there'll be more afore nightfall." While O'Malley spoke, Mr. Dougall leaned over and handed the letter from Kennington to Steven. After reading it, Steven stared at Forbred in disbelief.

"What about him?" Percy shouted, whirling his horse around, pointing his pistol at Forbred. "He's the murderer. You got the letter. Hang him!"

"This letter has nothing to do with the government of the United States of America," Steven declared boldly, after a moment's hesitation.

"Surrender, Captain Percy, immediately! You, men! Throw down your weapons!"

The Zouaves nervously looked back and forth between Percy and the Federal troops. The horses, sensing the tension in the air, paced and snorted. Fury poured from Percy's eyes, "Killing ain't murder. Not in a war."

"Surrender now, Percy. There's no reason for more men to die here today."

"There's your murderer," Percy whined, pointing again at Forbred.

"Surrender!"

"I don't reckon so, boys, not today."

Percy fired the first shot, narrowly missing Steven, but piercing the bonnet canopy of the wagon. At that instant, hell broke loose. Federal bullets ripped from every window; Zouaves returned the fire. Bucking horses threw eight dead riders, while others galloped off wildly. Black smoke filled the small courtyard. Pirou spurred his horse through the nearest window, shattering glass and crushing the unfortunate soldier in his path. Bloodied, he galloped through the west wing and out the front entrance, firing his revolver at anything that moved. Three other raiders followed his lead.

Mr. Dougall struggled to control his mules after shoving his wife to the wagon floor for safety.

Percy screamed as a bullet tore through his shoulder, then knocked Forbred off the stool as he attempted to escape. Another bullet tore into Percy's back as his horse reached the forest's edge.

Albert lunged forward, cutting the rope around Forbred's neck with his bayonet. The doctor plummeted to the ground, gasping.

"Troops, mount for pursuit!" came the orders from within the asylum.

Staggering, Forbred joined Steve, Thomas, and Ewan at the wagon. Once the Federals had raced off in pursuit of the Zouaves, Forbred was the first to speak. "Steven, please read the letter aloud."

Steven nodded.

Gasps, muttered cursing, and dead silence were the listeners' responses. Their eyes turned to Forbred for an explanation. Forbred silently prayed about what to say, but as soon as he opened his mouth, Mrs. Dougall cried out, "Dear God! Ana's been shot!"

Forbred leaped into the wagon, tore Ana's dress from her sleeve down to her hip, and discovered Percy's stray bullet lodged deep in her side. Weak and pale, Ana whispered so softly only her mother and Forbred could hear, "The eyes ... the eyes be those of my lovely Joseph." She smiled, her breathing now much more relaxed. "I'll be trusting the eyes ... windows to the soul they are." And she fainted.

"Lord, please let me help her," Forbred prayed before ordering Thomas to retrieve his instruments. But no one moved.

Forbred looked up, puzzled. "For God's sake, someone go for my instruments! I need to close these wounds and stop this bleeding!"

. . . . .

His heart pounding like a blacksmith's hammer on an anvil, Billy slowly climbed to the second floor of the Powhatan Hotel. Nervously, he stood outside Sally's room. He knocked gently three times, but no answer. He tried the doorknob, but it was locked. He knocked harder, and could faintly hear coughing. "Sally," he shouted, "it's me! Billy." He stepped back, about to kick the door in, when an elderly gentleman appeared.

"What in the devil are you doing, young man?"

"I'm trying to get to my son and my soon-to-be-wife," Billy shouted.

"I'm a doctor, and I will not have her disturbed."

Billy looked fiercely at the elderly doctor. "Let me tell you something, old man. I love that woman and I ain't seen her in almost two years. I'm fixing to get in that room. One way or another, ain't nothing in this world gonna stop me."

"Hold up a minute, son. She doesn't have very long to live. Her last few moments should be as peaceful as possible."

Billy felt sick, asking barely above a whisper, "What? What do you mean, she don't have long to live? What's wrong?"

"She's got tuberculosis, son. There's nothing I can do to save her."

His words hit Billy as if the entire brick jail had landed on his head. "I need to see her! Please, Doc."

The doctor gazed at the distraught man, then nodded and opened the door. Billy stood, drinking in the sight of the only woman he had ever loved. The rosy cheeks, sparkling eyes, and infectious smile had disappeared. Her face was white, her cheeks hollow, and her figure had shrunken. She looked like a doll resting in the large canopied bed. But he would have known—and loved—her anywhere.

The soldier took a deep breath and walked quickly to her bedside, ignoring the baby fast asleep in the crib. He groaned as he knelt beside her, "Oh God, no, Doc! Sally, you can't leave me now that we're finally together again!"

Billy slid into the bed beside Sally. He gently brushed her blonde hair off her face and whispered, "Sally, it's me, Billy."

A smile curved her lips as she struggled to open her eyes. She feebly clasped his fingers. "Billy Gibson, I've been everywhere looking for you … I almost found you at Point Lookout … but you had been sent here … I looked so long."

He was speechless. The strong man who had never cried in his life struggled to hold back his tears. They came as he cradled her in his arms. "It's okay now, Sally. You've found me. Everything's gonna be just fine."

Sally wept pitifully. "No, Billy, it's not all right. I tried to wait for you … tried to hold on, but I'm so very tired."

Gently, he kissed her forehead. "I'm here for you. I'm gonna take you home. Save your strength, don't try to talk."

"No, I'll never see Mississippi—but our baby will. I know you'll take good care of him," she turned her head slightly to look into his eyes. "Did you see him? He looks just like you," she whispered, then she began to cough violently. A small trickle of blood appeared in the corner of her mouth. Billy lovingly wiped it away.

"No, Sally, please! You can't die. The war's almost over! At last I can take care of you. I'll never leave you again," he sobbed.

She smiled, fading out of consciousness. He shook her gently, but he couldn't wake her.

"Doc!" Billy yelled. "Please, help!"

The old doctor appeared and hurried to the woman's side. Taking her wrist, he shook his head. "She barely has a pulse, son. It's almost her time."

"No! This can't happen! Please, Doc, do something!"

The doctor put his hand on the big man's shoulder. He didn't need to say more.

Holding her closely, weeping uncontrollably, and whispering

his love, Billy gently kissed the beautiful lips he had longed for and dreamed about for two long years of war.

Sally's eyes flickered open. She mouthed, "I love you … too."

And then her eyes dimmed and Billy rocked her lifeless body, caressing her face. "God, oh God, why did this have to happen?" he repeated over and over again, in anguish. Her hand slipped out of his grip and Billy knew that the woman he had loved so fiercely had left him. Holding her body tightly, he cried as he had never cried before.

Some minutes later, Billy was startled when a shrill cry broke the silence. He looked over to the baby's bed and saw his son standing, looking curiously back at him. "Well, hello, little fella," he whispered, tears streaming down his face.

Billy looked down at Sally once more, kissed her gently, and tenderly laid her on the bed.

The old doctor had been standing in the hallway. He walked into the room and sighed, "She's gone, son. Knowing her baby is with his father, she left us in peace. For the last two weeks, that's all she worried about."

Billy awkwardly picked his son up, hugging him tightly. "I'm your daddy, and I'll take good care of you," he promised, staring into the child's face.

The baby just stared at him, then looked back at his mother.

"I'll see that she gets a proper burial," the doctor promised. "You need to leave before the Yanks get here."

"I just can't leave her here like this," Billy cried in anguish.

"There's nothing anybody can do for her now, except let her rest in peace."

The baby started crying, reaching for his mother. Billy, still crying, realized he would have to follow the doctor's advice. He grasped the man's hand. "Sir, I appreciate what you did for her— more than my words could ever say. I haven't money to repay you, but—"

"That's quite all right. You owe me nothing. A friend paid for everything. Now, go with God."

Billy stuffed the baby's few belongings into a bag, then leaned over the bed and kissed Sally one more time. Burying his head on his son's tiny shoulder for a moment, he headed for the door.

Thirty-One

Enan McGinnis bolted into the doctor's office, grabbed the doctor's bag, and raced to the wagon. Forbred worked purposefully, searching for internal bleeding, then stitching and bandaging the wounds. Impressed by his surgical skills, the Dougalls sat on the wagon bench staring as he worked.

"Steven, help me move Ana inside where she'll be more comfortable." Again, no one moved and the doctor turned his head. "Please! For God's sake, you know me. You all know me."

"Do we?" someone asked.

"Can Ana be moved?" Steven inquired.

"Yes, the bleeding's stopped and there doesn't appear to be any organ damage. But she shouldn't travel! Help me move her inside."

Steven stammered, "I'm sorry, Forbred, but Mr. Dougall worked in the armory, Mrs. Dougall associated with the cabinet wives, and you have high-up Confederate connections. You'll surely all be imprisoned until this letter can be resolved—unless you leave right now."

"What?"

"Leave. Take the Dougalls and leave before the Federal troops return."

"I'm not leaving. It's not worth risking further injury to Ana."

The attorney pushed the doctor toward the wagon. "All of you must leave. O'Malley and the handlers will be safe. I'll see to it."

"Then let Mr. and Mrs. Dougall leave. I'll stay behind with Ana. Once she's well, she can meet up with her parents, and I'll go to prison."

Mrs. Dougall took his arm gently. "Forbred, you and your family will all be leaving now."

Steven hugged the doctor, pleading, "You once saved my life. Please, let me now save yours."

Forbred nodded reluctantly. "One day, my friend, we will meet again, if only to explain that letter."

"I don't need a letter to tell me who to trust or who my friends are," Steven said huskily. Thomas O'Malley and Ewan McGinnis nodded. "I left something very special behind in Harper's Ferry. A wise man once told me, 'Hold onto her, no matter what the cost.' I intend to go and do that."

Thomas O'Malley bear-hugged Forbred and said, "Me father taught me this blessing when I was a wee little lad, and today it just seems fitting: May the roads rise up to meet you. May the wind be at your back. *May the sun shine warm upon your face, the rain fall soft upon your fields …*" Tears welled up in his eyes as he finished, "… and until we meet again, me dearest friend, may God hold you in the palm o' his hand."

· · · · ·

Big Sam looked up just in time to see Billy staggering out the hotel's door.

"Where's the girl?"

Billy wiped his hands across his eyes. "Sally's dead, Sam. I just barely made it in time to speak to her before she passed."

Luther was stunned, "Dang, she was bad sick! I'm sorry, Billy."

"She was so weak … so frail … and then she was gone, just like that." Billy choked, then looked at his son and declared,

"And this here little man is going home with me to Mississippi."

"What's the little fella's name?" Sam asked, touching the baby's head.

Billy looked stunned. "I don't know!"

"You can call him Luther if you wanna."

Looking at the boy, Billy said thoughtfully, "Luther? Naw ... he doesn't look like a big brawler! I'll be thinking on a name ... Meanwhile, boys, there's no way I can do more fighting with this baby in tow, and I know y'all are wanting to find our brigade."

"I reckon we need to part ways here," Sam said, offering his hand. Sam gripped Billy tightly, staring at his friend fiercely. "Take care, Billy. One of these days, I'll see you back home."

"You sure you'll be okay by yourself?" Luther asked, concerned.

"Yeah. I ain't by myself anymore," he said, looking proudly at his little boy, his legacy from Sally and his gift from God. "Take care, Luther. Sam. Give Ulysses Grant hell from me!"

As Billy watched Sam and Luther quickly disappear into the chaotic mob, the baby started to sob. His father was crying again, too, crying for the woman he had lost and crying for the years they had lost together. And yet, another part of his heart was overflowing with joy because of the gift she had left him. *God, what could possibly happen next? In not much more than an hour, we blow up a jail. I find Sally and lose her again. Now I'm a daddy, without a clue about what to do with a baby. The Yanks will be here soon, and home is a long ways off!*

· · · · ·

"Column, halt!" Sergeant Cawley screamed louder than usual as the men stopped for yet another delay. Billy's head jerked around when he heard the command. *I'd know that voice anywhere!* He carried his baby to the steps of the hotel and found himself staring straight at the sergeant.

Sergeant Cawley stared back as though he were looking at a ghost. Finally, he shook himself and yelled, "Heavens to Betsy, if it ain't Billy Gibson hisself!"

Billy stared, speechless.

"Where in the hell have you been?" Cawley demanded to know, walking up to the corporal and grasping his shoulders with both hands.

"Got wounded and captured at Gettysburg, spent time at Point Lookout Prison Camp, been rotting in a Richmond jail for over a year …" Billy explained, as he searched the ranks for Zeke.

"Zeke's on back in the column. Good God, he'll be glad to see you! Zeke ain't smiled much since Gettysburg—" The sergeant lost his train of thought when he finally saw the baby in the soldier's arms. "Where did you get that baby?"

"This is my son, Sergeant, and it's a long story," Billy said, distracted. "Right now, I've got to go find Zeke." He briskly jogged along the column. Cheers erupted as veterans recognized their former corporal.

Tired of standing and marching, Zeke and Skeeter had been taking in all the sights. "Look yonder in them windows, Zeke! I betcha them's hookers up there." Skeeter pointed to a large hotel where pretty girls were waving and blowing kisses. Several hiked up their skirts and lowered their blouses. The boys were clearly distracted.

"I know it's hard to believe, but I ain't never seen a hooker up close," Zeke confessed.

"Me neither!" Skeeter admitted.

Daniel was in line behind them, but paid little attention to their escapades. His eyes were fixed straight ahead, waiting for a command. Suddenly, he glimpsed Billy walking toward them—with a baby. Daniel closed his eyes tightly, shook his head, and then opened them in disbelief. The two men made eye contact, but before he could say anything, Billy put his finger to his lips.

Billy stood just inches from Zeke, waiting for him to look his way. The baby jabbered something in Zeke's ear. *Dang if that don't sound like a baby right next to me, or else I'm losing my mind!* Zeke slowly turned with a puzzled look in his eyes, stared at the baby, and then Billy.

For a moment, Zeke wondered if he'd passed out—but only for a moment. He whooped and hollered and hugged his brother so tightly he nearly crushed the baby, who let out a Rebel yell protesting his treatment. Twisting, turning, crying, and laughing, the brothers greeted one another after their two-year separation. It was an unbridled celebration.

When Zeke could finally speak, he asked questions in rapid fire. "Where have you been, Billy? Where did you get a baby? I thought you was dead! What happened to you at Gettysburg? What happened after Gettysburg?" He continued barraging his brother with questions, wiping tears, and laughing all the while. That unmistakable grin had returned to his face.

Billy handed the baby to Daniel, who seemed to know what to do with him, and hugged his brother again as he answered him. "Wounded, captured, locked up in prison, exchanged, jailed, had a son … You know, the everyday life of a soldier," Billy joked. "I sure was hoping you were alive, little brother, 'cause the last time I saw you, yah didn't look too good."

Sergeant Cawley cleared his throat, "Boys, we need to be moving on. The road's been cleared for us."

The brothers stepped back and just stared at each other. For a moment, nothing else in the world—war, starvation, the chaos on Richmond's streets, the past, the future—seemed to matter.

"This is nothing short of a miracle," Daniel said, handing Billy his baby and grabbing the father for a hug.

"Hey, Daniel! How are you?" Billy grinned and scanned the ranks. "Where's Nate?"

Daniel and Zeke looked at each other. "Nate died in Spotsylvania," Zeke said quietly. "He saved my life in Gettysburg, killed the Yank that was fixing to kill me." Billy closed his eyes and shook his head.

"Column forward!" Sergeant Cawley hollered, with a big smile—for once.

After advancing a hundred yards or so, the column stopped again, and Zeke remembered to ask, "Who gave you the baby?"

Billy sighed, "I fell in love with my nurse in Gettysburg. She was someone very special. I loved her and planned on marrying her as soon as the war ended. This is my son, Zeke—and this is the first I've seen of him. Sally died in my arms not more than an hour ago."

"I got a nephew? Say, Billy, what's his name?"

"I had no time to ask, Zeke. Believe me, it's a long story." Billy looked down at the tiny boy chewing on his shirt collar, then announced, "Let's call him Nate. Pops would say it was 'the fitting thing to do,' naming his grandson after the man that saved his son's life. This way, Nate will always be with us, Zeke."

"Nate would like that," Zeke agreed, rubbing the baby's thick black hair. "Hey, Billy, he surely does look like a Gibson, poor little guy!"

Billy was talking nonstop about the last two years when Sergeant Cawley walked up. Smiling broadly at the brothers, he said, "Boys, what's left of this army is heading west, but you two are heading south. Get out of this war with that baby—that's an order!"

The men were stunned. They looked at each other and back at Cawley, "How's that?"

"Y'all heard me. The war is over for the Gibson boys. Now get out of here before I change my mind."

"Thanks, Sarge," Billy said huskily, holding out his hand. He and Zeke stepped out of the column.

"Take this rifle and cartridge box, just in case you run across any Yanks," Daniel instructed, handing Billy supplies from a nearby wagon. "Take care, you two! Look me up after the war." He saluted as the column began moving. Skeeter tossed a full canteen to Zeke and grinned. The two brothers stood silently and watched their brigade march off to the last days of the war.

"The war is over—and we lost," Zeke murmured.

"Come on, little brother," Billy ordered. "We did the best we could do. Now it's time to take Little Nate home to meet his granny."

Thirty-Two

Eleven miles from Bedlam South, Sergeant Boudreaux Pirou, Monroe Peltret, Pierre LaSalle, and Jacques Bourg slowed to a trot on a scrub pine ridge, confident that the Federal soldiers lost their trail when they crisscrossed through the smoldering back alleys of Richmond and then forded the James River.

Four lone Zouave raiders found themselves without a leader. Each man tended his wounds—cuts, bruises, lacerations, and a gaping hole in LaSalle's right thigh. Since they had ridden together by Captain Percy's code for years, they knew *Any man who falls behind gets left behind.*

Peltret broke the silence. "Sergeant Pirou, how many raiders you reckon survived the fight?"

The sergeant shrugged.

LaSalle fumed, "Don't know? How you 'spect to lead with *don't know*? Cap'n Percy always knew."

Snatching back on the reins, Pirou slowed his horse until Peltret and Bourg passed by, then chose to let his actions speak for his thoughts. He reached over and twisted the bloody bandage on LaSalle's thigh. Pain seared the man's body and he screamed in anguish, "You son of a—"

Pirou replied in a chilling voice, "I don't know. I'm not Cap'n Percy."

Pirou released his grip on the bandage, not bothering to wipe LaSalle's blood from his hand. He removed a piece of hardtack from his cartridge pouch, bit off a large chunk, and then threw the rest to LaSalle, a peace offering of sorts. Still agonizing from the pain, LaSalle caught the hardtack. Rejecting Pirou's *kindness* could be deadly.

Bourg spoke up to break the tension, "Where to now, Pirou?"

"Lynchburg. Get cargo."

"And then?" Peltret asked nervously.

"Wait for Percy." The sergeant kicked his horse into a faster trot. After curious glances at one another, the other riders followed his lead across two icy brooks, through battled-scarred woods, and through a shallow backwater marsh. It was more than an hour before any man dared speak again. "Sergeant," LaSalle's voice was filled with trepidation, "what if Captain Percy don't meet us, with all them Federals on our trail 'n' all."

Peltret interrupted saying, "After we get our belongings, I'm hightailing it to Mississippi, then on to New Orleans." Bourg and LaSalle nodded enthusiastically.

Pirou suddenly spoke up, with furious anger in his voice, "With Percy or not, I'm finding Bryarly 'n' killing 'im myself."

· · · · ·

Forbred navigated the wagon west on Cary Street. Rifle across his lap, Patrick Dougall sat beside him, aware that Federal forces were gathering in the southeast section of the city. Across the landscape, fires raged, smoke filled the air, soldiers and civilians ran dodging through the streets. The wagon slowed to a crawl while Forbred waited for an opportunity to merge into the mass of people going south on Fourteenth Street at Mayo's Bridge. Confederate soldiers took priority. Policemen and provost guards held up traffic while artillery wagons, cavalry riders, troops, and ambulances rumbled across the bridge. At last the wagon jerked forward and hard to the left, climbing the rise.

Ana was resting peacefully next to her mother, thanks to the sedative Forbred carried in his bag. Just after they crossed the bridge, Mrs. Dougall watched the engineers torch the north end of the bridge to protect the army's retreat. Suddenly, she shouted, "Joseph!—Forbred!—Stop the wagon!"

The wagon veered sharply to the right side of Hull Street, stopping beneath a willow tree close to the Danville railroad tracks. Panicked, the two men jumped from the wagon bench and rushed to the back of the wagon, asking anxiously, "Is Ana okay?"

Mrs. Dougall pointed. "Ana's fine, just fine. It's them boys I be worried about."

Puzzled, the two men scanned the thousands of refugees passing by. "Mary Margaret! We don't have time for these shenanigans," Patrick protested.

"Don't be daft, Patrick. I'm meaning them two soldier boys carrying that baby. Been watching 'em, and I know they need some help. I aim to help." Mrs. Dougall jumped out of the wagon. "Now make yourself useful, Forbred. Go get those boys 'n' that baby!"

As Forbred approached the men, Patrick Dougall protested once again. "You don't know what sort of ruffians these men could be!"

Mrs. Dougall took his hand. "Hush now, Patrick. I never saw a ruffian caring for a baby."

Pushing his way through the crowd, Forbred managed to get their attention. They struggled through the stampede to the back of the wagon, "You need something, mister?"

"Well, actually—"

Mrs. Dougall interrupted, walking up to peer at the baby. "It's you who might be needin' something, I'm thinking. Me name's Mary Margaret Dougall. That's me husband, Patrick. Our daughter Ana is in the wagon. This is Doctor Forbred Lytton."

Puzzled, the younger man wiped his hand on his trousers before extending it. "I'm Zeke Gibson. This here's my brother

Billy, and that little fella's my brand new nephew."

"We've got a long way to go, folks," Billy replied, shifting little Nate on his hip as the baby began crying once again. "Do y'all need help with something?"

"Me thinks you need help," Mrs. Dougall smiled, taking little Nate from Billy's arms. "Patrick, fetch the milk from that butter churn."

Billy hesitated, but the woman's gentle nature and motherly instincts won the day; soon she had the baby feeding as she swayed with him while the men talked among themselves. Patrick shared much-needed food and fresh water.

"Where you boys headed?" he asked.

"Calhoun County, Mississippi, sir," Billy said. "We're through with this war. It's time to go home." Trying to be polite, but not much on small talk, he asked, "Where are y'all going?"

"Well, that's a good question," Patrick Dougall said, scratching his head.

"To Calhoun County, Mississippi," his wife declared. Forbred and Patrick whipped their heads around to stare at her. "I need to be getting in the wagon," she laughed, looking at their faces. Forbred helped her aboard. Billy looked at Zeke, uncomprehending.

"She reminds me of Momma," Zeke chuckled, putting little Nate into Mrs. Dougall's outstretched arms. "Ma'am, I swear you even look a little like our momma."

Zeke sprang into the back of the wagon. Forbred and Patrick climbed onto the bench. Billy, dusty, dirty, and hesitant, stood at the back of the wagon. *I've seen the scum of the city and every conman in America. How can I trust these people? What do they want from me?*

"C'mon, Billy," Zeke urged. "It sure beats walking and totin' a fussy baby."

Mrs. Dougall reached for Billy's hand. "Son, your boy needs his father. Zeke needs a brother. 'N' we all be needing some friends."

Nodding, he whispered, "It's been so long since I was around decent folk …"

"Lost me son—almost lost me daughter," Mrs. Dougall told him, patting his hand. "A terrible thing this war." She looked down at little Nate and over to Ana. "Me thinks we could be helping each other, Billy Gibson."

Slowly his frown turned to a smile and the smile turned into a laugh—and in a moment, everyone in the wagon joined in. As Billy climbed on the bench beside Patrick and Forbred, the motherly woman asked curiously, "Billy, about this Mississippi o' yours. I'm sure it be a lovely country 'n' all, but will we be having to cross that ocean again?"

"Uh, no, ma'am."

Thoughtfully, Zeke looked at the passengers one by one. "Ma'am, did you say your daughter's name was Ana?"

She nodded.

"And your last name is Dougall?"

She nodded again.

"And your name is Mary Margaret and his is Patrick?"

"That be our names," Mrs. Dougall wasn't sure what to think.

"Did you have a son about my age, Michael Dougall?"

Suddenly, everyone in the wagon was staring at Zeke.

"Michael was me son, Ana's brother. Lost him we did to the army."

Zeke wrapped his arms around Mrs. Dougall like she was his long-lost mother. "I fought beside Michael and I was there when he died. He was a good friend and a good man, a man to make any family proud."

Mary Margaret and Patrick Dougall choked back tears.

"I reckon we have a lot to talk about," Zeke smiled.

Thirty-Three

It was almost dusk. Captain Percy had been riding hard all afternoon, rousted time and again by Federal troops. Doubling back, circling around, he hid in pine thickets and ditches. Finally, he climbed down from his horse, both of them exhausted and unable to go farther. Up ahead, the small pond and farmhouse showed no signs of people.

Unbeknownst to him, Percy's ride had accomplished nothing. He remained within two miles of Bedlam South. Stumbling to the water's edge, he collapsed, then leaned against a cypress tree and scooped water into his hat. He drank his fill, then poured water over his body. Ever since the fires of Bull Run, he routinely doused himself with water, to cool the burning scars and the terrifying memories. But now, instead of feeling relieved, Percy's skin began to crawl. Though only locusts and bullfrogs broke the silence around him, he heard …

Footsteps!

Percy ducked behind the tree, staring into the dusk and scanning the bank for intruders. A faint figure slowly materialized from the edge of the woods, barely visible in the heavy shadows. The captain drew his revolver and opened the breach. Only two cartridges remained. Laying the pistol in his lap, his hand patted jacket pockets, cartridge pouch, and folded shirtsleeve, finding no ammunition.

"I should kill you, you retard!" he shouted, recognizing the man as a former resident of Bedlam South.

The shadow made no reply. In fact, he simply sat at the water's edge and peacefully stared into the depths.

Percy shouted louder, "Leave or die." Still, no response. He raised his revolver, willing to sacrifice a precious cartridge, not in defense of his own life, but in cold-blooded murder.

With gun raised, he caught more sounds. *What was that?* Other figures dressed in long, tattered, filthy shirts—the unmistakable clothing of Bedlam South residents—appeared at the water's edge directly across from Percy. Something behind him ... breathing heavily ... Terrifying!

Percy whipped his head around in time to see his horse fall to the ground, gasping its last breaths.

"Captain Percy?" an eerie voice called out in the darkness. "You alone—huh?"

"Who's out there?" Percy panicked, firing a shot across the pond that ricocheted through the trees.

"You're a bad man, Percy ..."

The woods instantly came alive with footsteps and voices.

"Come out, you cowards!" he yelled, standing to his feet. The grass beneath him was stained with his blood. "I'll kill you all!"

"You won't kill *all* of us ... you can't kill all of us!"

"You a bad man, Percy."

Noises right behind him ...

Percy quickly whirled, firing his last shot into the darkness. It was nothing more than his dying horse shifting in the leaves. Percy's hand began to shake. *No bullets left and nowhere to run.*

Percy limped over to the carcass of his horse and grabbed his sword. Stiff-legged, he ran toward the farmhouse, quickly latching the door behind him. Gasping for air, he searched both rooms. Relieved to find he was alone, Percy stacked rubble behind the front door and braced the back door with an old table.

Pressing himself against the interior wall, he listened to the rustling leaves …

His pursuers drew closer.

Clack. Clack! CLACK.

What's that sound?

Paranoia consumed him. "Who's out there?" Percy shouted again, sweat pouring from his scarred face.

No response.

Clack. Clack! CLACK! Louder this time.

His head jerked around, sniffing the air. That sound. That smell! *Flint. Sulfur. Someone's using a flint-rock!*

The glow of crimson flames flared in the darkness. Dim at first, but raging threateningly within minutes, the flames encircled the shack. *Not fire! Anything but fire!* Percy's lungs burned as smoke filled the room. Gagging and coughing, he bent and grabbed a rag to cover his mouth.

"You're a bad man, Percy," the voice again cried out, echoed by dozens of other voices, "a bad man … bad man … bad man …"

"Retards! I should have killed you all when I had the chance!"

An army of ghosts surrounded the shack, quietly watching the flames climb the walls.

Percy had no path of escape. The captain's bloodcurdling screams filled the night. Smashing through the front door, he fell hard to the ground, somehow staggered to his feet, and lashed out with his sword. His uniform had caught on fire.

"Stop him! Don't let him get away," one man cried out.

"Let him burn," cried another.

Fighting for each step, the captain tried to reach the pond, but his body was engulfed in flames. He staggered, swayed for a moment, and finally collapsed.

The survivor of Bull Run's infernos had been burned alive less than two feet from the water's edge.

One by one, the men disappeared into the night. When only the glowing coals of the shack remained, a lone figure stood solemnly over the smoldering corpse.

"I tell you, Percy," Albert Wright grinned with satisfaction, "one day, I gonna kill you."

Albert kicked the charred remains into the water, watching as the tyrant that once had been Captain Samuel T. Percy quietly sank into the murky depths.

"Now, I go home, just like Doc said."

· · · · ·

By Monday, April tenth, word had spread far and wide that the Confederacy had surrendered. Billy and Zeke sat on the front porch of a modest country farmhouse somewhere in eastern Tennessee, reading a copy of a newly arrived dispatch announcing General Lee's surrender.

"What do you think this will mean to us back home, Billy?" Zeke asked.

His brother shook his head. "Things'll be different, no doubt about that. I know Pops is gonna need us now more than ever, to help with the farm and deal with any trouble."

"If we'd just had more men, ol' General Lee could've …"

"I'm glad it's over."

Zeke looked at his brother, shocked. "What?"

"I'm not glad we lost, but I've seen my fill of death. So many brave men and women on both sides … now either dead or helpless cripples." Billy thought of Sally's smile and the pain seared through his heart.

"I'll sure be glad to see Katherine again," Zeke admitted, then looked at his brother quickly. "I'm sorry, Billy. I know you're hurtin' over Sally. It just ain't right! Damn Yankees have ruined everything!"

"Maybe so, Zeke, but Momma would tell us, 'It's God's will.' I guess I'm beginning to understand what she means."

"What do you understand?"

"How to see God in everything around us and in everything that happens, like Momma always taught us to do."

Billy and Zeke both smiled, thinking of the way their mother talked about her favorite subject: … God.

"I don't see no good that's come from any of this, though," Zeke rubbed his stiff neck.

Billy teased him in an imitation of his mother's voice, "You're not trying hard enough, Zeke! God expects y'all to be looking for Him, too. He ain't gonna do all the work."

Zeke laughed. "Dang, you sound just like Momma. That's exactly what she'd be telling us, ain't it?"

"Well, let's try to figure this one out together, little brother," Billy began slowly rocking in the chair as little Nate lay asleep, draped over his father's shoulder.

"It took the war to get us out of Calhoun County …"

"Yeah, so?" Zeke wasn't willing to look for a divine plan of God in all their misery—yet.

"Gettysburg separated us. We both should have been dead."

"Okay, but a lot of men survived Gettysburg. Where's God in that?"

"I was captured and carried to a hospital for care. My wounds were the only reason I was kept in the area for over a month, just long enough to fall in love with Sally Stearns."

"Yeah, Billy—but Sally's dead."

"You're not trying, Zeke! Remember what Momma used to say: 'Think for yourself.' Sure, I miss Sally. I wanted to spend the rest of my life with her. But I have something from her, a little boy that I can love." Billy turned and glanced through the window at Mrs. Dougall. "There's lots of folks that lost somebody, but God's still at work. I've heard Mrs. Dougall crying at night, missing her son. She wishes he was still here, too."

Zeke gazed off in the distance and mumbled, "Michael was a good man. I miss him, too. "

"See? That's what I'm talking about. Look at all the time you and Mrs. Dougall have spent talking about Michael. You were with him when he died, Zeke. That will always make you special to her. That makes you like family."

"What's that got to do with God?"

Billy sighed, "She picked us out of the crowd, Zeke!

Thousands of folks escaping Richmond, and Mrs. Dougall just *happened* to pick out the one man who was friends with her son, who happened to be there when he died?"

"Okay, I'll give you that … it's sure enough strange."

"*Strange*?" Is it *strange* that we met in that same crowd, Zeke? I guess it's *strange* that I'm holding my son, your nephew?"

"Ain't *nothing* strange about li'l' Nate! Don't go putting words in my mouth!"

"Zeke, Mrs. Dougall found you, the last man to know Michael, in a crowd of thousands, only because I was carrying li'l' Nate … I wouldn't have had li'l' Nate without Sally loving me enough to search for me. I never would have met Sally without being wounded at Gettysburg, and I never would have gone to Gettysburg without this war."

"Are you saying God planned all of this?"

Billy didn't respond to Zeke's question. Instead, he reached inside his pocket and retrieved a worn, bloodstained pouch. Among its contents was a tintype photo of Sally and a handwritten note.

"Back when I first came to Barksdale's Brigade, I had a chance to listen to General Lee address a small group of officers. I'll never forget his words. They were meant for me, too, kinda like the way Momma describes reading her Bible. I took some paper and wrote the words down, and I used to read them sometimes when I was enjoying the fighting too much. I guess in a way, it reminded me of Momma."

"Well? Are you gonna read it to me or not?" Zeke's interest was aroused.

Billy carefully unfolded the note:

"*What a cruel thing is war, to separate and destroy families and friends and mar the purest joys and happiness God has granted us in this world. To fill our hearts with hatred instead of love for our neighbors, and to devastate the fair face of this beautiful world.*"

Zeke didn't say a word. Knowing Zeke was a lot like their

father, Billy didn't press for a response. He sat back and waited.

Billy was almost asleep when Zeke finally sorted it out. "Reckon General Lee saw God in all this—huh, Billy?"

"I reckon he did."

"It's gonna take me some time. I need to think on this for a while."

"Time, little brother, is the one thing us Gibson boys now have in plenty!

Thirty-Four

Forbred Lytton sat on a small stool beside Ana's bed in the farmhouse. He rarely left her side until her fever was gone and her green eyes sparkled once again. Ana had regained her strength, and Forbred knew it was now time to tell the truth about who he really was. *Oddly, I feel no fear or regret any longer. Somehow, I know in my spirit that everything will be all right.* He motioned for Mr. and Mrs. Dougall to join Ana as he explained the letter.

"I want to tell you the truth, the whole truth, and explain the lies in that letter from Lord Kennington."

"You don't owe us a tale," Mrs. Dougall protested. "We know you and we love you."

Ana, Forbred could see, remained skeptical.

"My name is Forbred Lytton, and I was institutionalized in Bethlem Royal Hospital at St. George's Field in Southwark for more than twelve years. That much is true … But I am not a murderer. I was a surgeon, a skilled surgeon with a prospering practice, until a tragedy changed my life."

"What happened?" Ana asked.

"My only sister, Milan, died giving birth to my niece Elizabeth." Forbred paused to answer the look on Mrs. Dougall's face. "I did not kill my niece." He picked up the story again.

"After Milan's death, Elizabeth and I were inseparable, spending summers and holidays together. She was the image of her mother. I loved her dearly."

Forbred seemed lost in thought for a moment, then continued, "One winter's day, while we were walking through the park, a snow rabbit bolted across our path and onto a frozen pond. Elizabeth chased it." The man struggled to go on, desperately trying to suppress the images flooding his mind. He whispered so low his listeners had to lean forward, "The most horrible sound on earth is the *cracking* of ice."

"Oh, merciful God," Mrs. Dougall's eyes filled with tears.

"In seconds, Elizabeth sank to the bottom. I rushed onto the ice to save her, but she was trapped beneath the ice. I pounded and pounded until I too fell through. It was probably only minutes, but it seemed like an eternity before I pulled her out. I tried again and again to revive her, but Elizabeth never regained consciousness. Whenever I close my eyes, I see her lovely face, pale blue in death. It haunts me."

"That's not murder, Forbred," Ana whispered, taking his hand.

"In losing Elizabeth, I lost my sanity. I blamed myself for her death. And so did her father, a very powerful man. He had no trouble obtaining a murder-by-insanity charge against me, and he insisted that I be committed to Bethlem Royal Hospital. I was devastated, so I offered little resistance."

"The devil's work!" Mrs. Dougall protested.

Forbred interrupted, "He felt justified in punishing me, Mrs. Dougall. For many years, I punished myself, considering Bedlam to be penance for my crime."

Ana asked why Lord Kennington wrote such lies to the Confederacy.

"When she married, my sister was Lady Kennington."

Mrs. Dougall winced.

"Lord Kennington was Elizabeth's father, my brother-in-law. He dealt with his grief through revenge."

Everyone sat in silence, lost in Forbred's tragic history.

Ana was the first to speak, "What about Doctor Bryarly? Kennington said you killed 'im.'"

"Doctor Bryarly was the kindest man I've ever known. When I arrived at Bedlam Asylum, he took pity on me. He tried to protect me from the vicious handlers and Lord Kennington. Sometimes he even protected me from myself. The doctor never gave up on me. I would fade in and out of sound reasoning, living in madness and lunacy for months, only to regain my senses and find him right there, once again working hard toward my recovery."

"How did he die, Forbred?"

"The night before he was to leave for America, we visited in his quarters one final time. On impulse or God's divine intervention, I know not which, Dr. Bryarly decided to smuggle me out of Bedlam and onto the ship bound for America. I climbed inside his shipping trunk and was loaded on the back of a carriage the next morning."

Forbred stopped speaking; images from the past flooded his senses. Ana leaned over to embrace him, whispering, "The dreams, Forbred! The dreams were real."

Forbred nodded. "On our way to the waterfront, we were attacked by highwaymen. The trunk smashed to the ground. I could hear the sounds of fighting, a single gunshot. Imagine the surprise of two bandits, opening the trunk seeking treasure, but finding me instead—a man who looked remarkably like their victim."

Mr. Dougall shook his head. "Must've scared the hell outta them fellers!"

"They certainly ran fast enough ..." Forbred paused, then continued the story. "Alone and frightened, I panicked. I put Joseph's body in the trunk and sank the trunk into a nearby canal. I knew if I returned to Bedlam, Lord Kennington would certainly have me hanged."

"But why pretend to be Doctor Bryarly?"

"To honor him, Ana. To honor the most admirable man I ever knew."

"Honor?"

"Wingate Asylum was his opportunity to show the world his advanced therapies in dealing with the mentally ill. I couldn't prevent his death, but I knew I owed the doctor my life. What better way to honor him than to carry on his legacy?"

"Forbred, that's why you wouldn't talk to President Davis!" Mrs. Dougall asked, struggling to understand the complexity of the tale.

"In part. I knew the president would discover I was an imposter, although the doctor and I looked remarkably similar. But I had already asked several cabinet members to obtain consideration for Michael without success. I knew the president would refuse."

Mrs. Dougall began softly to cry.

"I would have been unable to save Michael, regardless of my actions. But with my silence, I knew I could help save others. I also knew my silence meant I would sacrifice the bright hopes and dreams I had for the future ..."

Ana bowed her head.

"By choosing silence, I lost your love, but I helped save more than three hundred men barely surviving at the mercy of that sadist captain. Because I didn't go to the president, God used me to save lives. As I watched those men being released from Bedlam South, I felt myself releasing an old, dear friend: Doctor Bryarly. My debt to him is at last repaid."

"What o' your debt to me?" Ana asked.

"Debt?"

"Once upon a time, you promised me a wedding. And you'll be keeping your word, Forbred Lytton."

Forbred watched as Ana fell fast asleep, then joined the Dougalls and the Gibsons on the porch. *For the first time in fifteen years, I feel at peace. The war that raged within me and within my adopted country has ended, and we both bear the scars, but peace means hope, liberty, and the freedom to choose any path in life I want.*

A magenta sunset painted the western sky, while a gentle Southern breeze refreshed their spirits. In time, Forbred left the porch and walked down a cobblestone pathway to the nearby creek. Billy soon followed.

"Well, Doc, looks like you've done quite a job, keeping the family together."

Forbred put his hand on the young man's shoulder and pointed to the tiny boy sleeping in his arms. "Billy, you haven't done too badly yourself."

"Doc, was it worth it, the war? Was it worth the price we all paid?"

Forbred considered his answer. "I know a little about what you endured—I spent twelve years of my life rotting away in a prison. And I witnessed the depths to which men can sink—even basically good men. I don't know that anyone will truly grasp the meaning of it all, whether madness or folly. I'm just beginning to fully understand. "

"Understand?"

"That your answer really comes down to a single truth, Billy."

"What's that?"

"There are only two things worth living or dying for—and now you have them both—freedom and family."

References

During the long months of research for this book, dozens of historical newspaper articles, web sites, search engines, and book resources were utilized as inspiration and reference. Although all of these resources were important and contributed to our research, we would like to recognize a few exemplary works that were crucial to the writing of this book.

Frank R. Freeman's *Gangrene and Glory* (Associated University Presses, 1998).

Alfred Hoyt Bill's *The Beleaguered City* (Alfred A. Knopf, 1946).

Sallie B. Putnam's *Richmond during the War* (Library of Congress, 1983).

R. Gregory Lande's *Madness, Malingering & Malfeasance* (Brassey's Inc., 2003).

Susan Provost Beller's *Medical Practices in the Civil War* (Betterway Books, 1992).

Thomas P. Lowry's *The Story the Soldiers Wouldn't Tell: Sex in the Civil War* (Stackpole Books, 1994).

Roy Porter's *Madness: A Brief History* (Oxford University Press, 2002).

Robert Whitaker's *Mad in America* (Basic Books, 2003).

Thomas P. Lowry's *Don't Shoot That Boy! Abraham Lincoln and Military Justice* (Savas Publishing Company, 1999).

Acknowledgments

We have several people we wish to thank for their contributions to the book. Without each of you, this book would not have been published.

Norma Gill and Kay Hampson at gals2edit.com. Thank you for your prayerful support and encouragement through endless months of editing.

Cynthia Furlong Reynolds for your long hours in editing and counsel.

Lynne Johnson and Ann Arbor Media Group. We are grateful to Lynne for her patience and willingness to coach us throughout the process.

And finally, Tom Dwyer, Bob Chunn, and the Borders Group staff. Thanks for believing in the work and the authors.